How to Make a Pot in 14 Easy Lessons

Nicola Pearson

Nicola Pea

This book is a work of fiction.
No part of the contents relate to any real person or persons, living or dead.

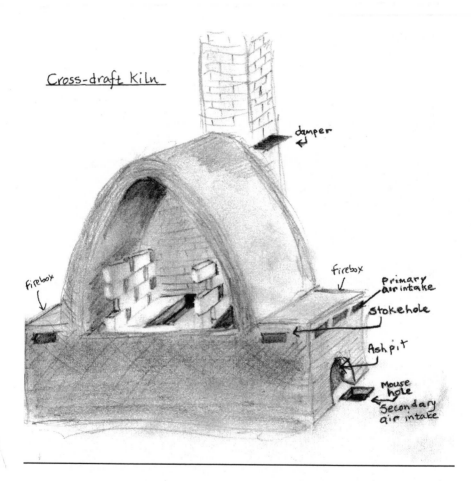

Cross-draft Kiln

damper

Firebox

Firebox

Primary air intake

Stokehole

Ashpit

Mouse hole

Secondary air intake

Acknowledgements

Many people helped me in the writing of this book; most notably, my editor, Jerry Ziegler, who patiently and always positively drew the story out of me; Pam Kopkowski who brought Jerry into my life; Sandee Butler for suggesting the lessons; Lesley Link, Nancy Johnson, Carole Schaefer, John & Joyce Arnold, Mary Lou Meader, Nancy Callan and the members of my book club, who were my first readers; my intelligent, insightful children who told me what did and did not work; my wonderful nephew, James Pearson, who kept after me to publish; and finally my husband, Stephen, who not only inspired this book by being a potter, but read the chapters over and over again until I was satisfied they were right. I don't think I can ever thank you all enough.

<u>Cover Art</u>:

Original cover photo by Lee Pollack; artistic rendering by Bobbi Jo Drysdale.

For Stephen,
the love of my life.

<u>Lesson 1</u>

Gather the Love

When deciding whether or not you want to make pots, you should first determine if you have the love. Otherwise there's really no point in getting your hands dirty.

Joe felt the sun on his broad shoulders as he leaned forward to assess the wet clay. He could tell by how shiny it was just how much longer it would have to sit before it was dry enough to use but he'd been muddying his hands in wet clay as a potter for 13 years now and he was still drawn to touch it whenever he could. He pushed against the sticky material with his right hand, evening out the thickness at one end of the long drying tray and then decided to do the same for the other end with his left hand.

He didn't have to do this. He had a perfectly adequate dough mixer sitting inside his studio that he used for making clay; but this clay had been trimmings from another potter who didn't make his own clay and, rather than waste it, he had brought it to Joe to throw in his mixer. But when Joe examined the trimmings he found dog hair and gravel and other impurities from the floor of the other guy's studio so he threw the trimmings into a blunger with an excess of water. The blunger, an oversized eggbeater, spun the two materials to a homogenous, creamy consistency, which Joe then poured through a kitchen sieve onto a cloth that he had laid on insulating firebricks in this wooden drying tray. He set the whole works on sawhorses alongside his garden and between the soft, porous firebricks absorbing the moisture and the heat of the sun, the clay was in the ideal place to dry. This was a labor of love.

It was also one of the best ways to make clay in Joe's opinion. Overwetting it and spinning it in a blunger, then leaving it to settle and dry in the sun meant the clay particles were more evenly dispersed than they would be in a clay mixer, creating a finished product with greater plasticity. Just the way he liked it for throwing. He'd make all his clay this way except it rained so darned much in the Upper Skagit he couldn't be sure he'd ever get it dry. So he only did it this way when he was recycling somebody else's clay and then only in the summer months. June was even a little early for this method but the last few days had brought cloudless, sunny skies and so Joe had jumped at the chance to get these trimmings dealt with.

He looked at his hands; they were covered in a thick, grayish coating of clay. He clicked twice in the side of his cheek and Magnolia, who had been rubbing her back in the sweet June grass a few feet away, flipped onto her paws and trotted over to see what was needed. Joe bent down and pressed a hand into each side of the brown dog's belly.

"There's a good girl," he told her and Maggie wagged her tail happily and pushed her nose up into his face. "Don't slime my glasses," he warned her before standing back to admire his handiwork. Satisfied, he looked at his dog and said, "Okay, let's go get our girl some irises."

❀

Lucy looked out the window of the plane and let her eyes stare over the expanse of gray tarmac at Kennedy International Airport. The plane had taxied away from the gate towards the runway almost 20 minutes ago and they still hadn't taken off. The pilot came onto the overhead speakers; "Another five minutes, folks, and we'll be on our way." The man sitting next to Lucy tipped his head down towards her and scrunched up his face. "They train them to lie, you know," he told her.

Lucy flashed him an amused look with her green eyes and smiled but then she turned away, not wanting to get drawn into a conversation. She just wanted to sit and think about being with Joe.

She was so excited to see him again after four months of them being apart but she had some other emotion going on at the same time. Fear, maybe? Lucy Carson was twenty-seven and had left her native England for France when she was twenty-two, then left France for New York City when she was twenty-four, in the hopes of doing theatre in as many places around the world as possible so she could go back to England and open her own theatre using the best of what she'd learned elsewhere. But now she was moving to Washington State, a place that had never been on her theatrical itinerary, and she was doing it for a man! She'd never moved anywhere for a man before and some part of her didn't really believe she was doing it now, particularly since she had no intention of settling down and getting married. But Joe had a special quality about him, a warm gravitational pull that made Lucy unable to resist drifting in his direction and she sensed that she might never meet anyone like him again. So despite her promise to herself never to get entangled in love, she found herself putting her theatrical journey on hold for a while and letting her heart take center stage.

As appealing as that prospect seemed every time Lucy pictured herself with Joe, she also knew there was something about this move that was bothering her because she'd been doing a lot of strange things recently. Like sleeping at weird hours, for long stretches of time. Just last week, she'd gone back to the apartment she shared with her roommate, Frank, around 5 p.m., planning to have a bite to eat and then work on her Master's degree thesis but as soon as she got through the door, she laid down for a moment on the couch and woke up 3 hours later when the telephone rang. It was Joe and he was shocked to find her sleeping at 8 o'clock at night. So was Lucy.

She'd also been forgetting things recently, some of them important things. Like the papers she was supposed to get for her professor from the library. Lucy had been this professor's research assistant for a year now and had never forgotten an assignment he'd given her. "I think I may be anxious about this move," she heard herself telling him to explain her omission.

"I've had that impression," the professor agreed, making Lucy aware that even others could tell she wasn't herself.

Lucy's thoughts were interrupted by the pilot again, who now told them that they were being delayed because of a storm passing across Long Island that they could see if they looked out the windows to their right. Her neighbor, Mr. Tall and Lanky, observed dryly that all he could see was blue skies. Lucy just nodded and smiled. She wasn't really paying attention. She was thinking how ready she was to leave New York and spend more than just a passing vacation with Joe. How *much* more would depend on whether she could overcome her fears when it came to love. And if she couldn't, well, as Joe had told her with his winning charm, at least Washington State was closer to Australia. And Australia was where she had planned to go next on her world tour of theatre.

Lucy looked at her watch. They were already an hour behind their scheduled departure time and it was getting hot inside the plane. She could feel her thick, wavy, reddish-blonde hair sticking to the back of her neck as a result of the New York heat broiling up from the tarmac. She fiddled with the air vent above her head but nothing happened.

"They won't turn those on till the plane takes off," her neighbor declared. Lucy rolled her eyes and Mr. Tall and Lanky saw this and laughed in agreement. Then he jumped in with, "I'm Malcolm, by the way."

Lucy took his proffered hand and shook it, saying, "I'm Lucy." Then she quickly turned back to her window, hoping to close him out again.

Lucy heard Malcolm stand up and open the overhead luggage bin. A few seconds later she heard the bin slam shut and felt Malcolm plunk down in the seat next to her again.

"Want a chocolate?" she heard him ask.

Lucy turned and saw a big box of good quality chocolates on Malcolm's lap. She grinned. Now she'd talk to him.

❦

Joe was picking his way slowly over the raised beds he'd made in his garden, carrying a good handful of irises, and stopping when he saw weeds that needed to be pulled around the young vegetable shoots he'd planted. He looked up when he heard somebody sound a car horn down in front of his house. Must be somebody had pulled in for the shop.

"Woof! Woof! Woof!" barked Maggie, and she loped down the graveled lane from the garden to the house to greet the visitor.

Joe followed, thinking for the umpteenth time that he really ought to build a fence around this garden, to keep the deer out of his vegetables. They'd already been snacking on his bush peas and chard, the two tallest crops this early in the season, and he certainly didn't want them in his tomatoes once they started growing. He let the irises swing at his side as he walked the 150 feet downhill, feet apart, toes turned out, the jaunt in his stride putting bounce in his bushy brown hair. Joe was thirty-three and at 5 foot 10, only average height but he had broad shoulders and well-built upper body muscles from years of wedging clay making him seem more formidable in stature. He had square-jawed good looks and a generous mouth, wore large, dark frame glasses and usually only shaved every third day, leaving just enough stubble on his cheeks and chin to make him look rugged. Not that Joe cared what he looked like; he just cared that he didn't have to take the time to shave every day because his facial hair didn't grow that fast. Today, though, he'd made a point of shaving to honor Lucy's arrival from New York. He cleared his throat noisily and spat on the ground by the cherry tree before coming around the corner of the house.

His visitor, a well-dressed woman of maybe fifty-five or fifty-six, slim with pointy, bird-like features, was standing beside a white Ford Bronco chuckling merrily as she petted his dog.

"Hi," Joe called out.

"Hi there," his visitor replied. "Did you do this?" She was pointing at the two large, white handprints on either side of the dog's belly.

"Yes, indeedy," Joe replied, holding up his right hand as if in evidence. "It's camouflage. So people can't tell us apart."

"Maybe if you'd made them in the shape of hibiscus," the woman teased, eyeing Joe's shirt.

Joe smiled and proudly smoothed one side of his Hawaiian shirt with his free hand. Then he dipped his head, so he could look at his visitor over his glasses with his hazel green eyes. "I got dressed up to go get my girl at the airport," he said, punctuating the "my girl" with a flirtatious lift of his eyebrows.

"Is that who those are for?" the woman asked, nodding at the flowers in Joe's hand.

Joe raised them up when she mentioned them. "Uh huh," he affirmed. "You think I'll get kissed?"

Some of the irises were white with lavender edgings on their petals, some were yellow and the rest were a deep chestnut color that looked almost too rich to be real.

"I think you might," replied the woman.

Joe gazed down at the blossoms that he was cradling in his large hands and could feel the woman watching him. He knew he came across as rough and gruff but that didn't mean he didn't love his flowers. He lifted his eyes and treated her to another of his wide, warm smiles; she blushed. Almost as quickly she snapped her head upright and asked, "Where's your girl coming from?"

"New York."

"How fun. Was she there on vacation?"

"No. She was living there!" Joe made himself sound suitably appalled.

"I take it you're not much of a city boy?"

"Not too much," Joe admitted. "Too many people for my taste. 'Specially in New York. You know what I heard on the radio the other day? I heard some guy describing New York as the second circle of Hell. And it was National Public Radio, so you know it must be true!"

"What was the first?"

"Dallas."

"Oh now," said the woman. "That's not fair. I lived in Dallas once and it wasn't that bad!"

"Were you hot?" Joe asked, baiting her.

"What?" The mischievous look on her face suggested she knew she was being baited but couldn't resist.

"Were you hot in Dallas?" Joe asked again.

"Well sure. Of course I was hot. I mean, it was Dallas."

"Well, there you go. Proves my point!"

The woman laughed uproariously. Then she stretched her manicured right hand out in his direction. "I'm Marianne, by the way," she volunteered. "Marianne Dunning."

Joe shook her hand, noticing the way the huge, turquoise pendant hanging around her neck picked up the blue of her eyes. "Joe Connors," he replied, then gave her a quizzical look. "Dunning?" he repeated. "Where do I know that name from?"

"You've met my husband."

Joe snapped his fingers and pointed at her, remembering. "The building inspector," he exclaimed.

"Uh huh."

"That son of a gun red tagged me!"

It was an indictment but he said it so good-naturedly that he made Marianne laugh. Joe noticed how the gold tips in her short, loose curls danced in the sunlight as her head bobbed to the rhythm of her laughter.

"You're not supposed to build without a permit," Marianne chided once she'd stopped laughing.

"That's not what I heard. I was talking to this building inspector once – not your husband, some other guy – and he said that none of the upriver people ever got permits. I figured he was giving me permission."

Marianne laughed again. "George told me you had said that." She paused and tipped her head up, gazing at the house Joe had built alongside the highway.

It looked like a gingerbread house with two steep gables pointing sharply towards the sky and a roof of overlapping, brown, cedar shakes. Underneath the roof, the house was made of alternating stretches of vertical logs and cedar shingles with a bay to the right that held the pottery shop. A series of small, mullioned windows circling the bay twinkled light from the inside out and there were identical windows on the second floor that had been arranged in triangles to accent the shape of the gables. The whole thing looked like something out of a fairy tale.

"George likes your house," Marianne told Joe. "I do too."

"Thanks. I wanted to build something that looked like it had always been here. Like it grew out of the ground."

He watched her eyes float over the thick forest on the mountain ridges behind his property and when she brought them back to his house, he could see her appraising the rough-hewn logs, the shakes and shingles abundant with growth ring swirls, the knotty posts holding up the roof over the front porch and the curves in the natural wood railings alongside the front steps.

She looked at him and declared, "You've done that, I'd say. Did you work with an architect?"

"Un uh. I told George – that's your husband, right?" Marianne nodded. "I told George when he asked about drawings that I didn't have any. I just drew it on the hood of my pick-up truck when I figured out what I wanted to build."

"Did the County accept that?"

"Nooooo. They wanted drawings. So I used a brown paper grocery bag from the shop, tore it open so it was one big sheet and drew the plans on the back of that. Then I took them down to the County. The woman behind the counter looked at them, kind of scratching her head – but she accepted them. And then she wanted three hundred some bucks for the permit. I said, "I don't have that kind of money!" but I could tell she was intractable on *that* subject so I said, "But I can make payments…""

"And she accepted that?"

"She didn't want to. "We don't usually allow people to make payments,"" Joe said, mimicking the County employee. "But I told her it was the only way I could do it. Take it or leave it. So she took it."

His bold, unapologetic manner provoked another burst of laughter from Marianne.

"Hey, people will work with you if you're willing," he added.

"And you were willing?"

"Well, no, not in that case. I would never have bought a building permit if that son of a gun husband of yours hadn't red tagged me. What do I need to give money to some pencil wielding knucklehead in a suit for just so he can tell me what I already know I can do?"

Marianne laughed again. A loud, staccato rumble made them both turn towards the highway, where a log truck was using its Jake brake in the long, shallow descent past Joe's house. The truck was loaded with huge diameter old growth fir logs and both Joe and Marianne watched it go by and sniffed deeply in unison, inhaling the tangy aroma of the fresh cut fir being misted into the air around them.

They grinned at each other, then Joe returned to his narrative. "But five years ago," he said. "I got a speeding ticket, going through Burlington, down below, and I had to go to the Skagit County Courthouse to contest it. The judge reduced it but I still had to pay a hundred dollars – I guess I must have been going fast. Well my girlfriend had taken my pick-up and left me to drive her piece of junk Mustang with the driver's side window that wouldn't roll up and windshield wipers that didn't work and it was raining – hard – so I had to drive fast!"

"Is this the girlfriend you're going to pick-up at the airport?" Marianne interrupted to ask.

"Oh good Lord, no," replied Joe. "The Mustang lady and I parted company quite some time ago. Anyway," he went on, drawing the word out to change the subject. "I told the judge that I didn't have a hundred dollars, "but I can make you some nice planters for the courthouse," I said. And he said, "Okay." So that's what I did." Joe leaned in towards Marianne and added with obvious pride, "Those planters are still there, right in the courtroom."

"Do they look anything like that one there?" Marianne was pointing at a planter sitting at the base of a big slab of cedar next to the steps to the front porch, on which someone had carved, "Sound Horn."

Joe turned and looked. It was one of his large, round, stoneware planters with mountains drawn on the outside. Mountains in the red slip with an ash glaze over that twinkled in the sunlight. "Probably," he said, twanging the word so hard it lost both letter bs.

"Do you have any more like that?" asked Marianne.

Joe sucked air noisily through his teeth because he really didn't want to say no, even though he knew he had to. "I'm pretty sure I don't," he admitted. Then his face lit up. "But I could make you one."

"That might be an option," Marianne replied, rubbing the point of her chin while still staring at the planter. "Although I need something right now. I have some begonias that need a pot for the summer....." she explained.

"I can never seem to get begonias to make it....." Joe told her.

"They need to be in the shade."

"Is that what it is?"

"Yes. They like it warm but they don't like direct sunlight. So if you can find a shady spot..."

Joe looked to the right of his house, at the area between the cherry tree and his garden. "Maybe under my vine maples...." he mused.

Marianne's face flashed sudden concern. "Am I holding you up from going to the airport?"

"Oh no," Joe replied. "Her plane doesn't get in until 3:30 this afternoon and what time is it now?"

Marianne looked at her watch. "11:15," she told the potter.

"Yeah, I wasn't planning to leave before noon 'cause it takes about two and a half hours to get to the airport from here. Plus Maggie and I always have time for customers. Don't we, Maggie?" The beautiful, clayprinted dog stepped towards her master, pushing her nose into the side of his leg. Maggie was a mix of Chesapeake and Short-Haired Pointer, which showed in the curl to her brown coat along her spine and in her long, slender nose. Joe let his free hand drop down to her ear and scratched it without thinking.

"How long's your girl coming for?" Marianne asked.

"Forever, I hope."

"Oh my. From New York City to here, that's a big change. Do you think she'll be able to take our rain?"

"I would think so," Joe answered. "She's from G.B."

"As in Great Britain?"

"Exactly right. So I doubt the rain will be a problem for her." Then he turned his roguish charm on his visitor and added, "I might though!"

Marianne chuckled. "I bet you might."

Joe looked at the pendant hanging around Marianne's neck again. "Come on," he said, moving towards the front steps of his house. "I'll show you into the shop. Maybe you can give me back some of that money George cost me…"

They'd been in the air for a good two hours when Lucy roused herself from a short catnap and peered out the window. She sat up, her curiosity piqued, and pushed her face closer to the window. Down on the ground, underneath them, were huge circles of land that had nothing inside them; no houses, no cars, no industry, no shopping centers. Some of them were dark brown with just the hint of a spiral inside them, others were more of a beige color. They must be agricultural, Lucy thought to herself, although she'd never seen anything like it. It wasn't just their size that impressed her, it was their perfect roundness and the complete lack of anything resembling a human habitation anywhere near them. What it must be, she thought, to have so much land you could create great circles like these that were seemingly isolated. Then she saw four of the circles sitting inside an even bigger square and again, they were devoid of anything suggesting human life in or around them. Except, of course, their very tidiness suggested human interference because the land would never be like that naturally. Some of the circles even had a line in them, going from the outside edge into the center, like a radius. Lucy was agog; she was pretty sure that the whole of England could probably fit inside one of those circles!

She glanced at her neighbor, Malcolm, to ask him what they were but he was fast asleep. She sat back in her seat again, thinking. She'd always been a bit bewildered by how big everything seemed in America compared to England. Like the highway that went past Joe's house; it was what they called a rural and scenic highway but it was spacious and wide, with well-delineated lanes for the two-directional traffic, not the least bit like the narrow, curvy, country roads of England with their tall hedgerows that blocked views so you had to stick to your lane for dear life when driving along them. Even Joe's house, which was pretty small when you didn't include the shop, seemed big to Lucy. Probably because the acreage around it was filled with pasture and trees and mountain ridges, giving the house the impression of being more spacious.

Lucy thought back to August, 1984, the summer she met Joe. He was in the process of building his house and he'd just nailed down the last of the floorboards on the second floor. Or what Lucy called the first floor. "Ground floor, first floor," she explained, pointing at the two levels.

"Nah, nah," Joe rebuffed. "This is America. We call that the second floor."

He'd led her up the ladder to the second floor and asked her to help him lift a hefty cedar log so it could become a post in one of the interior walls. They hoisted the 12 foot log to a stand together and then Joe had her help him guide it down onto a big old nail he had sticking up out of the floor to stop the post from moving once it was in place. It wasn't easy because the log was heavy, and tall, but they got it. "You can come back anytime," Joe commended, tipping his head down so she got a hit of those warm green eyes over his glasses.

And now here she was, two years later, going back to live in that little house. Was it a little house? Or a big house? Lucy thought for a moment. It was a fairytale house, that's what it was, because that's what Joe had made it look like. Lucy had seen shooting stars in the night sky over the second floor that first summer, something she'd never in her life seen before. Shooting stars in a sky that was absolutely laden with tiny twinklings. Big sky. Big land. She looked out the window once more, at the circles down on the ground. Big country, she thought.

❦

Joe pointed to the door on the right once they got up to the porch and told Marianne to head on in while he went and wrapped some wet newspaper around the stems of his irises. Then he disappeared through the door in the center of the porch.

The door to the shop, like the one to the house, was single pane glass with cross-grids set in an old wood frame that had been painted lavender and decorated with airbrushed flowers as if someone had been testing a stencil on it. Marianne peeked through one of the small squares of glass as she turned the handle. The pottery was displayed on tables made out of huge, rough-cut rounds of wood sitting on shortened tree trunks that billowed and twisted as they reached down to the floor. The far wall was made of the vertical logs visible from the outside, only they were flat sawn on the interior surface. Running the length of the logs was a slab of rich, dark cedar that Joe was using as a counter to display more of his pottery. To the right of the door was the bay holding five of the small, mullioned windows, and the early afternoon sunlight streamed in through them, lighting the pots on the display tables. It looked like a little gallery built by hobbits in a hollowed out tree trunk, one that was filled with treasures on every surface including the knotholes and root wads.

Marianne lingered on the threshold, as if appreciating the whole before allowing herself to explore the details, then she stepped inside the shop and quietly closed the door behind her. When she turned back around her eyes landed immediately on a first treasure. It was a pitcher, fairly narrow in the base, with a slender, cylindrical form that rose to an even narrower, but decidedly long neck. The whole thing was topped off with a delicate pout of a pouring spout and a wide, comfortable handle ran down one side, from the top of the neck to the middle of the base. Marianne picked it up with her right hand and balanced the bottom on her left, bouncing it gently as if surprised by the lightness of the object. Then she ran her thumb over some tiny flowers that had been carved into the body of the pitcher. The way their petals folded back on themselves and their stamen hung down exposed in the center suggested that they were alpine tiger lilies, a flower that grew alongside many of the trails in the North Cascades. Marianne smiled as she looked at the pot, then lifted it higher into the air and turned it around slowly, to admire its colors in the sunlight. The flowers were a soft, sky blue, the neck and spout were glazed a charcoal gray, and the rest of the pitcher, from the neck down, was covered in a matte, powdery pink glaze, making the pot, a piece of hard-fired clay, appear almost soft to the touch.

"A little wine to go with your cheese?" Joe asked as he came into the shop sipping some coffee.

Marianne lowered the pot and turned to look at him. "Is that what this is for?" she asked.

"Well, sure. It could be. But then again, it could be for anything you want it to be for once it's yours. Why? Don't you drink wine?"

"Oh yes, I drink wine. But not very often. And I doubt I'd ever decant it. I just think this would look great with some of my lavender in it." Joe watched her raise the pitcher to eye level again. "It would go so well with this pink."

Joe walked over to Marianne, set his coffee mug down on the center table and took the pitcher out of her hands. "I don't know why that glaze does that," he remarked, flipping the pot over to examine it on both sides.

"Does what?"

"Goes pink like that. It's really just a matte white but I changed the formula a couple of firings ago and it's been going that soft pink ever since."

"Well don't change it back," Marianne said, with a sing-song lilt in her voice. "I like it."

"That's what I've been hearing from other customers." Joe placed the pitcher back on the table, lifted up his coffee mug and walked around Marianne to perch on a bar stool he had sitting at the end of the long cedar counter. He propped his feet on one of the cross bars between the legs of the stool, so his knees were at a 90 degree angle to his waist and rested his hands, with the coffee mug between them, in his lap.

Marianne glanced once more at the pitcher on the center table then followed Joe to the counter on the outside wall. Except instead of walking its length to where Joe was sitting, Marianne stopped about mid-way, to examine another pitcher, this one with a ceramic cone coming out of its top. "What's this?" she asked.

"It's a drip coffee pot."

"Is that right?" Marianne sounded fascinated. "Does it make good coffee?"

"*I* think so. Here, I'll get you a cup if you like," and Joe shifted forward on the stool as if he were about to stand up.

"Oh no thanks," Marianne replied quickly, holding her hand up to suggest he need not go any further. "I'll take your word for it." She peered down at the coffee pot. "Does it take longer than the plastic coffee machines?"

"Probably."

"And people don't complain about that?"

"Not to me they don't."

Marianne swung her head from side to side and made a face. "I bet George would."

"You're s'posed to take a long time making coffee," Joe told her. "It's all part of the ritual."

Marianne sighed and crossed in front of Joe to look at the pots on the display table to his right. "George gave up rituals once he started making money."

"County pays that well, huh?"

"No, no, not the County..." Marianne took the lid off a cookie jar and ran her hand softly around the inside edge. "It's his hobby that's paying so well."

Joe had been leaning against the log wall but his excitement at hearing Marianne's words propelled him forward to an upright position, almost spilling his coffee in the process. "Did he finally design that computer program he had in his mind?" Marianne looked at the young potter, her mouth open with surprise. "Hey, George and I spent a long time shooting the shit after we were done with business," Joe told her. "And I had a good time talking to him. It was obvious he was into his computer stuff...."

"Yes, and you told him to go for it if that's what he really wanted to do....."

"I said that?!" Joe went for incredulity just in case he was in trouble here. "Were you not okay with that?"

"No, no." Marianne flapped her free hand around in the air, as if batting away Joe's concerns. "George came back so pumped up after he met you. He loved how you had a dream of building a house with a place in it to sell your pots and how you'd saved materials for it for ten years – isn't that what you told him?"

"Yep. Salvaged whatever I could from the local sawmill and from logging projects and by the time I was ready to start building I had piles everywhere on my 5 acres...."

"George found that inspiring. And he came home and stopped talking about designing a software program and actually did it. And I guess it's a great program because everybody wants it and they're all willing to pay him large amounts of money to get it."

"Well, hot dog! Way to go, George!"

Marianne looked back down at the cookie jar, making a little 'hmm' of doubt in the back of her throat.

"You're not pleased for him?"

"Well sure I am. It's just...." Marianne put the lid back down on the jar and left her hand resting on top of it as she looked at Joe. "These companies don't just want to buy his software program, they want him to work for them too. Which is good because George has now quit his job at the County...."

"Time for me to build an addition!" joked Joe.

Marianne smiled then looked down at the display table again. She opened her mouth as if to say something then changed her mind. She took a step forward and pointed at a shallow, lidded casserole dish, next to the cookie jar. "Can this go in the oven?" she asked.

"Yep. Oven safe, microwave safe and dishwasher safe. So where's George going to work?"

"That's the problem...."

Joe nodded as he sipped his coffee once more; now they were getting somewhere.

".....some of these companies are down in California, in Silicon Valley. And George is flying down there tomorrow, to finalize an offer."

"Oh." Joe paused. "So I guess you're moving to California."

"Maybe."

Joe saw her lips tighten, her eyebrows move together, creating lines of worry above her nose. He dropped his head again, to look at her over his glasses. "I take it you're not much of a California girl?" he said. He'd meant it as a joke but his tone was gentle because he could totally understand her reluctance.

"Not too much," Marianne confessed. She took a big, deep breath, as if plucking up the courage to address this issue, and Joe saw her shoulders relax when she exhaled. "I mean, I'm thrilled that George is finally being successful with his computer stuff but I'm not thrilled about the prospect of leaving Washington."

"How come he doesn't try for a job with that company in Redmond? The one that just went public. I'm always hearing about how well they're doing on the radio."

"They *are* doing well, Very well in fact. But.....I don't know, there's something about California that's luring George right now."

"The paycheck?"

"Could be," she answered, tracing the line of the mountains on the lid of the casserole with her fingers. "Or it could be all that sunshine. George has never had much tolerance for the rain here."

"What rain?"

"Well that's what I say." Marianne took the lid off the

casserole to look at the inside. "The trouble is," she continued, "what I say doesn't seem to matter to George all that much these days. And I'm beginning to think that part of the lure in California is my not wanting to go there."

"You think he wants to go without you?" Joe blurted.

Marianne lifted her eyes to meet Joe's and he could see relief in them, as if she were grateful that someone had finally said it. "I think so," she said. "He's been very distant these past few months."

"Maybe he's just freaked out that everyone wants him all of a sudden."

"Could be." She paused, then shrugged. "But even when his mind's not on the computer and I do everything he used to like me to do to make a relaxing moment for us, he can't seem to focus on me. Like I belong in the picture he had of himself in the past but I don't belong in the one he has of himself right now. Or in the future."

"Are you going down to California with him tomorrow?"

She shook her head no. "He didn't invite me." Then she put the lid back on the casserole and flicked her head towards Joe, smiling. "Have you ever taken your girl up Sauk Mountain?"

"Sure," he answered. "She loves to hike. The first date I took her on was a hike into Clear Lake."

"Where's that?"

"The other side of Jackman Ridge." Joe could tell from Marianne's expression that she didn't have a clue what he was talking about so he set down his coffee cup on the slab of cedar and headed for the door again. "Here. I'll show you," he offered.

Marianne trotted behind him as he jogged down the front steps and across the graveled driveway towards a grassy area on one side of his house that was lined with waist-high, Silver fir saplings. Joe stopped and pointed to a blocky ridge south east of his property that was covered in the dark green of alpine conifers. Or almost covered. "That's Jackman," he told Marianne. "And see that clear cut there?" His point drifted slightly to the right, indicating an ugly, bald patch towards the top of the ridge. "If you go up through that clear cut and over the top of the ridge you're supposed to be able to drop down into Clear Lake. But we never found it."

"And I suppose you're going to tell me you ran out of gas," Marianne joked.

"No, no, we really tried. We hiked and hiked and it seemed like all we were doing was going through one clearing after another and never getting to the ridge that we could see right above us. Plus it was hot and at one point I looked back to make sure she was doing okay and saw that her forehead was covered in bugs! So we bagged it. We had a lot of fun though. And I found out she was quite the hiker," he added.

Marianne's face softened and Joe sensed a little poignancy on her part. Here he was at the beginning of his journey of love and she didn't know where she was in hers. He reached out and ran his hand through the needles on one of the Silver firs, encouraging her to do them same with a nod of his head. She did and they both lifted their palms up to their faces and inhaled the piney scent with delight. They grinned at each other again.

"If only life were this uncomplicated," Marianne remarked, letting her hand drop back down to her side again.

Maggie came up to Joe with a stick in her mouth. He stepped forward and threw it for her, in among the vine maples behind his house, as Marianne gazed at Sauk Mountain.

The broad, knuckled top of the mountain was still covered in a good deal of snow but the spring greens were starting to peek through, suggesting the end of the long winter in the high country and the beginning of hiking season.

"How can anyone want to leave all this," Marianne sighed.

"I'm with you there," Joe agreed, bouncing back to her side. "We've got Baker, we've got Shuksan, we've got Sauk. This is some of the most beautiful real estate ever created!"

They stood together in silence, gazing reverentially at the top of the mountain that welcomed people to the upper end of the Skagit River Valley. Sauk wasn't very tall, at 5500 feet, but she looked much more inviting than some of the witches' hat peaks that towered above her further into the Cascades.

"Too bad George isn't here. On a day like today Sauk Mountain's enough to make anyone want to stay," Joe remarked.

"Oh, he's here," Marianne corrected. "I dropped him up at the Cascade River before I came here, so he could go fly-fishing…"

"For Sockeye?" Joe had been thinking about heading up to Bacon Creek to dip his pole in the water for some of his favorite salmon.

"That's what he said," Marianne replied

"Well that's a good sign," Joe suggested. "I mean, if he's fishing for salmon…"

Marianne's cheeks flexed with anger. "I don't know," she said. "I've just got this awful feeling that he's going to go down to

California tomorrow and never come back."

"What makes you think that?"

"I couldn't tell you," she replied. "But there was something about the way he announced he wanted to go fly-fishing today...." She paused, then pursed her lips before adding, "Maybe it's just been too long since I've seen his fishing pole!"

Joe smiled as he got an idea. "You know what you need?" he said.

"What?"

"A lovelight!" And he turned away from Marianne and strode back across the driveway.

"A lovelight?" she echoed, following him.

"Come on, I'll show you." And he bounded up to the shop again.

❦

Malcolm woke up shortly after Lucy saw the circles on the ground and explained that they were, indeed, crop circles. In Nebraska. Malcolm traveled a lot in the US, he told Lucy, on business. Sales. That's why he was heading out to Seattle. He had a pleasant, resilient manner and the time soon passed with the two of them gabbing about where they'd been and where they were going and why.

"You're moving from Manhattan to the mountains, huh? That's quite the change," Malcolm remarked, flicking his bushy eyebrows up in his forehead.

"Well not really," Lucy amended. "I might spend the summer up in the mountains but I'm going to start looking for work in Seattle as soon as I know my way around a bit and hopefully, I'll find a job and move down there. Then I'll spend my days off in the mountains with my boyfriend."

"What do you do for work?"

"I'm an actress."

"An actress?!" Malcolm was shocked. "An actress from London that's lived in Manhattan and now you're heading to the wilds of Washington to be with some guy. What is he, rich?"

Lucy laughed. "Hardly. He's a potter."

"Oh." Malcolm thought about this. He rubbed the little bit of hair on his chin with his forefinger as he looked up at the overhead vents. Then he looked at Lucy again. "My first wife liked pottery," he told her, "but she didn't like me. She took off one day and I haven't been able to find her since. Took our baby daughter with her. Nine months old. Want to see a picture?"

He was already reaching into his back pocket when he asked and Lucy nodded yes. She was surprised he was sharing this with her but, on the other hand, she was empathetic. Joe also had a daughter that he hadn't seen since she was a few months old and he didn't know where she was either. It was heartbreaking.

"That's her," Malcolm said, tapping on a wallet-sized photo of a plump, smiling baby. "Shelby we called her. She'd be 13 now. And I haven't seen her in all that time. I want to but...." He shrugged. He looked and sounded very matter-of-fact but Lucy was sure it must hurt. Well he probably wouldn't be telling her if it didn't hurt. Then, once again, he bounced on. "These are my other kids," he said, turning to the next photo in his wallet. "Jake and Zachary. And my wife." A smile curled the corners of his mouth as he confided, "She does like me."

Lucy smiled back. "Thank goodness for second chances, eh?"

"Amen to that."

Once Joe got inside the shop, he headed back towards the cedar counter and bent down to look through the wooden fruit boxes in which he kept his back stock of pots. Marianne came in behind him and turned to close the door but hesitated when she saw Maggie standing on the porch, looking into the shop with the stick in her mouth. "Can your dog come in," she asked.

"Oh no," said Joe. "She has a tail and tails can be hard on the pots." He turned and peered under the center display table at his dog. "Sit, Maggie," he said. Maggie sat and reluctantly dropped the stick on the porch in front of her.

Marianne closed the door and walked over to where Joe was kneeling on the floor. He swiveled towards her, holding a pot shaped like a hollow gourd on the palm of his hand. The pot had a wide base and a narrow opening at the top, with little heart cutouts all around the body. It was glazed purple and white. "Put a candle down inside this," he told her, sticking his fingers through the opening in the top, "and you'll have George buying you a ticket for the next plane out."

"Is that right?" Marianne reached out delightedly with both hands and gently cupped the object as Joe let go of it.

"I promise you it's true. That's how I got my girl to move out here from New York. With one of these."

"You sent her one?"

"No, I took it when I went and spent a couple of months with her last winter."

Marianne stopped staring at the candle lantern and raised a disbelieving eyebrow in Joe's direction. "I thought you didn't like New York?"

"I don't," Joe admitted. Then he grinned sheepishly. "But I like her."

"I guess you do." Marianne sounded very impressed. She closed one eye and tilted her face slightly away from him. "And you think it's the lovelight that won her heart?"

"I'm pretty sure."

"You don't think it's because you gave up two months of your life to live in a city you detest just to be close to her?"

Joe stood up, waving his head from side to side with sudden shyness. "I don't know," he countered. Then he nudged her with his elbow. "Maybe she just likes my fishing pole."

Marianne laughed, a deep, delighted belly laugh that seemed to release a surfeit of emotions that Joe guessed she'd been holding inside for too long. When she finished, she pointed at the lovelight and announced, "You know, I think you're right. I *do* need one of these."

"You want one with hearts?" Joe asked, crouching down to reach into the box again.

"Well that depends. What else have you got?"

"I've got stars and moons..." and he slid that one up onto the counter above his head, "....and one here with a coyote howling at the moon." Then he glanced around the gallery, to see if there were any others he was missing. "Oo! Oo! Oo!" he exclaimed and rushed over to a window to take a lovelight off the sill. "This one has swans flying over the mountains."

"Swans?"

"Yes. Trumpeter swans. And they always return to the Skagit Valley. So if you light this for George it might give him the idea that this is where he needs to come back to. Like the swans."

Marianne crossed the room and carefully took the candle lantern out of Joe's hands. She held it up to the light and turned it around, examining every inch of it. "Do you think I'll get kissed?" she asked with a glint in her eye.

"Guaranteed!" Joe declared.

And they grinned at each other for a third time.

Lucy felt her stomach lurch just as the seatbelt light pinged on above her head. "I guess we've started our descent," Malcolm remarked, stuffing some magazines he'd been reading into his briefcase before pushing it back under his seat. Lucy also began the process of stowing her personal items and she buckled her seat belt at the same time as Malcolm buckled his. He glanced at his watch. "Three hours behind schedule. I guess we didn't make up any time after that delay in New York," He shrugged. "Oh well. Doesn't matter to me. I was just going to head to a hotel and get ready for tomorrow anyway. Call my family. What about you? Will your guy have waited, do you think?"

Lucy lifted her shoulders and eyebrows. "I think so," she said. But she offered just enough of a smile to suggest she knew so. "After all, he waited two years for me to join him," she added. "I think he'll wait the extra few hours."

Malcolm grinned at her. "That's the spirit," he declared.

Marianne and Joe walked out of the shop and back towards the Bronco together, Marianne clutching a brown bag containing the lovelight and the narrow-necked pitcher from the center table.

"You tell George to leave some of those Sockeye for me," Joe teased.

"Will do," Marianne replied. "And good luck with your girl. What's her name, by the way?"

"Lucy."

"Is she a potter too?"

"No, she's an actress."

"An actress?!" Marianne stopped. She looked first to the right, then to the left, her mouth wide open. "She's leaving the lights and glamour and hype of Broadway to come out and live in the middle of *nowhere*?! I mean, it's beautiful up here but it's very rural. And pretty sleepy."

"Hey, I offered to build her a theatre," Joe said, feeling himself getting defensive. He paused and tried lightening the tone again. "And now that George has stopped working for the County…."

Marianne stared at him with her turquoise blue eyes and Joe wondered if she were trying to determine his value compared to the value of a career on Broadway.

"You don't think I'm worth it?" he asked softly.

"No, no, I would never say that," countered Marianne. "I'm sure your girlfriend finds you and your little pottery shop very charming. But....." She hesitated, and looked to her left again.

Joe followed her gaze out to the wide expanse of pasture next to his house and he knew that, all around him, beyond what either of them could see, was just more pasture leading into woods that turned into thick forests that climbed the mountain ridges. The only thing that cut through this abundant greenery was the highway and that could be pretty sleepy at times too.

"....for someone whose art form requires being in the city," Marianne continued, "living up here would mean she's got her work cut out for her."

"Don't I know it," Joe agreed. He opened the door of the Bronco and held it open while Marianne climbed into the driver's seat. "And you can be sure if there's anyone that can make things more complicated than they need to be," he said, pointing his thumb back towards his chest, "it's me!"

Marianne chuckled. She placed her bag of pottery on the empty passenger seat and started the engine. "I bet you'll be a great help," she reassured him. She buckled herself in, wrinkling her nose as she peered up at the sky through the open door. "They said it was going to rain later."

"Yeah." Joe turned slightly and also looked up at the sky. It was the kind of clear, dazzling blue that made him want to stand at the edge of a high mountain lake and fish. "You couldn't tell it by that sky but I'd better go cover my slow clay. Just in case."

"Slow clay?"

"Well that's what I call it. I make clay outside and let it dry slooooowly, under the sun." He closed the door for Marianne and waved as she took her foot of the brake, and let the Bronco drift backwards, down the driveway.

Then he paused and looked up at the sky again as he heard a plane passing overhead. Marianne's obvious concern about Lucy's living here had definitely got to him. Sometimes he wondered if his first marriage would have lasted if he and his wife had bought acreage closer to a city. Not that Lucy had agreed to marry him. No, he hadn't got her to bite on that lure yet. But Joe was persistent when he wanted something and he'd been hoping that Lucy would take the lure once she tried life out here for real. But what if he were wrong? The Upper Skagit was beautiful but it was a tough place to make a living. And these mountains were filled with the memories of many who had tried and failed. Was he taking Lucy away from everything that felt familiar or welcoming her to the adventure of a lifetime? He reflected on this as he walked back up to his clay and slid a piece of sheet metal over it. Who knew? He looked down at his dog. "We like it here, don't we, Maggie?"

The beautiful brown dog thumped her tail on the ground behind her. "Woof!" she replied.

Lesson 2

Preparing Your Space

Before you can settle into making pots, you need to create an appropriate workspace. Try to situate your studio in a place of calm and inspiration.

They stood for a long time holding each other at the airport, the crowd milling around them as people rushed to or from their planes. At first Lucy was a little taken aback at the sight of Joe wearing a shirt with flowers on it because, where she was from, men didn't wear Hawaiian shirts; but then she saw the bouquet of irises he was holding out for her and she threw her arms around his neck and kissed him deeply, unashamedly. They melted into each other's embrace and made the 4 months they'd spent apart disappear without trace.

That had been 3 weeks ago and now Lucy realized that what she needed at Joe's place was a project. She'd spent much of her time so far settling in, meeting new people and following theatrical leads. Joe had procured the number of an actress down in Seattle for her from one of the local loggers and this actress had been very helpful, telling Lucy about the hotline for casting information, dates of the general auditions, which theatres participated in them and giving her the names of various casting directors that accepted résumés. That, together with the connections Lucy had gathered herself, through the theatre work she'd done in New York, gave her all she needed to get started. Now she just had to wait for the summer round of general auditions to begin. And she didn't want to twirl her fingers, doing nothing, while she waited.

Not that she ever did nothing. She was already taking a role, helping Joe with sales of his pottery in the shop, but she needed something to fill in the time between customers. So she found herself standing in the downstairs of his house, hands on her hips, eyeing the space to see what needed to be done to make it more habitable. Joe had finished some of the downstairs walls and had made sure that the shop was ready by finishing sheetrock on the two interior walls and around the bay windows, but the rest of the inside of the house was a long way from being complete.

Lucy was wearing light blue shorts and a yellow t-shirt with a pair of flat, white shoes with little holes in the top of them arranged to look like flowers. Her slender limbs were slightly tanned from the amount of time she was spending outside at Joe's, walking, hiking and moving wood around for him. Usually Lucy avoided being out in the sun because her freckled complexion burned too easily but she always seemed to be on the move when she was out in the sun here so it didn't bother her.

Inside Joe's house, though, Lucy noticed that the sun was being kept at a remove by the opaque plastic he'd tacked up over the opening for the big picture window in his living room. The same was true in the kitchen where he had openings for two, good-sized windows. Lucy made a mental note to start saving money from sales in the shop towards the Thermopane windows Joe needed. She looked down at the plywood floor; there wasn't much she could do about that in the short term because Joe had talked about wanting to make tiles for the floor. Lucy might be able to lay the tiles, but she couldn't make them. And the bathroom posed a similar problem. She could finish the sheetrock on the walls in there but Joe wanted to cover them with hand-made tiles so she wasn't sure how much finishing the sheetrock actually required. Maybe none. And the kitchen needed cabinets and counter tops but, again, Joe was looking for the right piece of salvage wood to turn into cabinets and then he'd make tiles for the counter top.

Lucy walked slowly up the fir stairs that Joe had built. They definitely needed sanding and varnishing and maybe she could do that before Joe built a handrail on them. If he built a handrail on them. Apparently he liked the "open" look of stairs with no handrail. Lucy got to the top of the stairs and turned right into Joe's master bedroom. It was a beautiful, long bedroom, stretching 30 feet from the back to the front of the house, with gable dormers in the ceiling at the front end and a gable roof in the back. The two picture windows along the outside and back walls were also covered in plastic, like the ones downstairs. Only the windows in the front, small, wood-framed recycled windows with the cross bars in the center that sat above matching windows in the shop, were in place. Lucy looked up at the exposed insulation in the ceiling; the sheetrock needed to be hung in here but she definitely couldn't take that on alone.

She moved from the big bedroom to the smaller, second bedroom at the top of the stairs. It was another romantic, country bedroom with an opening for a side window that looked out at Jackman Ridge and a sloping ceiling that went down to a bigger window in the back wall that almost touched an apple tree. Lucy imagined that this room would be lovely in the spring, when that tree was covered in apple blossoms. She looked up, at the log beam running the length of the room in the middle of the ceiling. It hadn't been sanded or varnished and the natural look of the wood added to the rustic charm of the room. Around the beam, the ceiling and walls were covered in sheetrock that needed mudding and taping. Here's my project, thought Lucy; finishing this sheetrock.

She heard a car door close out front and stepped away from the center of the room towards the doorway, waiting for Maggie's bark. But Maggie didn't bark. Was she on the front porch, Lucy wondered? She stepped forward to the top of the stairs, running her fingers through her long, loose curls to push them away from her face as she looked down at the porch. If she didn't see Maggie, maybe she'd see someone coming up onto the porch, heading for the shop. But nobody appeared. Maybe she'd been wrong about hearing a car door close.

Lucy decided to see if there was a vehicle in the driveway. She walked around the stairwell to the right, into an open space between the gable dormers at the front and the back bedroom. It wasn't a very big space, maybe 8 feet at its widest, with the midpoint narrowing around a hexagon-shaped opening over the stairs that Joe had created in the 4-inch thick, tongue-and-groove cedar flooring he'd reclaimed from a demolished church. The space was filled with light from two windows in the sidewall, both of which looked out on Jackman, and from the recycled wood-frame windows in the front that repeated the design of those in the shop and the master bedroom. One day this would make a perfect space for an office, Lucy thought, as she eased past the extra pots Joe had stored in this area for now.

She glanced out the second of the two side windows as she went by and her attention was caught by something moving in a plum tree on the neighbor's property. She stopped. Was there something moving in that plum tree? She peered at what looked like a fluffy ball on one of the branches and then gasped as she saw a pair of eyes appear, then disappear in the fluff. She waited, squinting a little to try to determine what she might be looking at and suddenly the eyes came around again, then disappeared again. Was that an owl, she asked herself? It couldn't be. Owls were nocturnal.

She looked down, for the pair of binoculars that Joe sometimes kept by this window so he could watch the edge of the tree line around the pasture for wildlife and again, her attention was caught by something. This time it was a head of white hair at the top of a lithe, t-shirt and jeans clad body that was bobbing up and down along Joe's property line. Uh oh, thought Lucy. She had no idea what the owner of the white hair was doing but she thought she ought to go and get Joe. She glanced at the plum tree again; the fluffy ball was still there. Joe would probably like to see that too.

She jogged nimbly down the stairs and across the living room, out the opening for a future sliding glass door in the side of the house and leapt the four steps off the small porch there onto the ground. Then she hurried up the path worn in the grass, towards Joe's studio. She went past the outhouse with its stellar view of Sauk Mountain that she'd used until she helped Joe save enough to have his bathroom plumbed last summer. That was the first project she'd undertaken on Joe's house and she was very proud of that accomplishment. Not that it hadn't been without its trials; Lucy had saved a total of $350 but the plumber's bid came in at $650. Fortunately the plumber was willing to work with them and accepted firewood and pottery as the balance for his fee and the next thing Joe knew, he had an indoor toilet. And a shower, so he wouldn't have to keep going down to his friend, Sonny's house for a shower.

The path in the grass ended at the corner of Joe's garden, where it met the graveled lane coming up from the driveway. Lucy crossed the gravel, her gaze fixed on the studio Joe had built for himself 10 years previously after a disastrous fire had claimed the first structure he'd built on this property. That structure had everything in it, he'd told her; the shop, the studio and a living area, and the whole lot had burned to the ground very nearly taking Joe with it. Joe and his wife, Erica, were younger than Lucy at the time, only twenty-five, and they'd lost everything to that fire. Everything but some clothes that Erica had been washing at the Laundromat when the fire was happening. Lucy could imagine it would have discouraged most people from going on with their dream. But Joe reflected on the happening over and over again while he was lying in a hospital bed, recovering from the third-degree burns on his legs, and decided that what he needed to take from it was the art of decentralization. If he had a studio separate from his house and something happened to the house, at least he'd still have a place to work. And vice-versa. Joe's mother put a used mobile home on his property, so he and Erica would have a place to live, and when Joe got home, he scrounged enough reclaimed and scrap wood products to build himself a studio.

The result was another post-and-beam structure, single story and smaller than Joe's house at 20 by 24 feet, with a tiny loft area. That's where Joe was living the first summer Lucy met him, in the loft space under the metal roof, above the pots he was creating. She remembered how he used to croon down to Maggie the ballad after which she was named – *"Magnolia, you sweet thing, you're driving me wild!"* – and, since the dog couldn't climb the ladder up to the loft to be with him, she'd smack her tail happily on the wood floor. A beautiful wood floor made out of tight-grained, tongue-and-groove fir that Joe had scored from some massive rolling doors in a warehouse that somebody had asked him to take apart. Of course, the floor was hard to see, covered as it was in a fine sheen of clay dust but when Joe swabbed it out after every firing, he was always impressed with the quality of the wood. And the windows in the space were recycled too, single pane and large, to let in the natural light, though most of them were liberally coated in clay, especially the one by Joe's wheel. That was another project Lucy had in mind; to clean the studio so Joe could actually see the woods around it out of the windows.

He'd built himself a barn door on the studio and Lucy climbed the steps leading up to the narrow porch and rolled the door open. Maggie jumped up to greet her. "Well don't you look nice," Joe said as Lucy stepped into the space. He'd just finished putting handles on coffee cups and his hands were muddy and wet but he stretched his arms out to welcome his little redhead into an embrace. Lucy stepped forward and slipped her arms around his waist, kissing him, but drew back when his muddy hands got too close to her. "Don't," she chided, "you'll get my shorts dirty."

"Not if you take them off I won't," Joe teased.

"No such luck," Lucy informed him, tossing her head to get her curls away from her face. Joe couldn't help himself; she just looked so good. He stepped towards her again. "No really," she said, putting a hand flat against the center of his chest. "There's somebody down at the house."

"A customer?" Joe bent over to rinse his hands off in a bucket of milky water at the base of his clay bin.

"I don't think so. It's some bloke, messing around by your property line."

Joe frowned as he wiped his hands on a clay-encrusted towel. "Which property line?"

"The one at the side of the house, that you can see from the windows upstairs overlooking the pasture on Burns' property next door."

"Where there are all those blackberries?"

"Uh huh."

"Oh." Joe untied the orange and white striped apron he had around his waist and threw it on top of the towel on the clay bin. "He's probably eating my blackberries is all. Or talking to Daisy."

"The cow?"

"Uh huh."

Joe's neighbor, Clarence Burns, had one lone cow to keep his pasture down but the animal spent much of her time up against Joe's property line, hoping that somebody would talk to her. Sometimes Joe did, sometimes Maggie, and sometimes Joe's customers, particularly if they had children with them.

Joe turned back to the mugs he'd just finished. They were lined up on his wedging table, on a 1 by 12 by 4-foot long wooden plank that Joe referred to as a ware board, since he used a stack of these boards to put his pottery wares on before firing them in the kiln. He lifted the ware board holding his newly trimmed and decorated mugs, carried it over to one of the racks he'd made out of log posts and slipped it onto two dowels that protruded from the posts. There the mugs could dry at their own pace. "I was going over for coffee break anyway," he told Lucy as he turned off the overhead lights, "so I'll come check this guy out."

"Okay and I want you to look at this little bird I saw in the plum tree next door," Lucy replied as she rolled open the door. "It sort of looks like an owl but I don't see how that can be given that it's daytime."

"Some owls are diurnal," replied Joe, bouncing to his left to grab a pair of binoculars that were sitting on top of his clay mixer. He followed Lucy out the door. "I'll look from the front porch when I introduce myself to our mystery guest."

❦

They parted company at the corner of the garden, Lucy heading across the footpath to go inside and start water for coffee, Joe striding casually down towards the driveway with Maggie beside him. He came around the front of the house and saw a cherry red Mazda RX7 parked in the shade of his big cedar tree. He looked to the right and, sure enough, there was some old guy snacking on the blackberries growing at the end of the concrete slab on which Joe had built his house. The guy kept disappearing out of sight as he bent down to examine the pile of rocks Joe had sitting on the concrete slab.

Joe climbed the front steps and walked the length of the porch, putting himself just a few feet away from the old fellow. He lifted the binoculars up to his eyes and moved them over the branches of the plum tree. Yep, there was a pygmy owl on one of the branches, turning his head this way and that, hunting for his breakfast in the pasture below. He watched the bird, fascinated, while the guy in front of him continued to touch the rocks with one hand while slipping blackberries into his mouth with the other.

"You want anything to go with those berries?" Joe asked after a few moments.

"Oh no thanks," replied the man, barely glancing around to acknowledge Joe.

"Say, did you get these rocks from around here?"

"That depends," quipped Joe. "Are you missing some or something?"

"Because this gneiss I would expect," the man went on, letting Joe's dry humor pass right over his head and out into the field where the pygmy owl was still hunting from the plum tree. "But this marble..."

"Is that marble?" Joe was intrigued. He jumped down off the end of the porch and moved forward to join the old guy at his rock pile. "I always thought that was gneiss."

"No, no, this is definitely marble. This little grouping here," said the man, waving his hand over a small accumulation of rocks to his right, "with the greenish hue to them, now those are all gneiss......"

"See, now, I've only ever heard that called Finney Creek green because it comes from up at Finney Creek. And I always thought it was granite."

"Well that's what gneiss is," exclaimed the man, obviously pleased to have a willing participant in his knowledge. "Metamorphosed granite."

"I did not know that." Joe was joking but he actually loved the way this old geezer was getting down on his pile of rocks, popping his false teeth slightly out of his mouth as he concentrated. "What about this one?"

"Mudstone. Mudstone with molten silica. That's what that glassy line is inside this one – molten silica. You see, this mountain range, the Cascade Mountains," began the fellow, having sucked his false teeth back into his mouth and straightened his lean figure to a stand, "was formed when gobs and gobs of oceanic crust moved in-land and collided with the continental plate. Of course it didn't do that overnight - it took billions and billions of years – but what that *means* is that every part of the periodic table is to be found in the rock of the Cascade Mountains. *Every* part," he emphasized, using his right hand to sweep the mountain ridges around them while his left grazed the blackberries, "with *all* the blanks filled in. And what *that* translates into is every trace mineral you could ever wish for being found in the soil around here. Which is why the food grown in the Skagit Valley is *so **much better*** than food grown in areas of sedimentary or igneous rock." He crammed the blackberries he'd picked with his free hand into his mouth. "Good berries," he said through the juice.

"You should try the ones that grow wild up in the high country." The man turned a pair of beady blue eyes on Joe. "Dewberries, that's what we call them," Joe went on. "They're tiny, about the size of the tip of my little finger..." Joe lifted his hands and emphasized the point by pinching off the end of one pinkie with the thumb and forefinger of the opposing hand. His fingers were thick and blunt-ended and revealed that he was a potter by the half-worn thumbnails and the remnants of dry clay in the creases of every knuckle. "So it takes me about an hour to pick a pint. But you can't beat them for flavor. Oo, baby! It's like a burst of summer inside your mouth every time you eat one. "

"And they grow.....?" Joe could tell that the man was trying to sound casual.

"In the mountains around here," Joe replied. Then he laughed as the fellow tightened his lips in mock peeve. "You've got to buy a lot of pottery before I'll reveal my dewberry spots to you!"

He was joking, of course, but the man, with the efficiency of someone in pursuit of something they want, spun to face Joe's house. "Well then, take me to the pottery shop!"

Lucy went up to the back bedroom again after she put the kettle on, carrying a ladder and some tape for the seams in the sheetrock. She could hear Joe and his visitor talking when she got into the room, through the opening for the window, and she was surprised by how casual it all seemed. It was one thing for someone to ask if they could taste the berries in Joe's front garden but for someone just to stop and eat them – that would definitely cause a problem where she was from.

She positioned the ladder at the lower end of the ceiling and climbed it, tape in hand. Lucy grew up living in a semi-detached house, which meant it shared a common wall with the neighbors' house, a common wall through which the elderly neighbor's name – "SID-NEEEEEY!" – would float, loudly and repeatedly, every time his infirm wife needed him. Apparently Sidney was a little hard of hearing; or at least, he was when his wife yelled for him. The garden between the two properties, however, was clearly divided by a 5-foot high wooden fence but that didn't stop her parents from quibbling with Sidney over the greenery that sprawled in both directions. And the quibbles would lead to things like Sidney lighting a stinky bonfire of wet leaves when her mother put her clean washing out on the line to dry or her father getting out his shears and hacking away at Sidney's hydrangea bushes. Lucy hated to think what would have happened if Sidney had been caught filching her mother's raspberries.

But Joe was pretty easy about all that stuff. Of course, he'd grown up in an Irish-American family in Upstate New York, where friends, neighbors and the extended family wandered in whenever they felt like it to sit around the kitchen table and visit. Lucy's parents never really had anyone drop in. In fact, her mother used to make Lucy and her sisters hide under the kitchen table when somebody they knew ventured to knock on the front door, something that Lucy wondered about, a *lot*, until she grew up and understood what her mother was really hiding.

Lucy snapped her mind out of *that* thought before it could sink any deeper and smoothed a length of tape over a seam as far as she could stretch backwards on the ladder, then tore it off with her fingers. She climbed back down the ladder and moved it, to finish the last few feet of the seam. She thought about how a friend of hers at NYU had asked her once what ambitions she had other than work ambitions? What she wanted out of her everyday life? Lucy hadn't even had to think about that one. "I want to have a home where people can come anytime and share food at my table," she replied. She climbed the ladder again and smoothed tape from the tear down to where the sheetrock met the wall. Joe certainly seemed to share that ambition, she thought, as she heard the men discussing geology down on the concrete slab. Shared it and then some.

Once inside the shop Joe's visitor gravitated towards a large salad bowl that had green mountains carved into the outside and liberal splashes of purple and red on the inside. He turned it around and over comfortably in his hands, peering intently at all the colors.

"My name's Joe, by the way," said Joe as he came into the shop behind the customer. "And I make the pots."

"I gathered that," replied his visitor without taking his eyes off the bowl, "from the dots of clay on your glasses." Then he looked up and smiled at the young potter. "And I'm Sol."

Joe pulled a black and gold bandana out of the back pocket of his jeans. He removed his large, square-frame glasses and set about cleaning the lenses while he wandered across the room to sit on his bar stool. "And what do you do, Sol?"

"Well I'm retired now but I used to work as a petroleum

geologist."

"Really!" This was the first time he'd had a geologist in his shop. "No wonder you know so much about the subject. So tell me this, " he went on quickly, propping his now-clean glasses back on his nose. "Is 'gobs and gobs' a technical term?"

"It's in all the textbooks," affirmed Sol. He put the bowl back down on the table and made a good-natured, 'don't try to get the better of me' pucker with his lips in Joe's direction.

Joe laughed. "And where did you do your petroleum geology work?"

"Venezuela. For the most part." Sol picked up another wider, shallower bowl that was rich cobalt in color with gold flecks dusting the center. He stared at it for a good long while before he spoke again. "I worked for an American company down there. I still have an office at Lake Maracaibo and I own quite a bit of land down there that's just *dripping* with petroleum. I'm sure of it. If only I could find investors for the drilling."

"So that's where you live? Venezuela?"

"Part of the time. I have a son who's a fisherman on the coast and I spend part of the year with him. And I have a son here, in Gig Harbor, that I spend part of the year with. Right now I'm on my way to Idaho to visit my niece and her husband. And then I have a son in Boston and one in New York..." He trailed off, becoming more involved with the bowl than the conversation. "Say, I like this," he said, pointing to the gold flecks in the bowl.

"You know what that is?"

"Some kind of metal...?"

"No, that's wood ash...."

"Wood ash?"

"Yeah. I have a wood-firing kiln...."

"A *wood*-firing kiln?" Sol lifted his glasses and brought the bowl right up to his eyes.

Joe liked this old fellow's intensity and how he didn't seem to limit it to any one particular subject. "So how many sons have you got?"

"Seven."

"Seven?! You and your wife must have kept trying for a girl, huh?"

"Well they're not ours," Sol corrected. He lowered first the bowl, then his glasses back over his eyes so he could look at Joe. "No, my wife and I didn't have any children together. And we're divorced now. She divorced me, oh, about twenty years ago."

"But you adopted seven boys together?"

"No, it was just me that adopted the boys, although I don't have any papers on them. Nothing legal like that. But they all treat me as a father." Sol chewed on his dentures a moment and Joe watched his eyes narrow, as if he were searching for the best way to tell this story. "I met the first one in Caracas, just after the divorce. I was walking down the street, feeling sorry for myself, when this young man came up and offered to have sex with me for money. I told him, "No, no, I don't want to have sex with you. But I'll buy you a cup of coffee." We ended up in a café, talking, and I found him to be the most interesting young man. *The most* interesting," he reiterated, punctuating each word with a sideways turn of his head. "And I asked him, if you had a choice, and could be anything at all in the world, what would you be? And he said a doctor. So I put him through medical school in the US and now he's a medico in Boston." He smiled proudly. "That's my son, Eduardo."

Joe loved this guy! "And the one in Gig Harbor?" he asked.

"Pedro?" Sol put the bowl back down on the table. Apparently this was a story that required his hands for the telling. Maybe his hands and his arms and his legs by the way he was positioning himself. Joe leaned back against the wall behind his bar stool, to enjoy the show in comfort. "He was cleaning windows in Venezuela, in a house where I was a guest. The house overlooked Lake Maracaibo so it had *huge* windows, because of the view, and I looked up to see this young boy climbing around and over the windows, like it was nothing in the world. He looked like a *monkey* the way he was navigating those windows." He stretched his arms and legs this way and that in a perfect, theatrical re-enactment of Pedro's window-washing moves.

Joe laughed again. Sol, he determined, must be well into his sixties yet he was as lithe as a twentysomething and had the zest for life of a thirteen-year-old boy.

"That was Pedro," Sol went on, "and he was fifteen. And again, I asked him what he would do if he could be anything he wanted in the world and he said he'd be a vet. So I helped him get the education he needed and now he's a vet in Gig Harbor." Sol picked up the blue bowl again. "And I have a son who's an artist in New York City and one who's a physicist at Princeton University. And then Ramon, who owns a line of fishing boats in Venezuela..." He trailed off and looked quizzically at Joe. "Why a wood-firing kiln?"

Joe sat up, to explain his subject now. "Well for one thing there's a ton of waste wood around here…"

"From the logging?"

"Well that and from the shake mills. That's what I use primarily; cedar shake mill waste. It's available, it burns hot and fast and it's free. And when I started out that was a big plus. Now I usually pay someone to deliver it to me."

"So you make a living at your pottery then?"

"I wish." Joe smiled. "I usually tell people that I have enough money in my pocket either to drive to town or to buy groceries once I get there."

Sol shrugged. "You can always eat blackberries."

"I can if you don't get to them first!"

They both laughed. Then Joe jumped back into his explanation. "Plus the wood-firing's traditional. And it glazes the pots in its own special way. See this," he removed a mug from one of the hooks on the display table to his right, walked over to Sol and ran his fingers lightly over the unglazed foot of the mug. "See how bronzed the clay is on this side compared to the other? That's all wood ash. I get that a lot on the pots closest to the firebox in the kiln." He put the mug down on the center table and took the bowl out of the Sol's hands. "But I've never had wood ash float down inside a bowl like this before." He gazed admiringly down at the pot. This was what he wanted from wood firing but he'd never achieved it. Not until this bowl. "I think that's pretty special," he remarked.

"Museum quality," stated Sol, taking back the bowl with care.

"Yeah except after I got it out of the kiln and yodeled my thanks to the kiln gods, some dilettante potter from….well, I don't remember where she was from now…anyway, she told me that you can cheat by sprinkling wood ash in the bowl before you fire it." He looked Sol squarely in the eye and grimaced his ruefulness. "That burst my bubble, I'll tell you!"

Sol shrugged, a gesture of his resignation about some people in this world, and then rearranged his dentures before stating, "You know, I don't think I've ever seen a wood-firing kiln."

"Well, you'd better come with me then," Joe was already moving towards the door. Sol went to put the bowl back on the table but changed his mind before it touched the surface. "You can leave that here," Joe reassured him. "It'll be safe."

"Are you sure?"

"Here. I'll put it in the sold section." Joe took the bowl from Sol, bent over and placed it on the floor between two display tables, under a sign that he'd scrawled and pinned to the wall, which read, "THESE POTS ARE SOLD!"

"What if they don't see the sign?" asked Sol, obviously unsure about the whole arrangement.

Joe bent over and picked the bowl up again. 'We'll just put it in the house," he concurred, scrunching up his nose and nodding his head as if this were definitely the better choice. "That way no one will even see it."

Joe took four steps across the porch from the shop to the house and went inside.

"Hey, Lucy?" he called out.

"Yes?" Lucy called back from her position in the middle of the ladder.

"Where you at?"

"I'm upstairs in the back bedroom," replied Lucy as she climbed down the ladder and walked out of the room to the top of the stairs. "I thought I'd start on the sheetrock in here."

"Oh, good deal!" exclaimed Joe. "So I'm heading up to the kiln with Sol here…" He swung around and found his new friend gazing up the stairs at Lucy with a schoolboy smirk on his face. "And I'm leaving this bowl that he wants at the bottom of the stairs." Joe held the bowl up for Lucy to see then placed it on a 4-by-4 platform that was just inside the front door to the right. "Because he doesn't want anyone else to buy it."

"How much is it?" Lucy asked.

"I don't know," Joe replied. He turned the bowl over and found the price sticker. "Fifty bucks."

"What if someone offers me seventy-five?" she questioned and turned one side of her face towards Sol with the eye closed, to suggest she was playing with him.

The old fellow pushed his lips forward in a big pout. "Then I'll just have to offer you a hundred!" he proclaimed.

Lucy chuckled. "Don't worry," she reassured him. "I won't sell it out from under you." She looked at Joe again. "What do you want me to do about the kettle when it boils?"

"Just turn it off, would you. And maybe I can make some coffee when we get back from the kiln while you help Sol with his purchases in the shop."

"Sounds like a plan," Lucy agreed.

Joe turned back around and led Sol out the front door and down the steps.

"Who was that?" Sol asked from behind him.

Joe slowed down to let Sol catch up with him. "That was my sweetie. Lucy."

"I take it she's not from around here."

"Nope. She's from England. And she's really good at selling my pots." They walked in step now, around the house and up the graveled lane towards the studio and the kiln. "And if I manage to keep her around, I might start to make a living for real at my pottery."

"You'd better keep her around then."

"I'm working on it," Joe replied. He glanced back and saw that Sol had stopped to look at something up in the sky.

"Now if that's not worth the price of admission, I don't know what is," Sol muttered, his eyes fixed on Sauk Mountain sitting way above the trees at the back of Joe's property.

Joe followed his gaze to the top of the mountain. "Yeah," he agreed. "That's what got me to buy this property, that view of Sauk. I fell in love the moment I saw her. So did Erica." Sol wandered up to stand next to Joe, never taking his eyes off the mountain. Joe went on. "My wife at the time," he explained, "We were fresh out of art school in Kansas City, had just got married and wanted a place in the country where we could be back-to-the-land hippies. Well, it was 1975 – who didn't want to be a back-to-the-land hippie in the mid-70s?"

"I didn't," said Sol.

"That's 'cause you were down in Venezuela, eating Red Snapper with arepa while dancing the merengue."

Sol grinned broadly, as if that described exactly what he'd been doing. And he'd enjoyed it.

"But Erica and I had a plan to emigrate to Canada, open a little pottery business and live off the land. So we took our time, journeying across country, and got to the border here, in Washington State, only to have the Canadians turn us back. They didn't want us. Said they'd met their quota of Americans moving north in the early 70s…"

Sol nodded. "To escape being drafted into the Vietnam War."

"Exactly right. So we turned around and headed back east, opting to take the scenic route on this newly opened Highway 20, all the while thinking that we'd go back to Kansas, where Erica was from, but also thinking we'd keep our eyes open in case we saw something that appealed to us in land for sale." Maggie trotted over to Joe with a stick in her mouth and he stopped his story just long enough to throw it into the woods alongside his studio. Maggie gave chase and Joe picked up where he'd left off. "I think we would have missed the sign for this 5 acres, it was such a gray day, kind of typical for October up here - non-stop drizzle - although I didn't know that then, but I was so taken by all the trees that somehow I noticed the sign. We were past it by the time I saw it, of course, but we turned around, further up the highway, and came back to see what else might be on the property. And didn't really find much of anything. There were trees, a loafing shed for a cow, a creek and a lot – a *lot* – of moss. It was like we'd walked into a rain forest." He looked down and saw Maggie's stick on the ground in front of him and the dog staring up at him expectantly. He picked up the stick and tossed it into the woods again. "Which appealed to me because it was so different from Upstate New York and Kansas City but I certainly didn't get a very strong feel for this place. So I asked the owner, Clarence Burns, who's now my neighbor - along with his cow - if I could pitch a tent for the night. He said yes and the next morning, when I stuck my head out of the tent, the sun was shining and Sauk Mountain was out." He shrugged. "And I knew I was home."

The thought lingered as they both stared at the top of Sauk, bathed in the greens and russets of her summer splendor. Sol broke the silence. "Do you get clay for your pottery from that mountain?" he asked

"No. I tried but it didn't work. I fired a hundred grams of the local clay in the kiln but it fired out to almost nothing. There's no way it'll make a pot."

Sol nodded. "It's geologically too young."

"Is *that* what it is?" exclaimed Joe, fascinated.

Sol nodded again. "It's probably volcanic ash. Maybe from Mount Baker."

"Huh," Joe bent forward and picked up Maggie's stick once more. He threw it into the woods for her then moved on, leading Sol towards the kiln. "So I might be able to make a color with it."

Lucy was trying to smear sheetrock mud all the way up the

length of a seam in the ceiling when she heard the front door open and Joe call her name as he stepped inside. She lost her balance slightly on the ladder and the mud slid off the trowel and landed, with a plop, on the floor below her. She looked down at the gray mess, tutted, then climbed back down the ladder. She wiped her hands on one of Joe's old t-shirts that she'd been using as a rag, took the few steps to the top of the stairs and saw Joe waiting for her at the bottom, holding the blue bowl out in her direction. "Have at it," he encouraged with a smile.

Lucy trotted down the stairs and took the bowl out of Joe's hands. "What's his name again?"

"Sol."

Lucy nodded. She walked across the porch and into the shop and found Sol examining a cylindrical insert that Joe made for his teapots. "Is this for tea?" he asked turning the insert over in his hand.

"Uh huh, yes. It's a strainer, for loose-leaf tea. So you put a couple of tablespoons of tea down in there," she explained, pointing down inside the cylinder that Sol was holding, "pour your boiling water into the teapot and lower the strainer into the water to brew your tea."

Sol looked at the numerous holes that were peppering the insert. "And the tea doesn't come out through these holes?"

"Nope. The tea starts to expand as soon as it hits the water, so no, it doesn't go through the holes."

Sol gently lowered the strainer back into the teapot. "My niece would like that," he said, looking up at the English girl. "She makes a lot of tea."

Lucy nodded. "I like mine," she told him. "Joe makes them like that, with the strainer, because of a teapot his grandmother used when he was a boy. She was from Ireland."

Sol looked at the teapot once more and sighed. "I'm not sure my niece would prefer this green though," he said.

"That's Mount St. Helen's ash," Lucy explained with a tip of her chin towards the pot. "And Joe's not sure he prefers it either. The green's too dark and nondescript. He used it on a few pieces because so many people asked after it but he said he's not going to use it anymore."

"It's not like the green on the outside of that big salad bowl," Sol mentioned, looking over at a bowl with the green mountains on the outside. "That's the first piece I noticed."

"No," agreed Lucy. "That's much brighter. That's the green

slip Joe makes though, and slip is colored clay, not glaze. Did you see the flecks of lavender overlaying the green on the outside of that bowl?" Sol cocked his head curiously. "You should take it out into the sunlight. Then you'll see them."

Sol jumped at this instruction. He carried the big salad bowl out onto the front porch and walked down the steps until he hit the sunlight. "Say, you're *right!*" he exclaimed as all the colors on the bowl lit up. Lucy was carrying the blue bowl she'd been asked to watch over. She held it out in front of her so Sol could see how the wood ash floating on the inside became iridescent when caught by the sun. Sol's eyes bugged wide open. He thrust his false teeth forward excitedly out of his mouth then sucked them back in. "Maybe this is what old mossy needs," he said, nodding back towards the shop.

Lucy knew immediately that he meant the teapot. "No," she countered, "that glaze doesn't even pop in the sunlight. But there are plenty of others that do."

It didn't take them long to move pots of interest from the shop to the front steps so that Sol could examine them in sunlight. Joe heard all the commotion from the kitchen, poured a cup of coffee and headed out to join them. "What in the world are you doing?" he asked once he got to the porch.

"Say, you should set your pots out here to sell them!" Sol called out from down in the driveway where he was holding a mug in each hand up to the light. Lucy was standing beside him, patiently waiting with two more mugs.

Joe crossed the porch to the steps and went down two. He sat on the first step, took a swig of his coffee and then set it down between his feet. "I did for a while," he told Sol, "while I built the house. I had the pots on the display tables right about where you're standing, and I stuck a coffee can on one of the tables with a sign on it that said, "Leave Money Here." And you know what? People did."

"Is that right?!"

"I still sometimes go into the shop and find a check on the counter made out to the pottery with a price sticker or three next to it." Joe stretched his legs out down the steps.

"Hey be careful of my pots," Sol cautioned.

Joe looked down at the row of mugs, bowls and cream pitchers lined up on the lower steps to his right.

"These are all yours?" he asked, surprised.

"Uh huh. So don't break them."

Joe leaned back on his elbows and let his eyes dance over the mountain ridges opposite his house. He liked it when they were backlit by the soft blue of the summer sky. He looked up. The summers here weren't nearly as oppressive or suffocating as the summers in Upstate New York; he liked that too.

He leaned forward again and watched Lucy running her fingers gently over the surface of one of his mugs, pointing out all the colors to Sol. She was a girl who did well with an audience, that was for sure. Joe took another sip of his coffee and watched four cars sail by on the highway. Now if he could just figure out how to bring that audience to her, he'd be all set.

Lesson 3

Structuring Your Time

One of the most important factors in your success as a potter is how you organize your time. You can't go into your studio late in the day to throw pots and hope to have them dry enough to work on the next morning.

Almost two months after Lucy's arrival, Sonny pulled into Joe's driveway at 7:30 on a Sunday morning armed with the newspaper. Joe called Sonny his brother even though he wasn't really, it just seemed that way to both of them because they'd been born six weeks apart, right across the street from each other in Saratoga Springs, New York, and had been best friends from the start. And when Joe moved out to the Skagit, his best friend came to visit – and never left.

Sonny climbed out of his pick-up and started to take a leak against one of the fir trees in Joe's front yard. The air was soft and balmy, offering the promise of another fine, summer day and because it was so early in the morning, the highway was pleasantly quiet. A few blue jays circled overhead, giving chase to smaller birds while they hunted for free food, and the branches of the cedar trees around Joe's house rustled softly as the gentle morning breeze blew through them. Sunday morning was nature's time in the Upper Skagit.

Joe saw Sonny pull in through the glass in his front door, picked up his mug of tea and wandered out onto the front porch to join him. "Whatcha doing?" he teased.

"Watering the peonies," replied Sonny, without turning around.

"Don't they smell great?" Joe lowered himself to a sit on his top step.

"Not any more they don't," replied Sonny. Then he turned his head to the right and lifted it, enabling Joe to see his profile over the truck. "Hey, I just saw you in the newspaper. In the color supplement."

"Did I make it to the front cover?" asked Joe, scanning the trees around his house for signs of life.

"Uh uh, no. Dale's on the front. But there's a big picture of you standing in front of the kiln inside the paper. It's a good picture, too."

Joe gulped his tea as he honed in on a pileated woodpecker hammering for ants in the phone pole out by his rose garden. He was pretty sure it must be a pileated woodpecker because of the crown of red feathers on the top of its black and white head.

"You think you'll get any business out of it?" asked Sonny.

"Out of what?"

"Out of the newspaper article."

"Probably," Joe said. He didn't really care one way or the other. He flicked his eyes back towards Sonny. "Not if you stand out front peeing all day I won't."

Sonny loped around from behind the truck, rearranging his shorts as he did so. "You don't know that," he remarked. "That might be just the lure you need."

"Hey, I'd've been rich long ago if that were the case."

Sonny swung his rear end around to land a few steps down from where Joe was sitting. He was a big, burly guy with buzz-cut, sandy-colored hair and a crick in his shoulders from working as a carpenter that set him slightly off kilter in his posture. His size was at odds with his somewhat shy demeanor as well as with the boy-like fuzz of strawberry blonde hair on his limbs. Joe noticed a pronounced t-shirt line below a patch of red on the back of Sonny's neck; he must be working outside, pounding nails, to have scored a sunburn like that, Joe thought to himself.

"You want something to drink?" he asked his friend, holding out his mug of tea as if that was what was on offer.

"Nah. I just had breakfast at the café in town."

"That's where you saw the newspaper article?"

"Yeah. A lot of people were talking about it."

"In a good way?"

"For the most part. I guess some people thought it made us look like we don't work too much." Joe was studying the pileated woodpecker again and Sonny's eyes automatically strayed towards the phone pole and the bird. "I feel like I work all the time," he said, his tone mystified. He tipped his baseball cap up off his head and, with the same hand, rubbed his buzz cut vigorously before putting the cap back on.

"Me too," agreed Joe.

The woodpecker took off and both men watched it with the synchronization of thirty-three years of moments such as this shared together.

"Hey, you know what else I heard?" Sonny went on, changing the subject.

"I couldn't imagine." Joe was now watching a blue jay that was sitting in one of his Silver fir trees, eyeballing Maggie's dry dog food on the front porch. No doubt wondering when they were going to move so he could steal it, Joe thought to himself.

"The Kings are running in the Baker River."

Joe's head whipped around. "Is that right? You going?"

Sonny nodded. "I've got my gear in the truck. Have you got pots to work on?"

Joe shook his head no. "I don't throw on Saturday so I don't have pots to finish this morning. But I need to be back by 11 to throw for tomorrow."

"Yeah," agreed Sonny. "I don't want to be out there long either. I've got things to do."

Maggie trotted towards them from her morning jaunt around the property. "I should run up to the store, get Lucy a newspaper first," Joe told Sonny.

"I've got one in the truck she can have."

"Great! I'll go get my fishing gear then."

❀

Lucy came downstairs in her sweat pants and t-shirt and found the Sunday newspaper on the table with a note from Joe – "Gone fishing. Be back in a couple of hours." She glanced up at the burl wood clock on the wall between the kitchen and the living room; almost 8. That's good, she thought, with a big yawn. That would still leave her plenty of time to prepare for her audition down in Seattle this afternoon.

She wandered over to the kitchen and slipped her hands around the teapot on the plywood counter. It was still warm. Joe had some of his reject mugs hanging on nails on the wall above the counter and Lucy chose a big, round one with swirls of green and blue overlapping under a clear glaze. She filled it with tea, added a splash of milk and lifted the mug to her lips to take a sip. The tea was warm and strong and Lucy stood for a moment, her left hand wrapped around the belly of the mug, her eyes lost in the many shades of green she could see covering Jackman Ridge outside the window. She blinked and lowered the mug, thinking how much she liked to drink her morning tea in a round mug. She carried it over to the table under the picture window in the living room, set it down and picked up the newspaper as she sat on a battered, gold-colored couch that someone had given Joe. She folded her legs underneath her, picked up the tea again and sipped it as her eyes ran over the news headlines. President Reagan's response to the freeing of a US captive in Lebanon, Tenth anniversary of the earthquake in Tangshan, China. She turned the page; Lethal gas escapes from a volcanic lake in Cameroon, West Africa. Lucy spent a moment reading about the 1,200 people feared dead in that event and then her eye was caught by a photograph of Margaret Thatcher, with a caption about how she was set to open the new M25 ring road around London in October. Lucy didn't much care for Maggie Thatcher, She'd been very excited when a woman was finally elected Prime Minister in Britain but she wished it hadn't been Thatcher, who had made so many promises to women during her first election campaign, which had happened when Lucy was at university in London, and then she didn't do a thing for them once she was in office. Like that South London Women's Hospital that she promised to keep open if elected and then she let it close. It was depressing.

Lucy put the newspaper down on the couch beside her, yawned again and stood up, thinking about what she might eat for breakfast. Something sustaining, like bacon and eggs. She walked over to the kitchen and opened the refrigerator. There was bacon, but no eggs. She thought for a second. Maybe she'd wander up to Joe's chicken coop and see if there were any eggs in the nesting boxes. Joe only had one hen left and he let her range freely on the property so she wouldn't get lonely; but the hen did occasionally go back to the coop and lay an egg. Maybe Lucy would get lucky.

She walked up past the studio and garden to the ramshackle coop Joe had built at the base of a big maple tree by some huckleberry bushes. Lucy climbed up on the hunk of wood that acted as a step and peered inside. Sure enough there was one big, brown egg in the nesting box opposite the door. She leaned in and picked it up out of the cedar shavings that lined the nest. It felt cool and smooth against her fingers and she slipped it into the fleecy interior of the pocket in her sweats to take back down to the house.

Once she was in the kitchen again she lifted the precious egg out of her pocket and set it on the counter next to the teapot. She'd pour herself another cup of tea, make herself some toast and fry up the bacon and the egg. Too bad she didn't have some of her mother's homemade marmalade to go with it all.

But as she was lifting the bacon out of the packet to set it in the frying pan, she heard Maggie's low, steady bark. Lucy bobbed to her left and looked out the front door; sure enough there was somebody pulling in. She turned around and glanced at the clock on the wall again. 8:30. A bit early for customers. She rinsed her hands off in the kitchen sink and walked out onto the front porch. Two young women were climbing out of a Subaru station wagon. "Are you open?" they asked.

"Of course," replied Lucy. She hadn't brushed her hair yet but they probably wouldn't notice because her hair tended to look messy even when it was brushed. She showed them into the shop and spent 20 minutes with them, while they looked at every mug available. Apparently they'd read about Joe in this morning's newspaper and since they were on their way up to hike Sauk Mountain, they decided to stop in and check out his pottery. Lucy realized they were talking about the newspaper she'd just been reading in the house but she hadn't seen Joe in it. Nor had he mentioned anything about being in the newspaper. Or had he? Lucy wracked her brain while the girls compared mugs. Now that she thought about it, she did recollect a phone conversation with Joe, while she was still living in New York, in which he told her about hanging out with a newspaper reporter who was doing a piece about the people who lived in the Upper Skagit. And maybe he'd said that he was going to be featured in that article. She'd have to look when she got back into the house.

The young women came towards her, each holding a pair of mugs. Lucy added up the totals, wrapped the mugs in newspaper and put them in a bag with one of Joe's hand-made, silk-screened business cards. Then she took their money. She thanked them and nipped back indoors, crossing the living room to slip the cash she'd just made into the porcelain jar on a shelf by the couch where Joe kept his sales. She glanced at the newspaper as she walked back across the room. She really wanted to go through it and look for the article with Joe in it but she also realized that the ladies' impromptu visit might be an indication of how the rest of the day was to go so maybe she ought to get cleaned up. Lucy stopped and looked at the clock on the wall once more; it was almost 9. She made a beeline for the bathroom.

By 11 o'clock Joe's little pottery shop was packed and there was still no sign of Joe. There were six women in the shop, including Lucy, and a smiling, teddy bear of a man, who was accompanying his wife. A young woman of about Lucy's age, who had introduced herself as Ann from Seattle, had Lucy cornered by the door and seemed more interested in finding out her history than looking at the pots.

"So you were in New York before you came out here?" Ann asked as two of the other women in the shop, National Park Service employees, moved past her to give the mugs and bowls they had selected to Lucy. Ann was short with an unruly mop of dark hair and an infectious smile. And she wore big glasses that she had to keep sliding back up her narrow nose with her fingertips. She was obviously very intelligent and definitely tenacious with her questioning. Fortunately she was also easy-going and friendly.

"Uh huh," replied Lucy.

"Doing what?"

Lucy looked at Ann. Should she tell her? "Studying for a Master's degree in economics."

"You need a degree to work for Joe, eh?" teased the husband, obviously getting drawn into Lucy's story.

"Uh huh," replied Lucy, adding up the pottery for the Park Service employees on a little calculator. "A degree in varying concepts of time!"

The husband laughed. "How long did he tell you he'd be gone?" he asked.

"A couple of hours,"

"And it's been...."

"More than three." Lucy showed the total to her customers, who rummaged in their pockets for the cash.

The husband laughed merrily. "The fishing must be good, eh?"

"Let's put it this way," replied Lucy, smacking her lips together smartly. "It had better be!"

"I thought you said you were an actress?" Ann remarked, evidently trying to sort Lucy's story out in her mind.

"I am," replied Lucy, taking the cash from the Park Service ladies.

"Could we have a business card?" one of them requested.

Lucy pulled one off the little wooden stand that held Joe's business cards as well as brochures and ads for other local businesses.

"Then why do you have a degree in economics?"

Lucy sighed as she began wrapping newspaper around the pots she'd just sold. How could she explain to this person she didn't even know the convoluted nature of her life so far? That the choice to go to university to get a BA in French and Economics was more her father's than hers but she'd agreed because she thought his point about it being good to have a back up made sense. And because he promised to support her choice to act if she got a BA. Then when he reneged on that promise, she left the country and headed back to France, where she'd spent a blissfully happy year as part of her undergraduate degree, studying economics *and* theatre. The theatre was not part of her degree program but she'd been telling some guy in a Breton pub one night how upset she was to learn there wasn't a drama club at the University of Rennes, when he'd gifted her with the information that she should try the Conservatory of Drama in town. Lucy followed up on his suggestion, auditioned for a place and was shocked when they actually gave her one. From thereon her evenings were filled with acting classes - in French! Of course, she didn't tell her professors in London about all this because, well because she'd become used to hiding her theatrical activities. But then she'd taken a couple of bit parts at the Performing Arts Center in town and ended up in a photograph right smack on the front page of the regional newspaper. Which, somehow, got back to her professors and when Lucy returned to college in London, she found the photo pinned to the bulletin board in the French Department. She thought it had been put there to vilify her but no, they said, they'd put it up because they were proud of her. *Proud?* This was something new for Lucy.

So it was back to France that she ran after her father informed her that he hadn't helped her go to university just so she could be an actress and she spent two years in Strasbourg, teaching English as a foreign language to adults while acting whenever she could. Then she set her sights on New York. If she went back to being a student and got a Master's degree she would have a legal way to enter the country and she could pursue acting around that, like she did in Rennes. And since in England you couldn't change directions once you'd become a student, she thought she only had two choices – an MA in French or one in economics. She picked economics. The only trouble was, once Lucy got to NYU, her advisor didn't want her to do a Master's degree because he said her undergraduate degree from England already counted as a Master's. So he put her in the PhD program, with a full scholarship. "No acting though," he warned her.

"How do you know about my acting?"

"The letters of reference from your professors in London are filled with stories of your acting prowess," her advisor answered, not sounding the least bit impressed.

Lucy had done as she'd been told at first, but all that happened was she began to wilt and die without acting in her life. It was one thing, she realized, to try and fail, it was another not to try. She hated the PhD program, she hated New York, she hated life. Until one day she asked herself how her advisor would ever find out if she started acting and when she realized that the answer was, *he wouldn't*, she picked herself up and began knocking on stage doors. And before she knew it she was back to hiding her acting while earning credits in a PhD program, which she then quit when she'd accumulated enough for a Master's.

That pretty much summed up Lucy's way of dealing with life for too many years; hiding. Her pain, her dreams, herself. But then, how could some people understand what it felt like to discover you were good at something? Lucy had been called hard working, capable, persistent but never *good* - at anything - until she stepped on a stage at 17. And that made it what she had to do with her life. Joe understood that. He was at art school, learning to be an advertising artist, when somebody brought in a potter's wheel and showed them how to throw a pot. Everybody tried but Joe was the only one who actually succeeded. And when he heard all the students oohing and aahing over his newfound gift, he knew he had to make pots for the rest of his life.

Joe was direct, though, something Lucy loved about him, and because he was direct, he had a pottery business already and made art everyday. Lucy, on the other hand, was back to knocking on stage doors in Seattle, with a Master's degree in economics that she preferred not to talk about.

"It's a long story," she said finally, in answer to Ann's question. She picked up a recycled, brown paper bag from the grocery store and began putting the wrapped mugs and bowls inside it.

"Are there any more mugs with the fish on them?" It was the wife of the teddy bear asking the question, a tall, willowy woman, with deep, sea green eyes. She was looking at some fish mugs in the sold section of the shop.

"No, I'm afraid not."

"Do you mind if I look at these in the sunlight?" The last of the female shoppers, an older, fluttering, somewhat ethereal-looking lady, gave Lucy a pained look as she held out two salad bowls that were testing her decision-making ability.

"No, no, that's fine." Lucy replied.

"Are you going to be doing any acting here?" Ann asked.

"I think I'd like to order two of those fish mugs," said the wife.

"Only two?" asked the husband.

"I don't mean here as in up in the mountains here but down in Seattle. There's some really good theatre in Seattle...."

"How many were *you* thinking?"

"I know. I have an audition in Seattle later today," Lucy said, her stomach beginning to knot up at the thought that she may not make it if Joe didn't get back in time. She glanced surreptitiously at her wristwatch as she slipped a business card in with the pots in the grocery bag.

"So if we want more of something we can order it?" asked one of the ladies from the Park.

"At which theatre?"

"Yes. Yes, you can," Lucy answered; then turned to Ann. "At the Rep."

"That's a good theatre." Ann remarked, her eyes widening as her glasses slid back down her nose when she bobbed her head up and down to show approval. "They do a lot of plays that end up going on to productions in New York."

"Would Joe make me a bowl with ballet dancers in it?" asked the fluttery lady, skipping back in from the porch to look around the shop some more.

Lucy had no idea if Joe would make a bowl with ballet dancers in it and the knot in her stomach was beginning to make her think she might move *back* to New York if Joe didn't get himself home, like, right *now*! And, then, as if on cue, she heard the familiar chug of his Chevy pick-up slowing down to turn into the driveway. Lucy sighed inwardly, relieved that help was on its way, then smiled as she handed the grocery bag of pots to one of the Park Service workers.

"I wasn't thinking of anything very *specific*, you understand. I was just thinking that maybe in one of these large, shallow bowls that he makes he could put some brush strokes of color to *suggest* ballet dancers," the woman added, waving her arms up in the air gracefully to emphasize her point.

Lucy heard a truck door slam as she picked up a pen and some paper to write down the fish mug order. She stepped back from her position in front of Ann, to go around her and talk to the couple who wanted the fish mugs when suddenly Joe was on the porch behind her, standing in the doorway, holding a piece of rope with two big King salmon hanging from it.

"A roomful of beautiful women. My favorite," he joked and Lucy couldn't help but grin at his wet, happy self.

"I'm in here too," said the husband, stepping forward so Joe could see him.

"Hey, how're you doing, Roger?" greeted Joe. "I saw Ruth in there but I thought she was by herself this once."

"No chance," said Roger, his eyes alight with humor. "I'm like those Kings there; I took Ruth's lure long ago and she's been reeling me around with her ever since!" He laughed with full-bodied enjoyment. "Where'd you get those?" he asked, moving closer to Joe and peering with admiration at the salmon. "Those are beauties."

"Aren't they, though?!" Joe proudly held up his catch for his fishing buddy to admire. The fish were long and fat and their flesh was a delicate orange-pink encased in silvery scales. "I got them at the mouth of the Baker River. Man, did they give me a workout! I think I got everything I have on wet." Joe used his free hand to pull his clinging t-shirt away from his chest. Then a smile cracked his face again. "But I had a heck of a time doing it!"

"I'll bet you did!"

"Hey, I made your tiles," Joe told him, "if that's what you came for..."

"We thought we'd better come and get them before you upped the ante on us." Joe looked at him, confused. "Now that you've made the big time...."

"We saw you in the newspaper," explained Ruth.

Joe looked from one to the other, wondering what they were talking about. His time at the side of the river, fishing, had completely obliterated all memory of his being in the newspaper from his mind.

"Ah! Ah!" Roger pointed an accusing finger at the potter and grinned from ear to ear. "I'll bet you haven't even read it yet! You've been too busy *fishing*!"

Now Joe remembered. "Lucy's read it!" he argued, looking across at Lucy and hoping she would come to his rescue. Lucy made a face that suggested otherwise. "Haven't you?" Joe asked.

"I haven't even had time to look for it yet," she confessed. "I've been too busy with customers."

"Okay, okay, I'm going to help out," promised Joe. "Just let me wash these fish and show Roger and Ruth their tiles. What time is it?"

Lucy looked at her watch again. "11:15."

"Really? That late already? I'd better hustle if I'm going to throw pots."

"You remember I have to leave by 12:30 to get to my audition?"

"I sure do," said Joe. Then he gave the Park Service workers a bewildered look to indicate he had no clue of this fact. They laughed. Lucy rolled her eyes. "I'll just throw big stuff. Planters. It won't take me that long," Joe assured her.

The Park Service employees stepped out onto the porch with their newly acquired wares. "You make wonderful pottery," one of them told Joe as they started down the steps towards their vehicle. He bowed his head just a little. "Thank you," he said and spun around to face the door to the house. "How come these two salad bowls are sitting out here?" he asked, looking at the pieces on the cedar bench to the left of the front door.

The fluttery customer danced out to the porch again and put herself next to Joe. "I can't decide which one to buy," she said, with a pained expression.

"Why don't you just get 'em both?"

The woman smiled. "Okay," she agreed.

Lucy was floored. That's all it took for this lady to make up her mind? Permission?

"And I was wondering if you could make me one with ballet dancers in it?" the woman asked Joe.

"*Ballet* dancers?!!"

"I think your dog is hoping those fish are for her," Ann put in from the doorway to the shop. Then she let out a mellifluous chortle that made her small frame bounce and her glasses slide down her nose again.

Joe turned around to see Maggie's nose flexing lasciviously around the tails of the fish. "Grrrrrr!" he said to his dog. Maggie turned and scrutinized the front yard, as if she'd never even noticed the fish. "Okay, just let me go wash these," Joe repeated, "and then I'll head up to the studio." He looked in the shop at Roger and Ruth once more. "If you follow me up there I'll show you your tiles." Then he turned to the lady who was now proudly carrying both salad bowls back into the shop. "We can talk about your order while we're up there, if you don't mind joining us."

"Can I come too?" asked Ann.

"Sure," said Joe. As long as he could clean his fish and get out of his wet shirt, he didn't mind who came.

Up in the studio Joe pulled some used clay boxes filled with tiles out from under one of his drying racks while Ruth and Roger stood watching. Ann and the fluttery lady wandered around, gazing at the random decorations in the studio; things like the deer horns screwed into the log posts, colorful bird feathers hanging down from the beams in the ceiling and charcoal life sketches pinned to the walls. Joe unfolded a piece of brown, craft paper and spread it out on the floor. The paper had a series of boxes drawn on it with numbers written inside them, like something children would mark in chalk on the sidewalk to play hopscotch. Joe lifted the tiles one by one out of the clay boxes, glanced at the number he'd scratched into the clay on the back of each tile and matched it with its counterpart on the craft paper. An image began to emerge, an image of craggy, snow-covered mountains with swans flying in the foreground and the delicate pink of Joe's matte white glaze along the top to suggest alpenglow at sunset. And slap in the middle of the image was a series of grooves, grooves that looked like they didn't belong in this picture at all.

"What's that?" asked Ann, who had stopped her investigation of the studio and come over to look at the tiles. She was pointing directly at the grooves.

"That's a size ten, steel-toed, logging boot imprint," responded Joe, without masking his disgruntlement.

"You're kidding!" laughed Roger.

"I wish!" snapped Joe. He launched into an explanation without pausing for breath. "I had this logger friend come into the studio just after I finished doing the drawing on these tiles. They were laid out on the floor, just like they are now, on the craft paper, and I wanted them to dry, but not too fast otherwise they'd crack, so I had them covered with a piece of plastic. Anyway, this guy asked what was under the plastic and I told him it was tiles, and he asked if he could look at them and I said, "Sure, as long as he didn't get too close." Then, wouldn't you know it, as soon as I peeled back the plastic, he stepped forward, I guess to see better, and stuck the toe of his boot right into the wet clay!" Joe shook his head from side to side. "Some people just don't get the nature of what I do."

"Can you just make that one tile again?" questioned Ruth.

"If only it were that easy. The trouble is, if I do that, I'm almost guaranteed that the new tile won't come out the same color as these other ones because that's what happens with wood firing. The atmospheric conditions inside the kiln are different firing to firing so there's often a variation in the color response of the glazes. Which wouldn't matter if the tiles weren't mapped 'cause I could just put an off-color tile wherever we'd notice it the least. But as you saw on the craft paper, these fireplace surround tiles do have a map, because of the drawing on them, so I'd have to put the tile in the center where it belongs and if it doesn't work color-wise...." Joe trailed off with a groan. He pushed his hands up over his eyes, lifting his glasses above his forehead in the process. Then he propped his glasses back into place, combed his dark hair through with his fingers and smacked his lips together with frustration. "So I guess I'm making it again."

"Well if it's any consolation we came up to offer you some more money for these tiles," said Roger, nodding his head up and down at his wife as if seeking corroboration.

Joe saw Ann's eyebrows shoot up. The fact that he had the kind of business where people actually offered to pay more for their items than they'd been billed must have shocked her. He was shocked himself and wondered how he was going to handle this without embarrassing anyone. Fortunately Ann sidled away so if he screwed it up, he could at least do it semi-privately.

"Nah," said Joe, "it's not your fault I've had to make these tiles three times."

"It's not your fault either," Roger shot back. "First some of the tiles cracked in the kiln, now this footprint ....."

"And we know you didn't charge us enough in the first place." Ruth added.

Joe couldn't argue with that. He had seriously undercharged for this tile job but what did he know? It was his first major tile project and he had wanted the work. "Let's talk to Lucy about it," he said. "She's better at the money than I am."

"Why do you think we waited for you to get home?" joked Roger. "She's got a degree in economics. She might actually know what she's talking about!"

Everyone laughed. "Hey, the hearth tiles came out great!" Joe said, changing the subject. He pulled another clay box of tiles out from under the drying rack and began arranging the tiles on the floor at the bottom of the ones for the fireplace surround. "These are just field tiles," he explained, "so they don't have to be arranged in any specific way. Although they kind of do have an image on them but it's only suggested in the glaze work...."

"That's all I'd want for the ballet dancers," said the salad bowl lady, pulling herself away from some wildflower photographs Joe had pinned up on the wall next to his drawing station. "Something suggested."

"Oh I can do that," agreed Joe. "Some kind of image in slip?"

"What's slip?

Joe stopped putting the tiles down on the floor and looked up at her from his crouch. "Colored clay. I use it as an underglaze, to decorate the pots. Like on those salad bowls you bought?"

"Uh huh."

"The brush strokes of color, inside the bowls, were slip."

"Oh that would be perfect," the lady agreed. Then she waved one hand gracefully through the air and added, "Just brush them like ballet dancers."

"Okay, well pick a color. I've got blue, black, white, red and green slips. And we'll write it down in the shop and figure out a price," Joe told her as he went back to spreading out the tiles.

"And can you have it ready by next week?"

Joe stopped what he was doing again and looked at her over his glasses. "You're kidding, right?"

"Well it's my daughter's birthday next week and she's the one I'm getting it for."

"Six weeks, minimum." Joe declared. "That's what I tell people. It takes me that long to make enough pots to load the kiln. And then you're not guaranteed it will come out the first time. These folks have been waiting for their tiles since January," he added, nodding towards Roger and Ruth.

"Christmas then?" asked the bowl lady. She positioned the tips of her fingers on the sides of her cheeks and tipped her head just slightly, her eyes wide with hope.

"You bet," Joe agreed. Then smiled at her. "And maybe even sooner." She graced him with an excited flutter of her eyelashes, then danced away to stand next to Ann, who was examining the long, arching strands of horsehair in the calligraphy brushes on Joe's wedging table.

Roger edged to the right to get a better view over Joe's shoulder of the hearth tiles. "Those are perfect!" he exclaimed.

"I really like the colors," agreed Ruth.

The tiles looked like an abstract pastel in soft blue, grey and pink with just a touch of green visible in certain places. Joe stood up and explained the design, moving his hands in a circular motion like a magician over the tiles. "It's supposed to be a lake, reflecting the mountain scene that I drew on the fireplace surround." Ann and the bowl lady wandered over and everyone in the studio stood in the hushed cool, staring down at the hearth tiles as if picturing the mountain lake. Then Joe turned to Ruth and Roger. "You can take these ones with you today, if you want."

"Can we?" exclaimed Ruth. "Because then I could use the tiles to help me find the right carpet for the living room."

"Sure. I'll just put them back in this box." Joe bent down again to do just that. "And I'll make the fireplace surround tiles again for you in the next firing. In fact, I was going to make tile blanks today.......what time is it?" he asked, nodding at Roger.

Roger looked at his watch. "Almost noon."

"No way!" Joe stopped and held the tiles upright in the box with the palm of his right hand. "Well I guess there goes that plan!"

"I'm sorry. We're taking up all your time," said Ruth. She and Roger bent over hastily and began making stacks out of the remainder of the tiles.

"No, are you kidding? I'm the one that went fishing!" Joe argued. He added their stacks to the box of tiles.

Lucy suddenly leaned into the studio, her hands gripping either side of the open doorway, and looked in their direction. "There are three more customers in the shop, two dead fish in the kitchen sink and I'm hungry!" she announced.

Ann chortled. "Could you teach me how to be that forthright?" Lucy pushed her lower lip up like she wasn't kidding and Ann quickly jumped back in. "No, I'm just saying I could have used that kind of direct-speak yesterday when I found out that my boyfriend, Leon, - well, maybe now he's my *ex*-boyfriend – anyway, I found out that he took my brand new set of cookware back to the store and pocketed the money from it. He told me he hadn't but I checked and by the time I found out the truth, he'd taken off with his no-good cousin, Lester. That's why I came up here today; I decided I'd rather go visit the potter I'd read about in the paper than stew over how Leon's always pulling that kind of stunt on me."

Lucy stepped into the studio and slipped her arm around Ann's shoulders. "How about a nice chunk of fresh salmon?" she offered.

"No, no, I'm coming," Joe put in, jumping to his feet now that he'd finished putting the tiles back in the clay box. He hoisted the box up off the floor. "I've decided I'm not going to throw today. It's too late. And that way, I can make tile blanks first thing tomorrow instead of finishing pots from today." He stepped towards Lucy tucking the box of tiles into the crook of his left arm. Ann stepped back. "We're heading down to the shop now so I'll help the new customers while you get something to eat." He slipped his free arm around her waist and turned on the charm. "Would you help me with a couple of orders first though?"

Lucy tutted and pushed him away but he got the impression that she would. "Thanks," he whispered and gave her a quick peck on the cheek. He turned off the main light switch and led everyone out of the studio to head back down to the house.

❀

Lucy hung back to walk with Ann, thinking that she'd invite her to have some lunch, but Ann beat her to the punch. "I picked up some knishes from a Kosher deli on my way up here," Ann said. "We could have those for lunch if you like."

"Sure," agreed Lucy, feeling her stomach growl at the thought of the egg that was still sitting on the counter next to the bacon in the kitchen where she'd left them earlier. "What's a knish?"

"It's dough with meat and potatoes inside it."

"Oh. So it's like a Cornish pasty?"

"I don't know. What's a Cornish pasty?"

They laughed and a flock of tan and brown grosbeaks that were crushing seeds under the cherry tree scattered at the sound. Lucy looked up at the tree, which had been laden with golden cherries earlier this summer. Joe didn't know what kind they were but they were certainly plump and sweet and juicy and Lucy suspected the birds had eaten more than their fair share. Particularly since she hadn't taken Joe up on his suggestion that she preserve them.

"So are you a pottery aficionado?" she asked Ann once they'd gone past the tree and around the corner to the front of the house. "Is that why the newspaper article drew you up here?"

Ann shook her head. "No. I came because the newspaper article said that men outnumber women six to one in the Upper Skagit." She gave Lucy a sideways, sheepish look, which quickly turned into a cheeky smile. "And when I saw Joe's picture in the paper, I thought he was kind of cute so I was hoping he might be one of the single ones."

"He might be!" Lucy shot back. "If I don't get out of here on time for my audition."

Lesson 4

Throwing

The first thing to remember when throwing pots is that you're in charge; if not, you'll find clay a tricky and obstinate medium in which to work.

The trouble was that Joe could really wind Lucy up, and it was obvious he didn't even know he was doing it. Like the incident with the woman yesterday, the blonde woman with the Nordic accent and the beautiful bone structure. She'd driven up from Seattle, with a girlfriend, to buy some of Joe's pottery but she couldn't find anything she wanted in the shop. Sales had been brisk since the article in the newspaper and Joe was low on stock until he fired the kiln again. So apparently the woman had decided to order some goblets.

Lucy discovered all this when she found Joe sitting with the two ladies on the front steps in the sunshine, writing up a goblet order. She went to join them but noticed that the Nordic Goddess refused to acknowledge her. Instead the woman leaned in closer to

Joe and asked, "Who is that?" with what sounded very much to Lucy like distaste in her voice.

"That's my girlfriend," replied Joe.

The woman turned, gave Lucy an astonished once over with her cool, blue eyes and declared, "Noooo! She's not good enough to be your girlfriend!" and Lucy felt like she'd been slapped. She saw the woman's friend gasp at the rudeness of the remark and she waited for Joe to jump in with some kind of rebuke. But he didn't. He just went back to writing up the order. That's when Lucy felt her internal pressure cooker begin to steam.

"Why didn't you defend me?" she asked him after the women had left.

"I don't know," he shrugged. "What would you have had me say?"

The fact that he didn't know what he should have said just peeved Lucy further and she decided that was justification enough for her not to know what to say to him for the rest of the day! In fact, she only broke her silence when she asked for the keys to his truck this morning, so that she could drive to the airport. He handed them over but didn't try to mitigate her mood with an explanation. Or an apology.

Lucy sighed as she bounced along in Joe's pick-up truck. Going over and over it in her mind wasn't going to change anything. She let her eyes admire the tall, leafy corn plants, bowing gracefully to the summer sun in the agricultural fields of the lower valley, then she slowed to cross the railroad tracks and prepared to enter the freeway. She downshifted into second, indicated her turn and lugged the Chevy round to the left. This was it, she said to herself, as she accelerated down the ramp towards the southbound lanes; her first time driving on the freeway in America. Hopefully she'd find it as straightforward as Joe had said it would be.

She pulled into the middle lane and settled into a steady 60 miles per hour. She thought about how Joe had avoided eye contact with the Nordic blonde after her brash, unkind statement and she knew that a big part of what had happened was due to his social awkwardness. Joe was gregarious and articulate, even if he did play the dumb country boy for some of his friends, but there were many social situations that he just didn't know how to handle. Lucy secretly thought this was because his mother had never been able to teach him how to handle them because he was gone so much as a child. He'd been gone, he told Lucy, pretty much every weekend from the age of ten, camping out in the woods around Saratoga to avoid his father's drunken rages. When was he home to learn how to act in society? Sometimes Lucy felt like she was dating an alpine version of Lord Greystoke, from *Tarzan*; a man more comfortable in the wilderness than in society. Of course, that still didn't excuse him for not coming to her defense yesterday. After all, Tarzan defended Jane; where was Joe for Lucy?

She suddenly noticed that people were passing her on both sides and she glanced again at the speedometer. What had Joe told her? To do the speed limit or the speed of the traffic, whichever seemed best for the situation. She pushed her thick curls away from her face, sat up straight and put her foot down.

Stevie Ray Vaughan came on the radio in Joe's studio and he turned it up. Loud. He tied his apron around his waist and cut through the 25-pound block of porcelain on his wedging table three times with a thin bladed fettling knife. Joe didn't need to divide the porcelain further than this. He would if he were throwing large objects, like teapots of coffee pots; then he would slice the clay into measures that were approximately the right size, or weight, for each object. But today he planned to throw tumblers and coffee cups and he always threw off the hump for those.

He began wedging one of the measures of clay. Boy, Lucy had been mad at him this morning, he thought, as he started the rhythmic motion of pushing against the clay, then pulling it back towards him, and now she'd taken off for the airport. He continued pushing and pulling, evening out the consistency of the clay, until he'd made it resemble the hump on a camel's back. Then he lifted it up, slapped it in a circular motion around the outside, to emphasize the point of the hump, and carried it over to the ware board next to his potter's wheel. Why she couldn't understand that he just wasn't good at communicating with words was beyond him. He went back to the second measure of clay and began wedging again. Sure, he liked talking to people and could even be kind of entertaining sometimes but more often than not he'd say completely the wrong thing and end up with both feet in his mouth. And he'd seen way too many people wince at his bluntness to delude himself that he was good with words.

He finished the third measure and sat down at the stool in front of his wheel, throwing a towel over his lap to protect his jeans from clay splatters. No, he was better off communicating with clay. He spun the potter's wheel, doused it with water and ran his bare thumb across the surface. Then he slapped the first hump of porcelain down onto the center of the wheel. He wet his fingers, made the wheel spin faster, and cupped his left hand around the clay, to control it, while his right forced the point of the hump down. He gritted his teeth, breathing hard, using every muscle in his back and shoulders to convince the porcelain to go where his hands were telling it to go. Clay could be stubborn, unresponsive, but Joe had learned over the years how to get it to soften and yield so that, ultimately, he could make art with it. This was step one of that process; getting the clay centered on the wheel.

Stevie Ray blared out and Joe grabbed a wet sponge as he gathered more water with his fingers. He pushed the sponge into the clay with his right hand while pulling up with his left, encouraging the porcelain into a tall, spiral tower. The grayish clay rippled and resisted and Joe grunted, unwittingly, as he willed it not to bow out, away from where he wanted it to go. He cupped his hands around the spiral, exerting just enough force to turn friction into elasticity, then he changed directions and pushed down, puffing air loudly out of his nose as he compressed the tower into one, uniformly even, beehive-shaped cone down by the surface of the wheel. Joe thought working porcelain was like working gum; it had to be just the right texture before you could make a bubble out of it.

He dipped his thumbs into the center of the clay and opened it up, forming a crater on the top of his cone. He cupped his left hand around the bowl of the crater, brought more water to the project with his right, slipped the index finger of that hand inside the bowl and, with the middle finger on the outside, used them in a scissor position to pull up on the wall. Most potters didn't do it this way. They used one finger locked over a thumb to make the wall of a pot. Joe had even tried to show other potters how to do it his way, and when none of them could, he knew the scissor approach must be particular to him. Not that it mattered. He always managed to guide the clay to the shape of his choice. Today that shape happened to be a simple cylinder.

Joe rewetted his fingers and cupped the cylinder with both hands, to even out the thickness of the wall. He pushed his thumbnail into the base of the cylinder on the outside, to define it on the hump of clay, slipped his left hand inside the pot, and refined the thickness of the wall by running a small piece of Formica up the outside.

Stevie Ray turned into George Thorogood and Joe sang along as he dropped the Formica to replace it with a piece of credit card. Stiff rib followed by flexible rib. "B-B-B-B-B-B-Bad to the Bo-one, duh duh duh duh. B-B-Bad to the bone..."

He stopped singing and focused on edging the flexible rib up the side of the pot, all the while working to refine the thickness of the wall. Once at the top, he discarded the credit card, nodded his head hard with the beat of George's song, and then smoothed the walls of the cylinder with both hands again. He let the top of the cylinder flute outwards then back in with a simple movement of his fingers. Porcelain was a soft, delicate clay and Joe knew he had to talk to it gently otherwise it would fold and collapse under the weight of his fingers.

He pushed a dry sponge down into the bottom of the pot, to absorb the excess moisture, then grabbed a small piece of leather that was saturated with water. Joe ran the leather over the top of the cylinder as he finished it to a desired thickness. He had a teacher once who had told him not to end in a way that suggests you ran out of clay, so Joe's drinking vessels always had a lip of a certain thickness.

As a finishing touch, Joe took a wide brush loaded with red slip and ran it up and down the outside wall of the tumbler as he turned the wheel ever so slowly. He had an order for tumblers with raised, red mountains on the outside; tomorrow morning, when the cylinders were leather hard, Joe would carve mountains into the red slip.

He took his foot off the pedal and the wheel stopped abruptly. He picked up a length of string and sliced the tumbler off the hump. Using the forefinger and thumb of each hand, he gingerly transferred the wet cylinder to a ware board and then turned back to throw another one.

"Hi Joe!" someone shouted from behind him.

Joe jumped. He spun around to see Skye standing behind him. "You snuck up on me," he yelled at her.

"I didn't mean to," she said, "only your music's on so loud..."

"Hey, turn that music down, would you," Joe yelled. "I can't hear you over it." And without pausing, he went to work on another tumbler.

Skye turned the music down. Joe glanced at her quickly over

his shoulder. At 32, Skye was in the prime of her natural beauty. She had clear, olive complexion and eyes like big, blue sapphires that captivated the onlooker with their warmth and brilliance. Raised to be a dancer she was slender and graceful with long, chestnut-colored hair; but she had the hands of a farmer and the calling to match them and had danced herself away from New York City to grow organic berries and root crops in the Skagit Valley. Usually the dirt stains on her clothes and hands were a reflection of this but today she was wearing a sleeveless, chiffon dress in Impressionist blues and purple, with a braided leather tie at the waist and a pair of matching braided sandals on her feet. "Where are you off to, all dressed up?" Joe asked.

"Over to my dad's. It's his birthday today and I'm going to drive over to Leavenworth and have dinner with him."

"Cool." Joe was pulling up on another cylinder.

"I want to get a couple of cereal bowls for him and trade you for some potatoes…"

"Russets? From the farm"

"No. We sold all those. These are Yukon Golds, from my garden." Skye leaned to the right, as if mesmerized by the movement of the clay under Joe's hands.

"Wow. From your garden. I'm honored. How many pounds?' Joe cut off another tumbler and put it next to the first. He wet his fingers in the bucket behind the wheel and began working the clay again.

"About 30. Where's Lucy?" Skye asked, blinking her beautiful blue eyes away from Joe's hands and letting them roam to the right of his wheel.

"She went to the airport."

"The airport?!"

"To pick up Charlie."

"That's right! I forgot he arrived today." Skye looked at her watch. "When will she be back?"

Joe was pulling up on the wall of the next tumbler, his elbows out like wings beside him. "I think his plane was due in around 10:30 so, I don't know, maybe early this afternoon. If she comes back. What time is it now?" He sat back, folding his elbows down against his waist, and let the clay spin with greater freedom against his hands.

Skye glanced at her watch. "1:20. What do you mean, *if* she comes back?"

"She wasn't talking to me when she left this morning."

"Uh oh," Skye groaned. "What did you do now?"

"I didn't do anything!" Joe replied defensively. He turned and looked at Skye. "Honest. I didn't." Then he bent towards the tumbler he was working on and edged the piece of Formica up the sidewall. "It's what I didn't do that's got her upset," he muttered, focusing all the while on what he was doing.

He stopped the wheel and removed the excess clay from the Formica with two fingers, flicking it into a 5-gallon pail at his side. He picked up the red slip brush and turned back to the wheel to paint on the pot as he explained. "Some lady came into the shop yesterday and it was obvious she'd had too much to drink at lunch by the way she was acting. Plus I could smell the alcohol on her breath. Anyway, I was writing up her order when she said something about Lucy not being good enough to be my girlfriend."

Skye puffed exasperation from her lips. "What did you tell her?"

"Nothing. That's what's got Lucy mad."

"I don't blame her."

Joe dropped the brush back into the small bucket that held the red slip, cut the tumbler off the hump and moved it to the ware board. He began to make a fourth. "What was I s'posed to say?! This woman was drunk. You know what that's like. You grew up with a drunk just like I did. There's never any point in arguing with a drunk."

"Yes, but…"

"And I didn't want to give her statement any credibility," Joe went on. "It was a stupid thing to say. Lucy shouldn't have paid it any attention."

"Maybe not. But I can see why she's mad at you. And I wouldn't blame her if she picked up Charlie and just kept on going."

"Auhhh. She'll be back. She's got my truck, she has to come back."

Joe smoothed out the walls on the tumbler he was throwing, his hands covered in wet clay.

"That wouldn't have stopped Erica," Skye muttered.

The tumbler collapsed in on itself as Joe applied just a little too much pressure. "You got that right," he growled, then cut off the twisted, useless end of clay and flung it into the 5-gallon pail. "She's still got my daughter."

A painful silence hung in the air as Joe turned back to face his wheel, centering himself in the tangy scent of the wet porcelain before cupping his hands around it.

Skye's eyes drifted to the right of the wheel again. There was a photograph pinned to the unfinished sheetrock, a photograph of Joe's baby daughter, Madeline. Maddie. A beautiful, plump faced infant with tufts of reddish-brown hair who used to sit in her bouncy chair, not far from where the photo was pinned to the wall, contentedly hanging out with her daddy while he threw pots.

Joe heard Skye sigh behind him and turned back to catch her looking at his picture of Maddie. Skye had been present at Maddie's birth and missed that little girl almost as much as he did. Joe felt his stomach lurch. Yep, he couldn't think about that subject anymore, not while he was throwing. He stopped the wheel, picked up the red slip brush and slid it up and down the outside of the tumbler. He threw the brush back into its bucket, cut off the tumbler and gently transferred it to the ware board holding the others.

He ran his thumbnail over the surface of the wheel again, bringing all the clay he had left into the center. He didn't have enough to make another tumbler. Just something small.

He leaned forward, pulling his elbows close together to create a pot out of what was left of the porcelain.

"Maybe next time," Skye said from behind him, her tone light, suggesting how gauche she knew Joe could be when it came to communication, "you come to Lucy's defense, eh?"

"Yes, boss," Joe grunted.

"Hey, don't forget. I'm the one that brought her to you..."

Joe could never forget that. It was one of his favorite memories. Lucy, standing by his garden when Skye introduced him to her, telling Joe in her very British accent that she was going to build a 50-story, multi-office, financial building in the field next door. And he would have believed her – if her eyes hadn't held that teasing look when she'd said it.

"She'd never even heard of Washington State," Skye added, moving her eyes to the sloping ceiling above her.

It was true. Lucy met Skye on New Year's Day, 1984, when she moved into Skye's mother's loft apartment in lower Manhattan. The phone was ringing when Lucy came in through the front door and, not knowing anyone else was around, she picked it up. "Hullo," she said to the person on the other end.

"I've got it," said a voice and Lucy looked up, down and all around, in search of the voice. She hung up the receiver and waited, without moving, next to the phone, wondering what to do next.

Five minutes later she saw a beautiful young woman, of about her own age, padding towards her from the bedroom at the far end of the loft. It was Skye and she was wearing a bathrobe and some quilted-looking, bootie slippers that made swishing sounds when they brushed against each other.

"Sorry about that," Lucy said to Skye. "I didn't mean to intrude on your phone call. It was just ringing when I came in and I didn't know there was anyone else here." Then, reading Skye's blank expression, she added, "I'm Lucy, the new lodger." And she held up a key. "Elizabeth told me to let myself in." When Skye still didn't say anything, Lucy asked, "And you are...?"

"Skye. Elizabeth's daughter. I'm just visiting her, for the holidays."

Lucy smiled and nodded. "Where is Elizabeth anyway?"

"She went to Florida, for an acting gig."

"Well, that's a bit rude, isn't it?" Lucy retorted, favoring Skye with a scathing look to back up her comment. "You come to visit her and she takes off acting, in Florida."

Skye blasted out a long, loud, single-syllable laugh. "HAAAAAA!" and Lucy knew she'd made a friend.

After Skye returned to her organic farm in Washington State, Lucy received a letter, inviting her to come and visit that summer. "I can't!" Lucy wailed. "The scholarship NYU gave me doesn't stretch as far as subway fare, let alone a plane ticket." Then Lucy received a plane ticket from Skye, with a promise to feed her if she did some work around the farm. Three days into the visit, Skye took Lucy to meet Joe and stepped back when the sparks between them began to generate heat.

That had been two summers ago. Now Lucy had finished her Master's degree and had decided to tempt life with her potter, "I just don't want things to go wrong between you and Lucy," Skye told Joe.

"Me either!" he retorted. He used his pinkie fingers to form a long, slender neck on a tiny, pear-shaped vase, one that was just big enough to hold an avalanche lily or two.

"What are you making so hunched over like that?" asked Skye.

Joe sat back and revealed what he'd been working on.

"I've never seen anything like that in the shop."

"That's because I don't usually make things this small." Joe flipped over his whitened palms and held them out in front of him.

"My hands are too big." He sliced under the exquisite little object with the string. "Lucy will love it though."

"It's for Lucy?"

"If it turns out." Joe transferred the vase from the wheel to the ware board and immediately picked up the next clay hump.

"Hey, Joe, I really have to get out of here," Skye put in quickly.

He looked at her. "You didn't pick out the bowls already?"

"I did. But I want you to look at the potatoes..."

"That's right. I forgot about the spuds." Joe backed away from the stool, stepped down off the platform and threw his towel over the seat, muddy side up.

"And you've got customers in the shop..."

"I do?"

"And they're fighting over a teapot."

"Ah, no, don't tell me.....!" groaned Joe, throwing his head back in disgruntlement as he pulled off his apron. He dropped the apron on the clay bin and followed Skye out of the studio. "Oh well, I guess it's just my day to deal with people being pissed off at me."

Lucy rushed out of the asphalt spiral parking lot at the airport and ran quickly into the terminal, looking this way and that for an arrival/departure board so she could track down Charlie's gate. Not that there was much chance of finding him at the gate now, given how late she was. She was breathing hard and had a little burn going on in her lungs from running the length of the parking lot and then down two flights of stairs. She spied a clock on the wall; she was over an hour late. Then her eye caught the big board between the ticket counters with all the flights listed. She moved to her left and scanned it. Yep, his flight had arrived on time, 10:20, at Gate A7. She walked under the board and saw the sign for the gates to her right. Maybe she'd go to the gate anyway, just in case he was still there. But she'd have to hustle.

This is what she got for not trusting Joe's advice to wait until she was past Seattle for look for signs to Sea-Tac Airport. She'd had that in her mind and had meant to do it but then she'd seen a sign saying, "Airport Way," and she'd panicked and taken it and found herself in a mess of traffic in downtown Seattle. Lucy was terrible about directions. She could still remember being 10 years old and

turning the wrong way into oncoming traffic when she was out for a
bike ride with her dad. He'd yelled, "Turn!" but she didn't know
which way and, not understanding the nature of a dual carriageway,
she chose wrongly and turned into traffic. Fortunately nothing bad
had happened but when her father looked back and saw her mistake,
he'd come after her, furious, and made her get off her bike and walk
home and he'd never taken her out on a bike ride again.

Now here she was, still paying the price for her inability to
follow directions, standing at a gate at Sea-Tac where there was
nobody, not even a flight attendant to help her out. Where could
Charlie be, she wondered? She thought for a moment; maybe she
should check down in the baggage claim area.

She trotted towards the elevators leading down to baggage
claim, irritated with herself for letting this happen. And all because
she'd been too mad at Joe to go over the directions one more time.
Why? Because of some woman's bitchy comment. As if she hadn't
heard her share of women's unkind opinions of her looks. She'd
heard an equal amount of women's good opinions too. And men
seemed to find her attractive, so what did it matter? Plus, if Joe
didn't know how to say the right thing in situations like that, at least
he knew how to speak up at other times. Like with Ann, the young
woman who had visited the pottery the day the newspaper article
came out and had since become a friend. Joe had told her that his
girlfriend was looking for a place to live in Seattle, something Lucy
would never have thought to do, and Ann had offered to rent Lucy
the spare room in her little house in the Ballard neighborhood of
Seattle. Which was great because Lucy had got the job at the Rep
and was due to start rehearsals in September and now she wouldn't
have to worry about where to stay when the time came. He'd really
helped her out with that one, without being prompted. Lucy felt
herself soften at the thought of Joe's kindness. He was so good to
her. And he was letting *Charlie* come to stay.

She stepped off the elevator and turned to walk down the row
of baggage carousels, her eyes searching the displays above them for
Charlie's flight from New York. She saw it above the fourth
carousel along but the conveyor belt wasn't moving, there was no
luggage on it and nobody was waiting next to it. It was eerily quiet at
this end of baggage claim and Lucy turned a full circle, hoping to
find an attendant or somebody to help her. That's when she noticed
some unclaimed luggage over by the entrance to the carousel. She
walked towards it slowly, not really believing that it would be of any

assistance, and heard a noise. A noise like a brush moving quickly against plastic. She glanced across the unclaimed bags and spotted a tan carrier that was mostly hidden from view by two, hulking great suitcases. She shoved the suitcases to one side and bent down to peer inside the carrier. And there he was, standing up in anticipation of being released, tail wagging like crazy.

"Hello, Charlie," Lucy said gently to the well-whiskered black terrier.

"Ruf!" came the excited, high-pitched reply.

❦

Skye and Joe walked in silence down the graveled lane towards the driveway, their pace fluid and unhurried in the warmth of the August sun. It was a beautiful day and all the plant life along the way, from the billowing cedar trees to the dense, leafy rhododendron bushes, screamed life at its most vibrant. They reached Skye's yellow Chevy LUV, at the bottom of the lane, walked around to the back of it and stopped. "Did you get a sense of *why* these guys were fighting over a teapot?" Joe asked, as Skye undid the canopy window and lowered the tailgate.

"I think because it was the only one in the shop and they both thought they'd seen it first so then they got into a debate about who'd known you the longest..."

"I *know* these guys?! What do they look like?"

"One's really tall. Baldheaded, glasses. Said he used to be in the Navy maybe?"

"Kenny?"

"I don't know. I was trying to stay out of it, Joe."

"Good move." Joe reached into the back of Skye's pick-up and slid a box of potatoes out onto the tailgate.

"The other one's older, good looking, white-haired. He moved half your inventory out onto the front steps then he moved it all back in."

"That would be Sol," Joe remarked, turning the large, golden skinned potatoes over with his hand. "Lucy taught him to look at the glazes in the sunlight and now he empties the shop every time he's up here. I'm surprised he's taken on Kenny though. Kenny's much bigger than Sol."

"That came into it," Skye warned. "That's why I left to come find you. The Navy guy kind of squared off his shoulders at the other guy, like he was asserting his dominance physically, and the white-haired guy threatened him by saying, "I have seven sons you know!'" She laughed at the retelling.

Joe grimaced. "See, this is the kind of situation Lucy's good at. She'd know what to say to make it be over." He lifted the box of potatoes onto his shoulder and added, "I'd better go try to sort it out. These look great, by the way. I'll take 'em."

"For the two bowls? I already have them in my truck."

"You bet. Whatever. As long as that's good with you."

"Yep. I'm going to head out then. Tell Lucy to call me later." She glanced up as she pushed the tailgate closed again. "Hey Joe, look," she said, pointing up at the sky. "See that pink thing, floating just below the top of Sauk Mountain?"

Joe spun around and followed Skye's index finger. "Hang gliders," he said excitedly. "I'll get my binoculars."

He headed up the front steps to the house as Skye slammed the door on her pick-up and switched on the engine. Maggie, who'd been asleep on the porch, lifted her head to see what was going on. "Hey, Kenny. Hey, Sol," Joe called out, recognizing both men as he passed the door to the shop on his way over the porch. "Come check this out. Some guys are hang-gliding off the top of Sauk...."

He slipped in the house and took an immediate left, into a small pantry that he'd built for storing bulk foods and for the freezer he'd snagged from an auction. He put the box of potatoes down on the floor and grabbed his binoculars from where they were sitting on one of the shelves. Then he was back out of the house again and making his way down the front steps into the sunshine, with Kenny and Sol in hot pursuit. Maggie trotted after them.

He led the way across the front yard to his rose garden, for the best viewpoint. Skye waved as she headed east on the highway but Joe didn't see her, focused as he was already on the pink sail in the sky. For a good 10 minutes, he stood with the other men, passing the binoculars around and explaining how the warm draft, hitting this south face of Sauk Mountain, would rise upwards for thousands of feet, making it an ideal place for hang-gliders to ride the thermals. "All they've got to do is step off the wooden promontory that somebody built up at the trail-head, their sails get lifted by the air and, bingo, they're heading up, up and away."

"Where do they land?" asked Kenny.

"In a field belonging to one of my neighbors, just up the highway. It's the big pasture you see there on the left, 'bout a mile up the road. Mike's got his beef cattle in it."

"What must it *feel* like?" Sol wondered aloud, intent on what he was seeing through the binoculars. "To be at the mercy of nothing but air."

"Feel pretty scary to me," admitted Joe. "But then I'm not much of one for heights."

"I've parachuted out of a plane before. But never hang-glided," said Kenny. He smiled. "Maybe one day."

"You could go together," said Joe as he began to lead them back towards the house with Maggie at his heels. "If you can get past your feud over the teapot."

Joe saw Sol throw Kenny a peeved look.

Kenny just laughed. "Hey, it's my sister's birthday today," he told Joe, "and she wants a teapot. So I drove all the way upriver and you've only got the one."

"And I promised my niece, I *promised* her, that I would pick up one of the teapots next time I came this way..." Sol put in quickly.

"I don't know what to tell you," Joe began, shaking his head in resignation. "I make them as fast as I can...." He stopped suddenly and turned, hearing his truck coming up the highway. "Ah ha! Here comes my lovely assistant," he told the men, with a warning edge to his voice. "She'll sort you guys out, just you watch."

Lucy pulled into the driveway and waved happily at the three men standing in front of the house. She curled the Chevy to the left, around the Doug fir, and let it shudder to a stop in Joe's usual parking place. She jumped out of the cab, slammed the door on the driver's side, and moved speedily around the bed of the truck to the passenger side. "We made it," she announced.

"How'd it go?" Joe asked.

"Pretty well. I couldn't find him at first because I took the wrong exit off the freeway and so I was a bit late. But we ended up connecting in baggage claim." Lucy yanked open the passenger side door and leaned into the cab of the pick-up. "And I stopped on the way back at a fruit stand and got some fresh peaches," she said over her shoulder.

She turned back around to face the men, holding the tan carrier, then looked down at Maggie, who had come over to greet her. "I've brought you a friend," she told the brown dog. Lucy put down the carrier, opened the grated door and out sprang the little terrier.

"Well, hello there, Charlie," Joe said warmly. He was crouched down on one knee, his hands splayed apart to welcome the puppy. Charlie ran into his embrace and out of it and into it and out of it and then back into it and wriggled around in it, happy to have someone petting him so fiercely.

Kenny, an ardent dog-lover, stepped forward, warming instantly to the little pup. "Where'd you get him from?"

"New York City," Lucy answered, grinning. "My roommate, Frank, got him from the Pound a few months before I left New York to move out here, thinking he would be company after I left. But Frank was out working everyday and I was home, writing my Master's thesis, so Charlie bonded more with me than with Frank. And apparently he's been pining ever since I left. Loudly. And the neighbors have been complaining. So Frank asked if I would take him."

The two dogs, having sniffed the requisite greeting places on each other, suddenly bounded off together in pursuit of trees. As Charlie raced across the grass after Maggie, he leaped into the air, flinging all four legs straight out at his sides like a comic book hero in a bat cape. A few more paces and he did the same thing again.

"What was he in New York? A dancer?" joked Kenny.

The little animal's antics were very amusing

"I've never seen him do that before!" Lucy replied.

"He's found his bliss," said Joe. "That's what he's telling us with that little leap. He's finally out of that stinky, cramped, oppressive city where he was trapped in an apartment every day and yelled at for barking and in a place where he can run and play and be a dog. And he wants to embrace it all, right now, in a single bound." And Charlie leaped into the air again, flinging his little legs wide, as if to prove Joe's point.

"I'm inclined to do the same thing," mused Sol. "Every time I come up here."

"Okay," said Lucy, reaching back into the truck and pulling out a crumpled brown grocery bag. "Who wants a peach?"

"No, no," Joe was shaking his head. "Nobody gets a peach until this teapot thing is resolved."

"What teapot thing?"

"Apparently there's only one teapot in the shop," Joe explained to Lucy, "and both these guys want it."

Lucy looked at Sol and Kenny while her mind ran a mental accounting of the pots left in the shop. "But isn't it the green teapot, with the Mount St. Helen's ash on it?"

"Yes, and my sister loves green," Kenny said quickly.

"My niece said she'd be *fine* with green!" countered Sol.

"But didn't you buy your niece a little porcelain cream pitcher last time you were here? With blue mountains on it?" Lucy asked Sol. He nodded cautiously. She looked at Joe. "And aren't you working in porcelain right now?"

"I'm trying to," replied Joe, holding his palms, still white from the clay, out for her to see.

Lucy thought quickly; Joe was still throwing and often it helped a sale to see the artist at work. She turned back to Sol. "Why don't you let him make her a teapot to go with the cream pitcher? And we can ship it to her when it's ready."

"Well I'm throwing off the hump today so I'm making small stuff," Joe countered quickly. He knew what Lucy was thinking and he couldn't change horses in mid-stream.

Sol tipped his head back and partially closed his eyes, apparently contemplating something. Everyone waited to hear what he had to say. When he opened his eyes again, he looked directly at Joe. "Can we watch?" he asked.

"Yeah, I wouldn't mind that too," Kenny put in, giving his adversary a strong nod of agreement. "For a little while anyway."

Joe was more than willing to have an audience for his throwing. "As long as you understand that I'm not going to be making any teapots," he warned and spun around to lead them up the lane towards the studio.

"That's fine with me," Sol answered. "Besides, I still haven't made up my mind what I'm going to do about the teapot." He puckered his lips at Kenny, as if suggesting he shouldn't get too comfortable. Not yet anyway.

Lucy watched the three of them march around the house towards the studio and wondered if she shouldn't go too. She'd planned on spending a little time with Charlie, walking him around the property so he'd have a sense of where to go when he was outside. And, more importantly, where not to go because she didn't want him running out onto the highway. But he was romping happily with Maggie at the base of a thick, twisting maple tree in Joe's grassy front yard with its knee-high pockets of red, orange and gold roses, and Lucy decided he was safe for the time being. Plus if she went up to the studio she could maybe talk Joe into making that teapot. After all, Sol was a good customer and she wanted to resolve this teapot dispute with two sales if she could, instead of just one.

She zipped into the house with the bag of peaches and a pair of binoculars that Sol had handed her and put them on the kitchen counter. Then she turned right around and headed down the steps to the front porch. She wound around the house and stretched out along the graveled lane towards the studio, her arms swinging freely at her sides. It felt good to be out in the sweet, summery air after spending more than four hours in the truck. She heard a soft buzzing coming from Joe's garden and stopped alongside the cedar fence he'd built there earlier this summer. She saw a collection of bees nuzzling their way down into some of the pink and mauve snapdragons. There were snapdragons and aster daisies, nasturtiums and gladioli mixed in with the vegetables. And up against the rusty, sheet metal fence that the neighbor had put in to delineate his property line, there were tall, flowering hollyhocks in dark burgundy, yellow and white. The bees would have a feast today, Lucy thought to herself. She pulled herself away from the garden, swung around to the right, crossing the gravel in front of the kiln shed, and left the sun behind her as she climbed the few steps into the studio.

The door was open and Lucy slipped into the cool interior to see Joe already at his wheel, with Sol and Kenny standing behind him, their heads leaning to one side as they watched him work. She thought about how many times over the past couple of months she'd seen people standing in that very position, their silent stillness an indication of their fascination with the process. She sidled over to a spot behind the men without any of them noticing that she'd arrived and stood watching Joe throw. His shoulders were slanted heavily down, from left to right, the position he always adopted when centering the clay, and Lucy realized for the first time, how hard it must be to take this mass of gritty material and turn it into something so supple and buttery. Sensual even. She saw the muscles in Joe's back ripple under his thin t-shirt with the pressure he was exerting to make a smooth, centered hump from which to work. Then his back rose up straight and tall, like a conductor preparing for a crescendo, and his hands began to play the clay, dipping and pulling, thinning and smoothing, fluting the top out then back in with balletic precision until a tall, narrow cylinder emerged from the mass.

Lucy found herself marveling, yet again, that art could be

created from something as simple as dirt from the hillside. There was a magical, mythical quality to the notion, like the phoenix emerging from the ashes, or mankind emerging from dust. And yet what Joe was doing with his hands was very real, gliding easily over the surface of the clay, encouraging it steadily towards a thing of function and beauty. The radio was on low and Lucy could hear the whirring of the wheel and the soft, sucking sounds of the moisture trapped between Joe's hands and the clay. She thought about those hands on her skin and how they could make her give up all resistance too. And she asked herself, as she let her eyes drift up, to stare out the window in front of Joe's wheel at the dogs faking each other out around the rhododendron bush, what it was inside her that made her think those hands could hurt her?

Lesson 5

Trimming and Decorating

Once you have trimmed the bottom of your pot, you may want to consider decorating it. Nature can be a good source of inspiration for your motif but avoid the urge to copy. Instead, use your intuitive understanding of nature to create a vision that is uniquely yours.

For all the beauty of summer in the Upper Skagit, Lucy was beginning to think that September might be her favorite month yet. Joe had mentioned the warm, t-shirt wearing days and cool nights, perfect for hiking and fly-fishing some of the high mountain creeks that were low enough in September to reveal cutthroat trout hiding in their eddies, but he'd never said anything about the changing colors. The bright, lime greens and yellows of the summer season had softened into rich jades and ambers and there was something about these muted tones that gave Lucy a sense of belonging. Now she wasn't just a summer visitor anymore; she was here to see the changing of the seasons.

She thought about this as she stood at the kitchen sink running water down onto a pile of plates while gazing out one of the new Thermopane windows she and Joe had managed to afford at the end of August. She had watched the sunrise earlier, blushing fuchsia and mauve over the tops of the mountains, and now she was staring at clear beads of dew trembling on the leaves of an elderberry bush. Lucy had never really thought of nature as being compelling before this summer but now she almost couldn't take her eyes off it. Of course, usually she didn't see the sun rise, preferring to wait until it was up before she followed suit, but her parents were here, visiting from England, and they were early risers. So more than once in he past three weeks, Lucy had been treated to a Skagit sunrise spectacular and it made her a little sad to think that she wouldn't be here to see the daily changes autumn would bring to the colors of the trees blanketing Jackman Ridge.

But she was also excited to be starting rehearsals for her first show at the Rep. She looked down at the plates in the kitchen sink again and sighed. Sol had also been staying with them for the last few days, breaking his journey from Gig Harbor to Idaho. He slept up in the dome-house, a rustic, thimble-shaped cabin made out of cedar shakes and shingles that Joe had built up by the creek, but he ate his meals with them at the house. And looking down at the breakfast dishes, sticky with maple syrup from the French toast they'd all eaten, Lucy felt like she'd spent way too much time in the kitchen of late. She was looking forward to being independent in the city again, even though she knew she'd miss Joe. He had her heart that was for sure.

Just as she thought this, Joe came up behind her and slipped his arms around her waist. "When are you going to stop flinching when I come up behind you?" he whispered in her ear.

Lucy spun around to face him. "I didn't know that I flinched."

"Well you do."

"Maybe you startled me."

But Joe knew better. He rinsed his fingers off in the warm water running out of the faucet and splashed some of the moisture over his lips. "Maybe it's reflex from other events in your life," he suggested.

Lucy glanced across at her father, who was focused on the newspaper in front of him, completely oblivious to their conversation. She wrinkled her nose up at Joe, like she didn't want to talk about it right now. "Do you want to help me wash these dishes?" was all she said.

"I make the dishes. I don't do them," Joe joked as he wiped his face and hands on a towel he kept hanging on the stove. He chuckled when he saw Lucy's glower of frustration. "Seriously, I have to go to work. Get your mother to help," he told her.

Lucy looked around the living room, realizing she hadn't heard her mother's chatty voice since breakfast. "Where *is* my mum?" she questioned.

"Sol offered to drive her up to the farm so they could buy fresh corn for dinner tonight."

"Oh." Lucy turned back to the pile of plates and squeezed some dish soap onto a sponge. "She doesn't even like corn."

"Ah, but she hasn't eaten Skagit corn."

Lucy nodded, bobbing her head from side to side in total agreement as she lathered the first plate with soap from the sponge. She'd eaten corn only twice in her childhood in England and she'd found it disgusting both times. Then someone had served her corn in the US and what she thought she'd have to force down to be polite, she'd discovered was delicious. Now she looked forward to meals that included fresh corn.

Joe pulled her hair back off her shoulder and kissed her on the neck. "I'm going to finish my pots," he told her, "and then I think we should climb Sauk Mountain together. It's the perfect day for it."

Lucy looked out the window again, at the clear blue sky over Jackman. "Maybe," she replied.

"It might be your last chance for a while," he warned. He pulled away from her and went over to put on one of the wool shirts hanging from hooks on the stairs. He was right, of course. She was heading down to Seattle tomorrow, for the start of a 3-month acting contract; that would certainly put an end to hiking for this season. But this was also the last day of her parents' visit and she wasn't sure that it would be fair to go off and leave them for a hike.

Lucy turned towards the living room once more, wiping her hands on the towel Joe had looped back through the handle on the oven door. Her dad was sitting in his favorite spot at the end of the couch, where he could hear his financial news on the radio while doing the crossword puzzle in the paper. Even though he was overweight with thinning white hair and a matching goatee and mustache that made people tell him he looked like Father Christmas or Colonel Sanders, he was still quite fit, and some of Lucy's favorite times with him had been when they'd taken walks together. Maybe she'd ask him later if he wanted to try climbing Sauk. Give her mum a little peace and quiet while she packed.

Joe buttoned the top two buttons of the brown shirt he'd put on as he watched Lucy look at her dad. "Think about it," he told her.

"Okay," she agreed, and turned back to face the dishes once more.

Joe stepped out into the crisp morning air and inhaled deeply, enjoying the fresh chilled oxygen in the bottom of his lungs. The beginnings and endings of the days in September were definitely cold enough to suggest fall yet the middles were full of that balmy warmth indicative of a lingering summer sun. It was an appealing combination.

He trotted down the steps to the back porch and started up the path towards the studio, checking out his garden on the way by. He had potatoes that were so big, they were beginning to peek out from under the dirt, squash plants that had spread in all directions with dense, dark green gourds that needed collecting, a second planting of lettuce that looked like it was bolting already, carrots that were doing just fine and even though the nights were cold now, he still had a few tomatoes ripening on the vine. Yep, the garden was fat with food. Kind of overly fat, if he were to be honest. He could never keep up with all that he grew and he hadn't been able to persuade Lucy to work with him in the garden. "I'm an actress," she told him dramatically. "I don't like to get my fingernails dirty." But Joe suspected her resistance had more to do with her father browbeating her into working in his garden as a kid than it did with her nails. That was okay. Joe was prepared to give her all the space she needed – and Lucy was the first woman he'd met that needed so much space.

The kiln was the last thing Joe walked past before reaching the studio and this morning, he took a couple of steps to the left to examine it. He'd been wondering why the last firing had deposited so little wood ash on the pots. All he'd ever read about cross draft kilns was that they were great for blowing fly ash on the pots and he thought that maybe the flues between the fireboxes and the chamber were getting plugged. Joe kneeled on a 4 by 12 that he'd laid across cement blocks in front of the kiln and leaned into the chamber to examine the openings to the fireboxes. There were cracks around both of them. He stepped up onto the 4 by 12 and peered inside the chamber. The arch had pretty noticeable cracks too. That's what he got for using recycled materials to build the kiln in the first place. But then, what was he supposed to do? He hadn't had any money eight years ago when he built this kiln. He'd had to recycle.

He stepped down from the 4 by 12 and crunched across the gravel to grab a piece of firewood from the wood shed. It was looking like he'd have to build another kiln before too long and he still didn't have any money. Oh well, some things never changed. He rounded the corner to the porch of the studio, climbed the steps and rolled the door open.

It was warm inside the studio, from the small fire he'd built in the woodstove at 6 am, and he threw in the firewood he'd just picked up to keep it that way. He unbuttoned his outer wool shirt and hung it from some deer horns on the log post behind his clay bin. Then he tied on his apron and crossed to the wheel to trim the bottom of his pots from yesterday.

The radio was on, tuned to NPR, and he heard the familiar melody that signaled the top of the hour. Joe looked at the clock he had hanging in the corner by his wheel; 8 o'clock. For once it was keeping good time. He picked up the round piece of batting that held his Giffin Grip and clipped it onto his wheel. Joe loved his Giffin Grip. Before it had come along, he'd had to use wads of clay to stabilize his pots upside down on the wheel so he could finish the bottom. The Giffin Grip had three slender arms with curved pads at their ends. One, slow motion turn of the wheel and the arms moved inwards, gently clamping the pot in place. The wheel could then be spun freely without fear of displacing the object.

Joe picked up a leather-hard cereal bowl that he had thrown yesterday, turned it over, placed it on the wheel and let the Giffin Grip take a hold. He depressed the pedal of the wheel with his foot, spread his hands over a short piece of bamboo with a steel spring looped into the end of it and ran it around the edge of the bowl at an angle to create a foot, all the while thinking about what kind of kiln he might build next. He'd had a climbing chamber kiln before this cross-draft kiln and he'd loved that little hummer. It singed the hair off his knuckles every time he fired it but boy, it gave him some lovely reds and purples. And a lot more wood ash than this cross-draft kiln. Joe moved the spring loop inside the foot of the bowl and allowed it to remove a continuous coil of clay from the bottom of the pot. Then he stopped the wheel and discarded the excess curl of clay in a bucket behind him. Maybe he'd borrow the money to build another kiln from the bank and use new materials for once. Joe gently depressed the bottom of the bowl with his finger, put down the loop tool and flipped the bowl back over. He placed it on a ware board to his left.

"....56 degrees with a high today of 72," came the weather report from the radio.

72 degrees, Joe repeated to himself. They should definitely hike Sauk Mountain.

It was 8:13 exactly when Lucy heard Maggie bark. She glanced out the front door to see a silver Range Rover pulling into the driveway. The people in the front were peering up at the house while two beefy boxers hurtled around the small space in the back, shoulders and rumps colliding like bumper cars at an amusement park. "Ruh! Ruh! Ruh! Ruh! Ruh! Ruh!" they barked truculently as Maggie cavorted around outside the vehicle.

Lucy walked out onto the porch, wiping her hands on a dishtowel. The lady in the front passenger seat rolled down her window. "Are we too early?" she called out.

"Not at all," Lucy called back. Anything not to have to wade her way further through the interminable stack of dishes in the sink.

The woman didn't hesitate. She swung open the door to the Rover and jumped out, leaving the driver to park and deal with the dogs. She was casually but expensively dressed with pale linen pants and a dusky pink jacket that looked like it was made out of suede. It didn't seem to bother her that she'd got dog slobber on one of the shoulders and she swiped at it good-naturedly with a tissue. "Sheesh!" she said to Lucy. "Next time I swear I'm getting dogs that don't drool." The woman laughed, her lips dewy with freshly applied lipstick, and then she bent down and nuzzled Maggie with great affection. "I bet you don't drool," she told the brown dog. Maggie moved away to taunt the dogs in the Range Rover a little more and Lucy's eyebrows shot up at the sight of a brown, muddy stain she had left on the side of the woman's pants. The lady followed Lucy's gaze down to the stain, rubbed it with her tissue and then announced laughingly, "I guess it's just my day for dog goobers." That's when Lucy decided this was one zesty lady.

"Didn't you have another dog? A little black one?" asked the woman, swinging her head from left to right, as she looked down at the ground.

"Charlie," winced Lucy. It still hurt to have to explain what happened to Charlie. "Unfortunately we lost him to a car pulling into the driveway. He leapt off the porch to greet the visitor and leapt right under the wheels."

"Ohhhh!! That's too bad."

Lucy nodded and bit her lips together mournfully. Charlie had only lasted three weeks out here with them. She sighed, watching the boxers tremble excitedly through the window at Maggie. At least it had been three blissful weeks.

"You sent us a note about some baking dishes?"

That's right. Now Lucy remembered this dark-haired lady with the shiny red lips and infectious laugh. What was her name? Kathy? No, Caroline. Caroline Hazlehurst. And her husband's name was... Craig. Just as she remembered his name, Craig Hazlehurst appeared around the side of the Rover. He was slim and tidily dressed in jeans and a yellow polo shirt, and had a salt and pepper mustache and glasses under a baseball cap. "You didn't get the dogs out so they could go tinkle?" Caroline asked her husband as he moved towards the porch.

"Well I...."

"You don't mind, do you?" Caroline inquired of Lucy.

"No, not at all."

"Then, honey..." Caroline said to her husband, flicking her index finger towards the Rover.

Craig Hazlehurst automatically turned around and moved back towards the vehicle while Caroline loped elegantly up the front steps.

"I couldn't remember how many baking dishes you wanted," Lucy told Caroline as she pointed towards the shop, "so I put two in the sold section, under the windows, but there are more on the far counter. Why don't you go on in? I just need to turn the water off in the kitchen sink."

"Oh sure." Caroline remarked, crossing the threshold into the shop with the air of someone who didn't need to be told twice.

Lucy hustled back into the house and made straight for the sink to turn off the taps. "Could I impose on you for a cup of tea and

some of those cookies we bought yesterday?" her father asked from
across the room,

"I'm with a customer, dad."

"Oh." He paused, obviously thinking about her answer.
"Where's your mother?"

"She went to get us some corn for dinner."

"Well I'm rather peckish."

He was hungry?! How could that be? They'd had a big
breakfast not less than an hour ago. But then Lucy also didn't
understand why he couldn't get up and fetch his own tea and
cookies.

"It won't take you a moment," her father added.

Lucy heard Maggie barking again and glanced out the front
door. "Someone else is pulling in. Why don't you just help
yourself?" she suggested with a quick wave towards the cookie jar
and the kettle in the kitchen. Then she scooted out the front door.

A man in his mid-thirties with food particles around his mouth
and an exposed belly button from a shirt that was both too tight and
not properly tucked into his jeans was climbing out of a grubby
looking pick-up truck. "Joe here?" he called out to Lucy.

"He's in the studio," she replied, wondering who this person
was.

"Okay, well I know where that is. D'you mind if I head on up
there?"

Lucy shook her head no then watched him disappear around
the side of the house. Out of the corner of her eye she saw Maggie
leading the two frenzied boxers towards the woods with Craig
Hazlehurst staggering behind them, trying frantically not to be jerked
into a run at the end of the taut leashes. "I think your husband's got
his work cut out for him out there," Lucy told Caroline as she
walked into the shop.

"Oh he's used to it," Caroline replied dismissively. She was
looking down at four of Joe's rectangular baking dishes that she had
lined up side-by-side on the cedar counter. "You know," she said,
after a pause. "I think I'm going to take all of these. You see, we
have a number of buyers," she added, as if justifying her purchase to
Lucy, "that do a lot of business with us and I was thinking we'd give
them each one of these baking dishes as a thank you."

Lucy nodded. She didn't mind what the rationale was; four
baking dishes would be a great sale for 8:30 in the morning. But
knowing Joe's predilection for trading with people, she asked,

"What kind of business do you have?"

"Wholesale sporting goods. Tents, backpacks, sleeping bags….."

"Really?" Lucy felt her excitement level rising. "I don't suppose you sell canoes, do you?"

❦

Joe had finished trimming the bottoms of his cereal bowls and was examining the homemade tool he used for that purpose, thinking he'd better start hunting around for another chain saw that he could rob the steel spring out of to replace the loop on this one because it was getting dulled by the ceramic, when the door to the studio rolled open behind him. He dropped the tool on the ware board to his right, next to his buckets of slip, and turned around to see a man he thought he might recognize but he didn't know from where coming into the studio.

"Hi, I don't know if you remember me," the guy began, as he rolled the door closed and hovered next to it. Joe picked up the ware board full of cereal bowls and carried it over to his drawing station, glancing at the guy on his way by. He was fleshy and soft looking, with long, curly, dark hair and sun-darkened skin; maybe he'd met him at the Barter Faire? He balanced the ware board at a diagonal over the corner of the Formica counter top on which he had his drawing tools.

"I stopped by about a year ago to talk to you about some clay that got left on my property…"

"That's right!" Now Joe remembered, "You bought a piece of land on the east side that used to belong to some potters. Come on in," he encouraged as he moved one of the cereal bowls to a small wheel in the center of his drawing station. He switched on a desk lamp, sat down and picked up a dental tool with a straight point on the end of it. "I'm sorry, I don't remember your name."

"It's Lazo," said the man as he approached Joe.

"Lazo. Well, here, take a seat…" Joe pushed a wooden chair in Lazo's direction.

"No, that's okay," replied Lazo. "I've been driving for a long time."

"Yeah, you're from someplace outside of Brewster, right? Up on one of those ridges overlooking the town?" Lazo nodded. Joe started drawing on the bowl, moving the point of the dental tool swiftly and confidently through the blue slip, creating white lines that rose and fell, intersecting and overlapping to look like mountain ridges. "So did anyone come by and bid on the clay supplies those potters left?"

"Uh uh, no."

"So you still have them?"

"Not the clay and glazes. I took those to the dump."

Joe froze. "To the *dump*?!"

"Well nobody came by in a whole year and it was in my way…"

Joe snorted his exasperation - phuh! - put down the pointed dental tool and picked up one with a 90-degree bend in the tip. "How much clay did they leave?"

"Over a ton."

Joe stopped, his hand in the air, and looked hard at Lazo. He was wondering what this guy's problem was that he couldn't have found a school nearby to *give* the clay to? They would have come and got it, no doubt, and at least spared him the trouble of taking it to the dump. Lazo's face was expressionless, as if he didn't think what he'd just said was of any consequence. Joe pulled himself back to his pot and focused on removing a strip of clay from just below the rim of the bowl down to the top of his line drawing, using the bend in the tip of the dental tool to do so. He removed another strip right next to the first and another next to that. Having found his groove, he asked Lazo tightly, "So what can I do for you today?"

"Well there's a kiln that they left behind…"

"What kind of kiln?"

"Gas."

"How big is it?"

"Pretty big." Lazo pointed back towards the door to the studio. "Is that your kiln that I passed on the way in here?" Joe nodded. "It's about as big as that."

Joe removed the last strip of clay above his line drawing, scooped the trimmings off the Formica and threw them into a bucket at Lazo's feet. He knew Lazo was waiting for some kind of reply to his statement. Joe turned the small wheel once, to look at each part of the raised drawing of mountains he'd made on the bowl and then he moved it, with great care, from the drawing wheel back to the ware board. "Well, I don't fire with gas," he said finally.

"Yeah, but you could use the insulated firebricks, couldn't you?"

"Depends what shape they're in."

"They look brand new."

"Huh." Joe doubted that. He moved another bowl to the small wheel.

"I'm not kidding," Lazo remarked, haphazardly wiping the back of his hand across his mouth and knocking some crumbs to the floor. "It looks like they bought this place, set it up to function as a pottery, got all their supplies and then booked it in the middle of the night." He paused, watching Joe draw on the clay, then added, "And I don't have any use for a kiln. Or the bricks."

"The trouble is," Joe explained, "you're kind of out of my way over there. I usually only go east of the mountains once a year, for the Barter Faire, and you stopped in after that last year." Joe switched dental tools and shrugged at Lazo, "I couldn't afford to make that journey a second time for something I wasn't sure I could use."

"Yeah, but if you saw these bricks...."

Joe began engraving above his line drawing. "How much do you want for them?" he asked.

"I called the clay store in Seattle and they said I could get $1.50 a piece for the bricks."

"That's not much cheaper than new."

"I'm not saying I'd ask that much; that's just what they told me they're worth. I'd be happy to get the kiln out of my life 'cause it's in my way."

Joe contemplated this for a moment. He wasn't really ready to start acquiring materials for another kiln, even though it looked like he was ready to build another kiln, but he hated to think of those soft, insulating firebricks disintegrating in the winters they got east of the mountains. He let the drawing tool clatter down onto the Formica and stood up. "Okay," he said decisively. He moved towards the door, looking for a piece of paper on one of the shelves there. Lazo followed him. "Why don't you write down directions to your place..." He found the scrap he was looking for and picked up a short stub of pencil from his glazing table.

"Sure," said Lazo, taking both things and beginning to write. "I'll put my phone number down too..."

Joe watched Lazo write down his information as he spoke. "I won't make you any promises but maybe we'll stop on our way to the Barter Faire. That's in a couple of weeks." Joe rolled the door to his studio open and Lazo stepped out onto the small porch. "Can you wait that long?"

"I guess so." Lazo replied with a shrug. He gave Joe the suggestion of a smile before trotting, flat-footed, down the steps. "Just call me, let me know you're coming."

Joe tipped his face up to the sun; it was warm outside. He decided to leave the door to his studio open. He swung around and headed back to his drawing station, gathering his thoughts to get back to where he'd been before he stopped working. He sat down, rolled his chair in towards the counter and picked up the engraving tool. "Took a ton of clay to the dump!" he muttered angrily as he cleaned the end of the dental tool between the forefinger and thumb of his left hand. "I hope it gave him a back ache."

Sol's Mazda pulled into the driveway just as Lucy was helping load Caroline Hazelhurst's purchases into the Range Rover. Not only had the sporting goods rep bought four 9 by 13 baking dishes, she'd also bought a pie plate and asked Lucy to write up an order for some dinnerware. She'd pay for what she was taking with her today, she told Lucy in her no-nonsense way, and trade for the dinner service, if that's what Joe wanted.

Lucy's mother climbed out of the Mazda, carefully holding onto a big bag of fresh corn. "All right?" she said with a shy smile and nod in her daughter's direction. That triple action, the smile, the nod, and the lilting way she delivered the "all right?" was what Lucy thought of when she thought of her mother. She'd never forgotten going out to JFK to pick up her mum, who'd made the journey from England without her father, and over his objections, to visit Lucy in New York. Lucy's mother walked through the gate, saw her daughter, smiled, nodded and mouthed, "All right?" - and Lucy's heart jumped. There was something about that combination that suggested pride on the part of her mother, maybe for herself, maybe for Lucy; or, since her mother could never bring herself to say the actual words, what it really suggested was love.

Lucy peeked into the Mazda and saw Sol, sitting in the driver's seat, munching contentedly on a pint of blueberries while staring off at Jackman Ridge. It didn't take much to make him happy and she certainly didn't have to fuss over him as a guest.

"We'll send you some canoe catalogues," Craig called out to her as he climbed into the Rover.

"And you'll find out what kind of sleeping bags Joe's interested in?" Caroline added through her open window.

"I will indeed," she replied and waved them goodbye before following her mother up to the house. As Pam stepped through the front door, Lucy slipped back into the shop and picked up the Hazelhurst's check off the counter. She looked around, thinking she really ought to tidy a little since the Hazelhursts had moved a lot of pots around out while they were shopping. But then again, there were all those syrupy plates still to deal with in the kitchen.

Lucy walked into the house and heard her mother talking quietly, soothingly almost, to her father in the living room. "He just offered to give me a lift up there, Reggie. That's all. And we didn't spend too much time. We just bought the corn and came right back."

Lucy hesitated before turning the corner by the stairwell. Was her father *jealous*?! Lucy could tell that at 53 her mother still had a pretty good figure and thick, nut brown hair that fell in natural waves around her face but she'd never thought of her as being interested in other men. Or other men in her. But then, she'd never been around her mother when she was in the company of other men. Maybe this was why her father didn't like her mother going out to work; he didn't want her around other men. But, surely he couldn't doubt her fidelity?!

She felt the tension, though, as soon as she turned into the living room. And when she moved towards Joe's cash jar, sitting on the shelf by the radio, she glimpsed that look on her father's face; that tight-lipped, fixed-gaze look that told her something was up. The look that told her to run before the storm broke.

"Joe really wants me to climb Sauk Mountain with him," Lucy said quickly, to nobody in particular, as she dropped the check down into the jar.

"Oh go, go!" her mother voiced encouragingly.

"Well but I still haven't finished the washing up from breakfast..."

"I can do that...."

"And I didn't want to leave you on your last day here..."

"It won't take you that long, will it?"

"A couple of hours maybe."

"Well I'm just going to get your father's lunch and finish up our packing. You may as well go and enjoy yourself."

"You're sure you don't mind?" Lucy was asking the question of her mother but looking at her father. His eyes were still glazed with internal anger, making him oblivious to the conversation.

"Just go and have a good time," said her mother pointedly.

Lucy didn't need to be told twice. She hurried across the room and pulled a bottle of water out of the refrigerator that she'd seen Joe put in there in anticipation of the hike. She hustled from the kitchen to the stairs, grabbed her boots from under the coats and walked outside. She put the water bottle down at the top of the front steps and banged the bottom of her boots together, to get the dirt out from between the treads. Then she sat down on the top step to put her boots on.

Joe came around the corner of the house. "Did I hear a car door clo......whacha doing?" he asked.

"Getting ready to climb Sauk with you."

"Are you okay?" The set of her jaw told him otherwise.

"I'm fine."

"You sure?"

She stepped on his second inquiry with a terse, "Let's just go up the mountain."

Joe was taken aback by her brusqueness but left it alone. "You bet," he agreed.

"Do we need lunch or anything?"

"No, just some water for the trail."

"I've got that already." Lucy pulled the water bottle around from where it was sitting behind her on the porch.

"Then we're good to go once you get your boots on 'cause I've got my daypack already." He turned on the hose at the bottom of the steps and rinsed his hands off in the water while looking at Maggie. "You going hiking with us?" he asked. The brown dog swished her tail back and forth. "G'won then. Get in the truck." Maggie raced down the driveway and leapt into the back of the pick-up. Joe cupped one hand at the end of the hose and drank a little of the cold water, then he turned it off and flicked the excess moisture on his hands into the air. He looked up at the sky, which was clear and cloudless; the view would be perfect from the top of Sauk today. He wandered down the driveway to close the sign to the shop. It was a big wooden sign made out of some beautiful old growth cedar, with the top carved to replicate the top of Sauk Mountain and the name of the business, *Cascade Mountain Pottery*, carved and painted into the main body of the wood. The word, OPEN, in bold red letters stretched down onto a piece of 6 by 30 plywood that hung below the bottom of the sign and Joe could fold this in half and latch it, revealing smaller black letters that read CLOSED.

He did this on both sides of the sign and crossed the driveway again, heading for his truck. That's when he saw Sol, sitting in the front of the Mazda. He waved and Sol rolled down the window.

"Where are you off to?" Sol asked. Lucy came around the Mazda to join them.

"Up Sauk," replied Joe. "Want to come with us?"

Sol shook his head no. "I'm going to finish my blueberries and then head over to Idaho."

"Well drive carefully. Are we going to see you on the way back?"

"No I'm going to Boston, remember? To see my doctor son, Eduardo."

"That's right!" Joe remarked. He slapped the top of the Mazda twice with the flat of his hand. "Well you have a good time back there."

"And call us when you get back," Lucy added.

She climbed in on the passenger side of the Chevy as Joe jogged around to the driver's side. When she slammed the door closed beside her she saw her mother, standing on the front porch, smiling and waving a kindly good-bye to them. Lucy waved back, a pang in her heart for the distance that was about to open up between them again when her mother returned to England tomorrow. "Let's go," she told Joe before she could change her mind.

It was amazing how being almost 5,000 feet up on the side of a mountain could put everything in perspective. Lucy knew that Sauk Mountain was one of the reasons Joe had settled on his 5 acres in the Skagit, but it hadn't really meant anything to her when he'd told her that. Lucy had always been more of a people person than a place person so she couldn't imagine herself being drawn to somewhere because of the landscape. But standing here, on the narrow switchback trail that climbed through an alpine meadow on Sauk's south face, she began to think about it. With her right foot resting up on a flat rock in the corner of one of the switchbacks, Lucy leaned on her knee and looked out at the heat shimmering an incandescent blue over the mountain ridges on the other side of the valley. Then her gaze dropped to the Skagit River snaking silver through the lush, green landscape as it headed down towards the Puget Sound. Her life seemed pretty small in comparison to this, she thought to herself. Her problems even smaller. Maybe that's what Joe saw when he first looked up at the mountain.

She pushed on her right foot and propelled herself around the corner of the switchback. Her eyes traveled quickly over the rest of the trail, squiggling up the mountain, but came immediately back down to the rocky path under her feet. It was important to focus when moving along this trail because one wrong step could pitch a hiker downhill for a very long way. She walked quickly, using the balls of her feet to counterbalance the steepness of the trail, and caught up with Joe in a switchback that cut through a small outcropping of Silver firs and Mountain hemlocks. This was a good place to pause because of the shade created by the trees, the only shade to be had on the trail this side of the mountain. Joe was leaning against a conifer that seemed to have rooted horizontally in the trail bank and then changed direction to grow up towards the sky, creating a curve in its stump that could take the weight off a hiker's backpack perfectly. He was sipping from the water bottle when Lucy reached him. "Want some?" he asked holding the bottle out towards her.

"Thanks." Lucy took it and let the sweet, chemical-free creek water trickle down her throat. That was another thing she hadn't really understood at first; why the people here were so intent on protecting the old growth nature of this forest. "Wouldn't more trees grow if these ones were cut down?" she had asked Joe when he was cooking a slab of Skagit River salmon over an open fire a few days ago. "Not without damaging the watershed," he replied, "and we like drinking water straight out of the creek."

Lucy's father concurred. "The water we drink in England has been through eight sets of kidneys before it gets to us," he told the group around the fire. That had made things clear for Lucy. Crystal clear, she thought, as she sipped on the creek water again.

Joe walked to the tip of the switchback and put his binoculars up to his eyes. He glassed the tree line alongside the brushy clearing slowly, moving as little as possible. Lucy let her eyes wander to a cluster of crimson flowers growing further up the trail, in the sunlight, and Maggie snapped at a passing horsefly. It was peaceful here in the shade and the air tingled with the scent of the Silver firs around them.

Joe lowered the binoculars and took the few steps back towards Lucy. "Is that Indian Paintbrush?" she asked, leaning around him to put the water bottle back in his pack. Joe looked further up the trail, in the direction she had pointed. "Uh huh. And those yellow ones are Mountain Arnica." He started back up the trail again.

"Did you see anything?" Lucy asked, falling in behind him.

"With the binoculars? Nope. All the smart critters are bedded down right now, avoiding the heat of the day."

"Good for them. We should have taken this hike earlier too," Lucy agreed.

"Yeah, but I needed to finish my pots."

"And it took me a while to even make up my mind to go," admitted Lucy. "Although I don't know why. I *really* needed to get away from your house."

Joe stopped, stung by her remark. He turned and looked at her, his head cocked to one side, his mouth tight. He thought she liked it out here with him. He thought she loved the little house that he'd built. So what in the world was up all of a sudden? "Thanks!" he snorted. "And you're welcome. For giving you a place to be."

"No, don't take it like that," Lucy said quickly. "That's not what I meant."

"Then what did you mean?"

"Well, it's just....I feel like I've done nothing but *cook* for the last month. And wash dishes. And wait on people. And that's not what I want to do with my life."

"That's not my fault!"

"No, it's not. And I'm not saying it is."

"Then what are you saying?"

"I'm saying that I'm tired of being stuck in the kitchen. But I'm stuck there because there aren't any theatres upriver for me to work in."

"Well I'm sorry." Joe's words were apologetic but his tone was belligerent.

"No, don't be. It's not your fault," explained Lucy. "It's just the way it is up there. And I'm feeling a little oppressed by it, is what I'm saying."

"Oppressed?"

"Yes. You know. Suffocated. Hemmed in. Trapped."

"I'm sorry." Now he really did sound apologetic.

"It's not your fault. Honestly. I've just got to figure out how to make it work for me up here. Or if I even *can* make it work for me." She stepped forward and slid the fingers of her right hand up his forearm and over the curve of his bicep. "I'm not mad at you," she said, rubbing her thumb back and forth gently over the skin on his arm. "I'm just mad."

"Well that's good then," Joe decided, now that he understood what was going on. "As long as you're not mad at me. That's all I care about."

Lucy rolled her eyes - the things he worried about! – but then Maggie reappeared, barreling down the trail, and stopped next to Joe, panting up at him expectantly. "Go on," he told her quietly and followed her lead as she raced back up the trail. Lucy investigated the Indian Paintbrush more closely before moving on. It wasn't a very big flower but it grew on a leggy stem and had vivid red petals that sprayed out from a central point. Like a paintbrush, she said to herself.

Then it was onwards up the trail, with Joe pushing a vigorous pace. Lucy could walk the pants off Joe in any city situation, mostly because he lacked motivation to walk on concrete, but he could definitely outpace her in the mountains.

They got to the last switchback after 20 minutes of steady climbing and followed it around to the back of Sauk. This side was cooler because it was out of the direct sunlight and the rolling hillside on the ridge above the trail was covered in deep purple heather. Joe and Lucy stopped for a moment, enjoying the chill on their faces, and looked down into the cirque that cradled Sauk Lake. The steep, glacial, rock walls were coated in a rich, velvety-green grass that offset the turquoise of the water in the lake perfectly. A pika whistled to them from some coarse talus. Joe whistled back and Maggie gave chase even though the rabbit-like creature had already retreated to a hiding place safe from dogs and humans.

Joe and Lucy pushed on, across the part of the trail that side-hilled through the heather, disappeared under a permanent snow bank, then re-emerged on a wide, grassy ledge where there was the most magnificent panoramic view of the North Cascades. They stopped and gazed in awe at the snow-capped peaks sparkling all around them like a necklace in the sky. Mount Baker, Shuksan, Glacier Peak, Pugh, Whitehorse, White Chuck, these were the large jewels, clasped in a string of smaller, opalescent peaks and ridges. And the centerpiece today, dangling high in the sky, way off in the distance, was Mount Rainier.

"Let's go to the top, Lucy," Joe whispered when he realized that the highest peak in the State was on display. They followed the last few feet of the trail to the end and then stepping-stoned their way carefully up some sheer rocks to reach the summit at 5,500 feet. Lucy found a fairly flat rock and sat, trying to comprehend the scope of all that she could see around her. The air was refreshingly cool against her cheeks and her lungs radiated a heady burn from the hike. What a place to be, she thought to herself.

Joe stood a few feet away from her, gazing at the top of Mount Baker, which hung in the foreground, deceptively close, like a gigantic ice cream cone with a lick out of the top. Once he got his fill of the splendor, he moved towards Lucy and squatted down on another rock behind her, stretching his legs out on either side of her. He slipped his arms down around her neck, resting them one on top of the other in the center of her breastbone and pulled her back towards him so she could lean her head against his chest. They sat like that together, inhaling the view, for a good long while, totally at ease in each other's arms. Joe felt so content, sitting on top of his favorite mountain with his girl in his arms that he couldn't resist. "Will you marry me?" he whispered into the air.

Lucy didn't move but her insides seized at the sound of those words and suddenly she couldn't breathe. Why did he have to ask that? The one question that she couldn't answer. Well, wouldn't answer, because her answer would be no and she didn't want to tell him no because she didn't want to hurt his feelings. And she certainly wasn't going to tell him yes. Not to marriage. No way.

She waited, and when he didn't press it, she wondered if maybe she'd escaped with him thinking that she just hadn't heard. She waited some more, her eyes flicking over the undulations in the mountaintops opposite, and then slowly, very slowly, she let the air out of her lungs. She wanted to stay free as a bird, a bird soaring through the valley to rise up, up over one peak just to coast back down again before the next. She softened her gaze and noticed how the shade, falling in great swaths over the ridges opposite, turned the green of the trees a dark, inky blue. How the different light qualities made the ridgelines overlap, one over another over another. Just like on Joe's coffee cups. She lifted her right hand and pointed at what was in front of them. "Is that what you think of when you draw the mountains on your pottery?" she asked.

"Er yep," was all Joe said in reply. He knew she'd heard his question because his hands had felt her internal wrangling through the pulsing of her heart. And as soon as he'd felt it, he knew he'd pulled too hard. He needed to remember that he had to let the big fish play itself out before he could reel it in.

And Joe was determined to reel his Lucy in.

Lesson 6

Find Your Market

Once you have established a certain rhythm to your pottery making, you should take a moment to explore your customer base. Who are these people and what are they hoping to find in a hand-made object?

The Thursday evening before Barter Faire Joe was loading the camping gear on top of the pottery in the back of his pick-up truck when he looked up to see Pete's VW bus pulling into the driveway. He frowned. Pete was supposed to stay down in Seattle an extra night this week so that he could drive Lucy over to the Barter Faire. Joe leaned forward, seeing somebody in the seat next to Pete. Son of a gun, it was Lucy!

He leapt down off the tailgate, jogged over to the VW and pulled the passenger door open. "Tomorrow's rehearsal was cancelled!" Lucy burst out before he could say anything, "so I cadged a ride back up from Seattle with Pete tonight thinking that way, I could travel over to the Barter Faire with you in the morning."

"Hot dog!" declared Joe. "But what does that mean for you?" he asked, nodding at Pete.

"It means I'm going to go home and call Skye," Pete replied, chuckling. Pete was a cross between a dinosaur hippie and a debonair cad. He'd built a cabin in the Upper Skagit as a place for weekend retreats and future retirement but when his wife died of breast cancer he'd had to sell his home in Seattle and cash in his retirement fund to make the co-payments on her medical expenses. Now he lived Tuesday through Thursday in his VW bus down in Seattle, so he could work as a locations scout for TV shows and commercials, and the rest of the week at his cabin in the Upper Skagit. And he chased women in both locations. He wore his white hair back in a ponytail, had a trim, white beard and penetrating blue eyes. Pete was in his 50s so his target age for the opposite sex was thirtysomething. Although he'd take them younger. Or older.

"Well good luck," Joe told him.

"We'll see you over there," waved Lucy.

They turned and slipped their arms around each other, squeezing happily, with Maggie running circles around them, twirling her tail in the air. They were going to the Barter Faire!

Only Maggie wasn't going. "There are too many strange dogs over there," Joe admonished the next morning while filling the brown dog's water bowl from the hose out front.

"But she'll be all alone," Lucy protested.

"Not the whole time. Sonny'll come by and feed her in the mornings."

"You're not worried she might wander off?"

Joe shook his head no. "She won't do that, I took her to live with me in Concrete when I was building the house, and she freaked out being away from this place. She hated the city."

Lucy laughed. Concrete was a tiny town of about 600 people. Hardly a city.

"I finally came back here and moved into the loft of the studio to make her happy." Joe shrugged, curling the end of the hose back around a wheel rim he'd nailed to a fence post at the bottom of the steps. Then he looked across at Magnolia. She was lying on top of an old, brown wool shirt of his that he'd dropped on the porch as a bed for her. "She's not going anywhere."

"Okay," conceded Lucy. She trotted down the steps and slipped her hand in Joe's. "Can I drive?"

"You want to?"

"I've never driven over a mountain pass before. I think I should learn."

Joe nodded. "Okay then."

❀

They started their descent into the Okanagon River Valley with Joe peering at the dry, rocky landscape around them and Lucy braking hard to accommodate the slower pace of the traffic in front of them. "Sol told me there's a lot of overthrusting in the Okanagon," Joe said suddenly.

"Sounds saucy," muttered Lucy.

"No, it has to do with plate tectonics," Joe began, using his hands to illustrate his explanation, "and the movement of younger rock on top of much older rock."

Lucy thought that sounded even saucier but she kept it to herself this time. She let Joe launch into a description of molten lava and the geologic time scale while she surreptitiously tuned him out so that she could languish mentally in the wide, open terrain of Eastern Washington. It was all very brown and dry, with clumps of sage brush as the only vegetation in many places, but the lack of trees allowed the entire landscape to be suffused by sunlight and Lucy found that very inviting. Of course, she wouldn't like to live in this uninterrupted sunshine, not with her pale, English complexion, but it certainly did lift her spirits to be here now. And she loved the fact that driving through a steep, mountain pass had made a deceptively seamless transition from the lush rain forest of the west side to the rolling desert that surrounded them now.

"You doing okay?" Joe asked, thinking he'd lost her somewhere in the Tertiary Period.

"Uh huh," Lucy replied. She braked again, following the lead of everyone in front of her. "It's just too bad that I had to get behind all these slow vehicles again."

"That's what we get for stopping to look at that kiln!" Joe griped. That was the only thing that had thrown a damper on their journey, the interaction over the firebricks at Lazo's house.

They'd gone, as promised, to his property outside Brewster, lugging the truck slowly over potholed and washboarded dirt roads to get there, which made Joe extremely nervous because of all the boxes of pottery they were carrying in the truck. Lazo met them as they pulled past the gate, showed them where to park and then walked them over to two big, tidy stacks of firebricks. Lucy was impressed by the tidiness of the stacks and by the bright green, well-manicured lawn on which they sat.

"I thought you said it was still set up as a kiln?" Joe remarked.

"It was. But I decided to take it apart," Lazo replied. There was something in his tone that made Lucy look up. "I counted 500 bricks," he added, "and I want $1.50 a piece for them."

Joe took a startled step backwards. "That's $750!" he exclaimed. "I thought you said you wanted us to come and make you a bid."

"Well I want what they're worth," Lazo asserted, lifting his chin with an air of defiance. "And they're worth $1.50 each."

"Maybe." Joe answered, picking up one of the lightweight, honeycomb textured firebricks to examine it. He peered at the stacks, wondering if the ones on the inside were in as good shape as the one in his hand.

While Joe was gauging the quality of the firebricks, Lucy was gauging the man in front of them, thinking how his long, curly hair and sloppy appearance were so at odds with the exactitude of his demands. Maybe Cyrano de Bergerac had been right, she thought; maybe curly hair was a sign of a curly brain. "We brought everything we have with us," she told Lazo after a pause. "That's $350. Either we can go home and pay the bills with it or give it to you for these firebricks."

Lazo glanced down, picked up a crumb of something resting on the front of his shirt and flicked it away. "I want $750," he countered.

Joe whipped his baseball cap off his head in frustration. He hated to argue over money but there was no way he was going to let this guy push him around when he'd driven out of his way to do him a favor.

Lucy jumped in, hoping to solve the problem before it developed into a conflict. "We've only got $350," she said once more, this time with an apologetic shrug of her shoulders and eyebrows.

"I thought you said you weren't gonna ask $1.50 a piece," Joe balked.

"That was before I took the kiln all apart. Now I've got my labor tied up in them…"

"Well $350 is all that we have," Lucy impressed on Lazo, drawing his eyes to hers so he would be sure to see the truth of her statement. "Either you want it, or you don't."

Lazo blinked away from Lucy to look at Joe again, dismissing her authority in this negotiation. She gritted her teeth in irritation. The air was hot and still and she felt a bead of sweat trickle down the small of her back.

Joe folded his arms across his chest and gave Lazo a flat, tight smile, daring him to say no again. The little man looked down, retrieved another morsel of something from his shirt, then focused on the bricks once more "They're worth $750," he reiterated.

At this, Joe spun around and marched away. "Good luck getting it!" he yelled over his shoulder.

Lucy stood, momentarily taken aback by his departure, then flicked her eyebrows at Lazo, as if to say, "What did you expect?" She could tell by his expression that he really didn't care so she turned, without adding anything further to the discussion, and followed Joe to the truck.

As soon as she slammed the driver's side door, Joe began venting. "He hasn't got a nickel into those bricks, other than some sweat equity, and he wants pretty much what they're asking for them new down in Seattle! If he'd told me that yesterday when I called to say we were going to stop by I wouldn't have bothered."

"It looks like he's not going to get a nickel out of them either," Lucy remarked as she eased the truck past the gate and started down the access road.

"Yeah, no wonder none of the other potters bothered to stop by. They must know him!" Joe growled, frustrated with himself that he'd walked into such a trap. "You know what's going to happen to those bricks now? They're going to freeze and thaw and crack and freeze and thaw and crack until they're nothing more than a worthless pile of rubble."

They both lurched forward as the truck lollopped her way down into a big pothole. "Maybe he'll use them to patch up this road," Lucy finished dryly.

Unfortunately that little aside on their journey had put them right back behind an assortment of vehicles that they had overtaken once already, in the steeper sections of the Pass. The assortment that included a school bus with a stovepipe chimney sticking out of its top and curtains at the windows, a VW bus covered in lavender and blue bubble gum proclamations of peace and love, an aging, flatbed pick-up loaded with root crops and honey, home-made wine and straw bales and finally a tiny beater car that was being held together by stickers advocating such things as solar over nuclear, bake-sales over taxes. The hippies were on their way to the Barter Faire.

Lucy downshifted and followed the moving tribute to the 60s as they turned right, onto a road where a hand-made sign with flowers and a sunny face told them, "Barter Faire Ahead." It was the first of many such signs, pointing their way to a dirt road that climbed slowly, unevenly and exceedingly dustily up to the top of a barren ridge. Lucy tried using the windshield wipers to swat at the thick, brownish gray dust that was being sprayed up into the air by the slow-moving hippie-mobiles ahead of them, but it was no use. She was just going to have to try to see through it.

As they headed down the other side of the mountain, Joe pointed through the passenger-side window at an area below them where vendors were setting up tents and teepees and stalls for their wares in a large, open field made of the same dirty brown, floury soil that was coating the windshield. Only down in the field there were random patches of rough, leggy grass erupting out of the soil like hair out of a mole. "Looks kind of like North Africa, doesn't it?" Joe said, with a smile as wide as his face.

Lucy let the Chevy bump its way down the hill and then brought it to a stop behind the vehicles she had been following. Apparently they had reached the entrance to the fair. A big army truck parked to the left of them indicated this with a sign on a broad piece of cardboard that said "Entrance" hanging above its cab. The truck was holding a 100-gallon clear plastic tank, which also had a sign on it. This one said, simply, "Water." There were people here, milling about on foot, people with matted dreadlocks and lightweight, baggy pants that flapped around their thighs as they moved. Lucy watched two young women walk quickly around the water truck, their heads bowed slightly as they talked animatedly together. Both of them were slender and willowy, wearing long, sarong style skirts and skimpy tops. Lucy sighed. Not only would she never think to dress like that, she wouldn't look that free form and flowing if she did dress like that. She would always be an unstylish English girl, born too late to be a hippie and lacking the panache to fake it. Which was really too bad over here, at the hippie event of the year, because, apart from anything else, the jeans and sneakers Lucy was wearing were not meant for this oppressively hot climate. Lucy was eager to get out of the truck and change.

Her eyes moved away from the waiflike figures she'd been admiring and picked up another sign, hanging from the tailgate of the water truck. This sign read, "No Visible Firearms. No Alcohol."

"I thought you said people brought home-made wine to trade?" she remarked to Joe.

"Yeah, well they do. Just not openly. They used to be able to, until some guy brought a keg of homemade peach brandy one year. He left it out for people to taste, I guess so they could buy it if they liked it, only some guys tasted too much and set the woods on fire. So then they had to say no alcohol."

The cars in front of them began to move forward and a man with a clipboard and a heavy ponytail made entirely of blonde dreadlocks walked up to the driver's side window of the pick-up. "Hey, Rain," Joe said across Lucy to the aging hippie. "I was hoping we'd see you here."

"Haven't missed a Barter Faire yet," the man replied with a shy smile in Lucy's direction.

"No, I meant here at the gate. You know my friend, Skye, right? Skye from Star Route Farm?"

Rain looked upwards, pushing his lips together reflectively as he did so. He scratched his chin gently through his beard using the end of a pen. "Pickles and potatoes?" he asked hopefully.

"That's the one," Joe replied. "I don't suppose you know where she's camped out, do you? Or any of the Skagit contingent?"

Rain shook his head no. "I only just got here to take my turn at the gate so I don't know where anybody is. Except for us. I know where we're camped out."

"D'you bring flour?"

Rain nodded sagely. "A whole truck load of it."

"And where're you set up?"

"On the main spoke going through the center of the circle, over to the left," And, looking in the direction of the circle, he spliced through the air with the side of his hand to indicate the placement of his stall.

"Okay, brother," Joe said smiling. "We'll catch up with you later then."

Rain bowed solemnly in agreement, held a two-fingered peace sign up in front of his head and moved towards the next vehicle in line. Lucy watched fascinated. She didn't know people really acted like this. "Where to from here?" she asked Joe.

"Well we can either drive slowly around the outside of the circle or park the truck someplace for now and walk around looking for Skye."

"Let's park." Lucy pulled the truck around to the right because that was the direction all the other cars had taken, and took in a big whiff of air as she did so. "Something smells really good!" she said.

Joe pointed out the window past her, at an outdoor kitchen area set up under a big canvas tarp. "I think it's coming from over there."

Lucy glanced to her left. "Fresh Doughnuts," she read out loud. When she faced front again she spotted a grassy area where some people were leaving their cars and jerked the truck towards it. "Maybe I'll just park……..right here." She pulled up alongside an old station wagon that was camouflaged with airbrushed peace symbols, and let the truck rattle to a stop.

She promptly slid out of the truck, glad to be standing after such a long journey, and stretched her body in all directions. Joe hopped out of the driver's side after her, reached back in to retrieve his mug off the dash, then turned around and slipped his hand around her narrow waist. "This way I can start advertising the wares," he said, holding up the mug. He pulled her to him and kissed her excitedly on the lips.

She smiled at his obvious happiness and kissed him a second time. "Come on then," she said, slipping her hand into his. "Show me what all the fuss is about."

The Barter Faire was the only time Joe took his pots off property to market them and he'd been doing it every year since he moved to the Upper Skagit. He loved the abundance of organic produce and hand-made artifacts, he loved being amongst his hippie peer group and, more than anything, he loved doing business the old-fashioned way, goods for goods. He and Lucy made a beeline for the sweet, cinnamony smell they'd caught in the truck and found a lady with a thick, ginger braid that ran all the way down her back to her behind, frying doughnuts. Her younger assistant, who had a multitude of shorter, blonde braids clasped at the ends by wooden beads, was dealing with the public. She was taking orders and tonging the doughnuts from a tray onto napkins as people bought them.

"Is there coffee to go with the doughnuts?" Joe asked, holding up his mug.

"Uh huh," said the young woman and distractedly took his mug to fill it. But once it was in her hands she paused, lifted the mug to eye level and ran her long, delicate fingers over the mountain drawing. "Mom, it's a mug like your one," she said with barely contained excitement. Her mother glanced away from the circles of dough bobbing in the hot oil and towards her daughter, and then did an immediate double take and looked at Joe. "Where'd you get that mug?" she asked.

"I made it," Joe replied.

"You made it?" This obviously pleased and surprised the woman. She lifted the doughnuts she had just cooked out of the oil, tipped them onto a tray and sprinkled them with cinnamon sugar. Then she adjusted the heat down on the fryer, split six small doughnuts between two napkins and carried them over to Joe and Lucy herself.

"You gave us too many," Joe told her, looking down at the napkins he was being handed. "We only paid for two each."

"That's okay," she replied, her blue eyes dancing mischievously from Joe to Lucy. "You'll want three when you taste them."

"I'm sure we will," said Lucy, her stomach aching in anticipation of the sweet treat.

The doughnut maker, her hands now free, intercepted Joe's mug as her daughter reached past her to give it back to him full of coffee. She, too, held it up at eye level. "Somebody gave me one of your mugs once and everyday I have to fight Silka," she nodded in the girl's direction, "my daughter, to use it." She lowered the mug and passed it to Joe. "Did you bring any more of those to the fair?"

"Yes, ma'am," replied Joe, gulping down a mouthful of doughnut. "You wanna trade?"

"I do," said the woman, and moved back in the direction of her fryer.

"Are you making anything beside doughnuts?"

"We're making breakfast in the morning," Silka put in, pointing at a chalkboard hanging on a camper at the back of the kitchen area.

Joe glanced quickly at the selection; breakfast burritos, omelets, French toast. "Okay," he said, "well we just got here and we haven't set up yet but once we do, I'll come back and let you know where we are so you can come look at my stuff."

"See, we're already doing business," he told Lucy with a tweak of excitement as they moved into the middle of the outer circle, munching on their doughnuts. They began wandering, ostensibly looking for Skye, but taking the time to glance this way and that at the vendors who were already set up. Joe was interested in what was up for trade; Lucy was interested in the difference between the stalls. She noticed people perched on the tailgates of their trucks, burlap sacks full of fruit and vegetables open at their feet, people sitting cross-legged on blankets on the ground amid old books and candles, salves and home-made jams, people smiling out from between racks of tie-dyed clothing under square canvas and pole structures and people surrounded by fresh produce in colorful baskets artfully arranged on display tables. It reminded her of a souk she'd been to in Tunisia once only here she could understand the language. Kind of.

Lucy stopped at one of the produce stalls and picked up a small, green, ball-shaped article that was wrapped in a papery husk. "What's this?" she asked Joe,

"A tomatillo," he told her. "They make green salsa with those."

"Huh." Lucy had never seen such a thing. She picked up another one. They felt hard. She wondered if they would taste bitter, like unripe tomatoes.

Joe walked on to a big truck full of interesting slabs of wood. "Hey," he called out to a tidy-looking man wearing jeans and a checkered shirt who was building a fire pit outside the circle, at the other end of the truck. "I think I got some book-matched pieces of maple from you last year."

"Could be," replied the man. A woman with a neat, bobbed hair cut poked her head out of a tent near the fire pit. "I remember you," she said cheerfully. "You're Cascade Mountain Pottery."

"That's right!" agreed the fellow at the fire pit, recognizing Joe once he heard the name of his business. "Where are you set up?"

"Well we're not, yet. We just got here…"

"Will you come and let us know where you are once you do get set up?" asked the man. He pointed at the woman in the tent. "I promised my wife we'd get her another cereal bowl if we found you again this year." The woman's head bobbed up and down eagerly as she smiled at Joe.

"You bet," said Joe, lifting his hand up in the air as if to back up the promise. He moved off but hesitated as he caught a glimpse of something deep in the bed of the truck. He stopped. "You got any more of that cedar?" he called out, pointing at some boards in the back.

"That yellow cedar?" The man in the checkered shirt was too far away to see where Joe was pointing but apparently knew exactly what he was talking about. He nodded. "I've got a whole trailer full of boards I haven't even uncovered yet."

"Good enough," Joe called out and moved away, feeling Lucy's hand slip into his again as he did so.

A few steps more and they came up behind Skye trying on knitted hats in the middle of the walkway. The woman who had made the hats had them hanging from hooks on a long pole with a mirror at the top and she was carrying it around the circle, showing them when asked. Skye was looking at herself in a teal blue beanie that was flecked with beige and burgundy.

"It's a bit hot for a hat, isn't it?" Lucy joked, tapping Skye on her left shoulder while appearing at her right.

Skye pulled off the hat and spun around. "You guys made it already!"

"We did. Rehearsal was canceled for today, so I got back last night..."

"....and we left together his morning. Did you save us a spot?" Joe asked.

"Uh huh." Skye twirled the hat on her left hand and pointed with her right. "It's not that far from here. Just keep walking the way you're going and you'll see Pete's VW next to my pick-up on the outside edge of the circle. Opposite School Bus Mary...."

"Pete's here already?" Joe was moving in the direction of Skye's point, gently pulling Lucy behind him.

"Yeah. He's watching my stuff while I walk the circle. Well he was. I don't know if he still is. I've been gone a while and I haven't got too far!" She laughed, her single syllable laugh – "Ha!" - then she pulled the hat back on. "What do you think?" she called after Lucy.

"It's a lovely rich blue," Lucy called back, nodding. "Really suits your coloring."

She turned and jogged a few steps to come up alongside Joe, who was moving fast now, eager to get to their place in the circle. "I'll go back and get the truck once I know where we are," he told her, "and you can hang out with Pete."

"I'm surprised he made it over this early."

"Are you kidding? The chance to hang out alone with Skye?"

"She told me he's not her type."

"That won't stop him from trying."

Lucy nodded. This was true.

When Joe and Lucy caught sight of him, Pete was deep in flirtation with a barefoot maiden and they watched her hand him something before wandering away. "What d'you get?" Joe asked coming up alongside his friend. Pete turned, flashed Joe and Lucy a guilty smile, then unclasped his hand to reveal a beautiful, beaded barrette. "Is that for you?!" Joe asked.

"No, no," Pete laughed." Skye traded her for it. 'Least, that's what the girl told me." He turned and looked wistfully at the departing maiden. "I wouldn't have minded trading her something directly…"

"I'm sure you wouldn't.…"

"Nice sign," said Lucy, looking at a piece of butcher paper tacked to the back of a lawn chair that said, "Future site of Cascade Mountain Pottery."

"This our space?" asked Joe.

"Yeah. I tried to make sure there was enough room for your pick-up."

"Looks good to me. I'll just go get.…"

"Hey, before you go, I need to remember to tell you something. There was a woman here to see you.…" He narrowed his eyes, thinking hard. "With a bird name. Swan, I think."

"Black Swan?"

Pete shrugged and pulled a bandana out of his jean pocket. "She was wearing black," he offered before swiping his nose with the bandana and pushing it back in his pocket.

"Yeah, and she's short and kind of blocky built? But very fit looking." Pete nodded. "That's Black Swan, the Llama Trek lady," Joe affirmed.

"Okay. Well she's come by a couple of times already, looking for you."

"I'm not surprised. She's got pots coming to her." Joe turned around determinedly. "I'd better go get the truck."

"And somebody else came wanting to trade for candles," Pete called after him. Since Joe was obviously no longer listening, Pete turned to Lucy. "I guess he knows Joe's work."

Lucy didn't say anything. She was staring off at a fellow who was walking around wearing nothing but a loincloth, everything hanging freely underneath. The only other thing he had on was a guitar, strapped across his back. He reached a teepee, threw open the front flap and bent double to go inside, mooning Lucy every step of the way.

"Little culture shock?" asked Pete, following her gaze.

Lucy just tweaked her eyebrows in reply.

❦

An hour later the pottery was open for business. People began to sidle up immediately to the small sales area under the blue tarp and, once their appetites had been whetted by the few pots Lucy had put on the makeshift plywood display table, they delved into the boxes underneath. Lucy watched as ladies folded long, hemp skirts between their legs and squatted close to the ground, cradling cereal bowls in the palms of their hands to see if they felt like the perfect fit. There was something so reverential in the way they related to the pottery, Lucy couldn't help but be impressed.

The first trade she made was for a basket, made out of red willow. "Cool!" said Joe when she showed it to him. "What d'you have to give for that?"

"Two cereal bowls and a small candle holder."

"That seems fair. Why don't you put some pots in it and take them round the circle. See if you can't find something else you want to trade for."

"Really?"

"Sure."

"We can go together," said Skye, who'd just finished loading her little red wagon with pickles, potatoes and jams.

"You don't have to trade the pots you're carrying, just show them to people and tell them where we are and if they're interested in doing a trade they'll come find us," Joe explained.

"Don't you want me to wait until you've finished setting up the tent?"

"Nah, I'll do that later, when you're back. I think for now I'll sit out front and make a list of the things we want to trade for on some of that butcher paper Pete brought along. Do we have any magic markers?"

"I do," offered Skye. She pulled one out of the front pocket of the cotton dungarees she was wearing.

Joe took it and looked at it. "You got any color besides black?" he asked.

"I've got a green one and a yellow one," Pete called out.

"Black, green and yellow. Perfect," announced Joe. He looked at Skye and Lucy, who obviously didn't understand why just black wouldn't work. "I want it to look eye-catching," he explained. Their brows cleared immediately.

Skye picked up the handle to her wagon and began moving forward slowly. Lucy put three mugs and a lovelight in her new basket and followed. "I feel like little Red Riding Hood," she told Joe and Pete.

"Watch out for the big bad wolf," they warned.

Lucy looked at all the hippies dressed in flower power and open-toed sandals. "I don't think they're letting wolves through the gate," she joked.

"In this country, they come with a gun and a badge and they get through any gate they want," Pete called after her.

"They just have to be tall where I come from," Lucy called back. She turned and almost bumped into Skye.

"What do you mean, they just have to be tall?" Skye asked. She was looking at some interesting-shaped bottles of olive oil infused with cayenne peppers.

"Well to get into the City of London Police Force you have to be over 6-feet tall."

"Why?"

Lucy shrugged. "I think it's because you can be more imposing if you're tall and they use that against the criminals. You know, to intimidate them."

Skye turned and flashed Lucy a look of scorn. "That wouldn't work over here."

"It's pretty effective. Even Joe was impressed. When we went to see my parents that one Christmas, he watched some of our boys in blue get out of a police car and stride over to a bunch of kids like they were going to make mincemeat out of them. The kids were definitely scared."

"Hmm." Skye was still not convinced. She moved forward slowly, trundling her red wagon behind her. "What are you looking to trade for?" she asked Lucy.

"I don't know really. Whatever takes my fancy, I suppose. Joe said we should definitely trade for flour and some of the fruits.

Peaches and pears." Lucy leaned in closer to Skye. "Although I think he's hoping I'll put them up," she confided, "and I'm not planning on doing anything of the sort."

"You don't want to can them?"

"Nooooo!"

"How come?"

Lucy stopped and looked at Skye. "Do I look like the kind of girl who cans peaches and pears?!"

"I don't know how you'll get away with that. Joe's all about subsistence living....."

Well maybe he should can the peaches and pears, Lucy said to herself. Then she laughed, her mind skidding into something else in relation to Skye's comment. "When he came to visit me in New York and I got him that job, renovating your friend's rent-controlled apartment....."

"Kelley's place? On 60th and Park? She really liked the work he did for her..."

"Yes well, everyday, to get to her place, he took the subway down the West Side, then crossed through Central Park on foot. And he told me that he'd look at the squirrels in the park as he went by them and he'd wonder whether they'd have enough meat on them for a meal and how he'd go about hunting them if he lived in New York."

"That sounds like Joe," Skye admitted with a wry nod. "I'm telling you, Lucy, you're an Upper Skagit girl now....."

"No, I'm not. Not yet, I'm not," Lucy replied. "I'm still only trying it out..."

Skye stopped at a honey vendor and Lucy remembered that Joe had mentioned honey as a trade item. There was a table, loaded down with jars of the golden liquid sitting in front of a pick-up holding 5-gallon pails of the same. A skinny man came around to the table and smiled at Lucy and Skye. "If you want to try any of it, just let me know," he said pleasantly.

"Are you open to trading?" Skye asked.

"What have you got?" The man was peering over the table at Skye's red wagon.

"I've got a few potatoes but mostly jams, jellies and pickles."

"I'll take some pickles," the man agreed. Skye handed him a jar of pickles.

"And I've got pottery," Lucy offered.

"You've got what? Poultry?"

"No. Pottery," she said, more clearly now. She was used to people making this particular mistake so she held up a mug as a visual aide.

"Oh, pottery! Does it cost more because you say it that way?" the man teased.

"Absolutely," Lucy asserted with a straight face. Then she teased him right back, adding, "I'm really from Brooklyn."

By now the honey man was leaning across his display table, looking down into Lucy's basket. "What's that other thing you've got in there?"

"The lovelight?" Lucy lifted out the object to show him. "It's for candles...."

"And you call it a lovelight?" the man repeated taking a hold of the object. "I like the sound of that." He turned it around in his hands, looking at the colors before passing it back to Lucy. "You know, I think I may have done a trade for your pottery last year. But not with you...."

"No. You probably traded with Joe. He's the potter."

The honey man's eyes glazed over a little, as if he were thinking about something. Then he focused on Lucy again. "Have you got any teapots?" he asked.

She nodded. "A whole box of them."

"Do they come with a good cuppa tea?" Now he was imitating her accent.

"Only if you buy the cups to go with it."

"Boy, cups, a teapot, a lovelight! You'll own half my stock by the time you're done with me." The man laughed.

"Does that mean you want to trade?"

"I'm pretty sure we do. My wife said she was looking for a teapot. And I wouldn't mind getting another mug. Where are you set up?"

Lucy pointed back in the direction of their booth. "Over that way," she said, "on the outer circle. Next to some people cooking barbeque salmon over alder wood. And Skye's on the other side of us, with her stuff."

"We'll find you," the man told her. He motioned at the pint jars of honey on his table. "Pick a flavor," he told Skye, treating her to a flash of his warm smile again. Skye picked fireweed. She put the jar of honey down into her red wagon, looked at Lucy to indicate she was ready and they moved on.

"Where would you go if you didn't stay in the Skagit?" she

asked, picking up their earlier conversation.

"I have no idea," Lucy replied. "It's not like I'm really thinking of going anywhere else. It's just, I'm not sure I'm going to stay. Not yet anyway."

"Why wouldn't you stay? I thought you loved Joe."

"I do. It's just..." She glanced over at a group of people happily beating on bongo drums, all of them dressed in tie-die shirts and crochet, slouchy tam-o'-shanters that held the weight of their dreadlocks. "Well it's not England, is it?"

Skye spun around, her blue eyes filled with genuine concern. "Do you miss it?"

Lucy shrugged. "Sometimes." Sometimes she missed it like an ache in her heart but she loved Joe more than that ache so she tried not to think about it. "What I'm missing more right now," she told her friend, "is a loo. Is there such a thing at the Barter Faire or does one have to pee in the woods?"

"Oh no, one can pee in the outhouses," Skye responded, gesturing towards a row of mismatched wooden latrines set back away from the circle. Then she covered her mouth with her hand and confided theatrically, "Although one might wish one had gone in the woods when one sees the state of those particular accommodations!"

Lucy hustled towards them, deciding that they couldn't be worse than what she'd seen in co-ed urinals in French pubs. And she was right. The latrines, which seemed very "thrown together" with a toilet seat surrounding a hole in a sheet of plywood over the hole in the ground, were not exactly salubrious but she had definitely seen worse. "For the moment you have," Skye remarked when Lucy shared her observation. "Wait till you see those after an evening of eating, drinking and general rabble-rousing."

"Hmmm," murmured Lucy, still holding her breath to avoid inhaling the pungent odor the outhouses emitted. Maybe she'd rather not.

They continued on their way around the circle, cutting back towards their camp when they reached the main spoke across the center because by then, Skye had traded away all of the items in the wagon and Lucy had negotiated trades for soap, carrots and candles as well as for the honey. They agreed that it was too hot to walk the entire circle and time to sit in the shade of the blue tarp and let the guys go around for a while.

"Why didn't you just share a ride with Pete over the Pass?" Lucy asked, as they came to the intersection of the two main spokes.

"That's what I would have done."

"Burritos," said Skye, nodding to a food booth where a man was expertly folding beans and rice, sour cream and guacamole into a large, soft tortilla. "Those might be good for dinner."

"Um," agreed Lucy.

"Well you know, I thought about traveling over with Pete. But then I thought about what people would say if they saw him loading me and my pickles into the back of his VW bus. I wasn't sure I was ready to loose him on that fertile cesspool of gossipers."

"You're talking about the farm now?"

"Where else?!"

"I don't know, the whole Upper Valley seems pretty fertile when it comes to gossip."

"That's true," conceded Skye. Then her face moved through the contortions of high drama as she revealed, "They *loved* spreading the word about you."

"About me?! What on earth would they have to say about me?!"

"Are you kidding? The local potter bringing an actress in from New York?! A British actress no less. The phone lines were on fire with that news, girl."

"No wonder so many people turned up at the pottery to meet me when I first arrived. I thought it was because Joe had been talking about me."

"Well that was part of it. Plus he put up all those photos of you...."

Lucy blushed. "I know..."

They stopped at a small display of vintage jewelry. Lucy picked up a long row of jade beads that didn't have a clasp at either end and held it up to her neck. "That goes great with your eyes," Skye declared. Lucy looked at herself in a mirror; she really liked the beads. "Do you want to do any trading?" she asked the man who had come out of his camper to talk to her.

"No, we need to get money out of the jewelry," he replied. Then he gave Lucy a sheepish look. "It was my wife's grandmother's."

Lucy nodded. The beads came with some matching earrings and the set was priced at $150. More than she could afford. She laid the beads back down gently, smiled at the man and walked away.

"Well I'm glad you at least considered traveling with Pete," she told Skye as they moved further down the spoke.

"What's not to consider? He's very charming."

"And he'd give you the chance at a real relationship."

"He's fifty-five," Skye drawled. "I hardly think so."

"A fling then?"

"If only it were that easy." Skye investigated some dried apricots on a stall of mixed produce. "Besides, I'm still thinking about dating Gregg."

"The river guide?"

"Uh huh."

"But you told me he's a serial cheater."

"Well that's what I *heard*," Skye countered. "But like you said, the Upper Skagit is rife with rumor....." Skye pulled away from the apricots and turned to Lucy, her facial expression one of earnest innocence. "And he told me the other evening that he's always loved me."

Lucy smiled. "And you do so like those sweet words of love."

"Oh and you don't?!"

"Well maybe. But in my case, it doesn't matter. In yours it does. Because you want to get married and have children. I don't."

Skye's head bobbed to one side in surprise. "Does Joe know this?"

Everyone around them disappeared as the girls locked eyes silently in the middle of the crowded fair. "I've never made a secret of it."

"Well I bet he's hoping to change your mind."

Lucy squinted against the intense sunlight to look at the beige and brown of the mountains in the distance. Her mind flashbacked to that moment when she was a little girl, watching in horror as her father did that terrible thing to her mother. That thing that lived in the deepest recesses of her mind, guiding her every decision when it came to love. "It would take a heck of a man to change my mind on that subject," she whispered.

She turned and looked into the caring eyes of her friend again. Skye knew a lot of stories from Lucy's past but she didn't know that one. The big one. The one that had clamped closed that part of Lucy's heart that was supposed to trust. And maybe even to feel. Because sometimes Lucy was convinced that she couldn't feel things normally. Like how she'd ended it with her boyfriend in France, a man she thought she loved; she'd just walked away without even a glance back in his direction and not because anything was wrong in their relationship but because the time had come. Was that what she was going to do to Joe when the time came? Walk away?

Skye interrupted her train of thought. "Not all men are like your father."

"I know," replied Lucy. She glanced once more at the desiccated landscape around them as sadness washed through her, "But what if I am?"

She walked away, not wanting to hear any platitudes, and stopped only when she found a booth with an awning. "How do people survive in this heat?" she groaned.

"They hide a lot in the shade," laughed Skye. And she looped her arm through Lucy's and led them in the direction of their camp.

The heat of the day dissipated quickly when the sun went down and suddenly it was cold. Cold enough to put all the clothes back on that had been previously shed and add layers of wool and fleece in shirts, jackets, ponchos, hats, gloves, scarves, and socks in an attempt to protect every part of the body from the biting chill of the evening air. Joe and Pete built a solid campfire and pulled up lawn chairs as close as they dared to benefit from its warmth. "Seemed like you did some pretty good business for just getting here today," Pete remarked, as he kicked the end of a piece of wood in closer to the center of the fire with the tip of his Birkenstock clog.

"Yeah, it wasn't bad. I made more money than I did trades but it's early yet for trades. Tomorrow I expect it'll be the other way round."

"That one woman kept coming back...."

"Black Swan? Well I owe her for that llama trek I took with Lucy at the beginning of this summer."

"Was that when you went to the Sawtooth Wilderness?"

"That's the one." Joe tipped himself back in his lawn chair and grabbed another piece of firewood off the pile. He rocked back down onto the dusty ground and threw the pinky-yellow wedge of fir into the fire. Tiny orange sparks shot into the air as the fir snapped loudly upon ignition.

"I guess I never would have taken you for an organized trek kind of guy," Pete said.

"Not normally, no. But Lucy loves to walk and when Black Swan approached me last year about trading I thought, now that might be something fun for us to do. And it gave us a few days to reconnect once she got here after all those months of separation. Plus I've never really explored the Sawtooth Wilderness."

"Did you like it?"

"It wasn't bad," Joe said. "I'm more of a devotee of the thick trees we get on our side of the mountains but I liked not getting rained on every other day. And the views over the mountains were spectacular."

"And the llamas carried your gear?"

"Uh huh. That part was pretty deluxe, I have to admit. Except that one of them took off with Lucy's backpack."

"Took off?"

"Got spooked by something apparently. We weren't there. Swan walked with the llamas during the day and left us to make the hike to the next campout at our own speed. It was the last day and we were all s'posed to meet at the trailhead, where the van was parked, to take us all back into Chelan. We got there and waited and waited for Black Swan and finally she showed up and told us that one of the llamas had taken off running and disappeared. And it was carrying all of Lucy's stuff. Which was bad enough but it was also carrying this other guy's stuff and he was a photographer so he had hundreds of dollars worth of camera equipment in his pack."

Pete folded his tongue against the roof of his mouth and let out a whistle.

"Yeah, he was nice enough about it but you could tell it bothered him. A great deal. He wanted Black Swan to track the llama and find it if she could, which she said she was planning on doing. At first she promised to take care of both Lucy and this other guy, you know, make sure they got compensated for their missing gear. But when she found out about the guy's camera equipment she had second thoughts. She made a point of taking Lucy and me on one side to find out if we thought that the warning she had handed out at the beginning of the four day trek, about animals being unpredictable, if that was enough to get her out of having to pay for the camera equipment."

"What did you tell her?"

Joe's head was slumped down into his shoulders, for warmth, but he managed to give a slight shrug. "We told her we wouldn't handle it that way but it was up to her..."

Pete leaned forward and poked needlessly at the burning logs. "Was it expensive?"

"What, the camera stuff?"

"No, the trek."

"Not too bad. It's gonna take me a lot of pots to pay it off though..."

"I can imagine."

The two men were quiet for a moment, staring at the flames licking around and over the fir and listening to the sound of voices approaching and receding as people walked the outer circle even at this time of night. Joe tuned in to some people commenting on his candle lanterns, which he'd lit for effect, out at his display. He listened some more; they were definitely staying, "I think I've got a live one," he told Pete quietly and got up to go check. "Hey, how're you doing?" he asked of the young couple standing out in front of his display.

"You still open for business?" asked the man.

"You bet. We're like 7-Eleven, we never close," Joe quipped.

"Your partner...."

"Lucy?" Joe interrupted.

"She didn't tell me her name. The redhead."

"That's Lucy."

"Okay, well she showed me one of these lovelights earlier. I like them even better now that I see them lit."

"We could use one of those in the camper tonight," the lady said closely to the man, as if Joe weren't there.

The man directed his attention back to her. "We could. Which one do you like?"

Joe waited. The couple discussed the choices as if getting one were a fait accompli. They didn't need his help. Lucy had negotiated the trade earlier; he was just here to close the deal. The couple narrowed it down to a lantern with stars and moons and held it out to Joe.

"Can we get this one?"

"You bet..." He was about to ask what they'd brought to trade but they were already focused on their next item.

"Lucy said you had teapots too?"

"Uh huh. A whole box of them..."

The couple bent over together to look in the box and started a private conversation over which one they preferred. Joe felt like a fly on the wall again. He stuffed his gloved hands deep into the pockets of his parka and looked up at the sky. Barter Faire was always the weekend of the first full moon of October and tonight the huge, milky orb was illuminating the entire field with a serene white glow.

Joe could hear the drum circle starting up. He hoped they wouldn't drum all night again this year. It wasn't that the sound of the drumming bothered him so much as the fact that nobody seemed to drum to the same beat. They were terrible. Happy, smacking away on their stretched skins, but terrible. And he didn't relish the idea of another sleepless night spent listening to them.

"Do you have any mugs that might go with this teapot?" the man asked, holding one up for Joe to see.

"Are you looking for matching?' Joe asked hesitantly.

"No, no…"

"Good, 'cause I don't do matching too much."

"No, just something in the same family…"

"Well that we might be able to find. There's a whole box of mugs right here," Joe indicated, using his foot to point at something at his end of the display table. "You're welcome to go through it. Here, I'll even clear you a space…." He moved pots to one side on the plywood and set the fruit box full of mugs in the vacated area. "Now you don't have to dig around in the dirt to look at them."

"Is it warmer up there?" the man joked as he stretched himself to a stand, brushing the ground dust off the knees of his jeans.

"Yeah, that I can't promise you," Joe countered.

The woman also rose to a stand and tucked herself in close to her man, whispering opinions on the mugs while sharing body heat. Joe was almost inclined to huddle in behind them, to get a little extra warmth while he waited but then he saw Lucy bouncing towards him from the other side of the circle, her cheeks rosy from the cold, and he took heart in the fact that his own someone to stand close to was on her way.

"I'm glad you made me bring all these clothes," she told Joe as she stepped right up to him and nuzzled in close. The couple turned at the sound of her voice. "Oh, you made it!" Lucy beamed. "Did you find a teapot?" She looked at Joe. "This is the honey man I was telling you about."

"Honey!" Joe said loudly. "*That's* where I know you from. We did a trade…"

"…last year," the man completed with a knowing nod. "I hope you want more this year…"

"We do…"

"What kind of honey?" Pete asked, coming around the truck to join in the conversation.

"Raspberry, blackberry and fireweed."

"I got the fireweed last year and it was good!" declared Joe.

"Skye got that too," added Lucy.

"Do you think you want enough honey to cover all these pots?" the man asked, pointing at what he and his wife had amassed on the table.

"You bet," Joe replied. "I can take a couple of gallons at least and I'll get some for Lucy to have down in Seattle. Like a quart jar. And if that doesn't cover it, maybe Pete will get some and pay me for his." He flapped his hand in the air to indicate he wasn't worried about it. "One way or another we'll figure it out." The couple turned and smiled at each other. "You want me to wrap these up for you?"

"No, I brought a basket," the woman replied softly and, without enlisting Joe's help, began moving the objects from the table into the basket.

"Where's Skye?" Pete asked Lucy.

"Over talking to Dave and Shana. They're camped next to School Bus Mary. Look, she gave me these," and Lucy handed Joe one of two cookies she was carrying in her gloved hands. She looked at Pete. "I think she's got more if you want one. She was handing them out pretty freely..."

Joe looked at the cookie. "Who gave this to you?"

"School Bus Mary," Lucy replied as she lifted the cookie towards her mouth. Joe snatched it away from her. "Yeah, you don't want that," he said and took off towards the camp directly opposite them. Pete laughed.

"What did he do that for?"

"I'm guessing if Mary made those, they've got something more than just chocolate chips in them."

"Oh." Lucy lifted her head slowly in acknowledgement. Then she flicked her eyebrows at Pete. He smirked. "I would have eaten it," he told her.

"Well you'd better go and get it back then."

Pete looked towards School Bus Mary's camp. "Was Skye on her way over, do you know?"

"I'm not sure. I think she was going to the drum circle for a bit."

Pete nodded. "Maybe I'll do that too."

Lucy turned away from him as the honey people placed a teddy bear shaped container of blackberry honey in her hands and let her know that they were headed back to their camp. Lucy watched them walk away, their shoulders bumping gently as they swayed together, then apart, then together again, the way lovers do when they're thoroughly immersed in each other. Lucy could have gone with them, to ensure that Joe's end of the trade was collected without question, but she knew that wasn't needed. That was one of the things that appealed to Lucy about the Barter Faire already; how trusting the participants were. Trusting and non-confrontational. She'd witnessed a scene earlier that involved vehicles and a parking spot that would have provoked an outburst of bad language and temper in the city; but here, those involved just said, "You got it, sister" and "Right on, brother" and it was all over. And they didn't even look like hippies! Lucy loved it.

She felt Joe's arms slide around her waist as he came up behind her and placed his cold cheek against hers. "Did we get some honey?" he whispered.

"We got some honey," she replied and held the teddy bear up to show him.

"How 'bout I make you a cup of tea so you can try it out?"

"How 'bout you make hot apple cider instead. Then we can add some rum to it." Lucy's eyes sparkled with mischief in the moonlight.

"I like that idea. Might even help me sleep through the drumming."

❀

Joe was huddled over the campfire reading his book when Lucy put her head out of the tent the next morning and the first thing he told her was that he had a headache because of those "damn drummers, drumming all night long!" Skye seconded his sentiment when she crawled out of her tent and finally Pete slid open the door of his VW van, looked at them with bleary eyes and asked if anyone else had been able to sleep over those "goddamn drummers?!" Lucy had. She felt like she'd got a pretty good night's sleep despite the hard ground, the bitter night air and (apparently) the obsessive percussion.

At least she did until she started around the circle to gather trades and then she began to wonder if the all-night, off-beat hammering had somehow affected her memory's ability to rest because now it seemed to be playing tricks on her. First it was the flour lady, then somebody that Lucy had spoken to yesterday about a case of tomatoes and finally a fellow with hand-knitted, wool socks that she'd thought would make a great gift for Joe that told her no, he didn't want to trade because he'd already done a trade for Cascade Mountain Pottery. How could this be when none of them had traded with her and Joe was still back at their camp? In fact, it had started even before the flour lady, when Lucy had shown up to trade Silka a mug for some breakfast. The young woman had spun her head around to look behind her, the wooden beads at the end of her braids making gentle knocking sounds as she did so, and declared, "But we already got some mugs." She pointed at the two mountain mugs, sitting on the food prep table behind her. Lucy made a beeline back to camp, breakfast-less and hungry, and asked Joe what was going on.

Joe's hackles went up immediately. He pulled his elbows into his waist and waved his hands around in front of him, palms up, stating vigorously, "I've been sitting right here! How could I have taken them mugs?!"

"Well they got them from someone," Lucy retorted, pointing out the obvious.

Joe thought a moment. "Maybe they just came and bought them from Pete, when he was here watching the pots for us."

Lucy had accepted this at the time, since Pete was lost in line over at the outhouses and couldn't refute or confirm the statement, but now that she'd been turned down a fourth time, she'd begun to wonder. Why would Silka and her mother have paid for mugs when they knew that she and Joe were eager to trade? And why, given that Silka and her mother were both great looking women, would Pete not have mentioned making a sale to them? No, there was definitely something wrong in this situation and Lucy was determined to find out what.

She marched back to their camp and found Joe sitting alone, in a chair behind the display table, reading a book. "What's the matter?" he asked, picking up on her mood as soon as he saw her face.

"Did you get flour already?" she snapped.

"What? No! How could I....?!"

"Well somebody did a trade for flour with your pottery."

"That can't be....."

"I'm telling you, Joe, nobody wants to trade with me!"

"Did you ask Rain where he got the pots?"

Lucy shook her head no. "He wasn't there."

"You talked to Summer?"

"Who's that?'

"His wife."

"I don't know. I talked to some lady wearing a scarf wrapped around her head like a turban that was there with a baby and a toddler...."

Joe nodded. "That sounds like Summer."

Lucy hesitated then sighed. "I didn't think to ask her where she got the pots," she admitted.

"Well go back and find out...."

"Would you do it?" Lucy pleaded, coming around the table to sit in the empty lawn chair next to Joe. "They don't know me the way they know you....."

Joe looked into her eyes; he could tell this wasn't being as much fun as she'd thought it would be. "All right," he said, slipping a scrap of paper between the pages to mark his place in the book about the Indian mutiny. "I'll go. But first there's a guy down this way a bit that has a gun I want to look at again."

"Will he trade with you?"

"I doubt it. But I made some money already today. Silka's mom came by with a friend of hers, a cowgirl with a ranch just outside Omak. She wants me to make her two big bowls and she gave me a down payment. In cash."

Lucy nodded. She was hot already, even though it was only about 9:30 in the morning, and grimy from not having any way to bathe and from the film of fine dust that got on everything. Everything! She watched Joe walk away carrying a short stack of cereal bowls and a couple of mugs then she slowly closed her eyes and listened to the sounds around her. Sounds of something metallic chinking rhythmically to the beat of someone's walk, sounds of children running, their bare feet going "pouf, pouf, pouf " as they hit down on the floury soil, sounds of zippers on tents and wood snapping softly on the barbecue next door, sounds of words drifting closer then further away, the sound of clay pot grating against clay pot. Lucy opened her eyes.

"I'm sorry, I didn't mean to wake you." The woman was bending down, her eyes level with the pots on the display table, three fingers of one hand intertwined gently around the handle on the lid to a small jar.

"I wasn't sleeping," Lucy replied. Then yawned. "At least, I wasn't sleeping yet." She smiled.

The woman smiled back, her long, angular face coming to a point below her mouth. "What would you use a jar like this for?" she asked, looking again at the grapefruit-sized pot under her hand.

"That's a dream jar," replied Lucy. "You put your dreams inside it."

The woman lifted the small jar and took it down below the table, out of Lucy's line of vision, to look at it some more. Lucy didn't need to see her with the pot; she could imagine her gentle caress and her eyes, scanning every inch of the surface with eager pleasure. "And do they come true? The dreams?" the lady asked.

"Let's put it this way, that's not covered under the warranty," Lucy responded.

The woman laughed, tipping her head back so her leathery face was towards the sun. Then she turned to Lucy, placing the jar carefully back on the table. "It's very lovely," she said. "And I could imagine storing my dreams in it. I think I might have to have that one."

Lucy almost didn't want to ask, fearful that she might be rejected again. "Do you have anything to trade?"

"I do. I have soap." The woman stood up and held out a basket full of homemade soaps.

Lucy reached in and chose one of the cloth wrapped bars. Sandalwood. She held it up to her nose. The odor reminded her of the talcum powder her mother used to give her for Christmas. She put it back and picked up another; oatmeal/honey. That smelled good too. Now, this was the kind of thing she'd been hoping to find at the fair. "Can I take this?" she asked, pointing to the soaps in the basket. "Or do you want me to come to where you're set up?"

"I've got more back there at the camper," the woman replied, "but you can take any of these soaps that you want. I don't mind."

"I just don't want to lose the chance to trade with you...."

"Why would you......?"

"Did Joe take off?"

Both women turned towards the interruption. Pete was ambling their way, carrying a tall, white cardboard cup.

"Yep. He's on a mission."

"What kind of mission?" Pete nodded towards the soap lady. "Hi," he said meeting her eyes with warmth in his own.

"Is that coffee?" she asked.

"Yes. I found it at a place all the way over by the entrance gate. They're making doughnuts too."

Lucy stopped taking soaps out of the basket as she caught on to what Pete was saying. "Were there two ladies at the booth, both with their hair in braids?"

"Yeah. Silka and Twyla." He winked. "I got their names."

"And did you sell them two of Joe's mugs yesterday?" she went on.

"Uh uh, no," he said, with a slight shake of his head. "Why? Do you need me to do that? I can go back...."

"No, it's just...." Lucy paused, trying to get a handle on her emotions. It almost felt like she was going to cry, something she hadn't done in years. That didn't make any sense. Maybe it was the heat, upsetting her natural balance or the strangeness of the surroundings. Or maybe it was just the letdown she was experiencing after so looking forward to this weekend from Joe's build up. She looked at Pete; his gaze was kindly as he waited for her to go on. "Somehow they got mugs yesterday and if it wasn't from you and it wasn't from us......"

"Maybe Skye helped them?" Pete offered. "Where is Skye?"

Lucy shook her head from side to side. "She's volunteering over in the kids' play area and I asked her already. It wasn't her." She picked another soap out of the basket and sniffed it. Lemon Verbena. That elevated her spirits.

Pete just shrugged. "So where's Joe again?"

"Off trying to find out who's been trading his pots around...."

"I know already," Joe said from behind her. Lucy turned to see him swing a bag of onions off his shoulder and onto the tailgate of his truck.

"Did you get the gun?"

"Nope. The guy wanted too much for it." He came around to the table, pushing his thick brown hair away from his face. "Hi," he said to the soap lady.

"Are you the potter?" she asked.

"Er yep," he replied.

She held the candleholder out towards him. "What's this?" she asked, pointing to a green, crystalline glaze in the bottom on the object.

"That's a glass that I make from a formula," he told her. "Same type of glass they use to make chandeliers..."

"It's very pretty." The woman was studying it closely, running her index finger delicately over the surface of the glass.

Joe turned to Lucy again. "Yeah, so it's Black Swan that's

been trading my stuff around."

"Black Swan!" Now it all made sense to Lucy.

"She did get a lot of pots yesterday," Pete put in.

"Yeah and she's got more coming." Joe looked at Lucy; she grimaced. "It is what it is," he told her philosophically.

The soap lady held up the candleholder and looked at Lucy. "Can I get this too?" she asked.

Lucy, content to have someone to trade with, agreed readily. "Of course," she said. Then she thrust a bar of soap under Joe's nose. "Smell that," she told him.

Joe took a step back, momentarily unbalanced by the arrival of something scented in his face. "Oh that smells good," he agreed. "Get two. Then I want you to come look at a piece of stained glass with me."

Lucy stopped stacking soaps on the table in front of her and looked at him. "Together?" she asked.

"That was my general plan," he replied.

"I'll even watch things while you're gone," volunteered Pete. And, with a glance back towards the entrance gate, added. "Then I'll be here when the doughnuts come around." His eyes narrowed, snake-like, as he smiled.

The rest of the day was not a complete loss. Joe and Lucy traded for garlic, two pieces of the book-matched yellow cedar they'd seen on their way in, tools for Joe, earrings for Lucy and a beautiful 22-by-28 inch window of stained glass with geometric designs in amber, black and sand-blasted clear. Plus they bought some hand-made cheese from a lady whose cheeses were so popular, the line at her stand curled way around the circle before she'd even got the stock out of her pick-up. They just hadn't been able to get some of the staples Joe was used to trading for every Barter Faire. He shrugged; they were making quite a few sales from day visitors to the fair – they could always buy what they needed.

Early in the morning on Sunday, Lucy was alone at the pottery stand, watching the fair come to life as people began walking the circle to do business again. Everyone seemed to be moving a little slower today, maybe because it was Sunday or maybe because they were sleep deprived from yet another all-night drumming fever. Even Lucy had lain awake, urging them in her mind to shut up.

Except she was polite and said please, "Please shut up! Please shut up! Please...." And then they changed rhythms and her mantra expanded to add a curse word. Or two.

Lucy's gaze wandered to where a late-riser was crawling out of a tent further down the way. The guy stood up, scratched and then slowly moved forward across the walkway, trying not to make contact with any of the people that were already energized for the day.

"Where you going?" Lucy heard someone call to him.

"Outhouse," she heard him call back.

Good luck with that! Lucy thought to herself. She shivered as she remembered the mound of effluent she'd seen in those stinky cubicles this morning. She was looking forward to getting back to a place with a real toilet. A real toilet and a shower.

Pete came over to the stand, having put the morning campfire to sleep, and leaned against Joe's pick-up, sipping on some coffee. "How you doing?" he asked.

"I'm fine," Lucy replied. Except she wasn't. She was completely unsettled. Everything around her was so strange and then there was that conversation she'd had with Skye that kept nagging at her. She didn't want to lead Joe on but how could she ever make a life with him? With anyone, come to that.

She gave Pete a wan smile then turned in the opposite direction, to look down the row of vendors to her left. A familiar figure, wearing a black, wool poncho over baggy, black, cotton pants and sneakers was walking towards the stand. It was Black Swan, coming to get the last of her pots. She moved like she was all business, so different than most of the people Lucy had found herself watching at the Faire. "Hey there," the llama trek guide called as she got closer, her strident voice resonating in the quiet of the Sunday morning.

"Hey," Lucy replied and stood in greeting. Pete and Black Swan acknowledged each other with nods, then Pete went back to sipping his coffee from his lean against the truck while the two women chatted. They hadn't seen each other since the end of the trek and they talked about how relieved Black Swan had been when her roving llama was turned in a week after the animal had gone missing and then, also, that the backpacks had been recovered not far from where the llama had been found browsing. All the camera gear intact, thank you very much. They talked about Swan's growing business and how Joe and Lucy were still friends with the doctors they'd met on the trek. And then Black Swan began to sift through the few mugs left on the stand. Lucy took this as her cue and made her pitch. "Swan, could I ask that you consider getting one large item with your remaining trade rather than a number of small ones?"

Black Swan looked at her as if she were speaking a foreign language. "Why would I do that?"

"Well, Joe and I have been having trouble trading with some of the people here because you've gone ahead of us already and done a trade with Joe's pots."

"Yes, but if I get one large item I restrict myself to only being able to trade with one more person and I have more trades left to do than that."

Lucy nodded. She obviously knew this before she'd made her request but she was hoping Swan might get a sense of her needs too. "Fair enough," she said. "Well can I ask then that you vary the small items you get and not just take mugs because they're our biggest seller and if we can't trade then we need to make the money to buy the things we want."

"But the mugs are the easiest things to trade with…."

"I realize that…"

"…so I'd prefer to take what I know I can use." She put a fourth mug next to three others on the table.

Lucy took a deep breath and glanced at Pete, who seemed not to be paying attention to their conversation. She had been hoping this would be easier. "All right," she agreed. "Is there any chance that I can ask you to hold onto the mugs then, trade them a little later in the day? That way Joe and I might still be able to get some of the things we want…"

"But then I wouldn't necessarily be able to get all the things that I want."

Lucy's voice rose a level. "Okay, so how about we agree not to trade with the same vendors? There are plenty of people with fruits and vegetables…."

Black Swan cut her off. "I don't want to be told who I can trade with…."

Pete had been following every word; when Lucy's voice rose, he turned around and sidled away from the truck. "I'm not *trying* to tell you who to trade with," Lucy suddenly yelled and Pete immediately picked up the pace. "I'm trying to ask that you allow us to trade with some people too! But no, you don't want to find a way to work this out with us because it's working just fine for you.

You're like a monopolist the way you're doing business here, a monopolist that pretty much owns everyone at the fair and is blithely unperturbed by the fact that she's the only one able to do trades. We haven't been able to get flour, we haven't been able to get tomatoes, fruit, beans, candles – you name it, if it's something we want, Black Swan's been there ahead of us. If I'd known you were going to put a lien on every mug Joe brought to the Barter Faire I would have stayed at home and made you come and collect them,..."

In a flash, Lucy became aware that Pete was gone and that others were watching her. She swung around to find two pairs of eyes staring at her quizzically from the right. One of them belonged to Summer, standing with an infant on her hip, the other to Summer's friend. Both women had their heads tipped to one side, and they were looking at Lucy as if to say, "So this is a fight?"

"When I agreed to trade with Joe..." Black Swan began, pulling Lucy's attention back just as Lucy noticed Skye walking in their direction, her brow furrowed in concern.

"Yes, yes, I know – you're *owed* the pots." Lucy fairly spat the words out. "Nobody disagrees with you on that one. Have we stopped you from getting your share of the trade?! I don't think so...."

"You're trying to stop me now..."

"No, I'm *not*....!"

Pete arrived in front of Joe and announced that Lucy was "flipping out" just about the same moment that Joe heard her raised voice. He was in the middle of a negotiation over a puppy with School Bus Mary and he thrust the pup back into her hands and rushed off, telling her he'd be back.

It was all he could do not to run the few hundred feet back to his stand, he was so agitated at the thought of Lucy being upset. She *never* flipped out! "What's going on? Black Swan? Lucy?" he asked the minute he reached them.

Lucy got in first. "I was just trying to find a solution that would allow you and I to do some business at this fair but *she* didn't want to discuss a compromise..."

"It's okay. It's okay." Joe was circling in front of the stand now, both arms stretched wide like a traffic cop, as if this would keep the curious onlookers at bay.

"And I just came to get some mugs but apparently *she* doesn't understand the nature of our trade," Black Swan got in second.

"I *never* said you couldn't get the rest of your trade," Lucy defended.

"It's okay," Joe said again, this time touching Black Swan lightly on the forearm.

Swan jumped, as if she'd received an electric shot, but then she let Joe lead her away from the pottery stand so they could discuss the matter without an audience. His voice was low and soft as he talked to the llama trek guide about the nature of their agreement and Lucy bit down on her anger as she watched them pace further and further away, their heads bowed close together. Snippets of what Joe was saying drifted in her direction; "........talked about the Barter Faire....... no, because I knew I'd be cutting my own throat...... asked you specifically to refrain....... you agreed." Black Swan stopped suddenly and reared her head back, like a horse, shying away from a hand. Lucy looked away.

Suddenly she felt very exposed. She swallowed, ashamed and embarrassed that she'd let herself get so angry. How could she, a person who avoided confrontation at all cost, come to a peaceful event like the Barter Faire and start a fight?! This was so humiliating. She felt sick to her stomach.

And then Joe was back at the stand. "Give her whatever she wants," he said, "and let's be done with this." He pointed behind Lucy. "I was in the middle of something and I'm going to go back to it, if you don't mind." Lucy just nodded.

Black Swan marched back over to the stand and began to pick up the four mugs she'd set on the table. "I'm going to take these," she told Lucy definitively, "because that's what I want. And I'm going to take them now, while you still have them. But I'll consider trading them for something other than the things you listed as needing." With that, she walked away.

As Black Swan receded into the distance, Summer stepped forward and patted Lucy gently on the shoulder. "You can come get flour anytime," she told her. Lucy's mouth fell open, astonished that her outburst had provoked sympathy, not recrimination. "It's okay," Summer explained, "None of us likes the way Black Swan operates. We've just never had the courage to tell her that."

She and her friend walked off too, leaving Lucy to think she should at least have said thank you. But she was so torn up inside she couldn't say anything. And it wasn't the fight that had made her feel like that, it was the acceptance. It made her realize that it wouldn't just be Joe she'd be walking away from if she walked away from all this.

She turned to go and rinse her face off with a little cold water or something but Pete and Skye were standing behind her, looking like they knew something she didn't. Lucy opened her mouth to ask, "What?" when Joe stepped between them and placed a tiny brindle and white puppy in her hands.

And that's when Lucy fell apart.

Lesson 7

Handles and Lids

When making the handles or lids for an object be careful not to think of them as secondary. They are the very essence of functionality in your pot and, as such, should command as much of your attention as the creation of the object itself.

Of course, Joe had a plan when he got the puppy for Lucy at the Barter Faire. He always had a plan. He'd been half way looking for another dog ever since they'd lost Charlie and he was standing chatting to School Bus Mary when some guy thrust a puppy at each of them from an unwanted litter he was trying to dump. Joe looked at the all-brown pup on the palm of his hand and decided that he preferred the one Mary had been given. That puppy was brown in the body but had a white head with one brown ear. Perfect for Lucy.

School Bus Mary agreed to the trade when Joe returned from the argument and Joe moved forward with his plan to give Lucy one more reason to stay in the Upper Skagit. Of course, having a dog hadn't deterred Erica from leaving. She'd walked out on Maggie just as easily as she'd walked out on Joe, a fact that Joe hadn't regretted once because Maggie was such a faithful companion. But Lucy wasn't Erica and Joe decided that giving her a dog might give her a greater sense of belonging. Plus provide a companion for Magnolia as she got older.

The pup would have to grow some first though. He was so small that when Joe drove back to the Skagit, Lucy having left with Pete so she would have a ride all the way back to Seattle for rehearsal, the puppy made the entire journey lying under the gas pedal of the truck. Joe tried to discourage him, fearing he might crush him when he pushed down on the pedal but the puppy was having none of it. He liked it under the gas pedal.

Joe excitedly presented the puppy to Maggie as soon as he got home but the older dog lifted her nose high into the air and walked away, totally disenchanted with the little fellow. Joe sighed; the women in his life certainly seemed intent on teaching him patience.

❦

Lucy left the Barter Faire feeling a warm glow, as if someone had turned on a heater inside her that she didn't know she had in there. And it stayed with her for days after she got back to Seattle, right up until the moment she ducked out of a rainstorm and into the Ballard bungalow she shared with Ann after rehearsal one evening and hit the play button on the answering machine. "How dare you not be home when I need you?!" It was Joe, and the tone of his voice was not encouraging. It made Lucy do a double take.

"I have two flat tires and I'm stuck on the freeway north of 145th Street. I have no money and I don't have any way to get back to my truck except walk. So I need you to appear – like, right now – with money and a car." There was a pause while Joe obviously debated what to do next. Then, "But since you're not home I guess I'll just walk back to the truck and hope that you show up sometime soon. 145th Street," he repeated. "You can't miss the truck – it's got a cord of wood on it and it's listing like a one-legged pirate into traffic!" There was another pause then a final, heartfelt plea: "Save me!"

Lucy frowned. What on earth was Joe doing on the freeway at 145th Street?! He never said anything about coming down today. If this was a joke….. She grabbed the phone and dialed him at home.

No answer.

She thought again. If this was a joke and she spent the last of her money trying to get to him, then she'd definitely make him pay. And why would he even say come with a car when he knew she was afoot down here! She looked at her watch; 5:50. Rush hour. Delightful! Lucy clucked her tongue softly against the roof of her mouth, resigned to do what she knew she must do and swung into action.

She picked up the wet rain jacket she'd tossed onto a chair when she'd entered the bungalow and slid back into it. She retrieved her bag from the couch, pulled out her wallet and looked inside. $20. Hopefully that would be enough. She flipped through the phone book next to the answering machine, looked up a number, then dialed.

"A-1 Taxis" said the male voice when she got through.

"Oh, hullo," said Lucy in her best British accent. "Can you tell me if $20 would be enough to get me from 15th Avenue in Ballard to 145th Street on I-5 South?"

"I5 South?" the man repeated, as if that were a very strange destination.

"Yes. I need to rescue someone who's broken down on the freeway."

"$20?" Now he sounded peppier, obviously eager to participate in a rescue mission with a Brit. "Yeah, I think we can get you there for that."

Five minutes later, Lucy was sitting in the back of a Seattle taxi, heading north on Interstate 5. "We might be able to see that side of the freeway when we get up there," the driver told her helpfully. "It all depends where he's stuck. You said he was in a pick-up?"

"Yes, a blue Chevy. And it's old. Maybe 20 years old," replied Lucy as she looked out the window directly behind the driver. It was dark already, and still raining; probably not the most fun conditions for Joe to be stuck in.

"So, like a '66 then?"

"Uh huh. And it's got two flat tires."

"Two? They both go out at once?"

"I don't know. He didn't say. He just left me a message telling me to come and save him."

"We'll find him," said the driver, juicing the gas pedal heroically.

Lucy didn't doubt that they'd find Joe, she just didn't know exactly what they would do once they did find him. Hopefully Joe didn't mean it when he said he had no money; because if *he* didn't have any money and *she* didn't have any money then she had no idea how they were going to get out of this particular predicament.

Joe was thinking the same thing. Here he was, hauling a cord of wood down to Seattle so he could make the money to pay for the gas to come down and see Lucy, and maybe even take her out to dinner, but he couldn't sell the wood until he delivered it to the customer in Queen Anne and he couldn't do that until he had four functioning tires. And now he wouldn't have those until he made the money to replace his flat, which he couldn't do until he sold the wood! It was a mess.

And the worst part was, he knew his day was going to turn out like this. It was all Sonny's fault; he could be such a downer sometimes. Joe was in his studio, pulling handles for his creamer and sugar sets when Sonny showed up. Joe liked pulling handles. It was a rhythmic, repetitive, soothing action that demanded enough concentration that he could lose himself in it and today, Joe needed to get lost in something. He'd had that dream again last night, that dream where he ran into a burning building to save his potter's wheel and was sure that, this time, he could make it back out before he caught on fire. Only he didn't. He burst into flames just before he got to the door, the same way he did every time he had the dream, the same way it had happened in reality.

He wedged three pounds of clay into a fat cone, clasped the wide end firmly in his left hand, wet his right and pulled, first from one side then the other, squeezing down on the clay as if he were milking a cow, until it formed an abrupt icicle in his hand. Then he lengthened the thin end in a circular motion between his thumb and middle finger and flattened it between his middle and first, lengthened and flattened, lengthened and flattened until the clay stretched like taffy into a band about an inch wide by six inches long. The thick end of his fingers then snipped the length of clay off and laid it gently onto a cloth-covered ware board. Joe doused his right hand in water again and started over with the squeezing and pulling action.

He was on his third raw handle when the door to the studio rolled open. The noise made Joe jump and he accidentally tore the handle he was pulling. He threw the useless length of clay onto a small pile of scraps and turned around to see who had disturbed him. It was Sonny.

"No work today?" Joe greeted his friend.

"I went," Sonny replied as he lumbered across the studio and planted himself in Joe's drawing station chair. "But I got sent home."

"You got sent home?!"

"Yeah. Some guy from OSHA turned up at the site and wrote me up for wearing shorts."

Joe stopped, his fingers folded over the edge of the bucket of water on his wedging table, and looked at Sonny. "No kidding! He drove all the way upriver thinking he might find someone breaking the dress code?!"

"Nah. I think the building inspector turned me in. He was at the site a couple of days ago."

Joe began pulling on his clay again. "Did you get a fine?"

Sonny shook his head no as he yawned, lifted his baseball cap and rubbed the sandy stubble on his head. "Just a warning," he garbled through the yawn. Then he put his baseball hat back on. "But I ain't gonna wear shorts to work no more."

"You always wear shorts!" Joe scoffed. "Three hundred and sixty-five days a year you wear shorts."

"Yeah," Sonny agreed. "I meant I wasn't gonna wear them on the days when the building inspector's due to show up."

Joe nodded; that made sense. The clay broke off in his hand again and he flung it onto the recycle pile. He paused, took a breath and let his head nod down onto his chest.

"You all right?" asked Sonny.

"I've got a headache," Joe grunted.

"How come?"

"I don't know. Maybe because it's Thursday."

Sonny looked baffled. "You get headaches every Thursday?"

"No, Sonny, I was being facetious."

"Oh."

"I have a headache because I didn't sleep well last night."

"I never sleep well," Sonny reflected morosely.

"Usually I do. But I had that dream last night. You know, the dream where I catch on fire."

"Oh," Sonny repeated. He gazed up at the exposed insulation on the ceiling of Joe's studio and asked, "You ever worry that might happen again?" like this was the first time he'd ever thought of that.

"I think that's why I have the dream." Joe replied slowly, hoping Sonny wouldn't miss the irony this time.

But Sonny seemed to be lost in his own thought process. "I guess it could happen."

Joe tore the clay in his fingers again. "Goddammit!" he cursed as he tossed yet another unusable piece onto the scraps. He looked at Sonny.

"I'm just saying," Sonny justified.

"It's more likely that a tree could fall in the woods and come through this roof and land on your head!"

Sonny chuckled. "Shoot, that wouldn't matter any, hard as my head is."

Now Joe chuckled too. "You got that right." He carefully laid out a sixth band of clay then pushed the remainder of what was in his hand in with the scraps. He took two steps and drenched his hands in a 5-gallon bucket of milky water next to his woodstove, clucking at Maggie as she watched him with a doleful expression in her eyes. He suddenly noticed why she looked so miserable. "Hey, stop that!" he chided, flicking water into the air. The little brown and white ball of fur that had been attached to Maggie's hamstring rolled away across the floor. Then the puppy shook itself to a stand and trotted back over.

"Did you give that one a name yet?" Sonny asked.

"Uh uh, no. I'm going to wait till Lucy gets back and we'll name him together."

Sonny watched his friend wipe his hands off on a towel hanging over by the kiln. "It's cold today," he remarked.

"Should've worn long pants," Joe reminded him.

"Don't need to. It's good and warm in here."

"That's 'cause I've got the electric kiln going."'

"Oh. Did you see the fresh snow on the top of Jackman?"

"Yep. Be a good day to go sneak up on a deer or two."

"Is that what you're gonna do?"

"No." Joe walked back towards his wedging table and slipped three fingers of his left hand delicately into the top of one of the creamer pitchers he'd made. "I'm going to finish my pots from yesterday then load a cord of wood onto the pick-up and take it down to Seattle."

"You're going to haul a cord of wood down to Seattle? Today?!"

Joe picked up a tiny rake tool and dug furrows into the outside top edge of the cream pitcher, slanting them to the left and right, then repeated the action down by the bottom edge. "Yep."

"Why?"

"I want to go see my girl." He put down the rake, picked up a fettling knife and sliced the raw edge off one of the strips of clay he'd made. He gingerly picked up the length of clay, pressed the straight edge into the grooves he'd made at the top of the creamer and folded the clay back on itself, smoothing it flat with his thumb. Then his fingers slid expertly down the clay strip and pushed it into the grooves he'd made at the bottom of the creamer, leaving a tongue that he folded back on itself there too. Now that the handle was in place, Joe edged it out, away from the creamer, making it wide enough for someone to slip their fingers inside when using the object.

"I wouldn't haul a load of wood down to Seattle, not for nothing."

"I need the money." Joe was rubbing a small piece of the scrap clay in the palms of his hands. When he'd made a short worm out of it, he rubbed it against a cheese grater, to imprint a design, licked one side of it and pressed it into the top fold of the handle.

"What's that for?" asked Sonny.

"Reinforces a weak spot."

"Looks like a snail."

"It's a doo-hickey."

"Oh," said Sonny for the fourth time. Then he came to the point of his visit. "Can you come help me pour concrete before you leave?"

"I don't want to be driving through rush hour traffic," Joe replied as he crossed to a ware board with the now finished creamer and placed it there to dry. He moved back to his wedging table and drew the matching sugar bowl closer to him.

"It'll only take a couple of minutes."

Joe knew Sonny's couple of minutes only too well. He rolled out two scraps of clay, braided them together then curled the braid around the spoon hole opening on the sugar bowl. In Sonny's estimation, things either took two minutes or twenty; but they never did. They always took much longer. Way too much longer. He made another braid, raked the clay in two places on top of the lid, wet them and applied the ends of the braid to those spots. Then he pushed his thumb up under the braid, making a small arched handle for the top of the sugar bowl. He placed it next to the creamer to dry. "Let me finish my pots and load the wood on my pick-up and then I'll see if I can give you a half hour or so," he told Sonny.

The taxi driver yelped suddenly – "There it is!" They were heading north at high speed, along with the rest of the rush hour traffic, when they glimpsed Joe's pick-up sitting sadly on the shoulder of the southbound lanes at 145th Street. Lucy wanted the cab driver to pull off immediately but he couldn't; he had to go all the way to 175th before he could turn around. Lucy tensed as she saw the extra miles eating away at her $20 and the driver read her tension as a heightened sense of urgency. He wove in and out of the fast moving traffic, despite the fact that the rain was coming down in sheets, and hydroplaned to a white-knuckle stop on the shoulder behind the Chevy.

Both he and Lucy jumped out of the taxi, bent forward to protect their faces from the teaming rain, and ran towards the pick-up only to find it empty. Joe had left a note, though, inside a plastic sandwich bag that Lucy was pretty sure usually housed his carry-along toilet paper, and he'd pinned it to the windshield under the wiper blade. The State Patrol had also left a note, without caring whether it got rained on or not.

"I'm heading back to the pay phone to call you again," Joe's note read. And then there were some scribbled directions.

"Can you take me to the exit?" Lucy shouted over the noise of the traffic. She'd pulled the hood of her rain jacket up over her head and was scrunching her face against the raindrops that kept hitting it.

"That's where he is?"

Lucy nodded.

"Let's go then," the driver said determinedly. And they dropped their heads down again and charged back to the cab.

Joe was wearing a fedora, a red and black-checkered wool shirt and heavy-duty work boots so the rain wasn't bothering him hardly at all. The inane walk between the freeway and the payphone was beginning to irk him but he knew there wasn't anything he could do about it. Fortunately he had a bunch of small change in the ashtray of his pick-up. If he didn't get Lucy on the phone this time maybe he'd call Sonny and make him come down and save his ass. That would pay him back for hanging him up today.

Joe's foot kicked against something metal on the ground and he bent down to see what it was. "Huh," he said as he held the 8-inch length of pipe in his hand. It was solid and heavy and had grooves, like a screw, its entire length. He rolled it over the palm of his hand. He could use this in the pottery, to texture the handles. He slipped it in his pocket and moved on, feeling like the day wasn't a complete loss.

This was the second new texturing tool he'd found this week, the first being a plastic lid that had maybe sat inside a container of bullets since it was imprinted with a grid of circles with raised centers. That one made really cool designs on the various handles he put together.

"Why d'you do that?" Sonny had asked this morning when Joe ran a long bead of clay over the grid and then rolled it up, like a licorice whirl, and stuck it to the lid of another sugar bowl.

"Makes it more interesting," Joe replied, arching a second, undecorated, length of clay over the whirl and smoothing it into the return, to hold the handle in place. "Plus it shows an attention to detail."

"Looks like something you'd do in preschool."

"Thanks," said Joe.

"No, I'm just saying."

"Why do you think I like this job?" Joe asked as he moved the finished sugar bowl in a delicate cradle he had made with his fingers and put it with its mate to dry.

"'Cause you never have to grow up?" guessed Sonny.

"Something like that." Joe moved the last of the sugar bowls towards him and eyed his collection of decorating tools. Among them he had a rasp, a lemon juicer, an assortment of hollow, grooved tubes, part of the bell housing from a transmission, a heavy-duty, spiraled drill bit from an auger, part of an automobile jack, plastic grills that he thought may have come out of a computer and the timing chain from a pick-up, all of which were capable of imprinting a unique design on his clay. "You do a lot of detail work in the carpentry too," Joe remarked as he scratched some lines into the top of the lid. "I've seen you."

"At my house, maybe. But not on the job. Not unless the customer asks for it."

"Why not?"

"Takes too much time. And time is money."

"I can't be worrying about that. I don't get paid for my time as it is."

"Yeah but look at how long it's taking you to finish those – whatever it is you're making there…"

"Creamer sugar sets."

"Yeah, those creamer sugar sets. I bet if you made them all the same you could make more, then you'd have more to sell." Sonny paused as he watched Joe cut a clay snake into two lengths, roll them both over a piece of textured canvas for a diamond grid imprint, moisten them and place them one on top of the other in the lines on the lid. "You might sell enough to buy the sheetrock you need for your house."

Joe took a small scrap of clay and pressed it against the end of his thumb, making a small, curved button out of it. "There's a lot of things on my list before sheetrock, Sonny." He pushed the button into the top of the clay snakes he'd just affixed to the lid. That would be the handle.

"Sheetrock's good fire retardant."

"Don't tell me we're back to that again!"

"I'm just saying."

Joe smooshed a ball of clay on either end of the handle, reproducing the look of the button at the top. "I had sheetrock in that first house, Sonny! What I didn't have was water pressure enough to put the fire out because everybody on the water system must have been taking a shower at that moment. And the fire department was nowhere to be found. I have my own water system now and fire extinguishers everywhere." Joe pointed at one hanging close to his chimney in the studio.

"You were the one that brought it up," shrugged Sonny.

"Because it was giving me a headache and getting me down." Joe moved the last sugar bowl to the ware board to dry. "That's why I'm going to see Lucy."

"She's a cure for headaches?"

"She's a cure for down," Joe stated simply. He slipped off the apron he was wearing and sluiced his hands in the water bucket again. "Sometimes she's so positive she drives me nuts. She's like the Black Knight from that Monty Python movie – you cut off her arms and she'll tell you she can still fight." He dried his hands on the towel again and then reached for his wool shirt. "But then I find myself feeding off it. And when I get these days where I wonder what's the point of even trying again, I know I need to be with her."

"You'd better go then."

"I will. After I load this wood."

"If I help you load it, will you pour concrete with me?"

"Only if it takes two minutes," Joe mocked.

Lucy recognized his fedora and the bounce in his stride even before she could make out the color of his wool shirt. "Sound your horn," she urged the tax driver which he did, loudly and repeatedly. Meanwhile Lucy rolled down her window and threw her arms out of it, waving them around furiously so Joe would catch sight of her. But the dark of the evening and the heavy rainfall shrouded everything outside of the lights and noise of traffic going up and down 145th Street so Joe didn't even glance Lucy's way. He seemed oblivious to everything except walking down the street.

The cabbie swung hard to the left and pulled into a driveway a few feet in front of Joe, obviously intending to *make* him notice them. Lucy immediately flung her door open, jumped out and ran towards Joe, who stopped, his eyes registering both surprise and happiness, and then literally jumped with joy at the sight of her. He flung his arms out and began to trot towards Lucy, who was so moved by his obvious happiness at seeing her, she also flung her arms out and they collided into each other, like some corny scene in a major motion picture, and wrapped their arms around each other with joyous intensity. Joe launched instantly into a jumbled narrative about what was going on with his truck but Lucy stopped him, aware of the clock still ticking away in the taxi and the eyes of the cab driver on her back.

"You want me to stick around and help you guys?" the driver asked as Lucy handed over the $20 bill.

"No thanks," she replied smiling. "But thanks for getting me here."

And then they were on their own, in the rain, with no money between them. Joe grabbed Lucy by the hand and began walking her towards the service station where he'd found the payphone. "They've got a tire that'll fit my truck but it's new, so it's way more than I can afford. But I think I had the guy partially talked down in the price..." he explained as they hurried along.

"How are you going to get him to wait to get paid?"

"Yeah, I haven't figured that part out yet," Joe admitted.

Their problems increased when they got to the station and realized that the guy Joe had spoken with earlier was gone for the day and the new attendant was in no mood to care about their situation. They learned from another customer that he'd just served a lady who wanted him to live up to the "full-service" nature of the station and change her oil and when he wouldn't, because he was working alone and had too many other customers, she'd left screaming. He wasn't going to discount any tires for Joe and Lucy or make any kind of negotiated arrangement over payment. He did, however, take great pleasure in telling them that there was another place, "just down the road," with used and retread tires. "How far down the road?" Joe asked.

"125th Street."

"But that's twenty blocks!"

"Yeah. Have a nice walk," the attendant sneered and wandered off to share his bad humor with another lost soul in the shop.

"Now what do we do?" groaned Joe as they stepped outside.

Lucy thought for a moment, feeling the cold, October evening against her cheeks. She got a gleam in her eye. "Bobby Jo and Stan," she pronounced confidently.

"What?!"

"Bobby Jo and Stan," she repeated. "They live not far from here and she's always saying I should call if I ever need anything while I'm down here."

Bobby Jo was a customer; a petite, older lady who had skittered in and out of the pottery shop more than once this summer, while her husband, Stan, searched for the best place to fish on the Skagit River. The first time she came in she was so scatterbrained, it exasperated Lucy. Bobby Jo liked the cookie jars. She liked them so much she couldn't make up her mind between the three that were available for sale. She hemmed and hawed and touched and agonized until Lucy's patience was steaming through her teeth and then, suddenly, she disappeared out the door saying, "I'll be back." Lucy doubted it. She thought Bobby Jo's parting statement was about saving face until the sweet little lady reappeared a few moments later, and bought all three of the cookie jars, teaching Lucy not to dismiss any customer in her mind, no matter how irritating they appeared at first. She and Bobby Jo became firm friends, then Joe joined them and eventually Stan was persuaded to get out of his truck and come into the shop on the promise of fish talk with Joe.

Stan spent more on pots than Bobby Jo ever had proving to himself that you couldn't take a salesman anywhere because he'd talk himself into buying way too much. He managed to get Joe to reveal one of the best local fishing holes though, so he didn't begrudge him the sales.

"Do you have their number?" Joe asked warily.

Lucy nodded. "The only thing is," she added as she took a dime out of Joe's outstretched hand, "I think they said they were leaving for California today."

Joe shrugged; of course that would be the case. Because nobody else had a neighbor like Sonny who might delay them from leaving on time. He stepped away from the payphone, not wanting to crowd Lucy as she punched in their number, or maybe so he wouldn't have to hear bad news directly. He looked up at the night sky. The rain had stopped and the sky was suddenly clear, with a bite to the air that suggested it would be cold up home. He hoped Maggie and the new puppy would be okay sleeping outside in the kennel tonight. At least they had each other, assuming Maggie would let the puppy get close enough to snuggle. And at least they'd eaten today which is more than he could say for himself. He thought he might grab something on the fly after the concrete pour, which had gone pretty fast, all things considered; only then Sonny had wanted to stand around and shoot the shit with the concrete truck driver instead of driving Joe home and Joe had joined in because – well, what else could he do? It was 3 o'clock when he finally walked through his front door and he knew he was destined to sit in rush hour traffic on an empty stomach. He just didn't know that he'd be doing it on two flat tires!

Joe realized that his thoughts had carried him all the way to the other side of the gas pumps and he looked around to see Lucy giving him an excited thumbs up from the payphone. Great! They must be home. Joe hustled back across the paved area and caught the end of her conversation with Bobby Jo.

"And Stan knows where it is?......145th right now but the one we need to get to is on 125th........Okay, good, good. And you're sure he doesn't mind...?......Well if we get this all resolved in time, we'd love to." Lucy smiled at Joe and reached for him with her free hand. She noticed how cold his hand was and drew him in closer to her until she could feel his body up against hers and his breath on her cheek. "Okay that's wonderful," she said into the phone. "We'll be here."

She hung up and swiveled around to face Joe, enjoying the scent of the woods he seemed to carry with him everywhere. "Stan to the rescue!" she announced, her eyes shining with excitement. "He knows where we are and he knows the place on 125th. I think Bobby Jo said he buys his tires from them. He'll be here in about five minutes."

Joe pulled her out of the phone booth and spun her around, pleased as punch at her resourcefulness. When he set her down, he wrapped his arms tightly around her as she slipped her hands inside his wool jacket, to warm them against the heat of his body. He still didn't know how he was going to pay for the tire but he didn't care so much anymore. They'd find a way. "What time is it?" he asked, pulling back to look into Lucy's eyes.

She freed her left arm from his wool shirt and glanced at her watch. "Twenty to seven."

Joe winced. "Let's hope this other place is still open."

The World War II veteran showed up driving a dark red Mercury Cougar – "the wife's car," he explained, when he climbed out. He had on a long, camel hair coat and cap, and looked much different than when Lucy and Joe saw him upriver, all garbed up for fishing and driving a shiny Ford pick-up. But his change of costume didn't seem to alter his friendly nature. His automatic response to their financial situation was to whip out a Gasmart credit card. "We can buy that tire here if you like," he told them, pointing at the big Gasmart sign swaying in the wind over the pumps. Lucy and Joe looked at each other; did they really want to go back inside and deal with that surly attendant again and pay the price he was asking for the tire? "Or not," said Stan when they hesitated. "We'll do whatever you want. Just let's do it quick. My dinner's getting cold."

The three of them huddled and agreed that the best thing they could do was head back to Joe's truck, grab the one wheel with the flat that he'd already changed out, and then go to the Gasmart station at 125th Street.

Coasting smoothly and stylishly on the leather seats in Bobby Jo's Cougar made short work of the to-ing and fro-ing on the freeway and Lucy relaxed in the back as Joe described to Stan how he'd got the first flat tire back in Everett and changed it out only to have the spare get a flat at 145th Street. "Where are you taking the wood?" Stan asked, once he'd got the story straight.

"To this TV producer that my friend, Pete, knows. He wanted firewood and Pete thought of me so I decided I'd come down and visit Lucy and make some money while I was at it."

"I wish you'd've told me you were coming today. I would've cashed my paycheck," Lucy put in.

"I wanted to surprise you," Joe told her. "Plus I didn't know we'd need your paycheck."

"Would the firewood have covered the price of that one tire?" Stan inquired.

"Not hardly!" Joe scoffed. "That's why I didn't want to buy it. It's ludicrous what he was asking for that tire!"

"Welcome to Seattle," said Stan.

"Hey, how'd you like that fishing hole I sent you to?" Joe asked and sat up in his seat, an indication that they were onto his favorite subject.

Stan threw a horrified look in Joe's direction. "That railroad grade was covered in brush!"

"Was that a problem?"

"I nearly scratched up my truck!"

"Oh. I guess I don't notice those kind of things."

"I know. I've seen your pick-up."

Joe laughed. "Yeah, I take that old girl everywhere and she never complains."

"Except when you bring her to the city," Stan remarked.

Joe shook his head ruefully. "I knew that tire was dicey when I spun it loading the firewood. I should've checked." He looked out the window at the view of the city from the freeway, cringing at the thought of all the money being spent on electricity. Seattle was lit up like a bauble on a Christmas tree. "And my 30 mile spare was worthless," he added after a beat, "'cause that's exactly how far it went before it punked out on me - 30 miles."

"What did you expect?" Lucy piped in again from behind them.

"More than that!"

"And he says I'm optimistic!" Lucy told Stan. He laughed.

"Hey, I was stuck in the center lane when it died on me," griped Joe. "It could've at least waited until I changed into the slow lane."

They were about to turn into the second Gasmart station and Lucy slid forward in the back seat to tease Joe a little. "I bet you were hoping that spare would take you all the way back home."

"No!" scoffed Joe. "I'm not *that* stupid." Then he rubbed the bristle on his chin with his hand, a mischievous smile lighting up his eyes and his mouth. "But I wouldn't have minded if it had got me to Queen Anne, so I could deliver the wood. That way I would've at least made the money for a new tire."

"How far's Queen Anne from 145th Street?" Lucy asked Stan.

Stan nodded his head from side to side. "About 20 miles?" he guessed.

Lucy slumped back in her seat. "Dream on," she muttered to Joe.

"Yeah, yeah. You would've dreamt too if you'd been hauling a cord of wood through rush hour traffic."

❀

The second Gasmart station had a young man in attendance with curly blond hair and large blue eyes and Lucy held his gaze as she explained their situation. She could tell he wanted to help, he really wanted to help; "Only thing is," he explained a little sheepishly, "the used tire shed is locked for the night and the boss is the only one with a key to it."

"So where's the boss?" asked Joe.

"Gone for the day," the young man admitted. Then seeing the look of defeat on their faces he quickly added, "But we've got lots of tires inside here. We'll find you one."

He wasn't kidding either; there were about half a dozen shelves to one side of where they'd been standing that were just crammed with tires, one right next to another, with no room for air in between, and the attendant, Joe, Lucy and Stan paraded along those shelves, slow step by slow step, looking for that one 15-inch tire they needed for the truck. But it wasn't there. At least, not as far as they could see. For as brightly lit as the main entryway and sales area of this station were, the overstuffed rows of tires had to manage with a single, grimy fluorescent tube flickering amongst the cobwebs a few inches from the ceiling. But not finding the tire immediately didn't faze the attendant. "There's got to be one here," he said trotting back to where they had started their search, Joe two steps behind him.

Lucy looked at Stan. She was tired of inhaling the bitter smell of so much rubber and besides, she was pretty sure she wouldn't recognize a 15-inch tire if someone laid it in her lap. She nodded for him to follow her and crossed the red and white-checkered linoleum floor towards two seats by the main window in the front. But someone beat her to the seats; another customer, who was leaving his vehicle and waiting on his daughter to come and pick him up according to what he was telling a pleasant-faced, older woman sitting inside a tiny booth in the center of the sales area. A booth that reminded Lucy of a box office, with its large plastic window in the front and a slot at the bottom of the window for money to change hands.

Since they couldn't sit, she and Stan hovered by the front door, chatting. They talked quietly about Lucy's acting job at the Rep, their voices being the only noise in the station other than the occasional buzz from the overhead fluorescents and the jangle of the doorbell when a customer came in to pay for gas. The man in the seats flipped idly through a magazine and the woman in the pay booth stared aimlessly straight ahead between customers.

Suddenly a loud yelp of excitement was heard from among the shelves of tires and everyone jumped. Lucy and Stan moved towards the sound and found Joe holding onto a tire while the attendant was down on his hands and knees, reading something off the side. "Yep, it's a 15-incher all right," the attendant confirmed.

"We found one!" Joe grinned.

Lucy looked at Stan who was peering at the tire, frowning. She got the impression he wanted to say something but was holding back. Behind them the doorbell jangled loudly and they heard voices. Stan glanced up at Joe, then the attendant, then looked back down at the tire again. "It's bald," he grumbled.

"Yeah," the attendant admitted.

"Yeah," repeated Joe. "But look, it's only ten bucks." He was pointing at the chalked-on price on the side.

Stan turned to Lucy, hoping to get an opinion. She just shrugged. The price seemed right for their budget. "We can always use it just to get you back home and then you can change it again," she told Joe.

But Stan's reaction was obviously making Joe think twice. "You're not in favor?" he asked the salesman.

"Can't you do any better?" Stan asked the Gasmart attendant.

"We can keep looking," he told Joe by way of a reply.

Stan nodded. "I think you should."

Stan led Lucy back across the squares of red and white on the floor and noticed that the customer who had been waiting for his daughter had left, so the chairs were empty. "He doesn't want a bald tire," he assured Lucy as he invited her to sit in one of the seats. "And you don't want him to have one. Imagine what he'd be like if it blew out on the way to deliver that firewood."

Lucy thought about this and then decided that she probably didn't want to imagine what Joe would be like if that happened. The bell jangled on the front door and she watched a woman with a little boy enter, cross directly to the pay booth, and encourage the child to put the money through the slot. He stood on tiptoe, lifted up his hands and pushed some dollar bills through the opening at the bottom of the plastic window. The cashier smiled indulgently at the little boy and handed him a receipt. He swiveled around on his toes, passed the receipt off to his mother then sprinted back to the door, his mother trotting behind him. The cashier smiled across at Lucy and she returned it with a half-hearted lift to the sides of her mouth. She was tired and hungry. And she really didn't care for the caustic aroma of this place.

Stan looked at his watch. "8:30 already," he said. "I might be too late for dinner by the time this is over."

"Oh I'm so sorry, Stan."

"Don't be," he replied nonchalantly. "It's not as if it'll kill me to miss a meal."

Lucy felt guilty. Here she was, moping over her situation, when Stan, whom she hardly knew, was still in his work suit and tie, with patent leather shoes that looked like they must be pinching his feet, missing his dinner. Yet he was prepared to wait as long as it took until this was over. Lucy shook off her petulance, sat up straight and gave the cashier more of a smile.

Joe came out to the sales area carrying a brand new, 15-inch tire. "Look what we found!" he gloated.

"I know it looks flat," the attendant said quickly, holding one hand up in front of him towards Stan as if to suggest he had an explanation. "But it was smashed between the other tires, so most of the air's out of it. Once we get it inflated, it'll be fine."

He sped off before Stan could offer an objection but Stan seemed fine with the choice. "As long as it's not bald," he told Joe.

"And maybe you'll even get your dinner," Lucy added, looking at her watch. She smiled at Stan then leaned her head back and closed her eyes. Joe brought up the subject of fishing and he and Stan were off comparing lures and line weight, reels and locations. Lucy opened her eyes when she heard the attendant come back. He was shaking his head disconsolately. "I can't find this tire anywhere in the books so I'll have to call my boss for the price."

"You'd better do it then," Joe encouraged.

The young man hustled across the station once more and disappeared into the pay booth with the older lady, who was holding the phone out to him, apparently with the boss already on the other end. The young man spoke into the phone then listened, nodded, scribbled something down, then listened again. He put the mouthpiece to his shoulder and said something to the woman who immediately bobbed down and asked, through the slot at the bottom of her window, "How are you planning to pay for this?"

"Credit card," Stan, Joe and Lucy replied in unison and Stan held out his Gasmart card as proof.

The woman looked at the blond-headed attendant as he repeated this into the phone and then they both turned and looked at Stan and Joe. They did not look happy. This time the cashier unlatched a lock on the window and pushed it open so she could look at them directly when she made her announcement. "You can't pay by credit card unless you let us put the tire on the truck," she said, sounding sad.

"What?!" Joe and Stan exclaimed. Lucy leaned back in her seat and looked up at the ceiling; why couldn't they get a handle on this situation?

"Company policy," the woman offered apologetically.

"Something to do with security," the attendant added.

"Let me talk to this guy," Joe demanded, crowding himself into the booth with the cashier and the attendant. Stan walked over also and stood in the entryway to the booth, holding the door open with his hip.

Joe talked on the phone first to the boss then handed him off to Stan, who said his piece then handed him off to the attendant, who did more nodding than talking before handing the phone back to Stan and, at this point, some deal must have been struck because Lucy watched Stan hang up the phone and give his credit card, with a flourish, to the cashier. She took it, made an imprint of it and everyone in the room breathed a sigh of relief that this was finally coming together. All that remained was for the attendant to inflate the tire onto Joe's wheel and they could be out of there.

But even that turned into a fiasco. The tire had been so squashed between the other tires that the young attendant could not inflate it fully onto the wheel. It just would not grip the rim. He tried and tried and tried while Joe became more and more frustrated. When it was obvious to all of them that this was just not going to happen, the attendant went back to call his boss again. He hung up the phone and then braced himself to tell them the news. "He says there's another gas station, not that far from here, where they've got a bigger machine for pumping air into tires and he says you should take the tire over there."

Lucy, Joe and Stan all jumped on this statement,

"What if it's closed?"

"What if it won't work any better than your machine?"

"How much are they going to charge us?"

The phone rang before the attendant could answer any of their questions. It was the boss again, He'd called over to this other station and yes, they were still open, yes, they could inflate this tire onto the wheel in less than two minutes and no, there would not be a charge. Joe, Stan and Lucy looked at each other; what choice did they have? They thanked the two people who had helped them so kindly and headed on their way.

It didn't take them long to find the third gas station of the evening and, as promised, a worker there inflated the new tire onto Joe's wheel before they could blink. They took a moment to share a look of disbelief that they hadn't come to this place first, and then they threw off the regrets and headed back to the truck, as fast as Stan could legally drive.

"She's still there," Joe announced in relief as they pulled up behind his lonely Chevy sitting at the side of the freeway. "And it doesn't look like anyone's messed with the wood."

"Have you got a jack?" asked Stan.

"I've got three," Joe nodded. He jumped out of Stan's car, reclaimed the new tire from the trunk and rolled it through the puddles on the shoulder of the freeway towards his truck. Lucy and Stan followed. It wasn't raining anymore but the cold of the evening had definitely set in and Stan pulled up the collar on his coat while Lucy huddled down into her jacket. They stood as close to Joe as they could so it would be easy for him to turn to them for help.

Of course, the flat was on the outside of the vehicle so Lucy was terrified that one of the passing vehicles on the freeway would take Joe's legs with it on the way by but what made it worse was that

Joe had to keep shifting around as he fought a losing battle against physics with his pick-up. He'd jack it up in one spot only to have it not budge in another because of the weight of the firewood in the bed, which meant he couldn't get the axle high enough to liberate the wheel with the flat. The whole process turned into one of jacking then holding that spot with a block of firewood, jacking somewhere else and holding that with more firewood until all three jacks were fully extended and an entire row of firewood was propping up the underside of the truck.

Joe sloughed off all offers of help during this process, letting his frustration propel him into hyperactivity, while Lucy stood listening to Stan talk about his upcoming visit to his sons in California as she eyed the passing traffic anxiously. "I don't suppose you have a jack in your car, do you?" she asked him at one point to cover the stream of expletives she'd just heard erupt from Joe's lips.

"To be honest I don't know what I have in that car, it's so new," replied Stan. But the question made him curious so he wandered off to dig through the Cougar.

Lucy shook off the raindrops that were beginning to fall again on her head. "You should put your hood up!" Joe yelled out, from under the truck. She spun around and watched him, huffing and puffing one of the jacks into place. "I'm fine," she yelled back. "It's not raining that hard."

Joe jumped up and raced around to the tailgate of the pick-up, leaned forward and grabbed a piece of firewood. "Well don't be catching a cold on my account," he cautioned. "They won't like it at the theatre if you lose your voice." He slid back under the truck and began forcing the firewood into the space he'd created under the axle. Lucy turned to face the oncoming traffic and saw Stan, trotting towards her, a massive hydraulic jack hanging down from one hand. "Look what I found," he beamed. Lucy looked down at the wheel of the truck, which was now high enough in the air to come off, and wondered silently why he couldn't have found that earlier.

Joe felt no need to be silent when he emerged from under the truck and saw Stan holding his new treasure. "Boy, I wished you'd've found that sooner!" he griped.

But now, finally, it was quick. The flat came off, the new tire went on and Joe and Lucy thanked Stan profusely, promising to send him a money order for the tire as soon as they got home.

"No, no," Stan replied dismissively. "Bobby Jo's planning to give those cookie jars she bought from you to our boys when we get down to California but she wants one for herself. So maybe you could make her one?"

Lucy felt the warm glow start up again inside her.

"I can do that," Joe agreed as he wiped the rainwater off his glasses with a bandana. "D'you know if she wants a drawing on it?"

"I don't think she's worried about that but she said something about the handle."

"Okay," Joe prompted.

"I guess she saw a handle on one of your pieces that looked like a fish swimming?"

"You got a pen?" Joe asked Lucy. She nodded. The rain was falling more steadily now and the cold of the night was settling into her fingers and toes and around the back of her neck and she imagined the same was true for the others. But no one seemed bothered by the cold as Joe flipped his hand over and began drawing an undulating fish on his palm. "Like that?" he asked Stan.

"Is that easy to get a hold of? Because, you know, she has a touch of arthritis in her hands...."

"I could make it a fat fish, so she has something to grasp," Joe offered, drawing arcs at the side of his sketch to indicate a belly on the fish. "Or," he said, struck by a new idea. "I could make it a fish leaping and attach it at the mouth and the tail, so she can get her fingers in underneath the handle."

Stan paused, and Lucy suspected he was asking himself whether he should move this far away from what Bobby Jo had said she liked.

"You know what?" Joe went on quickly. "Why don't I just make a couple of different jars with fish handles on the lids? How's that sound?"

"Sounds like a deal," Stan declared.

"And if you want we'll use my truck to get to that fishing hole next time you're up."

Stan smiled and sealed both deals by shaking Joe's hand.

Once inside the Chevy, Joe turned the heater up full blast. "Come on, come a little closer," he told Lucy and she bounced along the bench seat to sit next to him. He glanced at the watch he had hanging from a dial on the dashboard; it was after 10 already. "I'm sorry about dinner."

"I don't care," shrugged Lucy. She laid her head on his shoulder. "I'm just glad you're here."

Joe felt his spirits lift. He was glad he was there too. He blew on his hands, looked in the side-mirror and watched the Mercury Cougar roll smoothly out into traffic. He put the Chevy into first and chugged out into the lane behind the Cougar. Next time, he told himself, as he worked up through the gears, he wouldn't let Sonny talk him out of his warm studio to do something that would delay him getting down to..... Oh no, he thought. No, no, "*No!*" he groaned out loud.

"What?" said Lucy.

"The studio,"

"What about the studio?"

"I left the electric kiln on!"

Lesson 8

Bisque Firing

No matter how warm your studio, a first firing, or bisque firing, is recommended for your pots. Not only will it strengthen them, so they can be handled more easily, it will also make them dry enough to absorb a glaze.

The next morning Joe woke to the sound of a siren squealing in his ear. What in the world....? That was way too loud to be out on the highway. Unless.... His heart leaped into his mouth; maybe they were down in his driveway. He swung his legs out of bed only to have them hit a wall. What the...? How come his bed got turned around? Then he remembered, he was at Lucy's house, down in the city. No wonder the siren sounded so loud. He swung his legs the other way out of bed, slumped forward and balanced his forehead on the fingers of both hands. He sat for a moment, going over all the things that had woken him during the night. Then he gave both sides of his head a vigorous scratching. How could he have left home without checking on the electric kiln?

He reached for his glasses, slid them up over his nose and read the clock; 9 o'clock. 9 o'clock?! He never slept that late. But he never stayed up past 10 usually either. He'd wanted to drive home as soon as he realized he'd left without checking the electric kiln but he still had the cord of wood on the truck and wasn't going to drive it all the way back upriver. And it was too late to call Sonny and ask him to go over and check the kiln and his studio. Now it was too late to call him again, because he would have left for work already.

Joe smacked his lips together; oh well. He stood up, climbed into his jeans and tugged his t-shirt over his head. Then he took three steps towards the door, opened it, and walked out into the living room. He was stopped by the sight of Ann, sitting cross-legged on the couch in front of the counter that separated the living room from the kitchen, staring fixedly out ahead of her. Joe glanced to his left to see what she was staring at; he saw nothing. "You all right?" he asked. Ann didn't reply. She looked almost catatonic, she was so still, and it worried Joe a little. Plus she looked like she'd slept in her clothes, her brown hair was even more straggly than usual and he was pretty sure she was supposed to be at work. Joe took one step forward. "Ann?" he asked again.

Hearing her name, Ann turned towards Joe, her eyes unseeing from behind her large glasses. It was as if she were somewhere else entirely. "I don't know what to do," she whimpered.

Joe's inclination was to go over and give her a hug, to comfort her, but she looked so tiny and tense, sitting nursing her obvious angst, that Joe feared if he touched her, she'd burst into a million pieces. Like an over-vitrified pot. "Bout what?" he asked, trying to bury his concerns about his electric kiln.

"About my yukkie boyfriend," Ann replied.

"Which one's the yukkie one?" Joe queried.

"Leon," Ann replied, grimacing. "I've only got one boyfriend."

"I thought you dumped him last summer?"

"I did. But then, two weeks ago, he walked into my office at the School District with his cousin Lester and asked if he could borrow my truck for a couple of hours......."

"Okay, hang on a minute," Joe interrupted. "Let me make sure I've got this straight. Leon?" he questioned. "Is he the guy that would take things you bought back to the store and get the money refunded without telling you?"

"Uh huh."

"And didn't he steal some jewelry or something from you?"

"Well he never admitted to that."

"But it disappeared when he was staying with you, right?"

"Right." Ann nudged her glasses back up her nose and changed positions slightly as Joe forced her to focus a little.

"And doesn't this Lester deal drugs?"

"Yes. Pot. Leon does too, when he's with Lester."

"So tell me you said no to him borrowing your truck."

Ann bent one knee up and turned to face Joe more fully. "The thing is," she started, a slight whine creeping into her tone, "they told me it was for a family thing. And he's a Tlinget from Alaska and family's very important to the Tlingets. And I'm a Jewish girl from Connecticut and, you know, guilt's kind of important to us." She let out a deep, throaty chuckle but Joe didn't join her. He was waiting for the rest of the story. Ann let her smile fade and she looked down at her hands. "And they were in my office, in the middle of the day! Leon never comes to my office. And he looked so strange and soulful and out of place and I guess I was so glad to see him. And Lester was saying it was an emergency so even though I knew I shouldn't, I handed over the keys to my Toyota." Joe just looked at her, expectantly. "I haven't seen him or the truck since," she added finally.

Joe couldn't say what he wanted to say so, instead, he said, "You got any coffee?"

Ann nodded sadly and Joe could tell that she knew she'd screwed up. "In the kitchen," she said and turned back to stare at the window on the wall opposite her again.

Joe poured himself a large cup of coffee and helped himself to a bagel from a bag on the kitchen counter. "Have you reported it stolen?" he asked as he sliced the bagel in two and put it in the toaster oven.

"I tried," Ann explained. "But the police said because I gave him the keys the truck wasn't technically stolen."

"Sounds like something they'd say." Joe pressed the button on the toaster oven and took a sip of coffee.

"So I rented a car and drove around all the motels south of the airport, because that's where Lester said he was staying......." Ann stopped abruptly and Joe wondered if she were fighting back tears. He stole a glance at the back of her head over the kitchen counter.

"No sign, eh," he stated for her.

"No. So then I spent another evening driving to all the bars where they hang out and drink but I didn't find them there either." Ann let her head drop and when she spoke again, her voice echoed in her lap. "I'm just scared he's going to head back to Alaska and I'll never see him – or my truck - again."

Joe had planned to wait by the toaster for his bagel to finish toasting but he picked up his coffee and came around from the kitchen so he could make eye contact with Ann as he spoke. "You know what I'd do?" he offered as he perched on the edge of an armchair to one side of the couch. Ann looked up at him. "I'd stake out the Alaska ferry terminal, see if I couldn't catch him in the act of skipping town with my truck."

"I called to see if he'd made a reservation," Ann volunteered, then fell silent again.

"He probably won't, if he suspects you're looking for him." Ann pushed her lower lip up and nodded. "When does the ferry head up to Alaska?"

"Fridays at 2 pm. Today."

"Okay, then you should go down there, see if he shows up."

"Yes, but what will I do if he does show up?"

"You get your truck back!" Joe commanded. "Stand in his way so he can't drive onto the ferry, reach in and grab the keys, yell, scream, make a scene. You've probably got something that proves you own it, right?" Ann nodded again. "Take that with you, case anyone asks."

"Will you come with me?"

Joe shook his head from side to side. "I can't. I've got this wood to deliver and Lucy to pick up from work. Then I have to get back upriver because I forgot to check my electric kiln before I left yesterday."

"I thought you fired with wood?"

"I do. The electric kiln's for bisque firing." Joe stood up and headed back to the kitchen, wanting to avoid the look of disappointment on Ann's face. "If you want I'll give you a ride down to the ferry terminal."

"What I want is your .38," Ann replied quietly, looking down at her hands again.

"I wish you'd've told me that yesterday." Joe pulled the bagel out of the toaster oven. "I'd've brought it down with me."

There was a moment of quiet while Joe buttered his bagel thinking that Ann was reflecting on yet another missed opportunity.

Then Ann said, "It's probably just as well you didn't. I'd have shot him with it, then I'd be the one in trouble."

Joe nodded; he couldn't disagree with that. He took a big bite out of one half of the bagel and walked back into the living room with the rest on a plate.

"Why do you need to check on your electric kiln?" Ann asked as Joe plopped himself down into the armchair.

"'Cause if it doesn't switch itself off, the pots could melt. Or burst," he answered as he finished his mouthful. Then added, "Or worse."

"Worse?"

Joe took another bite of bagel and chewed slowly before articulating his greatest fear. "The studio could burn down."

"Oh." Ann obviously hadn't thought of this. "What's bisque firing?"

"You fire the pots to a low temperature so then they'll absorb a glaze."

"You fire your pots twice?"

"Yep." Joe took another swig of coffee and looked at the woodstove in the corner of the living room while Ann stared straight ahead again. He was trying not to think about his kiln stuck at red hot.

"I hope Leon didn't just abandon my truck in the middle of some road because it ran out of gas," Ann said. She looked at Joe. "You know, I think I will ride with you down to the ferry terminal."

"All right," Joe agreed through his last bite of bagel. "But I want to leave soon. And I want to deliver the firewood before I go anywhere else."

Ann shrugged. "I'm ready," she said simply. Joe glanced at her hair and suddenly Ann's face lit up with an impish smile. "Maybe I need to brush my hair first?" Joe didn't say anything. Ann pulled herself up off the couch. "All right," she said, then cupped her hand around her mouth and nose. "Maybe my teeth too?" she added before exhaling into her palm. "Definitely my teeth," she determined, wrinkling her nose in distaste. Joe made a face that said he was glad she figured that out by herself and Ann chuckled again.

Queen Anne was divided into two sections; Lower Queen Anne, neighboring the Space Needle and the Seattle Rep, and Queen

Anne Hill. Joe had to go up on the hill, to one of the fancier houses, to deliver his firewood and he was grateful to have Ann in the truck to navigate his way across town without having to pull too many of the hills with his load. The truck was making a frighteningly eerie grinding noise at low speed so Joe was also grateful that Ann knew how to avoid areas of heavy traffic.

Plus she helped him back the Chevy down a very tight alley to get to the TV producer's garage at the rear of his high-end town house. Once there, Joe was instructed by the producer not to dump the wood in the alleyway but to place it carefully inside the garage, making sure that none of it touched the carpet on which he parked his Porsche. Joe scratched his head as he assessed the situation, wondering why anyone would park their car on carpet? "I don't usually stack the wood I deliver," he explained to the producer. "Not unless I get paid."

"Well how much would it cost to have your stack it?"

"Another twenty bucks."

"How about I give you ten?"

"How about you give me thirty?"

The producer furrowed his brow, momentarily confused by this change of direction. "Okay," he agreed finally, "a hundred dollars for the wood and the stacking. And you'll make sure none of it touches my Porsche."

Joe threw off the firewood as cautiously as he could, took his money with a smile and rethread the truck, forward this time, down the alley away from the house and towards the main road that would take him sailing down Queen Anne hill and around to the Rep, where Lucy was working. "What time is it?" he asked Ann as they came to the major traffic light that connected Queen Anne Avenue and Roy Street to the tiny coffee shops and restaurants in Lower Queen Anne. By the look on her face she was fixated on her problems again and she didn't hear him. Joe leaned across her and turned the watch hanging from the dash towards him. 11 o'clock. Lucy was supposed to be off at 11:30. He probably didn't have enough time to swing down to the ferry terminal with Ann then make it back here by 11:30. "You mind coming with me to get Lucy?" he asked.

This Ann heard. She looked grateful when she replied, "Not at all."

The light changed to green and Joe pulled forward, trying his best to ignore the grinding sound as he worked his way up through the gears. "Get over," Ann instructed, pointing across Joe's line of sight, "so you can turn left onto Mercer."

Joe followed her instruction quickly and unquestioningly, not really caring about right of way in this sea of urban traffic. A horn sounded behind him. "Oh yeah?" he challenged into his rear view mirror. "Have you looked at my truck? You think I care if you hit me?"

Ann chortled and held the door handle as the truck careened around the corner onto Mercer.

"I'm not usually this aggressive," Joe reassured her.

"You have to be down here."

A traffic light brought them to a halt where Mercer switched from two-way to one-way and Joe let his gaze wander over the posters in the window of the Tower Books to his left. The light changed and somebody beeped a horn again, to spur Joe on. "I'm going. I'm going," he grumbled and then winced as the truck grumbled much more painfully from second to third gear.

"Now get in the right hand lane," Ann advised with a quick look out her window. Joe saw a driver react by gesticulating at this sudden move and then he lost sight of the driver behind his truck.

They turned right onto Warren and chanced upon a parking spot in front of the Rep's stage door. "See, things are looking up," Joe told Ann. "You coming in?"

"No. I'll just wait here."

"Come on," Joe remonstrated. He threw open his door and caused another driver to honk at him. "Well, excuuuuuuuuuse me!" he yelled, closing his door to let the driver get past him in the narrow street. "You'd better come with me," he told Ann. "I obviously can't be trusted in the city."

They crossed the street together and went into a small foyer that had two interior doors leading off it, one to the administrative offices and one to the stage. Ann looked at the attendant buzzing people through the doors and whispered to Joe, "Are you sure they're going to let us in?"

At that moment the stage door swung open as someone came out and Joe strode through to the inside with complete self-assurance, holding the door ajar behind him for Ann. "What do I know?" he rationalized when she looked at him quizzically. "I'm just a dumb country boy."

Joe followed the route that Lucy had taken him down once before, along a narrow, hushed, dimly lit corridor to the green room, where the actors hung out when they weren't needed on stage. The windowless room wasn't green at all. The walls were painted cream and the carpet was burgundy with small black and brown flecks running through it. At the far end there was a counter spanning the length of the wall, with cupboards and a small refrigerator underneath it and a sink, microwave, coffee maker and some mugs on top. Two round, glass-topped tables with metal and upholstery chairs around them took up much of the space in the room and close to the door there was a love-seat couch and three easy chairs in the same cream of the walls, flecked with colors similar to the carpet.

Joe put his head inside the door, to look for Lucy, and an actress with bright orange hair, who was enjoying a cigarette break while reading a paperback at one of the round tables, saw him. "Are you looking for someone?" she asked.

"Lucy," Joe replied.

"She's on stage."

"Oh."

"You can go out into the orchestra and watch if you like."

"I won't get arrested?" joked Joe.

"Not unless you try to steal the seats," the actress joked back. Her voice, and the laugh that came with it, were husky indications of the fact that she was a smoker. Ann remained silent, her attention taken by the framed posters of previous productions filling the walls of the room.

Joe waved the index finger of his right hands around in the air. "Can you tell me which way?" he asked.

"I can do better than that," the actress replied. She took one last, long drag on her cigarette, closed her book and stood up, stubbing out the butt in an ashtray on the table. She blew a long plume of smoke into the air before adding, "I can show you."

"I didn't mean to put you out."

"Oh it's no trouble."

She led Joe and Ann through a maze of soundproofed, carpeted corridors and pointed them towards some burgundy curtains made of heavy velvet, indicating that was their entry to the orchestra. Then she disappeared behind the stage.

Joe and Ann pushed past the soft curtains into the main stage orchestra. A large fan of comfortable seats, upholstered in the same burgundy of the curtains, tilted up away from the stage towards the soundproofed, black wall in the back. The floor had the same carpet as the green room and the corridors, so Joe and Ann were able to climb the shallow steps towards the back of the orchestra without making noise. The house was fully lit and, aside from a table in the middle front of the orchestra, where Shari, the stage manager, was sitting, running the rehearsal, Joe counted a half a dozen people scattered throughout the seats, watching. He slipped into a seat close to the aisle, under the balcony and motioned for Ann to sit next to him. They both sank down into the springy cushions and slid the seats forward, to watch in comfort.

The stage was bare except for a large canvas suspended center stage, in the middle of which was a square of red paint. Lucy was next to this painting, listening to two other actors, downstage and to her left, who were heatedly discussing whether good promotion could sell this piece of nothing art. One was convinced that if you spun the right line, people would buy just about anything. Or, as his character put it, "Bullshit sells dog shit!" [1]

Joe blasted out a raucous laugh that echoed through the theatre, causing the few actors sitting in the audience to titter. Lucy spun towards the laugh, recognizing it as Joe's, and opened her eyes wider hoping to signal him to silence. She didn't want him disturbing the rehearsal. But Joe, who had seen way too much crappy art make it because some glib advertiser could put the right spin on it, loved this pithy summation. He settled further into his seat, putting one knee on the back of the seat in front of him, and chuckled at the dialogue, marveling that Lucy didn't seem like Lucy in her character. A few lines later a character reiterated that bullshit sells dog shit and Joe burst out with another crude, "Haw! Haw! Haw!" This time, everyone else laughed with him, including Ann, including the actors onstage, including Shari, who jumped up and said they should run it again, so they could practice their comic timing with this audience. Only one man seemed bothered. He rose from his seat alongside the stage manager's table and moved up the aisle towards Joe. Ann slunk further down into her seat.

"Am I bothering you?" the potter asked when the slim, dark-haired man came almost level with him.

"Not at all!" the man rebuffed. He kneeled on the seat in front of Joe, leaned forward, folded his hands together on top of the seatback and confided, "I'm the playwright…"

"Ah!" exclaimed Joe. He grabbed the man's right hand and

---

[1] From "Red Square," by Theodore Faro Gross

pumped it enthusiastically.

"....and I just came over to make sure you had tickets to opening night."

"I think so. I think Lucy said she got me a ticket..."

"You're a friend of Lucy's?" Joe nodded. "Okay, well if she didn't get you a ticket, let me know because I will."

Joe grinned at the man. "I'm pretty loud," he warned. "That won't be a problem?"

"Are you kidding?! The way you laugh at my lines, I want you at every show..."

"Yeah, that's not gonna happen," Joe cautioned, thinking about all the work he had waiting for him up home. "But I might come a couple of times...."

"Quiet in the house," interrupted the stage manager with a glance in their direction. The actors had started the scene again.

"As long as nobody yells at me," Joe whispered quickly.

"I'll make sure you get a seat near me," the playwright whispered back. "That way, no-one will mess with you. I promise."

By the time Shari swung around to shush them again, they were both staring fixedly ahead at the stage. Joe for sure didn't want to get yelled at by Lucy.

❀

But when rehearsal was called at 11:30 and she bounced off the stage and came tripping up the aisle to greet him, there was no sign of disapproval from Lucy. Joe noticed that her eyes were sparkling and her face was alight with pleasure. He wanted to think it was because of him but he knew that it was acting that did this to Lucy. Being on stage was her nirvana. "Did you bring me lunch?" she asked as she planted a kiss on Joe's lips.

"Was I supposed to?"

"Well no," she shrugged. "I was just hoping." She looked at Ann and smiled. "What are you up to?"

"I'm going to stake out the Alaska ferry terminal and see if I can't catch Leon trying to sneak on with my truck."

Lucy's eyes grew wide; she was impressed. "We should go with her," she told Joe.

"No, no, I don't want to be a nuisance...."

"I've got to get back upriver," Joe snapped. Lucy's face filled with surprise; Joe nearly always helped. "Because of the electric kiln. Remember?" Lucy gave him a nod although she didn't understand why a little extra time to help a friend would make a difference to whatever had happened with the electric kiln.

"What time's the ferry?" she asked, spinning towards Ann.

"2 o'clock. But it's okay, really. Joe gave me the idea and he's helping me out by giving me a ride to the terminal."

Lucy glanced at Joe again. He had that look of single-mindedness on his face, that look he got when he wanted to go and work in the studio and didn't want anyone to stand in his way. She knew this single-mindedness was one of the reasons he was making it as a potter but she didn't necessarily like it when he used it against her. "Let's just go and get some lunch and we'll see what time it is when we're finished," she said.

Joe stood up feeling decidedly tense. Lucy slipped her arm through his, leaning into him as they took the steps back down towards the curtains leading to backstage. They walked side-by-side through the narrow corridors and feeling her against him, her long, loose curls brushing the skin on his cheek, her perfume delicately scenting his every step, Joe relaxed.

"We should stop at the bank first, so I can cash my paycheck," Lucy said.

"I've got money from the firewood."

"Did you deliver it already?"

"First thing," Joe nodded. They'd reached the lobby where he and Ann had entered the theatre and Joe pushed the stage door open, letting the women pass ahead of him to go outside. The air was bitingly cold and both Lucy and Ann folded in on themselves and faced back towards the door to protect against the wind. Lucy zipped up her rain jacket, tucking the collar as high as she could around her neck and Ann pulled her wool hat down over her ears. Only Joe seemed impervious to the elements in his fedora and his wool shirt. He strode across the street to the truck with Ann and Lucy tucked in behind him, as protection against the wind.

He unlocked the passenger door for them and then went around to the drivers' side and jumped in. In one continuous move he started the engine, turned the heater up to full blast, and pulled out of the narrow parking spot onto the street. Immediately someone tooted their horn behind him. "What the....?!"

Ann laughed. "We've decided the city drivers don't like Joe," she told Lucy.

"But when I pulled out just then," Joe justified, pointing back over his shoulder as he drove past the Key Arena, down a side street towards 1st Avenue, "there was nobody coming! It's not my fault he was speeding when he came around the corner."

"They do move fast down here," Lucy agreed.

"Yeah, so what am I s'posed to do? Wait until there's no traffic around at all? I'd be pulling out of that parking spot at 2 in the morning!"

"I think you're just supposed to ignore all the honking," Lucy told him.

"Yeah, that's about as useful as telling me to ignore all the beggars in New York," Joe grumbled.

Lucy smiled. She turned to Ann and explained. "When Joe came to visit me in New York he was really bothered by all the street people that approached him for money...."

"Or tried to sell me drugs. 'Crack the whip. Crack the whip,'" Joe imitated.

"I told him - just ignore them! - but he couldn't...." Lucy laughed as she prepared to tell a story on Joe. Ann smiled in anticipation. It was warm now in the front of the pick-up and the three of them were relaxing into each other's company. "One day, we went to my subway stop in Washington Heights and had to buy tokens. There was this fairly young bum, standing at the booth, asking people for money, and of course, when we got close enough, he asked us too. "Just some money for my subway fare," he said. Well, Joe took one look at his coat...."

"It was beautiful," Joe interjected. "A long, camel hair coat - like the one Stan was wearing last night......"

"...and he said, "Man, your coat's nicer than mine!"" Lucy mimicked Joe's outraged tone perfectly and Ann laughed at her acting of the scene. "And the bum got so angry that Joe had tried to talk to him, he started flapping his arms and screaming, "You want my coat?! I'll *give* you my coat!!" He practically chased us down the tunnel towards the subway."

"He didn't chase me!" Joe contradicted, as if it were a point of pride that he not run from another man.

But Lucy just went on with her story to Ann. "I told him, you can't be talking to these people....!"

"Yeah, but that's not in my nature, to ignore people like that. They're human too."

Lucy shrugged. She didn't want to think about all the beggars she had ignored in Strasbourg when she lived there. Beggars that sat on the walkways outside the shops in the center of town, their legs stretched out so people either had to step over them or go around them to get anywhere. "He's definitely better off living in the mountains," Ann murmured, nudging Lucy with her shoulder.

"That's what his father said," Lucy murmured back. She remembered because the comment seemed to come out of the blue. Joe had taken Lucy up to Saratoga from New York City to meet his parents over Christmas the previous winter. At one point, she and Joe's dad, Frankie, found themselves sitting at the kitchen table, sharing a quiet moment together. Lucy was thinking about the discussion she and Joe kept having about where they would live if they decided to make a life together – England or Washington State – and Frankie was reading his newspaper, smoking a cigarette. Then suddenly, it was as if Frankie reached into her mind and knew her private musings because he looked up towards the ceiling in the kitchen, exhaled smoke from his cigarette, and said, "You'll never get that boy out of those mountains." Lucy blinked. Some part of her wanted to say, "Well, we'll see about that," but she knew he was right. And she was impressed that he cared enough about his son's well being to make that clear to her.

Joe changed gear as the cars ahead of him moved forward. "Is that your truck?!" Lucy asked, appalled at what she was hearing.

"Yep. But it goes away when I get into fourth and pick up speed."

"I don't think you're going to gain much speed on 1st Avenue," Ann told him. She was looking ahead, at all the people holding up the traffic as they crossed the street between the shops in the busy downtown area. "Why don't you take a right on Broad and drop down to Alaskan Way. You can drive past the ferry terminals and park where there are no meters and then walk back up to 1st to find some lunch."

Joe hooked a right immediately and went down an intensely steep hill towards the water of the Puget Sound. He crossed the railway lines used by the trams that took tourists up and down the waterfront and by the freight trains that came through Seattle, and turned left onto Alaskan Way. This road was wide, with two lanes of traffic in both directions. It paralleled the calm waters of the Puget Sound to their right and the noisy, heavily trafficked viaduct above them and to their left. Joe drove past all the parking lots for the Pike Place Market, all the turn offs for streets leading into downtown and all the ferry terminals before he finally pulled to the left and parked under the Alaskan Way viaduct, not far from the Kingdome. Ann was right; there were no parking meters this far down Alaskan Way. Pete had mentioned that too, but he had also mentioned that his VW bus had been broken into three times already when he left it in this area, so Joe double-checked that both doors were locked before he walked away from the pick-up.

Leaving the Puget Sound behind them they walked quickly, the two girls hunched over against the cold, up Jackson towards 1st Avenue. "Let's eat at the bookstore," Lucy suggested.

They stopped at the curb on 1st, where a divider between the lanes boasted quite an inviting stretch of greenery for a busy downtown street, and glanced left, to check for oncoming traffic. There was nothing coming and even though the light was against them, Joe grabbed Lucy's hand and started moving across the road.

"No, don't," she objected. "You know I got that jaywalking ticket."

"I'm not standing around in the cold for nothing!"

"You got a jaywalking ticket?!" Ann exclaimed. "I've never heard of anyone getting a jaywalking ticket in Seattle before."

Almost immediately they heard the high-pitched whoop, whoop of a police siren to their left and they all three turned to see a cruiser coming around the corner towards them, blue and reds flashing, the driver motioning for them to step back to the sidewalk.

"See, see!" hissed Lucy as they followed the driver's directions and climbed back onto the sidewalk. "What did I tell you?! Now I'm going to get another ticket...!"

The cruiser pulled over to the curb a few feet beyond them and a buff, young, Seattle police officer, wearing dark glasses, whipped out of the driver's side, leaving his partner in the vehicle, and asked to see Joe's license.

Ann giggled at their situation. "Wouldn't it be funny if after living in Seattle for six years," she whispered to Lucy, "I finally get a jaywalking ticket?"

The officer took off his dark glasses and looked at the license. Then he looked at Joe. His eyes narrowed. "Concrete," he said. "Isn't that up by the Baker River?"

"Yep," Joe replied. His mouth was tight and Lucy could tell he was prepping for whatever kind of altercation the cop wanted to throw his way.

"I've heard the Steelhead fishing's pretty good on the Baker," the young police officer said, his gray eyes alight with enthusiasm.

Lucy turned away, not believing that the one subject this officer would think to bring up would be fishing.

"Yeah, I've heard that too," Joe replied, stepping back slightly as his whole body posture changed with the subject. "But you couldn't prove it by me. Now the Skagit, that's different. I've at least had one on the hook on the Skagit..."

"D'you catch it?"

"Un uh. I got it right up to the boat and then it got away..."

"You were boat fishing?"

"That's the only way I've ever come close to a Steelhead. Now the guy I was fishing with, he caught his limit. But he was bait fishing with sand shrimp, bouncing them along the bottom of the river."

"What were you using?"

"Rapalas mostly - those spinners that look like tiny fish? So we were fishing very different styles and I guess mine didn't work. Not for the steelhead it didn't. I caught some Dollies though."

"Dolly Vardens?"

"Uh huh." Joe grinned. "They're great fishing. You can pull one right after the other into the boat."

"Not so great eating, I heard."

"I smoke them," Joe confessed, "and they taste fine to me." He pointed across at Lucy, who was huddled into her clothes, inwardly wishing they'd get this over with so she could go into the warm and get something to eat. "My girlfriend, she's from England, and she loves smoked salmon. She thinks they taste great. Don't you, Luce?"

Lucy replied with a tight smile. The officer looked over at her then slowly down at Joe's driver's license one more time. "You probably don't have a traffic light in Concrete, do you?" he remarked, shaking his tight cropped, blond head affably as he handed the license back to Joe.

Lucy's jaw dropped. She looked at Ann who was grinning.

"No," Joe told the police officer. Then he feigned thinking about it, narrowing his eyes and puckering his lips as he tipped back his head for a second. "We've got a couple of stop signs but the closest traffic light is thirty miles away."

"Well next time, remember we do have them down here," the officer said, moving quickly back towards his cruiser. He threw a half salute and a smile in their direction, slid back into the cruiser and then he and his partner were gone.

"I gave that other cop my British driver's license and told him

I'd only been in the country three weeks!" Lucy protested as they crossed the road towards the bookstore. She was miffed that she'd been given a ticket and Joe hadn't.

"Yeah but listen to you. You sound way too educated," Joe told her. "Me, he figured I was just a hick from the sticks that had never seen a traffic light before..."

"No he didn't," grumbled Lucy. "He thought you were someone who could give him tips about Steelhead fishing!"

"Whatever works, baby," Joe joked as he held open the door to the bookstore for her. "Whatever works!"

They ate heartily in the cozy basement under the bookstore on Pioneer Square and then hopped back in the truck for the short journey to the Alaska ferry terminal. "Wish me luck," said Ann, as she reached for the handle on the passenger door to let herself out.

"What are you going to do?" asked Lucy.

Ann glanced at the vast, gray concrete dock, extending from Alaskan Way out towards the Puget Sound. Beyond the dock, the blue of the water stole her gaze and took it towards the snow-capped Olympic Mountains, shining in the distance on this cold October day. She glanced back towards the busy street every driver had to cross in order to get into the lanes for the ferry. It was just 1 o'clock but there were a few vehicles already parked in some of the lanes. Then she looked at the stark, gray terminal building, with its long row of windows out to the water, and saw people milling about inside. Ann shrugged in reply to Lucy's question and wrinkled her mouth into something of a smile. If she waited on the dock, she might lose herself to the call of the Olympics so maybe it was better that she wait by the street. "I think I'll sit on that bench outside the terminal building," she replied, pointing behind them. "I can see down Main from there, just in case he comes that way."

"You can see down Main from here," Joe informed her.

"From your truck, you mean?"

"Yeah."

"But you're leaving..."

"That's okay." Joe turned and looked out his side window, not wanting Lucy to think she'd won. "We'll wait with you."

"What about your kiln?"

"It'll be what it'll be. The damage is already done if it didn't switch itself off."

"Has it ever not switched itself off?" Lucy asked.

"Last time I used it," Joe said, turning back to face her.

This gave Lucy pause. "What happened?" she asked.

"Well nothing because I was there to monitor it. And when it didn't get to temperature in the time that I thought it should, I switched it off manually. I think one of the elements is going out."

"There he is!" Ann shouted. She jerked the door of the truck open and was gone so fast that Lucy and Joe didn't have time to do anything other than gape after her. Since she was heading for the front of Joe's truck, they faced forward and saw a small, red Toyota pick-up with a white canopy driving past, moving towards one of the central lanes. Then Ann came into their line of sight, marching her short, busty body determinedly across the concrete in the direction of the vehicle. When she caught up with it, they watched her yank open the driver's side door and start yelling. Lucy and Joe couldn't make out what Ann was saying but she was leaning forward, thrusting her jaw out aggressively. Slowly, two young men climbed out of the Toyota and stood on either side of it, their expressions shamefaced. Joe and Lucy watched Ann throw herself into the driver's seat, slam the door shut, then the reverse lights came on and the vehicle squealed backwards, away from Leon and Lester. It spun around and they could see Ann gripping the steering wheel, glaring straight ahead, as she drove hard towards Alaskan Way.

"I guess she didn't need me after all," Joe remarked, reaching forward to turn on the ignition. But the Toyota paused longer than necessary in the entrance to the ferry terminal and suddenly the back-up lights went on again and the little pick-up arced furiously back towards Joe's Chevy. "What in the.....?!"

Joe rolled his window down, expecting Ann to pull up to talk to him, but the Toyota curved around, away from his Chevy. He and Lucy watched as Ann drove her Toyota back towards Leon and Lester, who were both still standing in exactly the same positions Ann had left them in, their faces an indication that they hadn't really caught up with what was going on yet. The vehicle stopped inches away from them, and Ann threw open the door and pounced in Leon's direction. "ARE THERE DRUGS IN THIS PICK-UP?" they heard her scream. Both Leon and Lester nodded their heads slowly, up and down, up and down. Yes. "THEN GET THEM THE FUCK OUT!" Ann ordered, pointing savagely towards her truck.

Leon inched cautiously around Ann and reached behind the

driver's seat and pulled out a backpack. Then he shuffled quickly back to where he'd been standing. Lester didn't move. Ann jumped back in the Toyota, spun it around and punched it towards Alaskan Way again.

"Do you think....?" Joe asked in the quiet of the pick-up.

"I don't know," said Lucy.

Joe didn't know if he should start up the engine or not. He watched the Toyota sitting in the entrance to the terminal again, not moving. The light was in Ann's favor but still she didn't pull forward. "What do you think she's....?"

"I don't know!" Lucy repeated. She was tensing up. Why didn't Ann just quit while she was ahead?

But apparently Ann didn't feel like she was ahead. Not yet, she didn't. They watched her put the Toyota into reverse for a third time, spin it around and drive once more towards the still stationary Leon and Lester.

Lucy's stomach tightened. She hated confrontation and Joe didn't, so if this little situation came to blows, Joe was sure to get involved. He never shied away from a fight, particularly when it came to defending someone he cared about. Not that Lucy had ever seen Joe fight - except verbally - but he'd told her many times he was good at it. His two older, and much bigger brothers had used him as their punching bag when he was a kid and they'd taught him that he was going down no matter what, so he may as well go down fighting. As a result, Joe approached any confrontation, even verbal ones, with a provocative, devil-may-care defiance and Lucy knew, only too well, that it was the unexpected you had to fear when people felt provoked. She willed Ann to stay in her truck.

But it didn't work. Ann climbed out of the Toyota yet again and thrust her hand out towards Leon. "Gimme some money!" Lucy heard her demand.

Leon cut his eyes almost imperceptibly towards Lester, who slipped a hand inside the pocket of his parka. Joe took this as his cue. "I'm going over there," he said, pushing his door open.

"No," pleaded Lucy.

"I ain't scared of those guys!" Joe scoffed, already out of the truck. He left the door open, so as to avoid making noise, and Lucy caught a whiff of the salty sea air. She missed the sea, the constant companion of her childhood. She pulled her eyes away from the scene by the Toyota and fixed it on the blue of the water. There were no mountains around the sea of her youth, just France somewhere beyond what she could see on the horizon. Or maybe the Netherlands if she was looking in that direction. Although the seaside resort town where she'd grown up was on the upper bank of the Thames estuary so really, if there was land on the horizon, it was Kent. But if she was looking far enough to the southeast she could make believe she was seeing France. Lucy brought her focus back to the Puget Sound and lost herself in the small, frothy waves being stirred up on the surface by the wind.

Joe walked forward, keeping himself behind Ann so he could watch the standoff without being obvious about it. Like stalking a deer. He saw Ann with her arm outstretched, the boyfriend – maybe now for real the *ex*-boyfriend – and his cousin looking towards her but not at her, with flat, non-committal expressions.

"I mean it," he heard Ann snarl at Leon. "Give. Me. Some. Money!" Then he heard Leon mumble, "I don't have any money."

Ann's head snapped around to face Lester, who just raised his eyebrows as if to say, me neither. She slapped her hand down on her leg.

"Everything okay here?" Joe asked once he got close enough for her to hear him.

"Yeah," was Ann's bitter reply. "This truck better not break down on me on the way home!" she hissed at Leon and Lester. Then she climbed back in the Toyota. "Thanks," she said to Joe before pulling the door towards her.

"Need me to follow you home?" he called out without taking his eyes off Leon and Lester. They held their positions without meeting his gaze.

"Maybe just as far as the viaduct," Ann answered. And then she slammed her door and took off towards Alaskan Way for the last time that day.

❧

Ann's words turned out to be prophetic. She went to pull onto the Alaskan Way viaduct and Joe watched, from two cars behind, as her truck come to a stop, followed by a long pause during which it remained stopped, then her hand came out the driver's side window and lethargically waved back and forth in the air as an indication for other drivers to pass her. "Ah, shit," he said and stepped on his emergency brake as he unbuckled his seat belt. Lucy began to follow suit. "No, you stay in the truck," he told her. "I'll go find out what's going on." Horns echoed down the line of vehicles behind him. "Yeah, yeah," he grumbled without looking at any of them.

"You stuck?" he asked Ann when he got to her window.

She didn't answer, probably because her lips were clamped firmly together in anger. Finally he received a terse nod.

"Okay," said Joe, having assessed the situation and figured out what he was going to do. He hustled back to his truck, keeping his eyes averted from the irate motorists who were edging past him to get onto Aurora. He hopped in the Chevy, grabbed a hold of the top of the bench seat with his right arm as he looked out through the rear window, then quickly reversed while there was no-one behind him. "We're going to push her off the road," he informed Lucy as he made his maneuver.

"Is she all right?"

"No. So let's do this quickly, before she loses it completely."

He left his pick-up in the mouth of a parking lot underneath the viaduct and he and Lucy legged it back to the Toyota. He motioned her around to the front and they both assumed the position, hands apart on the front of the hood, one leg back and flexed, ready to walk forward while pushing on the Toyota. "Put it into neutral," Joe yelled out to Ann. She did. Within minutes they had the Toyota moved back away from the entrance to Aurora and tucked tight into the curb in front of the parking lot, with enough space for motorists to zip by onto the viaduct.

"What was it? The clutch?" asked Joe when Ann had finally composed herself enough to climb out of her truck and join them on the narrow curb alongside the parking lot. It was cold under the viaduct, and dark, with nothing around them that looked even vaguely natural. It was as if they were in a linear, concrete cave with traffic roaring above and around them, completely impervious to their presence. Ann nodded miserably. "I can tow you someplace if you like," Joe offered.

Ann shook her head no. "Your truck sounds sick enough without having to pull mine around Seattle. And I don't want you to get stuck in rush hour traffic again." She nudged her glasses up her nose and then wrinkled out a small smile. "But thanks."

"What will you do?" asked Lucy. She felt a sudden poignancy for Ann's aloneness in the middle of this teeming city and didn't want to leave her stranded.

Ann looked down the road, first one way, then the other. "I'm going to find a payphone and call my dad." Her eyes moved in all directions behind her glasses, thinking the decision through once more. Then her shoulders straightened, her chin lifted and she stated with a firm nod, "I'm going to call my dad."

Lucy and Joe could tell she'd made up her mind so they did the only thing they could do; they left her to it.

❀

The Chevy stopped the eerie grinding sound once Joe got her on the freeway but started it again as soon as he turned onto Highway 20. And this time, it wasn't only at low speeds; it was all the time. Joe and Lucy rode with the noise churning in the pits of their stomachs, willing it to go away. But it didn't.

"Should we pull over?" Lucy asked after she'd heard enough to make her really worried.

Joe's face tightened. "I'm not stopping till I either get her home or get her to Odell Richard's," he declared.

"Who's Odell Richard?"

"The mechanic in Concrete."

"But...."

"I'm not stopping," Joe stated. He wasn't going to be talked out of this decision. He was going to drive the Chevy as far as he could because the closer he got to home, the easier it would be for him to walk if she suddenly quit on him.

Lucy held her tongue and tried not to focus on the sound. She looked out the window and let her mind wander over the past 24 hours. Between the truck, the tire and the electric kiln, stability was expensive. And onerous. She wasn't sure she was ready to face this much responsibility yet. She thought about Leon and Lester, who also didn't seem to want to face responsibility, and wondered if they'd ended up taking the ferry to Alaska now that their ride at the other end had fallen through. She wondered what Alaska was like. She looked at the mountains they were driving past, their white peaks as glossy as the icing on a Christmas cake, and decided that Alaska sounded too far from the theatre. That's what it was like.

She turned back to Joe. She could see the muscles in his cheeks flexing as he gritted his teeth against the sound. And he had a hold of the steering wheel with a tense, white-knuckle grip.

Joe felt her eyes on him. "I just don't want to get stranded," he said, emphasizing every other syllable as if speaking in pentameter.

Lucy didn't say anything. She knew his mind was made up and her teeth were clenched too tight to speak anyhow. So rather than let herself picture what might happen when the parts making the grinding sound finally ground themselves apart, she ran lines. She was almost at the end of the first act when they reached Concrete and Joe turned off the highway and rounded into the mechanic's garage on the corner of Main.

"What's going on?" drawled an older, white-haired man with a Mark Twain moustache and a lump of something down in the corner of his lower lip. He was standing in the paved area in front of the garage when Joe and Lucy pulled in, wearing a pair of grubby, blue and white striped coveralls and blithely wiping his grease-stained hands on a blackened rag.

"That's Odell," Joe whispered to Lucy as he held open the driver's side door for her to climb out. He'd already explained to her that Odell's folks were tar heels, from North Carolina, and even though he'd grown up in Concrete, he had the slow, tight-lipped twang of his heritage. It was a twang heard frequently in the woods of the Upper Skagit. "My truck's making a real bad grinding noise," Joe explained as he came around the vehicle towards Odell.

"Well I heard that," puffed the mechanic. He got down on one knee and bent his head under the back of truck. He reached out to touch something with his right hand and shot it back to his side almost as quickly. "Yep," he announced morosely. "You've blown the rear end." He got up and shook his right hand as if it hurt, then wiped it again on the rag. "I 'bout burned myself. That's what you get for overloading it."

"Overloading it?!"

"I seen you, put a ton of wood on this truck! And she's only a half ton." Odell walked slowly around the Chevy, as if he could see the damage from the outside. "Now you've blown the rear end. You're lucky she brought you this far,"

"So what are you saying? I've got to get a new rear end?"

"I'm saying you've got to get a new truck!" Odell twanged. He waited a moment for the information to sink in, then added, "Better make it a three quarter ton." He winked at Lucy. "Then you can put *two* tons on it!" Lucy smiled. "Need a ride home?" he asked.

"If you don't mind," Joe replied gratefully.

"I was offering her, not you," quipped Odell. Joe laughed.

They piled into a red, Ford pinto Odell kept at his shop. "I was thinking of selling this to you," Odell told Joe as he pulled out towards the highway. "But it'ud be for your girl. Not for you. So she can get to her acting in the city."

Lucy blinked; she had no idea this man knew so much about her. But then again, Concrete was a really small town.

Joe looked at Odell. "Seriously?" Odell just nodded. "Well how much do you want for it?"

"I don't know. Couple'a hundred dollars. And maybe a pot for the wife. You do pigs?"

"Pigs?!"

"Yeah. She likes pigs."

"I guess I could do a pig. What do you want it on?"

"I don't know. Something small. Don't want her to think I'm spoiling her."

Joe laughed and winked back at Lucy. He was feeling so much better now that he was nearing home. "What do you think?" he asked.

Lucy bugged her eyes out at him. What did she *think*? He had a tire to pay for on a truck that had been pronounced dead by the very man who was trying to sell him a car when he knew they needed another truck, an electric kiln that had kept him up half the night and what was left of the money from the cord of wood after paying for lunch. And he wanted to buy her a *car*?! Was he crazy?

"Yeah, maybe we should check on the electric kiln before we start splurging on automobiles," Joe said, seeing the look on her face. Too right, thought Lucy. "Although Ann might appreciate you having this in the city while her truck is getting fixed."

Lucy looked down at her hands. She hated to imagine what Ann was thinking right now after all she went through today. How could Leon have done that to her? She blinked her eyes back up at Joe. The look on his face was so persuasive, with his beguiling half smile, laughing hazel eyes and his brow raised expectantly. She felt her resistance soften like butter in the sunlight and the edges of her mouth twitch upwards. He was crazy all right. Crazy in love. With her!

Maybe it was time she stopped hovering around that, like a hummingbird at a feeder, and started to take it seriously.

Lesson 9

Glazing

If you want to distinguish yourself as a potter, you should develop your own glazes. Your pots may be the right weight, perfectly formed and functional in the extreme but it will be their surface sheen and its color that first draws the eye.

The trouble was, Lucy was feeling out of sorts and she didn't know why. She leaned back against the slab of Formica counter top in the kitchen and eyed the venison roast opposite her. She sipped her tea as she contemplated. Maybe it was culture shock; that feeling when everything suddenly appears unfamiliar, something that was exciting at first but after a certain time, just jarred. That would make sense. She'd been here about six months now and that was how long it had taken for culture shock to kick in when she'd lived in France.

She ran her fingers over the smooth surface of the mug in her hands and then looked down at it. It had finger mark waves of green on it, a soft, sea green, with just a few overlaps of dark, cobalt blue. The light coming in the kitchen window behind her hit it just right for her to see accents of mauve and red. She'd never noticed them before. She brought the mug to her lips again and sipped another trickle of tea.

Then again, maybe it was the conversation Joe had had last night with Skye, about his daughter. It had seemed so intimate, so complicit, and Lucy had felt left out. Didn't Joe know she wanted him to be able to see his little girl again too? "Of course I know that," Joe had insisted, looping his arms around her so she'd feel loved. "But the whole reason she stopped in was to tell me that someone on the farm had run into Erica and found out where she was living. And Skye was there, when Maddie was born. She's missed her ever since Erica took her away, just like I have. So I guess I thought she'd be the right person to ask." Lucy had let herself be convinced but secretly, she thought she would have been the better one to ask if Joe should send his five-year old one of his candle lanterns for Christmas. Or, at the very least, she thought he could have told her before he told Skye that he'd been thinking about doing that. Lucy realized she'd felt her first streak of jealousy and she didn't like the bitter taste it left in her mouth.

She drank some more tea then set her mug down on the counter, sighing. What did it matter anyway? Eventually Joe was bound to find someone better than her, someone like Skye, who was beautiful and who understood life in the Upper Skagit so much better than she ever would. Or someone with a lot of money, who would give his business the backing it needed. She tutted loudly. Why did she let her mind go to these places?

Lucy snapped out of it and stepped towards the venison roast. How was she supposed to cook this thing? She didn't have that much experience cooking red meat because she didn't have that much experience eating it. Not that she'd ever been a vegetarian, not like Joe; he'd been a vegetarian for 10 years, from his time as an art student all the way through his first years of living in the Skagit. Right up until the day when one of his newfound, tar heel friends had offered to take Joe fishing. "But I don't eat fish," Joe had told him by way of a no.

"You don't have to eat it," his friend intoned tightly. "You just have to catch it. And enjoy being out in the woods."

Joe agreed and noticed that as soon as their vehicle left the paved road, heading for the mountain lake, he stopped thinking about his next fight with Erica, and started getting drawn into the natural world around him. And then he didn't go back to thinking about the next fight again until their car hit the paved road on the way back out. In those early years of trying to make it as a potter, Joe had forgotten just how relaxing fishing could be. And, as he watched his friends reel in their catch, he decided that if he killed it, he could eat it.

Lucy pulled down the three recipe books Joe had on a shelf next to the cook stove. One was entitled "Vegetarian Cooking" so she discarded it immediately but she looked through the others for something involving venison. There was a recipe for a roast but it required red currant jelly and juniper berries. Lucy wasn't sure that Joe had either and since today was Thanksgiving Day, she wasn't sure the shops would be open. "Maybe I'll give mum a ring," she thought to herself. She picked up her tea and crossed to the rocking chair next to the woodstove. She set her tea on the woodstove while she lifted the receiver off the wall and dialed her parent's number. She sat down into the rocker and stretched out onto the hearth. The woodstove had legs just tall enough for her to slip her stockinged feet underneath and warm her toes. She heard the double ring of the English telephone and leaned forward to retrieve her tea. Then she settled back for a good natter with her mum.

Over in the studio Joe was also looking at a recipe; a recipe for a new liner glaze he wanted to test. He'd scratched it down after seeing it in one of his ceramics magazines, and filed it in his glaze notebook under the heading 11-10 Test 835E29. He began reading the ingredients; corn stone, nef. syn, S1O2, EPK. He may have failed chemistry in high school but, by gum, he was good at it now. He remembered proudly the lady chemist from the company down in Hamilton who had wandered into his shop one day. She arrived at a time in his life when he felt about as defeated as a one-legged man in an ass kicking contest. His house had burned down, he'd lost pretty much everything he owned and six months after recovering from the third-degree burns, he was working in a talc mine further upriver, when the boss plowed into the side of him with a backhoe. As Joe lay dying on the ground, his lung collapsed, his liver smashed into tiny pieces, his boss begged him not to tell anyone how it had happened, promising to take care of him if he agreed. Joe had given his word, in between gasps as he struggled to catch his breath, and kept it when he arrived at the hospital. The boss, however, immediately forgot his promise once the danger was over and, overwhelmed by their crushing poverty, Joe's wife, Erica, left him, taking baby Maddie with her. That was when the lady chemist stepped into Joe's world and after a spirited back and forth between them about glaze chemistry, declared, "I'm about to quit my job and you're by far the most qualified person I've spoken to on the subject. Would you like my job?" Joe thought about it for 2 seconds as the woman tipped her head to one side, waiting for his answer. She was offering him thirty thousand dollars a year, a generous salary for 1983, plus benefits at a job that was within 20 minutes drive of his home, a rare gift in the Upper Skagit. But he couldn't do it. "Nah," he told the chemist, "I'd go brain dead." Then he sold her a pot.

"And that, my love, was my one chance at making a living from chemistry," finished Joe, when he related the story to Lucy. "Well, apart from the years of my misspent youth, of course," he joked.

"Why didn't you turn your boss in, when he didn't come through for you?" Lucy asked.

"Because I gave him my word," Joe replied. He could still feel pretty bitter inside when he thought about it though. Joe focused on the recipe. He pulled a plastic tub of ball clay down off the shelf above his glazing table, unscrewed the lid, and tapped a measure of the powder into a bowl on his scale. He kept tapping until the scale started to tip and then he dropped the measured amount into an old sour cream container. He put the ball clay back and popped the lid off a tub next to it labeled barium carb. He tapped and measured, tapped and measured all the way down his ingredients list until his sour cream container held what it needed for the new glaze. Then Joe went outside the studio and grabbed a 5-gallon bucket of rainwater from underneath one of the gutters on the roof.

Lucy watched him from her seat in the rocking chair. It had stopped raining, finally, but the moss on the vine maples between the house and the studio was still dripping plentifully, giving the illusion of more rain. "Happy Thanksgiving," chirruped her mother when she knew it was Lucy on the phone.

"Oh thanks," replied Lucy. Thanksgiving didn't really mean anything to her. She'd only had three, since coming to America and two of them she'd spent alone. The third she'd spent with a Greek classmate from NYU and they'd gone to a movie and eaten pizza so she didn't think that counted.

"Are you cooking a turkey? Isn't that what they eat at Thanksgiving?"

"Well, yes. But no," replied Lucy. "I mean, they eat turkey but we've been invited to a potluck in Rockport where everyone is supposed to bring something they grew, harvested, hunted or raised. So we're taking a venison roast. Only I'm not sure how to cook it because last time I roasted venison it just dried out."

"Well it's lean, isn't it, so it probably doesn't need very long to cook," her mother told her. "If it were me, I'd cook it slowly, in one of those casseroles Joe makes. You know the ones I mean? With the lid. Like the one he gave your dad and I. Do you have one of those in the house?"

Lucy thought about the green covered casserole sitting on a shelf in the pantry. "Yes. Yes, we do."

"Okay, good," said her mum. "So I'd puncture the roast in a couple of places and squeeze a bit of garlic in the holes, then put it in the casserole with some kind of soup mix. Do you have oxtail over there?"

"Not that I've seen," replied Lucy distractedly, as she watched Joe carrying a bucket of water towards the porch of the studio.

"Well you want something hearty," her mum explained.

"How about French onion? I think I've got a packet of French onion soup."

"Yes, that would work. Mix it up and pour it over your joint of meat, add some wine, if you have it, and some carrots, and cook it in the oven on low. Between gas mark two and three. That would be..." and she clicked her tongue against the roof of her mouth as she calculated, "...oh, three hundred degrees on your oven?" Lucy laughed. "What?" asked her mother.

"No, I was just laughing at the puppy." Lucy could see the dogs through the sliding glass door, racing up the hill to catch Joe before he went back into the studio. "He chases after Maggie like he really doesn't want to get left behind but as soon as he catches up with her, he nips at the back of her legs. So then she runs even faster."

"That's the new puppy? Max?"

"Yes."

Lucy could see how much Max had grown in the two months they'd had him but he was still no match for Maggie when she was trying to get away from him.

"Whose house are you going to in Rockport?" her mother asked.

Lucy focused again on the conversation. "Dave and Shana's. I don't know if you...."

"Oh yes," interrupted her mother eagerly. "Aren't they the ones with the tree farm? And she grows raspberries? You took me there once." It was hard for Lucy's mother not to be part of her everyday life, so she liked joining in mentally whenever she could.

"That's the one."

"And they invited a group of people over for Thanksgiving, did they? Will Sonny be there with his wife?"

"I expect so."

"And everyone's supposed to bring something they had a hand in cultivating in some way. Sounds a bit like our Harvest Festival."

Lucy thought back to the annual service in the little church associated with her primary school; the way people brought loaves of bread and baskets of fruit to share with the poor as a celebration of the seasonal bounty. And then they all sang, "We plow the fields and scatter," at full lung. It was one of the few services that was well attended and one that Lucy could actually get her mind around, even as a child. "So how long should I cook this roast for?" she asked her mother.

"Depends on how big it is. If it's from a Blacktail deer it's probably not very big,"

Lucy looked back at the roast on the counter. "No, it's not."

"What time is your potluck?"

"2," said Lucy.

"And what time is it now?"

Lucy glanced over her shoulder at the maple burl clock. "10," she answered. Then she did a quick mental computation, adding on 8 hours for the time difference, and realized it was early evening for her mother and that the drafty hallway she was standing in to talk on the phone, was undoubtedly cold. Lucy wiggled her toes under the woodstove, wishing her mother didn't have to be cold.

"Well if you pop it in the oven in the next half an hour, I think you'll be all right. You can always turn it down if it's ready before you leave. Should be nice and tender."

"Thanks, mum."

"Of course." There was a pause and Lucy could hear the unspoken longing coming down the phone line. It was interrupted by the sound of her father barking out her mother's name. "I'd better go. Your father wants his pudding," her mother finished hurriedly, sounding very put upon. "Bye now."

"Bye," said Lucy. She sat for a moment, lost in thought, mesmerized by the warmth from the woodstove. Then she blinked, gulped down the last of her tea and got out of the rocker. Back to the roast, she thought pragmatically.

Joe poured a measure of water into the sour cream container and mixed it into the ingredients vigorously. Once he'd got an adequate slurry, he sieved it into a mayonnaise jar then poured it back into the sour cream container. He reached down and picked up a bisque fired tile from a pile under his glazing table and dipped one side of it into the new glaze. He looked around him and spied a plastic lid with some dried green slip on the underside. He pulled it towards him and moistened the slip by sprinkling a few drops of rainwater on it, then dipped a paintbrush in the color. He used that to write the glaze test number and the date on the back of the tile.

Every firing Joe made a half dozen glaze test tiles. He hadn't set out to become so proficient in chemistry but he couldn't afford to be dependent on the clay store for his glazes because they were expensive. So he tested, observed and adjusted to get glazes that would work at his temperature more out of necessity than passion. When he thought about it he realized that it was the random effects from the kiln on his glazes that intrigued and pleased him more than the ones he could adjust scientifically. Things like the matte white glaze, for example, which had suddenly turned a soft shade of pink in the wood kiln when he added an element of talc from the local soapstone to the mix and yet, fired in the electric kiln, it stayed matte white. What was it in the talc that went pink on contact with fire? And the red, which was so fugitive in his wood kiln that he couldn't very often promise it to his customers. Sometimes it came out brown red, sometimes burgundy, china red, maroon but more often than not, the copper in the red fled into the flame, leaving the pot it was on to come out beige. Then it would move through the kiln and re-vaporize onto other pots, making them blush with a red they weren't expecting. This random migration of the red could turn Joe's blue glazes purple, could highlight his greens with lilac and lavender and, quite often, could add a touch of rose to the ordinarily white surface of his porcelain pieces. But at its best, the red would stay on the pot of its origin and come out a delicious shade of raspberry with maybe some flecks of teal and mauve throughout. Then it was a prize. Joe could never predict any of this and he liked that. He liked that atmospheric conditions in the kiln were the final arbiter of his work. It meant that he didn't have that much control over the finished look of his objects but that was more than compensated for by the abundance of surprises. And surprises kept him challenged and challenges kept him reaching as a potter.

Now that his glaze tests were finished, Joe lifted the bucket of rainwater up to his glazing table and added a little more to each of his main glazes. He had five buckets sunk down into the counter on which he did his glazing, labeled CLEAR, RHODES CLEAR, WHITE, CuO MATTE and BLUE MATTE. He went from one to the next pouring in a measure of water and then stirred each of them with a wooden stick. Some potters used hydrometers to measure the specific gravity of their glazes but Joe didn't. He just knew what the glazes were supposed to look like when he saw it. As long as they resembled heavy cream he was good to go. He walked the length of the table, peering down into each bucket. Yep, they looked like heavy cream all right. He switched off the light over the glazing table and began to take off his apron. The dogs, who had been lying quietly by the woodstove jumped up, realizing the boss was on the move. Joe leaned over to rinse his hands in the water bucket on the floor by the stove and felt the puppy jumping between his legs, as if trying to see inside the bucket, "You want a drink, little buddy?" he asked and cupped some water in his palm for Max to lap. Max sniffed it then jumped around, uninterested, and bounced over towards Maggie. Once he reached her, he tipped his head sideways and began chewing on her hamstrings. Maggie turned and snapped at him, then extended both front legs out towards him and play bowed. "Okay, let's go, you guys," Joe said and rolled the door open.

❀

Lucy was standing outside the studio, wearing one of Joe's gray and blue wool shirts over some tight-fitting jeans and staring intently at a scrap of paper in her hands. Her hair looked gold in the mid-morning light and fell thickly across her shoulders in an extra curly jumble, probably from all the moisture in the air. Joe's heart did a sudden somersault. "Have you finished?" she asked, looking up to meet his gaze.

"For today I have," he replied as he buttoned the top two buttons on the brown wool shirt he was wearing. Joe had been a devotee of natural fibers ever since the day he got burned and somebody had reached out to touch him and made a permanent handprint on his arm out of the acrylic sweater he was wearing. "Now I'll let the glazes sit overnight, so all the minerals can get completely saturated. Then tomorrow I'll start glazing." He looked at the piece of paper in her hands. "What's that?" he asked.

"I think it's one of your orders," she answered. "But it's wet, because it was lying on the ground outside your studio here, so it's a bit hard to read." She held it out to him with a stern look. "People put money down on these orders, you know. You really ought to get yourself a notice board instead of sticking them under a piece of glass on your wedging table."

"Nah," rebuffed Joe. "I don't need a notice board." He pulled a bandana out of his back pocket and blew his nose loudly. "What I need is a mask, so I can protect my sinuses when I make glazes." He pushed the bandana back into his jean pocket and took the order from Lucy. "Hang on a sec," he told her before heading back into the studio to put the order back under the piece of glass.

Lucy turned her attention to the dogs while she waited. They were playing tag around her legs and she reached down and scooped Max up in her arms. Instantly he began lapping at the underside of her chin, his body wriggling in happiness. Lucy bent her head forward and kissed him noisily at the top of his nose, to thank him for all the good loving he was giving her.

"Did you go for your walk?" Joe asked, interrupting their sweet doings as he rolled to the studio closed once more and trotted down the steps.

Lucy put Max back down on the ground and watched him go right back to chasing Maggie. "Nope," she replied. "I just put the meat in the oven." She slipped her hand in Joe's and they began ambling down towards the house. "I was hoping that maybe we could go on a walk together, since it is Thanksgiving today." Lucy knew that Joe found her walks in the park too tame so she took whatever advantage she could to try to talk him into one. "Aren't you supposed to take the day off?"

"Probably. But I don't get vacation pay." Then he narrowed his eyes, as if struck by a sudden realization. "Come to think of it, I don't get paid at all."

"Ha, ha," mocked Lucy. "It would just be a short walk – the Scenic View Trail. And we could take the dogs."

Joe followed her up the steps to the back porch and Lucy slid open the glass door.

"Did you make coffee?" he asked, surprised by the inviting aroma that hit the back of his throat.

"Yep," attested Lucy, wiping her feet on the mat by the sliding-glass door.

"Then sure, I'll come for a walk in the park."

Ha! Lucy thought smugly. That wasn't so hard after all.

The ground under the trees in the State Park was like a wet sponge from the heavy rainfall of the previous few days but the blanket of boughs, leaves, and grape-sized, dark brown hemlock cones that covered the trail contained the excess moisture so walking on it was not an issue. The dogs ran enthusiastically back and forth, stopping occasionally to pee on a fern or sniff the residual scent of another critter that had been there before them, while Lucy and Joe both found themselves with their faces tipped slightly up, enjoying the rich, loamy scent of the newly wetted earth and the tingle of the clean air against their cheeks. Lucy's eyes swung left and right, embracing the countless variations on the color green she could see around her. She remembered reading somewhere that if you wanted a room in your home to be welcoming, you should color it green. She stopped to study a patch of moss that was made of long, delicate threads that were so pale a green they were almost yellow. Was it welcoming or comforting? Or maybe relaxing? She didn't remember exactly. What she did remember was that green was the most frequently used color in living rooms because it encouraged people to want to be there.

Joe stopped and tipped his head up to try to see the top of a tree. "Will you look at that," he said in quiet awe. "People say that Rockport State Park has some of the most impressive old growth trees for this low an elevation and you look at a tree like this and you know it's true. This one's got to be hundreds of years old."

Lucy craned her neck, trying to see the leaves on the tree but all the branches were so high up in the air, it was impossible to distinguish anything other than huge clusters of dense dark green backlit by the sky. "What kind of tree is it?" she asked.

"It's a Doug fir."

"How do you know that?"

"By the bark. See how thick and sinewy it is?" The pattern on the bark looked like the outside of a peach pit to Lucy only much longer and thicker. "And this one," Joe went on, pointing to a tree behind them, "that's a cedar. See, its bark is thin and vertical and peels off in strips. You couldn't do that with a Doug fir." Joe looked at the blocky buttress swell at the base of the cedar. "And no matter how old a Western red cedar gets, its bark never gets thicker."

Lucy was trying to remember what the trees looked like in Priory Park, where she played as a child in England. She could picture the brook, Prittle Brook, and the well alongside it, both of which encouraged the original Saxon village of Prittlewell and the establishment of the priory. Then the village grew in its south end, moving down towards the sea rather than west towards London or north towards the agricultural land of Essex county, and over time that growth turned into the town of Southend-on-Sea, which absorbed the village of Prittlewell. That's where Lucy grew up, in Southend-on-Sea, and she played in the park that had been built to preserve the memory of the village and protect the ruins of the old priory. Lucy thought about the maze at the old priory and how she and her sisters would run through it over and over again, hoping to lose each other. But it wasn't that big a maze and the hedges that separated one route from another were neatly trimmed so you could see heads over the top of them. The brook was much less cultivated and encouraged muddy, woodsy-type games but the water looked like it was covered in fecal matter and smelled putrid so their mother cautioned them not to get too close. But what kind of trees grew in that park? There weren't that many, not like in Rockport State Park, but there must have been horse chestnuts because her brother collected the acorns to play a game called conkers with his school mates, where the acorns were hung from strings and smashed against each other in the air until one broke. And Lucy remembered at least one big oak tree that sprawled like a large umbrella over the wide expanse of manicured lawn in front of the tennis courts and food pavilion. It was a park designed to meet the needs of the people rather than one set up to capture and preserve the essence of the earth; her trees. Definitely a different way of looking at the universe, Lucy thought to herself.

The dogs came back to find out what was causing the delay so Joe and Lucy moved on, following the trail around a bend alongside a creek bed. The creek had cut a deep groove in the earth here and crashed and splashed its way over the smooth rocks that lined its bed as it headed down towards the river. Joe pointed out the abundance of sword ferns covering the opposing bank. "I always thought ferns were a forest floor kind of plant," Lucy remarked.

"They are."

"Then why do they grow out of trees here?"

"What do you mean?"

Lucy pointed at a group of small fronds, shooting out of the trunk of a maple tree.

"No, no, that's not a fern. You know what that is?" Without waiting for an answer, Joe moved towards the shoots and pulled one out at the root. "It's natural licorice," he explained and carefully removed the outer skin from the stem. Then he held it out to Lucy. "Chew on that."

Lucy put it in her mouth and bit down gently on the exposed stem. The taste came slowly; the taste of something a little spicy, almost hot on the back of her tongue, yet sweet. Something molasses like. Joe peeled another shoot and then broke it lengthways in two, exposing a dark seam in the center. "See," he said, before putting the root in his mouth. "The Native Americans chewed on this to keep their breath sweet."

They continued on, following the trail around another bend to where it ran parallel to the river. They could only see glimpses of the turquoise water, which lay below the park through the trees, but what they saw danced and sparkled in the mid-day sunlight. They were moving quickly now, enjoying the freedom to stretch their legs in a forest that was both densely treed, yet gave them a path that was unencumbered by blow down. A noise to their right made them turn just in time to see a small, Blacktail deer bound across the trail behind them and disappear over the side of the bank, heading down to the river. "We probably woke her from her bed," Joe whispered and clapped twice, to bring the dogs to him so they wouldn't chase the deer. The dogs came immediately, their breath making great clouds of steam in the air around them. "Good job," praised Joe, then freed them with a hand signal.

They walked on, moving away from the river now and back into the thick of the trees. "So what time are you heading back to Seattle tomorrow?" Joe asked.

"About 8 o'clock."

"In the morning?!"

"Of course in the morning. I have a show at 7:30 tomorrow night, remember?"

"Then why so early?"

"Because I have that interview in the morning, for the telemarketing job."

"Oh, that's right," Joe remarked. "I still don't understand why you want to go for that."

"Because!" Lucy exclaimed, having gone over this already with him. "My show closes in a couple of days and I can't just sit on my hands for the next two weeks, waiting for the next one to start. I have to do something."

"You could stay up here."

"Easy for you to say!"

The sharpness of her tone caught Joe off guard and he became instantly defensive. "Fine then! Don't stay."

"I've told you before, it's hard to make it work up here," Lucy explained, stopping and turning towards him on the trail so he could sense her frustration rather than her anger. "And you've got your life and your business and I think that's great, I really do. But I don't want to end up being just an addendum to you. Plus you've got all this history up here and all your friends have been part of that history so I don't know that they're necessarily my friends or even all that interested in who I am really."

"Skye's your friend."

"I know but she met me in New York. She knows my dreams, my goals, the inner Lucy. I think the people up here look at me and think I'm just stepping into something you and Erica created."

"But Erica *didn't* create this with me. Admittedly, she and I found the 5 acres on Sauk and started a life together but she bailed when things got tough. Not that I'm blaming her," he added quickly, "'cause it was bad. Real bad. It was just too much hardship in too short a period of time and I don't think she trusted me to make any dream come true. Except for Maddie." His eyes softened when he said his daughter's name. "She was a dream come true for us." He blinked and stepped a little closer to Lucy. "You came along just when I was beginning to turn my dream into reality. You can even claim credit for helping me put up those log posts on the second floor of the house. Whatever it is I have going here….," he was pointed off the trail, down river, in the direction of his house and the pottery, " …will be *our* creation, if that's what you want. And people will see that. You've just got to give them time."

Lucy turned her face away from him, not wanting to make eye contact while she thought about what he'd said. She looked at the footbridge coming up and the dogs, who were already lapping at the water in the creek underneath it. "Maybe you're right," she said finally. "Maybe I just get frustrated."

"Well if that's all it is," said Joe huskily, 'I think I have the cure."

"No I didn't mean that kind of...." Lucy said as she turned back to face him. But he was gently lifting the hair off her shoulders with his hands and she felt the skin on her neck shiver with pleasure. "Then again....." she amended softly.

He leaned forward and their lips met, warm and desirous against the chill of their faces. They kissed deeply, savoring the sweet taste of love in the quiet of the forest, until Lucy felt Maggie's nose nudge gently into the palm of her left hand. She broke away, chuckling down at the dog, but Joe tipped her face back towards his and held her eyes with his own. "We just have to make the pottery yours as well as mine," he told her. "Find your niche. You've already proven yourself as my number one salesperson."

"And on that subject," Lucy cut in, her spirits renewed from their little conversation. She looped one arm into his and led him across the footbridge. "I've had an idea."

"Uh oh."

"No, no, it's a good idea. At least I think it's a good idea."

They stopped to admire the mammoth cedar tree on the other side of the footbridge. Lucy had snapped many a photograph of guests standing by this tree, trying to hold hands around its girth. Three or four people together could not do it, the tree was that massive. They paid their respects, by silent accord, and walked on.

Lucy went back to her idea. "You said you don't have that much of a Christmas season up here, not once the Pass closes, so I was thinking, you're going to do a firing pretty soon and the guest book in your shop has lots of names and addresses of customers down in Seattle and since I'm down there already, why don't I host a pottery party at Ann's place. If she'll let us."

"A pottery party?"

"Yes. Kind of like a Tupperware party only with pots," Lucy clarified. They turned the corner onto a section of the trail that used to be the old highway. There was gravel and hardpan under the organic material on the surface here and enough room for them to walk comfortably side by side.

"Would I have to come?" Joe queried.

"You'd better!" Lucy retorted and then realized he was teasing her. "You'd be the guest of honor."

"When do you want to do it?"

"I was thinking the weekend after next. You'll have the firing done by then, won't you?"

Joe nodded. He whistled and the dogs came running. "Don't get too far ahead of us," he told them. They panted in agreement and trotted alongside Joe and Lucy for a distance.

"That will give me enough time to make a flyer and send it to your Seattle customers. And I'll make some hors d'oeuvres for people to eat..."

"Hors d'oeuvres," mimicked Joe. "Sounds a bit fancy for me. Can't we just give 'em buck steak and eggs?"

"I don't think you have enough for that."

"You think that many people will come?"

"I don't know," Lucy replied honestly. "But we'll find out."

"And all I have to do is bring the pots down?"

"And talk to people. Be your usual charming self. That's the main reason they'll come - to see you. And maybe to get some pots as Christmas gifts."

They reached the scenic view at the end of the trail and stopped to stare out across the Skagit River at Suiattle Mountain. Unlike her craggier, snow-capped neighbors, Suiattle Mountain was a gentle bell curve of a mountain, with a smaller, flattened protuberance at the top. Some people called her Squaw Tit Mountain and it wasn't hard to see why. She was discreetly covered in inky-green conifers, which made her a fitting backdrop to the shimmering turquoise of the Skagit River. "Look," said Joe, pointing across Lucy's line of sight to a blue heron flapping languidly down the length of the river. They watched without speaking, amazed that such an ungainly, prehistoric looking creature could move through the air so gracefully.

"Well, what do you think?" Lucy asked. They were leaning on a short, split-rail fence that the Park had erected to protect people from falling over the side of the bank. It was a good 100-foot drop down to the river.

"'Bout what?" he replied.

"'Bout the pottery party."

"Oh." Joe turned towards her. "Yeah, I think it's a great idea. If you don't mind doing the work."

Lucy smiled into the warmth of his eyes. "I love you," she said.

"I love you too," he smiled back. "The only thing is," he cautioned slowly. "I just have to say..." He paused as if looking for the right words. Then his face filled with cynicism. "Really, Lucy?! A tele*marketing* job?!!"

And he took off running before she could cuff him.

❀

"What's in there?" a voice whispered eagerly somewhere to the right of Lucy. Lucy swung around to see Katie, a neighbor of Dave and Shana's, peering, bright-eyed, around her arm. Katie was only about five feet tall so seeing over most people's shoulders was not an option.

"Venison," Lucy answered, peeling the towel she'd wrapped around the hot casserole dish back off the lid and then tipping it so they could see inside. Heat poured from out of the casserole, carrying an appetizing aroma of something meaty with it, and Lucy set the lid back down just as Katie's mouth made an "o" of excitement. "What did you make?" Lucy asked.

"Roast goose." Katie pointed proudly at her dish.

Lucy leaned forward and smelled herbs and butter and a little onion, maybe. "We butchered two of our geese," Katie went on, "and since they were old, I decided to cut them up and cook them in sauce, to soften them a little. See," she said, pointing at the dish they were in. "I used my Cascade Mountain Pottery baking dish."

Lucy nodded her approval. Katie was a little older than Lucy and much more wiry in physique but Lucy liked her because of the great enthusiasm she gave everything and the constant gleam in her eye that came with it. "One of my favorite meals when I lived in France," Lucy confided to Katie, "was confit d'oie."

Katie inhaled excitedly. "What's con-fee dwuh?" she asked, exaggerating the pronunciation for the fun of it.

"Goose that they preserve in its own fat. So, really, it's just home-canned goose. But it's delicious. And the people that gave it to me cooked some French fries in the fat after they took the goose out and they were the best French fries I've ever had."

"Mmmm," agreed Katie. "Sounds yummy,"

"Why do you keep geese? For their eggs?" Lucy asked.

"No, although I do eat whatever eggs they lay for me. No, I

keep them mostly because they weed my crops."

"Oh."

"Yup. They don't eat the plants, just the weeds that grow around them, so they're really handy to have around. And they honk when people pull into the driveway, so they're kind of my alarm system too." She looked at the small mounds of meat covered in a brown sauce in her rectangular baking dish and sighed. "But these ones weren't honking or weeding anymore. So...." The gleam came back into her eye. "...time to become Thanksgiving dinner." Then she covered her mouth with her hand and giggled, like she'd been naughty.

Two other people arrived in the kitchen at that moment and Katie spun around to greet them. "What did you bring to eat?" she asked,

Lucy moved slightly so she could see pretty much the entire downstairs of the small home that was filling with people. Like many of the back-to-the-land-ers who moved to the Upper Skagit in the mid-seventies, Dave and Shana had spent the majority of their savings on acreage, for farming, and built a house out of whatever was left over. What they ended up with, essentially, was one room downstairs, one up, none of which was finished and all of which was built around their heat source, a woodstove. Lucy noticed that the overstuffed furniture that usually took up most of the space around the wood stove, along with the dogs, had disappeared somewhere out of sight, so that Dave and Shana could put in three, long, trestle tables, arranged like the letter N, for their Thanksgiving guests. The plywood floor had been swept clean, the mess of boots and shoes usually by the front door were in a tidy row and the tables, covered in white paper, held a variety of hollowed out gourds with candles in them. It was primitive and very rustic but it was also very welcoming.

Lucy watched the people arriving, carefully carrying their dinner contributions over to the tiny kitchen. Most of them were a little older than her, 30 to 35, and they had all made a decided choice to stay away from the rat race of the city and live a life of voluntary simplicity in the country. Many of them worked seasonally for the National Park Service, so they got the winters off to work on their places and spent summers in the woods. The rest were either organic farmers or carpenters. Lucy noticed that most of them were wearing their best jeans and smart or attractive tops that suggested they'd made an effort to "dress" for dinner. She also noticed how comfortable they were with each other.

This was where Lucy fell down in the up-valley potluck situations; she had trouble feeling comfortable. Which surprised her because she had always been an outgoing type of person and didn't have difficulty making conversation. Maybe it was just common ground that eluded her up here. She didn't know enough about farming or conservation and they didn't know enough about theatre. Not that they didn't try; these were educated, kind people who wanted to accept Joe's girlfriend into their group. But Lucy tended to find that after a few faltering questions and answers, the conversation inevitably petered out and she was back to looking at the room. Undoubtedly it was her fault. She just didn't fit in this particular socio-economic slice of life. Which didn't bother her - Lucy was content enough inside her own head not to worry about fitting in - but she did hate standing around, being bored. There were way too many things to accomplish in a day for that.

"Can I ask you something?"

Dave was suddenly in front of her, a red-headed, red-bearded gentle gnome of a fellow, who'd found his life partner in New Jersey and together they'd searched for a place to grow things that wasn't the Garden State. Dave knew pretty much everything there was to know about the indigenous plants of the Pacific Northwest, could discourse for long periods about bamboo and enjoyed the occasional dive into the world of psychology. Lucy tried pulling what little she knew of those three subjects to the forefront of her brain. "Of course," she replied.

"When did Joe start making tree mugs?"

Lucy smiled to herself. Ah, the pottery. The one subject everyone could relate to in this crowd. She looked at the mug that Dave was showing her; it was definitely one of Joe's but instead of his usual mountains, it had trees drawn on the outside. "I don't know," she replied. "I just remember there were a couple in the last firing."

"Well Shana brought this one home...."

"Yeah and I brought it home for me but every time I go to use it, Dave's using it." Shana was now standing next to them and joined in the conversation as if she'd be part of it from the start. She gave Dave a disapproving look to back up the tone she'd used about his constant filching of her mug.

"I didn't know we had his and her pottery now," he remarked affably.

"We don't," Shana shot back. "We have her and her pottery. So don't keep using my tree mug." And she laughed. Shana was petite and muscled, with angular features, smooth brown eyes and definite farm worker hands. She used those now to pull her long dark hair off her shoulders and snap it back into a ponytail.

"But they're trees, Shana," explained Dave and took a defiant sip out of the mug while she was watching him.

"I know. So buy your own." And she took the mug, drank a little of whatever he was drinking and then handed it back to him.

"Can Joe make me one like this?" Dave asked Lucy, holding the mug up for her to see.

"He could come close," she offered hopefully.

"With this red on it?" Dave was pointing at a sunrise of red, just over the trees, up by the lip of the mug.

"Hmm. I don't know." At that moment Lucy felt Joe's arms slide around her waist and his chin nestle down over her shoulder. "Can you make this red again?"

"Maybe. Give it here." Joe let go of Lucy and grasped the mug in both hands.

"I'm going to start glazing tomorrow and I have some tree mugs made for this next firing so I could try to do this again." He paused, examining the mug carefully. "See what I do," he explained to Dave and Shana while Lucy listened in, " is I like to use an accent glaze at the top of my pots. So for this mug, I swirled a matte white liner glaze on the inside first, then I dipped the lip and the top of the handle in my copper green."

"Green?! But it's turquoise," pointed out Shana.

"Yes, because the copper green goes turquoise in my wood kiln."

"Which one's the copper green?" interjected Lucy, picturing the buckets on Joe's glazing table.

"The CuCo3 matte," Joe answered quickly. Lucy placed it in her mind while Joe went on with his explanation to Dave and Shana. "So then I dipped the bottom two thirds of the mug in my clear glaze and where the copper green and the clear met, it turned red." He held the mug up at eye level one more time. "Yeah, I think I can do that again. But these other bits of red," he said, pointing to accents in the body of the trees, "those were just 'the kiln giveth' type of effects. Those I can't guarantee." He returned the mug to Dave.

"Well if 'the kiln giveth' any more like this, let Dave know. And make sure he giveth you the money out of his pocket in exchange," Shana joked dryly. "Hey, talking of pockets," she said suddenly and dug down in the front pocket of her jeans. "Skye dropped off a pie for us on her way to her dad's this morning and left this for you." She pulled out a dog-eared business card and handed it to Joe. "One of the potato harvesters took his wife to an Arts and Crafts Fair in Bellevue and ran into your ex. I guess she's making jewelry now and had a booth there. He got that thinking of you." Joe looked at the card. There was an address on it. "Happy Thanksgiving," Shana said softly.

Joe's heart skipped a beat as he looked at the crumpled business card. Maddie. This might be the first step in getting her back into his life. He felt Lucy lean into his upper arm, sliding one hand around him to rest on his hip; the rest of the room fell away as the two of them, along with Dave and Shana, quietly absorbed the significance of this little piece of paper. "Thanks," he managed finally.

"You're welcome," said Shana simply. Then she turned to Lucy. "Can you help me with something."

"Of course."

"See that bag on the floor over there?" She was pointing at a brown paper grocery bag tucked in the kitchen behind everyone's legs. "That's full of paper plates, plastic forks and cups and I want to put them out someplace that suggests the beginning of the food line only I don't know that there's any space left in the kitchen...." She looked overawed by all the food on the counter.

"I can take care of it," Lucy reassured her. "Would you mind if I put some of the desserts on the tables?"

Shana looked from the counter in the kitchen to the tables then to Lucy. "No, I think that's a great idea," she stated, obviously surprised she hadn't thought of this herself. "Whatever you need to do so we can all put some food on our plates. And you," she said, turning to Dave. "I need you to get the ice that I put in the freezer in the barn and put it in the coolers on the porch with the beer and sodas in them."

"Got it," said Dave.

"I'll help," added Joe, following Dave to the front door.

Lucy moved the berry cobblers, apple crisps and pumpkin pies to center spots on the trestle tables and then emptied the grocery bag of the plates, cups, napkins and forks. She'd seen a large, hand-made basket full of hats over by the front door. She edged through all the people in the room, emptied the hats into the grocery bag, then crossed back to the kitchen and lined the basket with a clean dishtowel from one of the cabinet drawers. She refilled it with the dinnerware and placed it at the end of the counter, on a bar stool she'd moved from under the phone hanging on one of the kitchen walls. Satisfied, she turned her attention to the buffet.

Along with the venison and roast goose, there was a meat dish made from someone's grass fed cow and platters of grilled salmon, caught in the Skagit. Lucy interspersed these with whole grain and tofu entrees that weren't her taste but knew the vegetarians among them would like them, then moved on to the many potato, squash, green bean and kale side dishes. Finally she made a grouping of the beet, carrot and green salads in front of some jars of nectarine chutney and green tomato salsa that someone had brought. She stood back and assessed her handiwork. It looked pleasing and appetizing; a veritable array of people's pride in the bounty of their gardens. A veritable sharing of their wealth. Like Thanksgiving and Harvest Festival all in the same room. Lucy was pleased. She glanced up to see Joe coming through the front door, carrying a stack of lawn chairs for people to sit on. She caught his eye and he smiled across the room at her. Now she felt comfortable. Very comfortable, in fact.

And for some reason, it scared her.

Lesson 10

Share Your Gift

The season of giving is a good time for you to reflect on what it means to have a gift for creativity; because a gift is only a gift if you share it with others.

Lucy woke up in a cold sweat and tried to bring the room into focus. Where was she? The shadows didn't look right for her bedroom in England, yet she was sure she was there. She struggled towards full consciousness but it was painful, as if her body didn't want to be where her mind was pulling it. She looked again. That couldn't be the window and if it wasn't the wardrobe then where was she? She listened to the sounds on the street behind her but even those she couldn't make fit with the sounds of her childhood. Her heartbeat slowed, distancing her from the nightmare she'd just exited, and she realized that she was in Seattle now, in the spare bedroom at Ann's place.

She rolled over and pulled the blankets up over her head, hoping to close out the scene that had just screamed through her mind. But the blankets were no help. Not now, as an adult, any more than they were when she was a little girl of 7 and she had run from the horror, seeking solace under the covers on her bed. She remembered lying in a tense knot, waiting for the darkness to close out the terrible thing she'd just witnessed. But it kept on playing in front of her staring eyes, like a film on a continuous loop, until it was seared onto her psyche, branding her forever - Child of a Man Whose Anger Knows No Bounds.

Lucy slid out from under the covers and sat up, folding her legs over the edge of the bed. She wished Joe were here. Without him she felt like an unloved sweater; musty and mothballed. She stood up, slipped into her thin, cotton nightgown and tied it around the waist as she padded across the room to the door. Quietly, so as not to wake Ann, she opened her bedroom door and followed the glow from the remaining embers towards the warmth of the woodstove in the living room.

She sat cross-legged on the floor, as close to the cast iron box as she could get and peered in the arched, glass window on the front at what was left of the fire she and Ann had built. It was one of those wet, dreary, cold December evenings in Seattle and Lucy had got back to Ballard after working at the telemarketing company wanting something that would take the dull out of her spirit. Ann agreed and they'd each brought in an armload of Doug fir firewood from the stack Joe had given them and watched as it snapped, crackled, curled and flamed in the stove. There wasn't much left of their fire now; just some dusky coals and a little residual heat in the room. If Lucy wanted more out of it, she'd have to go outside and get wood again but the sound of the rain hammering against the roof of the bungalow dissuaded her from that idea. Plus it was after midnight and she had to get up early in the morning for the pottery party so she couldn't afford to sit too long being hypnotized by a fire. She pulled a green throw blanket off the armchair next to her and covered her legs with it. Ann's cat, a sprightly tabby named Scrabble, jumped down off the couch and trotted across the room to climb into the hammock of warmth made by the blanket between Lucy's feet and her torso. She let him settle then ran her hand around the curve of his spine as he purred appreciatively.

What haunted her most about that terrifying incident between her parents was why. *Why* did her father do such a thing? As a teen,

Lucy had found herself wishing her father were a drunk, to give a reason for him being the way he was. But then she was embarrassed for that thought, listening to the tales of people like Joe and Skye who'd grown up with alcoholics. Lucy knew her father had a short fuse from all the times he'd hit her; but the way he'd treated her mother sat like bile at the back of her throat.

"You weren't there," her older sister, Jackie, had accused on the phone this morning, when the conversation had suddenly swerved towards the worst thing they'd ever seen. They had *never* spoken of that moment before. Never.

"Yes, I was," Lucy retorted.

"No, you weren't," Jackie threw back. "I was alone at the top of the stairs when he did what he did."

"No, Jackie. Meg and I were there too. All three of us saw it."

"Saw what?" Jackie questioned, her tone provocative, like she still didn't believe Lucy.

Lucy swallowed before answering. This was hard. "He had mum face down on the floor, across the mat inside the front door, and she was sobbing and pleading, "Stop it, Reggie, stop it," because he was......he was....... *stamping* on her." Lucy paused, waiting for her sister to say something but the line was silent. "And I remember the three of us standing there, our little bodies rigid with fear, screaming, "Stop it, daddy. Stop it!" But he didn't hear us. He was just so...*frenzied* with anger."

There was a long pause before Jackie stated, "He could have killed her, you know."

As if Lucy hadn't thought of that. "Why would he *do* such a thing?" she cried.

Jackie sighed. "People get hurt, Lucy, and they hurt back. As if that might move the pain out of their hearts. You know how tough dad's childhood was. And then his time in the army, when he was forced to learn about terrible acts of torture."

Lucy bristled. "That's no excuse."

"I know," agreed Jackie. She paused again, as if thinking about something, then added, "But maybe one day it'll be an explanation."

Something popped inside the stove and Lucy looked up from her thoughts to see a tiny flame burst into life. She watched it flickering blue and orange until it burned the gasses that were feeding it. Then it died.

She couldn't believe that her sister had cut her out of that memory and she'd said as much to Joe when she called him after the conversation with Jackie.

"She's the oldest," Joe explained. "It's her job to protect you and Meg. So she reworked that memory in her mind until she did her job."

That made sense. The cat flipped onto his back and a bead of light that was sneaking through a gap in the curtains to the left of them hit him perfectly on the belly. Lucy turned towards the light, hoping to see the moon coming around the shoulder of Sauk as she often did at Joe's house, but it was just the light from a street lamp. She ran her fingers down the length of the extra soft fur on the cat's belly and he stretched pleasurably.

She was glad she had Joe to explain that stuff to her because all she'd ever managed to do was run from it. She'd run and she'd run, thinking she was leaving it all behind her only to turn every now and then and find it loping along beside her. How far was she going to have to run, Lucy wondered, to get past it altogether? Or had the time come, maybe, for her to stop running and face it?

Joe blew in from outside with his signature smile and mountain man garb. Lucy marveled that she'd fallen for a guy who wore red and black wool shirts and suspenders to hold up his jeans but then he pulled her to him and the thrill of his skin against hers and the faint scent of wood smoke in his hair made her not care how he was dressed. They kissed and he ran his hands appreciatively over the soft wool of her sweater. "This is nice," he remarked.

Lucy looked down at the loose knit, ivory top she had put on to dress up her jeans but not make her look to formal for the party. "My sister knitted it for me."

"Feels good." Joe stepped back and touched one of the long, slender pieces of ivory she had hanging from her ears. "Are these the ones I got you at the Barter Faire?"

"Uh huh."

"They look good too." He ran his fingers along the edge of her chin and kissed her lightly on the lips once more. Then she looked past him, out towards the street in front of the house.

"Where's Skye's truck?" she asked. Skye had gone back to New York for a month, to visit her mother, and had loaned her truck to Joe while he looked for another one to buy.

"Pete brought me," Joe explained. "He wants to do some

Christmas shopping in town so he offered to bring me and the pots down, leave us here while he went shopping, then he's going to swing by after the party and pack up what's left and I can ride back up to the Skagit with you in the Pinto. After we meet up with Maddie." Joe had gone ahead with his plan to send a candle lantern for Christmas to his daughter and was rewarded with a letter from her mother saying she was ready for them to visit and when she'd found out that Joe was coming down to Seattle today, she'd decided dinner in a restaurant would be the easiest. "We have to help him unload the pots first though, and it would be nice if we could give him a cup of coffee to go. You think I can start a pot of coffee?" Joe asked, looking towards the kitchen.

"I've already got one going," Ann called out as she emerged from the narrow bathroom behind the kitchen, wrapped in a towel, her hair wet from the shower.

"How's by you?" Joe called out.

"Pretty good," she grinned back. "I have a new boyfriend."

"Is that right? This one's got his own vehicle, I trust."

Ann chortled as she disappeared into her bedroom, opposite the bathroom. "A beemer," she announced, popping her head back out the door.

"Allriiiiiiiiight!" teased Joe. "I hope you invited him to the party."

Lucy heard Ann's bedroom door close from the tiny front porch where she was standing, looking up and down the street for Pete's VW bus. "Where did he park?" she called back in to Joe.

"He went around back. Doesn't Ann have parking there at the end of the yard behind the house?"

Lucy came in and closed the front door quickly against the cold. It wasn't raining this morning but it was frosty, as if winter were really setting in. "Yes, but there's only room for one car and I've got the Pinto parked there because somebody called the police when they saw it sitting for more than a couple of days on the street and they came and left me a warning note to move it."

"Yeah, people in the city will do that." There was a knock on the back door. "That's probably Pete," chuckled Joe, "wanting you to move your car again."

Lucy opened the back door to find Pete standing there, holding a box of pots. He was wearing jeans with turn-ups, his Birkenstock loafers and a white turtleneck that offset the blue of his eyes perfectly. "Where d'you want these?" he asked as he continued on into the house.

"Just put them on the floor in the living room somewhere," Lucy replied. She walked across the back lawn, following Joe, and pulled another box of pots out of Pete's VW, which he'd left idling in the alley behind Lucy's Pinto. Presumably he didn't think he'd be there long enough to warrant parking it.

And he wasn't wrong. It didn't take the three of them more than a few minutes of back and forth to get all the pottery out of the VW and then Pete was on his way and Joe and Lucy were in the living room, wondering how to organize the space for the party. Ann came in to join them once she'd pulled on some jeans and a sweatshirt and she stood, brushing out her wet hair, while they discussed ways to maximize the space. Joe lobbied to move all the furniture except the table into Lucy's bedroom so they'd have a place to display the pottery and room for people to move around it but Lucy thought they needed somewhere for people to sit. In the end it was Ann who had the best idea; she suggested turning the couch 90 degrees, so it was against the outside wall, and moving the table closer to the center of the room so they could put the pottery on the table as well as on the counter top divider between the kitchen and the living room.

"Where will we put the food?" Lucy asked.

"Over next to the refrigerator," Ann replied. "People won't mind going into the kitchen for their cheese and crackers."

"And I brought some apple cider," Joe added, "which I can warm on the stove in there for people. Unless you want me to light a fire in the woodstove and leave the cider on top of it."

"I think it'll get too warm in here if we have a fire," Ann countered.

"And I want to put some of the bigger pots on the hearth with maybe a couple of pieces on top of the wood stove," Lucy put in.

"Okay, whatever," agreed Joe.

"Is that what's in the big saucepan?" asked Lucy. "Apple cider?"

"Uh huh. Be nice if we had a cinnamon stick to put in it."

"What's a cinnamon stick?" asked Lucy.

Joe and Ann just looked at her. Ann laughed. "I'll find us one," she told Joe.

❀

An hour ahead of schedule the place was ready. There were pots on all the available surfaces, silver fir boughs that Joe had brought down from the mountains hanging here and there around the room, a menorah sitting in the window and a single strand of colored lights over the counter top divider. The little bungalow had the aroma of fresh, mountain fir and warm apples. Lucy and Joe felt like they'd done their part; now all they had to do was wait and hope that people would show up.

They didn't have to wait long. The party was supposed to start at noon but they heard voices coming up the front path at 11:30. The doorbell rang and Joe jumped up from the couch and opened the door to a woman with dark frizzy hair and dimples.

"Connie!" he yelled and wrapped her in one of his big hugs.

"We thought we'd come and see what our favorite potter looked like outside of his habitat!" the woman joked as she stepped over the threshold. She ran him up and down once with her eyes, then beamed. "You look the same," she teased. Three other people wandered in behind her; she introduced them to Joe as her boyfriend, her sister and her sister's boyfriend.

"And this," Joe said to Lucy, "is Connie, who used to live upriver and was one of my first customers in the Skagit..."

"I bought a coffee pot the first time I stopped."

"Well I don't remember that much," Joe admitted. "Ten years is a lot for my feeble brain."

"Yes, but I use it every day. My coffee pot," Connie laughed, "not your feeble brain."

"Durable, huh? I can tell I'm not going to get rich off you if you keep my pots that long," joked Joe.

"You might, if you keep doing events like this. I just brought my sister today but if you do this again I might bring my whole family."

"And Connie's from a good Irish family, like me," Joe explained to Lucy. "Lots of siblings."

The banter was underway and before they knew it, others were coming up the path to join the party. It was Sol, with his son, Pedro, from Gig Harbor. Pedro was a solidly built Venezuelan who was friendly enough to Joe and Lucy but he looked uncomfortable and excused himself shortly after he got there, telling Sol he'd be back in a couple of hours to fetch him. Sol walked him out.

A few minutes later, he was back at Joe's elbow. "I had a jar already picked out," the older man said, jabbing the air with his finger. "But when I went to say goodbye to Pedro, that fellow over there…" - he nodded towards Connie's sister's boyfriend - "took the jar out of a pile I'd started, and he doesn't seem to want to let go of it!"

Joe glanced over at the boyfriend; he was way taller than anyone else in the room and had a pretty firm grasp on the pot. "I don't know what to tell you," he whispered to Sol. "Except you're going to have to find a better place for your stash, I guess."

Sol pushed his lips up towards his nose, like a baby rejecting food, then popped his false teeth out of his mouth. He marched to the corner of the room and picked up some mugs that Joe assumed were part of his "pile," went to the front door and exited the house. Joe felt his anxiety level go up a notch at the idea that he might have to chase after his friend but as Sol stepped outside, Stan and Bobby Jo stepped in. Joe moved forward to greet them and could see Sol arranging the mugs in the middle of the lawn. "Hey, I made your cookie jar," Joe announced to Bobby Jo. "Actually I made three, so you'd have a choice."

"Yes, and I heard you're going to take my husband fishing in your truck so that his won't have to get scratched up," Bobby Jo replied.

"Well not that truck 'cause I don't have it anymore."

Stan winced. "What happened?"

"I burned up the rear end when I drove it down to Seattle that time and she died the next day on my way home."

"With the new tire on her?" Stan looked crestfallen.

"Yeah, but that was the first thing I took off when my mechanic told me I couldn't drive her home." Sol slipped back into the room and Joe watched him whisper something to Lucy. "Now all I need is another truck that will fit that tire."

"What are you looking for?"

"A three-quarter ton Chevy." Lucy glanced out the front window then nodded at Sol, who left her after that for a box of cereal bowls on the floor at the end of the couch. "And I'm thinking I want a four-wheel drive. Except, of course, they're all way more than I was hoping to pay. Plus I need one of the elements replaced in my electric kiln….."

"I've been meaning to ask you about that kiln," Ann interrupted as she came over to join them. She'd been talking to Connie but now Connie had to help her sister choose a lovelight.

Joe shifted around to include her in the conversation. "Turns out it was fine that day I came down with the wood but it became less and less predictable about switching itself off so I finally got someone in to look at it. The guy's an electrician who rebuilds kilns for his local school district - and his wife likes my pottery." Joe winked at the others. "I'm hoping we can make a deal. Talking of which," he went on to Stan and Bobby Jo. "That tire cost way more than one of my cookie jars so I'll give you whatever I owe you on top of the pot."

"I think my wife was hoping for some cereal bowls," Stan said, looking down at Bobby Jo. She fluttered her eyelashes at Joe.

"Whatever you want," he told her. The doorbell rang again and Joe looked at Lucy across the room, "Where are those cookie jars I made for Bobby Jo?"

"In the boxes of pots that we left in my bedroom."

Sol's head perked up at the mention of pots he hadn't seen. "I'll help," he offered and trotted after Joe who was already disappearing through a door off the living room.

"We have cider in the kitchen if you want," Ann pointed out to Stan and Bobby Jo.

Lucy let in four more people, none of whom she recognized. The tips of their noses were red, from the bite in the air outside, and Lucy could tell they were grateful to come into the warm. They smiled expectantly as they looked around, probably hoping to see Joe, but when they didn't, they allowed themselves to get drawn into the flow of the room, drifting around the table from the front door to the woodstove, browsing the pottery. Then Joe appeared from the other room and the greetings rang out. He left Bobby Jo and Stan with Sol hovering behind them while he went to chat with the newcomers and Ann took over opening the door while Lucy dealt with the first sales.

This was turning out better than she'd hoped with new people arriving at increasing intervals now that they were well past the noon start time. Lucy glanced at her watch; actually it was only 12:30. Maybe people were arriving faster than she realized. She overheard a woman reintroducing herself to Joe. "I don't know if you remember me," the woman started. "But I'm Marianne Dunning...."

"The building inspector's wife!" Joe interrupted.

"Well not anymore," she corrected.

Joe's face fell. "Oh, you guys didn't work it out, huh?"

Marianne laughed, and her gold-tinted curls bobbed as she

shook her head from side-to-side, realizing his mistake. "No, no, we're still married." She leaned closer to Joe and whispered out of the side of her mouth, "The lovelight was a big hit."

"Ah, what'd'I tell you!"

"In fact, I was hoping you had some of those here today because I want to get a couple for gifts." Joe turned immediately, to go and find the box of lovelights, but Marianne stayed him with a hand on his forearm. "But my husband's not a building inspector anymore, remember?"

"Oh sorry, you're right. The *software* designer's wife."

"Software *architect*." She gave him a small smile. "Technically."

Sol disappeared out the front door again, this time with one of the jars that Bobby Jo had rejected.

"Well what do I know," Joe rebuffed. "I'm certainly not the person to talk to about computers."

"That's a lady from my church," Bobby Jo whispered to Lucy, who had come over to see what she thought about the cookie jars. Lucy looked back at the elegant lady who was now telling Joe about moving to Seattle because her husband worked for Microsoft. "I put the invitation flyer you sent us on the bulletin board downstairs and I guess she saw it." Lucy gave Bobby Jo an admiring nod and the older woman giggled. "Maybe now we'll become friends."

"You should go over and introduce yourself," Lucy encouraged.

"After I choose a cookie jar," pronounced the World War II vet's diminutive wife.

But she probably wouldn't, Lucy thought to herself. She'd noticed that was the one thing that wasn't working so far at the party; the mingling. People obviously appreciated the pottery and having it come to them for once instead of the other way around but they seemed shy of each other and shy to help themselves to the food.

And then, as if on cue, the actors showed up. They couldn't afford the pottery but they came for the party, for the free food and for the chance to make new friends and they weren't shy in the least to admit it. There were 3 guys who had understudied with Lucy in her first show at the Rep. and then Missy, with the orange hair, who'd done *Red Square* with her. Missy had brought her mother along and as she introduced her around, sounds of her deep, mellifluous voice and smoky laugh filled the walls of the little house, making everybody feel more comfortable. Curiosity drew the pottery customers towards the actors and the room began to hum with stories of shows seen and shows performed. The actors made themselves at home with plates of snacks from the kitchen and when they sensed a general inhibition on the part of others to delve into the food, they showed their plates to people they'd just met, saying, "You should try this smoked salmon. It's good."

"Is that salmon from the Skagit River?" Connie asked as she tripped happily across the room to get some.

"Yes, ma'am," Joe replied.

"Maybe next time we'll do this at my house," Connie laughed. "Especially if you promise to bring salmon."

Joe grinned. Any excuse to go fishing. Before his mind could wander to the banks of the Skagit River he turned his attention back to Marianne. She'd filled him in on how much she was enjoying living in the city because it put her close to her grandchildren and now she wanted to hear how things were going between Joe and his English actress.

"Lucy?" asked Joe, surprised. "That's her over there." Lucy turned when she heard her name and saw Joe pointing at her. She smiled at the woman who was talking to Joe and Marianne smiled back. "Well it's still going," he said. Then he leaned in and whispered to Marianne, "Otherwise you wouldn't be seeing me here, that's for sure."

Marianne laughed. "I wondered," she said.

Lucy had gone back to wrapping a pot for Connie's sister. Joe looked at her as he spoke to Marianne. "No it's going great, to be honest. She's making it work for herself down here in the city, with her acting. Hey," he said, his mind zinging to an associated thought. "You should take your grandkids to see her in *The Secret Garden* at the Children's Theatre."

"Oh I read about that." Marianne rubbed her forefinger and thumb on her chin, thinking. "Somewhere. I don't remember where. That opens in the New Year, doesn't it?"

Joe nodded. "January something. Oh, here's Beth," he added, looking at the dark-haired, dark-eyed, rosy cheeked actress who'd just walked through the front door. "Hey, Beth."

"Hey, Joe."

"She's going to be in *The Secret Garden* with Lucy," he explained to Marianne. Then he beckoned Beth over with a nudge of his head as she acknowledged her presence to Lucy with a small wave.

"Smells good in here," Beth said as she walked towards Joe and Marianne.

"Apple cider," Joe boasted.

"From the apples on your tree?"

"Yep. Beth's a master gardener as well as an actress," Joe told Marianne.

"When's *The Secret Garden* open?" he asked Beth.

Lucy heard him billing her new show as she was putting pots into a bag for Connie's sister. It sent a vein of warmth through her, like drinking sweet liqueur, and she realized this was the first time she'd heard someone she loved brag about her acting. What made it even more poignant was the fact that it was a man who lived way out in the woods supporting her, a man who knew very little about theatre when he met her. But then Lucy didn't know anything about pottery when she met Joe.

She handed the bag of wrapped pots to Connie's sister and let her eyes roam the room for a moment. This was their two worlds coming together – her theatre and Joe's pottery – and it was working pretty well now that the initial resistance was over. But then sometimes two opposites could come together to form a cohesive unit given the right encouragement. Like Joe's pottery; what was that but earth and water, molded together to make a vessel. And a vessel that could stand the test of time if it was heated by fire. What had Joe said? Durable.

She took a baking dish and two goblets out of the hands of the next customer and turned to wrap them just as Ann approached her with a plate of food and some cider. "Joe wanted you to get some of this before it all went," said her roommate.

"Oh thank you!" said Lucy, "I'm actually famished so your timing's perfect." She looked behind her. "Could you put it on the woodstove so I can finish helping these customers first?" Lucy took the price stickers off the pots and gave the couple their total so they could write out a check. Then she looked over at Joe hoping to acknowledge his gift of food from a distance.

Sensing her eyes on him, Joe looked across at Lucy. She mouthed 'thank you' to him, pointing to the food behind her, and he nodded. He watched her, talking animatedly to some people as she wrapped their pots in newspaper. She was definitely more comfortable in this setting than he was. He got nervous around so many people, and embarrassed when they complimented his work.

He watched the couple she was talking to laughing with her; Lucy was definitely the outward to his awkward. The yin to his yang.

Lucy finished her sale with the couple and immediately picked up the apple cider Ann had poured for her. She sipped it repeatedly, enjoying the feel of the sweet warmth on her parched throat. She took in the room once more, letting her eyes settle on Joe, who was deep in conversation with the people around him. They were talking about talent and Joe was saying that if the Creator of the Universe had given you a gift, you should use it; because a gift was only a gift if you shared it with others. He looked like he was having a good time and to a certain degree he was, but Lucy knew that inside of himself he was uncomfortable. They were so different, she and Joe, in so many ways, and yet they both wanted the same thing; to be good at what they did. She remembered whispered, excited conversations that first summer they were together; dreams of his pottery featured in ceramics magazines, dreams of people seeing her work on stage and screen. Dreams that they'd never voiced out loud before. The trouble was, Joe didn't want to go places where people could see his work and Lucy didn't want to hide anymore. And yet, she thought to herself, here he was. And suddenly she saw the harmony in their togetherness, like waves on a sandy shore. Like earth and water.

As soon as she could see it she felt herself pulling back and she gritted her teeth in irritation. What was it with her and this knee-jerk aversion to marriage and commitment! Wasn't Joe a good man? A solid, dependable guy who might stop her from being so flighty, center her even, if she gave him half a chance? So why did she have to be this way? She broke off some of the salmon with a plastic fork and put it in her mouth. It flaked onto her tongue and she tasted cracked pepper and smoky brine around the flavor of the fish as she contemplated the answer to her question. She was scared to be talked out of her dreams, she supposed. Scared she'd have to kowtow to some man for the rest of her life. Her eyes dropped to put some brie on one of the crackers and she saw her problem as clearly as if it were written on the plate. She was scared. Lucy bit into the cracker and watched Bobby Jo introducing herself to Marianne. Everyone was scared, she thought to herself. And it was no excuse.

"Lucy, I want to introduce you to mama," a voice she recognized said to her left.

Lucy slipped the plate of food back onto the woodstove, wiped her fingers on a napkin and extended her right hand eagerly towards

Missy's mother. "Thank you for coming," she said.

"So how'd we do?" Joe asked, seeing Lucy adding up the sales as he came back in from loading up Pete's VW. She and Ann had moved most of the furniture back into place in the living room and were just waiting on Joe to help them with the couch. Except right now, Ann was sitting, zoned out, on the couch, petting the cat idly with her right hand, while Lucy did the math.

Lucy put a finger up in the air, for Joe to wait just a moment, then she looked up. "Really well. We made over $500."

"You're kidding?! That's more than I made in the shop the entire month of November."

"Maybe now you'll be able to buy another used truck," Ann said, her eyes still glazed over. Then she blinked and tipped her head to one side, looking at Joe.

"I don't know about that," he responded. "I probably have to pay bills with this."

"Why?" queried Lucy. "This money's like a gift you weren't expecting. You should put it towards another truck and use your regular income to pay the bills."

"I don't have a regular income."

Lucy stood up from the table where she'd been doing the computations and slipped her arms around Joe. "You know what I mean." They gave each other a hug, glad that the party had been such a success, then Lucy caught sight of the time on Ann's microwave. It was almost 6:30. "We should get going," she told Joe.

They turned the couch back around to its position in front of the counter top divider, teasing Ann the whole time about the fact that her new boyfriend had not shown up. "I don't think he's much of a pottery guy," Ann told them. "He is taking me to the theatre tonight though."

"Oh?" Lucy commented. "What are you going to see?"

Ann chuckled. "I don't remember. He's taking me to some off-the-wall place up on Capital Hill." She shrugged. "I guess I'll tell you tomorrow. Are you coming back tomorrow?"

"No. Monday morning," said Lucy as she headed into her bedroom to fetch her stuff. "I'm going straight to rehearsal at the Children's Theatre so I'll see you Monday night."

"I really do appreciate what you did for us today," Joe told

Ann as he slipped on his wool jacket and hat. It was dark already outside and cold; cold like the moisture in the air had started to freeze. "You got your share of what we made, I hope?"

Ann looked at a small grouping of cereal bowls and mugs on the counter behind her and nodded. "I did," she said. She yawned. "Good luck tonight." He looked at her as if he didn't get what she meant. "Seeing Maddie," she qualified.

"Oh yeah," he replied. He glanced at Lucy as she came back into the living room. She'd slipped into her raincoat and had her backpack slung over her shoulder, ready to leave. "I'm trying not to think about it, I guess. Not until I get there."

"Are you nervous?" Lucy asked, as they walked across the back lawn, hand in hand, towards the car.

"Little bit," Joe replied. He ran his thumb over the top of her fingers, enjoying how soft her hand felt against his. "But I'll get over it."

❦

The reason they'd chosen a restaurant in Seattle for the meeting with Maddie was because she and Erica lived in Issaquah now, on the east side of Lake Washington. Erica had wanted Joe and Lucy to drive out to her house after the pottery party but driving was one of Joe's least favorite things to do, especially in the city. "I can't promise I'll be in a good mood if I have to drive all the way out to Issaquah," he told Erica, "and I don't want to do that to Maddie." Erica had pushed but when Joe countered with the suggestion they make the meeting some other time, she capitulated. Maddie was eager to see her daddy.

Pete had recommended a pizza place overlooking Greenlake; it wasn't very expensive, the atmosphere was cheery and they could probably find something on the menu that would suit a 5-year old, he said. Joe and Lucy slowed to a crawl in front of the brightly lit restaurant and peered at the name over the door. They couldn't stop because there were too many cars behind them and there was nowhere to park but this was definitely the place. Lucy edged the Pinto around the corner and drove three blocks up one of Seattle's hilly streets looking for a place to park. They found one right underneath a street lamp in a block of well cared for houses that boasted brick arches over the windows and doors and lots of pointy rooflines. Joe stood with his feet apart and hands in his pockets, looking up at the detail work as Lucy locked the Pinto. She came around the car, slipped her arm through one of his and hustled him down the street, not because they were late but because it was too cold to amble.

"I'm hungry," said Lucy as they pushed the door to the restaurant open and the smells of cooked dough and sauces, garlic and onions hit the back of her throat.

"Me too," Joe agreed. "I only hope my stomach will settle down enough to let me eat." He'd already seen Erica, sitting in a booth over by one of the front windows and he imagined that the person she was smiling at, the person he couldn't see because the vinyl backed bench seat was too tall, was his daughter, Madeline. Last time he'd seen Maddie she was a chubby, brown-eyed baby with smooth, sweet-smelling skin and almost no hair on her head. Undoubtedly she wouldn't look like that anymore.

Lucy started to walk towards the counter diagonally opposite the front door, where a waitress was leaning forward, jotting down a phone order, but Joe caught her by the elbow and gently tugged her back towards him. "They're over here," he told her quietly. Lucy turned to see a woman with shoulder-length, reddish-brown hair looking their way. She had an elfin face with caramel brown eyes and when she stood up to greet them, Lucy was struck by her graceful, slender form. She reminded Lucy of some of the hippies she'd seen at the Barter Faire and she instantly felt intimidated. But as she shook Erica's hand she remembered what Joe had told her many times; that Erica's wackiness definitely overshadowed her good looks.

The greetings between the adults were clipped, terse even on Joe's part, but the atmosphere began to soften when he slid into the booth next to his daughter. "Whatcha drawing?" he asked, looking at the marks Maddie was making with colored crayons on the paper place mat in front of her. The little girl began pointing at the different loops and lines on the paper as she launched into a clear explanation of the story she was telling with her picture. "I wanted to put a horse in," she finished, "but I don't know how to draw a horse." And then, for the first time, Maddie turned her big brown eyes on the man sitting beside her. "Do you know how to draw a horse, daddy?"

Daddy. It was the word Joe had been wanting to hear for so long and yet it sounded strange coming from the lips of this little person beside him. This little person who now had a full head of thick, reddish-brown hair and a face shaped like his. How much he had missed in the last four years. He bit down on the anger that threatened to heave out of him and ruin their time together and reached for the crayons. "What color do you want the horse to be?"

❧

The dinner didn't last much more than an hour. Not only were Joe and Lucy tired from a day filled with people and all sorts of internal anxieties, but Maddie showed signs that this was past her bedtime when she slid out of the booth and began skipping her way between the other tables at the restaurant. "This probably wasn't the best time," Erica conceded, looking across at Joe who was watching his daughter spin in circles to make her dress balloon out at the bottom. "Maybe we could come up to your house next time," she offered. "Maddie has memories of being in the studio with you."

"Me too," Joe shot back, though he doubted Maddie could really remember something from so young in her life.

The thing that Lucy noticed most about Erica was how spacey she seemed. She'd be talking about one thing then her mind would wander away to something else, some remembrance of time spent with Joe in the past; a remembrance that he apparently didn't share in that way at all. He kept his eyes on Maddie, dancing around the restaurant, as Erica launched into a rambling narrative about how she'd never meant for so much time to elapse before putting Maddie back in Joe's life. How she just kept thinking that once she got her life together.....

"So when am I going to see her again?" Joe interrupted sharply.

"Well I'm supposed to be going away for a weekend sometime after Christmas with my new boyfriend only I don't remember when exactly. But I was hoping I could bring Maddie up to your place and leave her there with you for that weekend."

"I think she should come for a visit before that weekend so it's not a total shock to her to be left in a strange place with people she barely knows."

"It's not a strange place," Erica insisted. She tipped her head to one side and her face took on a look of gentle confusion. "She remembers it."

Lucy could sense there was a "between-the-lines" conversation going on here and since she wasn't privy to it and since she didn't have a clue what a child may or may not need to feel secure and grounded, she excused herself to go to the restrooms. She slid out of the booth and Maddie ran right up to her. "Where you going?" she asked.

"To the bathroom."

"Can I come too?"

"I don't see why not," Lucy replied, looking back at Erica for approbation. Erica nodded and for the first time, Lucy could see that she was pouting, like a sullen child. She didn't know if the pout was directed at her, for being willing to take Maddie along to the bathroom, or at Joe for not yielding immediately to her wishes. She decided it was probably just as well she was leaving them to figure it out.

When she and Maddie returned, Erica was staring fixedly out the front window and Joe was at the counter, paying for the dinner, wearing his wool jacket and hat as if he were ready to leave. Maddie skipped to her daddy and he swung her up into the air and sat her on the counter so she could help him with the money for the waitress.

Lucy walked over to the booth and picked up her raincoat. "It was good meeting you," she said to Erica as she slid her arms into the sleeves. Erica turned and gave Lucy an unfocused look, as if she'd been far, far away in her thoughts. "Did you decide when the next visit would be?" Lucy asked.

"I'll call," Erica promised airily; then smiled across the restaurant at her daughter.

Maddie ran back towards them and Lucy bobbed down close to the floor, to say goodbye. "I look forward to seeing you again," she said to the little girl with the dimples in her smile.

The 5-year old swayed from side to side, coyly, and Lucy didn't quite know what to do. She had almost no experience with small children and in England she wouldn't do more than give her a peck on the cheek because that's the kind of affection she and her sisters gave to each other. She leaned forward, to act on this impulse, and was surprised to feel Maddie's little arms go up around her neck in a warm hug. Lucy responded by squeezing her round the waist then she stood abruptly and headed for the door, throwing a quick wave back in Erica's direction.

Joe was already at the door, his right hand resting on the long, metal handle. As Lucy walked towards him he pulled the door open to let her go out ahead of him. They trotted down the steps to the restaurant side by side and then swung around the corner to head up towards the car. Joe set a grueling pace and Lucy got the impression it wasn't because of the cold this time but because he just couldn't wait to get out of there.

She began to think that maybe there was something in the interaction between Erica and Joe that she'd missed, maybe when she was in the bathroom with Maddie or maybe even before. Something that had been aimed so specifically at Joe it had gone right over her head because he certainly seemed tense right now.

Two blocks up and a safe distance from the restaurant, the explosion happened. Joe began spitting and snarling, frothing and raging in a way that Lucy had never seen before. As she climbed into the car next to him she looked at him astounded, watching his jaws snap at the air like an attack dog at the end of its leash. What in the world could have had made him so angry, she wondered?

And who in the world was this man?

Lesson 11

Loading the Kiln

Loading your kiln is an exercise in balance itself. Not only will you have to decide which pieces you want to fire, you will also need to determine the optimal size, number and placement of your pieces so as to allow heat to move freely among them.

Joe knew he'd blown it, letting Erica push his buttons the way she had until he couldn't stand it any longer and he flipped out. But seeing Maddie had made him realize just how much time had passed with her out of his life and all he could hear coming from Erica's mouth was more reluctance to let them be together. Unless it suited her needs, of course.

Still, the best thing he could do, he told himself, was not let it get to him and he went into the New Year determined not to lose Maddie out of his life again. Which would give him two goals for 1987; to build a new kiln and to find a way to hold this little unformed, unrealized family of his together.

Three weeks later, though, in late January, Joe was still alone in his little house. Lucy was down in Seattle, Maddie was in Issaquah, only the dogs kept him company as the first major snowfall of the season gathered in deep, downy layers outside the windows. At 2 in the morning Joe was fast asleep under the eaves in his bedroom, Max was asleep on the floor next to him and Magnolia was downstairs, twitching in silent dreamland next to the warmth of the woodstove. Everything was perfectly still and peaceful, with the snow sound-proofing the countryside around their slumber. Then someone opened the front door.

Maggie leapt up immediately and charged the intruder, barking with all her might; "Woo, woo, woo, woo, woo, woo, woo!!" Joe shot awake at her signal, threw his legs out of bed and kick-started Max. "Go check it out, you lazy mutt!" Max tore down the stairs, barking like he was going to rip whoever had come in limb from limb, while Joe slipped his hand under his bed and grabbed his Ruger Security Six revolver. He grasped the handle in his right hand, steadied it with his left and cocked the hammer. He moved, swiftly but stealthily, out of his bedroom and around the corner of the stairwell, his finger poised alongside the trigger.

"Don't move!" he ordered whoever was at the bottom of the stairs. "I've got a gun and I don't have my glasses on."

"I'm not moving. I'm not moving," begged a male voice. Joe knew it probably wasn't the fact that he had a gun or that he might not see well enough to shoot him without killing him that was scaring the man; it was the two dogs, barking voraciously at his crotch that had him terrified.

"Who is it?" he grunted.

"Your neighbor. Ricky."

Joe quickly ran through all the neighbors around him; none of them was named Ricky. "Who?"

"Ricky Weaver. From Ranger Station Road."

Marblemount. No wonder he couldn't place him. That was nearly 15 miles up the road. But Joe remembered him now. He lowered the revolver down to his side and released the action. "Whadya need?"

"I swerved, just down the road here, trying not to hit a deer and I went into the ditch. I was hoping you could pull me out with your truck."

"What time is it?"

"I don't know," fibbed Ricky, "It's late though."

No kidding! thought Joe. "All right. Let me get my pants on. Wouldn't want to scare you again, seeing me with no clothes on."

"Can you call the dogs off?" Ricky asked timidly.

"Oh. Sure," Joe responded. Then commanded the dogs: "Go lay down." Maggie moved back to the woodstove and Max trotted upstairs, following Joe into the bedroom. Joe bent down to slide the revolver back under the bed as Max snuffled around him, looking for affection. "Yeah, lot of help you were," Joe told him caustically. Then he pulled on his jeans and prepared to go out into the cold.

"Holy mackerel!" he exclaimed, when he stepped out of his front door and saw how much snow was on the ground already. His voice bounced off the trees, echoing his shock across the valley and he heard a lone dog bark a single response before total silence descended in the neighborhood again. The three-quarter moon that hung in the sky above them illuminated the landscape, showing every inch of it to be white. White with a coating of fresh snowflakes that twinkled intermittently like sprinkles on a wedding cake. When Joe had gone to bed there were maybe only 5 inches of snow on the ground; now that amount looked to have doubled and his eyes fixed on the flakes, floating down from the sky, as he marveled that something so small and spread out could end up accumulating so rapidly. Of course, that shouldn't surprise him, he thought to himself. After all, he'd grown up in Saratoga Springs, New York, so if there was one thing he'd learned early and repeatedly it was that snow could pile up fast. Much faster than it could be shoveled away. That was one of the things he loved about life in the Pacific Northwest; no matter how much it rained, you never had to shovel it.

"You think you'll make it to Marblemount?" he asked Ricky.

"Oh sure. It's not that bad," Ricky fibbed again.

"Yeah but it'll be snowing worse up there. Have you got four-wheel drive?"

"Nah. But it'll be okay. Once you get me out of the ditch."

Joe caught the distinct aroma of alcohol and wondered if Ricky had really swerved to avoid a deer or if he'd just missed seeing the edge of the road because he was slightly toasted. "So whereabouts are you stuck?" he asked.

Ricky pointed back towards Concrete. "Just down the road a-ways, by the boat launch."

Joe nodded, picturing it; right after the big bend in the road at the top of Faber Hill. This guy was lucky not to have ended up in the river. "All right, let's go get her," he said, having willed himself to walk out into the weather.

He turned and grabbed a broom he had sitting next to the front door, took three paces to the top of the steps and then leaned over to make sure he knew where he was putting his feet. Immediately he felt icy crystals hit the back of his neck and slither down into his shirt. He put one foot forward and sank down into the cold, wet, white stuff, past the top of his hunting boot, up to the middle of his shin, where it began seeping through his dry jeans and socks to get to his bare skin. He definitely wished he were still in bed.

He noticed that Ricky's legs and feet were already wet, no doubt from walking up the highway in the snow. Plus he probably had some internal heat going on from the alcohol he'd consumed. Ricky took the steps without missing a beat and they both trudged across the driveway to Joe's truck.

Joe's new, four-wheel drive, three-quarter ton, Chevy pick-up truck. New to Joe, that was, because the truck itself was 12 years old and previously belonged to the guy who made the upriver deliveries for UPS. It was blue, like the Chevy that Joe had worked unto death, but a darker shade of blue, and very straight, from the engine grill all the way back to the tailgate. Joe knew he'd soon fix that, tossing firewood on it the way he did, but it was great to have bought something that didn't start out looking so hammered.

Sonny had found this vehicle in the classified section of the local paper, and Lucy had insisted that Joe finance it with the revenue from the pottery party.

"How do you normally pay your bills in the winter when you're not making much from the pottery?" she'd asked him when she was trying to justify her argument.

"I sell firewood."

"Okay. And you can't sell firewood without a truck, right?"

"Right."

"And I thought you said that the Highway Department doesn't usually reopen the Pass until the beginning of fishing season?"

Joe nodded. "April 17th."

"Well what we made at the pottery party was a nice little windfall but it wasn't enough to tide you over till April 17th. You should buy another pick-up. If you can find one for that kind of money."

Of course, that was a problem at first. Joe had made up his mind that he needed a four-wheel drive, so he could get into the mountains to find dry firewood when they were deep in snow. It never made any sense to him why people had to wait until the last minute to call him with their wood needs but they did. And more often than not, while they were inside, protecting themselves from the inclement weather, he was out in the worst of it, getting them more wood. But it was how he supported his pottery habit in the winter months so he couldn't complain. However, getting stuck was not part of the deal in his mind, so he decided it was time to upgrade to a four-wheel drive. Only all the used four-wheel drives were about twice what they'd made at the pottery party and he was just about to call his parents and ask for a loan when Sonny showed up with that one lucky ad.

Joe grasped the top of the truck bed with his right hand, wiped the snow off the handle to the driver's side door and pulled hard, nearly hitting himself in the face. He was going to have to learn not to yank on this door the way he did his old Chevy. He grabbed the steering wheel and bounced himself onto the bench seat, knocking his feet together to get off the worst of the snow and then swung around and turned the key in the ignition. "Don't you just love that sound?" he commented to Ricky, who'd heaved himself into the passenger side of the cab.

"What sound?"

"The sound of your truck starting when you want it to start," Joe said with satisfaction.

He didn't wait for an answer. Ricky looked content enough not to have been eaten by the dogs to worry about whether a pick-up would start or not. Joe turned the defroster to high, put the truck in neutral, stepped on the emergency brake and slid back out to broom the snow off his windshield. He got most of it off the hood at the same time, then threw the broom over his firewood racks into the bed of the pick-up. Still feeling a certain amount of pride he locked the hubs, climbed back into the cab and put the truck in four-wheel drive and reverse. He let off the emergency brake, pushed down on the gas and the truck shuddered tentatively as the tires encountered slime instead of traction. "Come on, Nelly, you can do it," Joe encouraged, pushing down further on the gas pedal. He'd had her up in Osterman today, over by Finney Creek, where he had a permit to cut wood and even though he'd made himself some ruts through the snow, driving back and forth these last few days, there was still enough accumulation for him to know that this truck could do what he was asking of her right now. And she did. They backed up through the 8 to 10 inches of snow in the driveway and pulled forward onto the highway.

Joe turned right and the truck gained a little speed as the tires felt the traction of the tarmac. He turned the windshield wipers on and tried the high beams. Instantly the snow was coming straight towards them, blinding them from anything that might be on the road. Joe switched back to low beams and kept the truck at a steady 20 miles per hour. He could see long, dragging tracks in the snow on the other side of the road; human tracks. Ricky's most likely, from when he walked from his truck to Joe's house. He drove about a mile and a quarter and saw Ricky's two-wheel drive Datsun, pointing down into the ditch at Faber Landing. That doesn't look so bad, he told himself.

Joe did a wide, slow U-turn across Highway 20 and positioned his truck on the shoulder. "You steer and I'll pull," he told Ricky as he slipped on a pair of work gloves he had in the cab.

Ricky scuffed forward through the snow again to get into his pick-up while Joe hitched a logging chain between the two vehicles. As soon as he bent over to tighten the end of the chain on the underside of his truck, a snowplow came roaring by, throwing a tidal wave of dirty snow directly at him. "Shit!' yelped Joe, leaping to a stand and causing the frigid mess to slide down from where it had landed on his head to the one part of him that was still dry - his face.

"Did that get you?" Ricky hollered from the safety of his pick-up.

Joe didn't answer. He wiped his face in the crook of his arm to get the last of the sludge off and went back to his chain. It was good and tight. He stood up, hitched up his wet jeans and trudged over to Ricky's window. "You really ought to put some firewood rounds in the back of this pick-up. Give you some ballast when it snows," he advised.

"Wasn't snowing when I left today," Ricky argued.

Joe gave Ricky a tight smile. There were some people that just didn't want to hear it. "Keep your foot off the brake," he told him. "I'm gonna pull you straight back."

In a matter of seconds his good deed was done. He hopped out of his Chevy again, recovered his chain and smacked the bed of the Datsun twice. "You're good to go," he yelled.

"Thanks," Ricky yelled back. He revved the engine on the Datsun, which slid a little as it climbed the snow bank on the shoulder but made it back onto the highway. Joe watched it settle into the fresh, compact tracks left by the plow. Beep, beep Ricky signaled as his little Datsun carried him away and Joe waved through the falling snow.

He hopped back in his truck, glad of the warmth coming from the heater that worked so well, and buckled up picturing himself crawling back into the cozy cocoon he'd made in the blankets on his bed. Hopefully it would still be warm.

He followed the Datsun's tracks up the highway and in less than two minutes was back home. He sat for a moment, fatigue suddenly reminding him what time it was, then slid wearily out of the truck and trudged back up to his front door. Maggie barked and ran to him when he opened it. "Good girl," he told her, dipping his face into hers as he rubbed her behind the ears. "Now go back to bed."

Joe followed her across to the woodstove and threw another log into the fire. He climbed out of his wet clothes right there, by the stove, and walked back upstairs naked. He stepped over Max, back into bed and shivered as his cold body hit the cold sheets. "Where's Lucy when I need her," he muttered to himself. Then he rolled over, cocooned the blankets around him again and fell, almost instantly, back to sleep.

6 o'clock came way too soon for Joe that morning. At least, he assumed it was 6 o'clock. He hadn't heard the alarm yet. He reached over to turn the lamp on next to his bed but nothing happened. Power must be out, Joe thought to himself. He yawned then fumbled around for his glasses. On second thought, he realized, it must be after 6 because what had woken him was daylight coming through the window next to his bed. And daylight in January never happened before 7.

He turned towards the window and saw rolling dunes of white snow everywhere. The apple tree had big splashes on one side of its trunk, thick, half-moon crescents in every crook and finely balanced layers the length of every branch. The vine maple next to the apple tree was so laden with snow, it had been forced into a full, all-the-way-down-to-the-ground bow, plugging the access to the crawl space at the back of the house. Joe yawned again, hoping he wouldn't need to get in there to work on his water for some reason.

He lay in bed, thinking for a moment. He'd planned to load his kiln today since he'd spent quite a bit of time away from the pottery this past week and needed to get back to stay balanced. Loading the kiln meant a lot of back and forth between the studio and the kiln shed, carrying ware boards full of pots, and that was not going to be easy in this snow. He'd have to make sure he shoveled out an adequate path and dressed warmly. He wondered how long the power had been out and whether he'd be able to squeeze a hot shower out of the residual heat in the water tank.

He rolled over and looked at Max, who was standing beside the bed, watching him. How come you're not getting up, boss, he seemed to be saying. Joe heard Maggie downstairs, moving from one foot to another as she waited at the front door to go outside. "Urgh," he groaned and swung his legs out of the bed to hit the cold, wood floor. The cedar was beautiful to look at and its thickness made it wonderfully functional but he was beginning to think he should trade for a sheepskin rug at next year's Barter Faire, to soften his landings when he got up in the morning.

He reached into the shelf unit he'd built under the dormer roof at the back end of the bedroom and pulled out a t-shirt, socks and jeans while Max headed downstairs to join Maggie. Joe followed him down and peered out the window next to the front door. He guessed there was about two feet of snow on the ground. "Nah," he told the dogs, "you guys are going out the back door. That way you can plow me a path up to the studio."

He walked around the stairwell, reading the time off the battery-powered clock on the wall as he did so. 7:30. Boy, he'd slept in. Good thing it was Sunday. He made a stop at the woodstove, opening up the drafts and the door, and saw that there was a nice bed of coals still going. That was one advantage to having been pulled out of bed in the middle of the night; he'd managed to keep the fire going by stoking it. He threw on a couple of chunks of wood and then walked over to the sliding glass door. The snow on the back porch was up to his knees at least, with about a three-inch gap from the door to the accumulation. If the dogs took their exit at high speed, they'd never see what they were getting into until they were in it. He clicked twice, in the side of his mouth, and they came running. He slid open the door and Max barreled ahead without slowing down. He was half way down the porch steps before he stopped and looked up, wondering what this stuff was blocking his way. Not so Maggie. She'd seen the conditions and had slid to a halt, right next to Joe. "G'won," he told her impatiently. "You're making it cold in here." But Maggie didn't appear to be convinced, especially now that Max had stopped. Joe trapped his clothes between his bare legs, reluctantly leaned forward and grabbed a handful of snow. He made a quick snowball and threw it way out, in the direction of the studio, Max took off after it, leaping and jumping through the thick snow with joyful abandon. Maggie glanced woefully up at Joe. "Hey, at least I made him go first," he told her, holding his clothes in his arms again and encouraging her out with a nudge to her rear end. He closed the sliding-glass door behind her and headed for the bathroom, wondering if he'd pay for his trickery with a cold shower.

Down in Seattle Lucy zipped off stage, tearing at her clothes as she piled into the dressing room. It hadn't snowed that much down here, not compared to what Joe had told her on the phone this morning they'd got at his house, but the couple of inches that had dropped on the city had thrown everyone into a tizzy. Lucy herself had waited at the bus stop for almost an hour before she realized that she wasn't going to get to the matinee at the theatre by bus today. Fortunately she'd left herself enough time to rush back home and take the Pinto. Her dresser, on the other hand, had relied on public transportation and called the theatre just before the show went up to say that she wouldn't make it in time to help Lucy with her big costume change.

Lucy stepped out of the Mrs. Lennox dress and into the padded underskirt that she had to wear as the maid, Martha. She was fumbling to attach it in the back when the girl that usually worked the box office rushed into the tiny changing room. "What goes on next?" she asked hurriedly.

Lucy pointed at the one rack holding the costumes for all three of the women in this cast. Backstage at the Children's Theatre was definitely not as spacious as backstage at the Rep. "That padded corset," she told the girl, who grabbed it and slipped it up over Lucy's arms. She stood behind her, securing the Velcro, as Lucy stepped out of one pair of shoes and into another.

"You really are skinny, aren't you?" the girl remarked.

"What do you mean?" Lucy leaned away from her and grabbed the floor-length dress she wore on top of this.

"You look so plump on stage as Martha."

Lucy just rolled her eyes as she bent forward to step into the dress. She walked past this girl every day on her way into the theatre; surely she knew what Lucy really looked like. But recently, at auditions, she'd noticed directors dropping their eyes to her hips when she mentioned she was playing Martha in *The Secret Garden*, as if looking for her fat. Had they never heard of padding, she thought to herself.

She pulled her arms into the dress and the girl zipped it up in the back as Lucy grabbed her apron and began moving towards the stage. "The hat! The hat!" the girl called out from behind her. Lucy ripped off Mrs. Lennox's hat and fumbled it into the box office attendant's hands. "Thanks," she whispered and bobbed down to check in the mirror that her braids were still spiraled tidily over her ears. Then she made a mad dash to be in place for her first entrance as Martha.

Joe's kiln was a single chamber in the shape of a catenary arch, named after the curve made by a heavy chain hanging freely from two points. Except the arch of the kiln was a mirror image of that hanging curve, going up instead of down. It looked like a giant grandfather clock, built out of castable refractory clay, and it held about 150 pots. Joe had built bourry fireboxes on either side of the chamber, two brick rectangles that came about half way up the sidewalls of the arch, and looked like two great shoulders on a torso. They worked on a downdraft principle, so he stoked them from the top, the wood burned on grate bars half way down the firebox and the embers fell into the ash pit below. Then the fly ash and heat was pulled into the chamber by the vacuum at the top of the sixteen-foot tall brick chimney. At least, that was the theory. So far, in the eight years Joe had been using this kiln, the one thing that disappointed him consistently was how little fly ash made its way onto the pots. And he couldn't see the point of firing with wood if he didn't get ash on the outside of the pots, except that it used up the waste material from the shake industry. But it was a lot of work to be doing it to use up somebody else's waste product. Joe wanted the artistic benefits too.

The first thing he did before loading the kiln every firing was to check for any ash that might be blocking the mouse holes since they were pivotal to the success of his firings. Both sides looked clear today. Next he raked the ash pits in the fireboxes. Joe looked over his shoulder at the narrow path he'd dug in the snow between the studio and the kiln shed. Maybe he'd sprinkle the ashes on that today, add a little traction to the icy ground. He walked back over to the studio and grabbed a dustpan he had hanging on a nail outside the door, then stopped, on his way back over to the kiln, and looked at the towers of snow on top of the fence posts around his garden. They looked like those bearskin hats he'd seen on the Beefeaters in London when he'd gone that one Christmas with Lucy; except these, of course, were more like polar bearskins. He wondered if Lucy would be able to make it up here tonight after her show. He heard the dogs barking on the front porch and waited to see if he heard a car door. He doubted anyone would be driving into his place in this weather but he never knew. It could be Sonny, coming up the hill from his place on cross-country skis, wanting to visit at coffee break. It was getting to be that time.

Oh well, whoever it was would find him. Or maybe it was just the snow falling out of the trees like exploding clumps of powdered sugar that was setting the dogs off. It was too cold for him to be standing around doing nothing.

Joe sprinkled the ashes on his path then went into the studio and got some stoneware clay and a wad of ceramic fiber. He walked back out to the kiln shed and turned on his portable radio. The unmistakable mellow tone of Miles Davis filled the little area under the sheet metal roof and Joe let himself imbibe a few beats before stepping inside the 35-cubic foot chamber to begin his pre-firing examination of the castable for cracks. Yep, just as he expected. The crack between the arch and the front wall of the kiln had definitely gotten wider in the last firing. No wonder that firing had dragged out to 20 hours; he must have been losing a lot of heat through this crack. He pulled off some fiber and stuffed it into the crack. Then he rolled out a length of stoneware clay between his palms and thumbed it over the opening. There was one on the other side of the door too. He filled that the same way. Joe looked up. Holy mackerel! There was a huge crack at the top of the arch that ran the depth of the kiln. If that got much bigger this arch might lose its ability to be self-supporting and collapse in on itself. Joe was glad he'd made an appointment at the bank tomorrow. He hated borrowing money because he was always terrified he wouldn't be able to make a payment, given his erratic income, but he definitely needed to build a new kiln. And the little bank in Concrete had worked with him when he had to pay off Erica; he was pretty sure they'd work with him again. The only other time he'd bothered them was when the interest rate had dropped on mortgages and Joe had gone in and asked Bill Sr., the manager, if he could borrow what he owed them, pay them off and then borrow the same amount back at the lower mortgage rate. Bill Sr. suppressed a small smile. "Are you telling me you'd like to refinance your mortgage?" he asked.

"Would that get me the lower interest rate?" Joe replied.

Bill Sr. nodded. "I just have to talk to the loan committee," he added gravely. Joe knew that the loan committee was Bill's brother, Ben, and that they met over coffee at the café in town. He expected he'd hear the same thing tomorrow, when he asked him for some money to build another kiln.

Joe worked for what seemed like a long time patching the cracks and crevices inside the chamber of his kiln, accompanied by such greats as Wynton Marsalis, Artie Shaw and his orchestra and Ella Fitzgerald. When he stepped out his hands and nose were both numb with cold and he was very ready for some coffee. He switched off the radio and walked down to the house, the snow scrunching under his boots with every step. He banged his feet on the back porch, which he had dutifully shoveled off before heading up to the kiln, then slid open the back door and stepped into the warmth of his little home. He crossed immediately to the woodstove and picked up the kettle that was gently steaming on its surface. Plenty of water for a pot of coffee. He put the kettle back down and slipped off his wool jacket. He hung it on a hook behind the stove so it would be warm when he went to put it back on and then he stoked the fire.

He picked up the kettle once more and carried it over to the kitchen counter. He pulled his coffee pot towards him, took the used paper cone out of the ceramic filter and put in a fresh one, then loaded it with three heaping spoonfuls of ground coffee. Joe lifted the kettle once more and poured enough hot water into the filter to fill it. He thought about the first kiln he'd built on this property, with three, climbing chambers and a single firebox. He was pretty sure he was going to build another one like that, only bigger. And maybe two chambers instead of three. Joe lifted his eyes, and stared out the window. There were tracks in the snow, coming from the back corner of the pasture next door towards his house. The tracks were big, rounded it seemed like, heavy....

"Hi there."

Joe jumped, slamming the kettle down onto the counter as he did so. "Geez!" he said, spinning around to see his new neighbor, Laura, standing on the stairs behind him.

"You scared the shit out of me."

"Sorry," said Laura, pulling her mouth down at one corner.

"S'alright," Joe reassured her. "I had kind of a short night so I guess it made me jumpy."

"You were up late?"

"No. I just had someone needing me to pull them out of the ditch in the middle of the night."

"You went out in this?!" Laura turned and peered through one of the panels of glass in the front door. "I couldn't even get my car out of my driveway so I came over on snowshoes."

"I see that." Joe was looking at the tracks again. "You must be what got the dogs excited."

"They were barking, yes. But I was carrying a bunch of my art supplies so I couldn't pet them."

"You started setting up already?" Joe looked at her, pleased. Laura and her husband, Jimmy, had bought the property next door with another couple. They called themselves New Age hippies, which Joe thought was an oxymoron because, from what he could tell, you needed a lot of money to follow some of the New Age gurus and money had never stopped anyone from being a hippie. But so far he liked all his new neighbors and found them to be sweet relief from the old curmudgeon who had sold him his 5 acres and then tortured him about their mutual property line for the ten years that they'd lived next to each other.

Laura was an artist, like Joe, only she made paintings instead of pots. Since she and Jimmy were in the process of building a house on the far edge of their land, Joe had agreed to rent her his little back bedroom so she could make art while waiting for her own work space. Lucy was not thrilled with the arrangement. Joe looked at Laura, coming towards him in the kitchen; she was somewhere in her 30s, curvy yet slender, with a flamboyant, arty dress style and thick, luxuriously dark hair. She was definitely attractive, with that generous mouth that she nearly always held in a smile, but Joe wasn't interested in her. Not in that way. And she was married, for goodness sakes. What was Lucy thinking?

"Well you said it was okay...." Laura replied, as she sashayed towards him.

"Yeah, no, it's fine," Joe reassured her. "But you should know that Lucy's coming up tonight and she's bringing our friend, Sol, with her. And he'll be sleeping in that back bedroom."

"Oh, I only put a couple of canvases and some paints in there. Just what I could carry. I'm sure they won't be in the way."

"Good enough. When are you going to start making art in it?" The last of the coffee was draining down into the pot and Joe reached behind Laura, to lift a mug off one of the nails he'd banged into the wall above the kitchen counter.

"I don't know. I think I'm going to wait until this snow clears before I bring the rest of my stuff."

"That could be a long wait," Joe said, looking out the window at the snow again as he poured a mug of coffee. "You want some?"

Laura wrinkled her nose as if thinking about it. The dogs suddenly jumped up on the front porch and began barking again. Joe picked up the coffee pot and walked it to the woodstove, looking out the windows in the front door as he did so. "Here comes Sonny on his skis. He must have smelled the coffee."

"It does smell good."

"Well there's plenty….." Joe set the coffee pot down on the woodstove, to keep it warm for the rest of the day.

"No, I should get back," Laura responded, looking at the maple burl clock on Joe's wall. "Jimmy wants to hang insulation."

"Uh oh. Well good luck with that! Don't forget, Sunday is sauna night. You guys might need one after hanging insulation."

Laura's brown eyes lit up at the invitation. "Can we make snow angels?"

"You can if I can. And I'm planning on it."

"Here." Laura pulled something out of her pocket. "This is for you." The noise on the front porch increased as the dogs jumped around in excitement at Sonny's arrival. Joe took the check from Laura. "Thanks," he said, looking at the amount. "My banker will be pleased when I deposit this."

Sonny slipped in through the front door and smiled shyly at Laura. "Hi," he said.

Laura stared down, wide-eyed with astonishment, at his bare legs. "Aren't you cold?" she asked.

"Nah," he told her.

Joe laughed. Nobody ever understood Sonny's penchant for shorts.

Laura made her eyes even bigger at Joe as if to say she thought Sonny was crazy then she offered a little wave goodbye and headed out the door. "Have a good coffee break," were her parting words.

"Did she buy a pot or something?" Sonny asked, nodding at the check in Joe's hand. He trotted over to the kitchen to get a mug for some coffee.

"No. This is rent, for the back bedroom." Joe endorsed the back of the check and left it sitting on the table he had pushed up against the picture window in his living room.

"Oh, I thought Lucy wasn't in favor of that."

"She's not," Joe remarked, "but we need the money." He sat down, with obvious pleasure, in the vinyl armchair he'd bought for a buck at a down valley thrift store. "If I'm to build a new kiln, we do."

Lucy stepped out of the theatre into the twilight. She loved this time of day. There was something about the light quality that made her feel like she belonged, no matter where she was. She remembered walking through the narrow, cobblestone streets of Rennes, France, on the way to the Conservatory of Drama at this time of day, school children passing her, wearing their smart uniforms, laughing and talking in rapid fire French, people bustling in both directions, the smell of buttery croissants and sweet pain aux raisins coming from the bakery that fronted onto the street, and she, in the midst of all this, was one of them. She could never quite understand why she felt like that at this particular time of day, but she did.

She walked quickly towards her car, running her fingers through her thick, curly hair, to release it a little further from the lock-down she'd put on it by braiding it for the show. When the costumer had insisted she wear her hair like that Lucy had cried and cried because of what her father had told her when she was 16; that she was a real plain Jane without her hair loose around her face. But so many little girls had come up to her after performances and told her how pretty they thought she looked and could she tell them how she did he hair like that, that Lucy had stopped being so upset about it and had even started to warm to the hairstyle. She smiled, thinking about the sweet look of sincerity on the faces of some of those little girls. Working for the Children's Theatre was pretty grueling, with its two school shows every weekday as well as evening performances and matinees on weekends and no full day dark, but the children made it worth it.

Lucy got to her Pinto, unlocked the door and slipped gratefully into the driver's seat. It was cold outside. She blew on her hands while she waited for the heater to warm things up. The show had been good this afternoon. Shelley, the assistant stage manager, had come to them after curtain and squeezed herself narrowly into their dressing room to avoid exposing them to the young men in the cast who found their own dressing room so claustrophobic, they tended to hang around outside the women's. That way they could stretch their legs without cluttering up the wings of the stage. Shelley told Lucy and the other women in the cast that the enthusiastic crowd they'd heard from the stage had been a full house, which surprised everyone given the snow in Seattle. But she also went on to tell them that if the schools were closed the next day, they would cancel performances. Lucy's spirits sank when she heard that. She loved playing Martha and the last thing she wanted was for them to cancel shows. She backed around and pulled forward to the paved road that led through the entrance to the Woodland Park Zoo to the Poncho Forum, where the Children's Theatre performed. Most of the snow was gone here, as far as she could see. She would take that as a good sign.

Lucy turned out onto 50th and headed straight for Aurora. She had to go downtown to the ferry terminal and pick up Sol. He needed a break from staying with Pedro in Gig Harbor and wanted to come up to the mountains. Sol liked sharing himself amongst his sons but they didn't necessarily want to share him; so when he made up his mind to move from one son to another, it caused conflict. Right now, he was preparing to go and spend some time with Ramon in Venezuela, and in order not to face Pedro's feelings on this subject, Sol had decided to go and be with his favorite potter. Joe wasn't one of Sol's sons, although Lucy had overheard Sol referring to her as his daughter-in-law once or twice, but Joe was a great listener. And Sol did love to stand and regale him with stories of the billions and billions of dollars worth of oil he thought was under the land he owned the drilling rights to down in South America. Plus Sol liked riding up into the mountains with Joe, to hunt for rocks. More than once Joe had slammed on the brakes on a logging road at Sol's insistence and gone up a bank to retrieve some interesting slab of geology that Sol just had to have for his collection. A collection he kept in Joe's front yard, to touch and admire every time he came up to visit. The first time Joe did this for Sol, he hauled the rock down to the pick-up and went to slide it into the bed when Sol stopped him, obviously distressed. "Oh no," he remonstrated, "don't put it there. It'll get scratched up."

Joe looked at him, mystified, "Where am I supposed to put it then?"

"In the front, with me. That way I can take care of it."

Joe obliged him, even though it made no sense at all to him, and continued to oblige him for the rest of the outing until Sol's lap and the bench seat between them was covered in rocks. Fortunately Lucy had never ridden along on one of those adventures. She could only imagine where she would end up if Joe's work gloves, firewood wedges and spare coats were relegated to the floor to make space for the rocks on the front seat.

The traffic ahead of Lucy slowed approaching a light on Aurora. Lucy took her foot of the gas and glanced at a woman on the sidewalk, who was being pulled along by three big dogs on leashes. Lucy thought about the story Joe had told her this morning on the phone, about the middle-of-the-night intruder that Max and Maggie had successfully pinned in the doorway. Joe was right; if that guy had been able to see the dogs he would have noticed that their tails were wagging like crazy and that they were only barking so loudly because they were pleased to see him. Lucy smiled when she thought about this. Then she noticed that the vehicle ahead of her slid a little in the rear when it stopped at the light. Uh oh, she thought to herself, maybe the snow wasn't gone after all. She gripped the steering wheel and focused on her driving.

Joe didn't go back to loading the kiln after coffee break because, with the power out, Sonny was at a loss as to what to do with his day so he offered to help Joe hang sheetrock in his bedroom. Joe jumped at the offer and they nailed and cut and lifted and carried sheetrock for a good hour until the ceiling in Joe's bedroom was almost covered. Then the power came back on and Sonny got ready to head home. "You coming back for sauna later?" Joe asked, as Sonny snapped his cross-country skis back onto his sneakers at the bottom of Joe's front steps.

"I might. If it hasn't started snowing again."

Joe looked up at the sky. "Is it supposed to snow again?"

"That's what the paper said."

Joe walked to the end of the porch and looked at Jackman Ridge. This morning the cloud cover had been at about 7,000 feet; now he could see that it had come down, and it was snowing at the top of Jackman. By tonight he imagined it would be snowing again at the house. He hoped Lucy would make it up here before then.

Sonny took off and Joe walked back into the house. He looked at the clock; 11:30. Not enough time to get involved in loading the kiln before lunch and too much time to think of making lunch already. Joe was always at his best if he stuck to his routine. He decided to call Lucy instead.

"Good. You haven't left for the theatre yet," he said, when she picked up after the first ring.

"No. Not for another fifteen, twenty minutes," she replied, pleased to hear his voice. "I thought I'd better give myself a little extra time since it snowed a bit down here last night."

"A bit?!" mocked Joe. "Well, let me tell you about what we've got going on up *here*." He launched into a colorful retelling of the snow and the dogs and Ricky Weaver and the dogs again and eventually wound around to Laura surprising him by being in the house when he was making his mid-morning coffee. He could almost feel the hackles on Lucy's neck go up when he mentioned Laura's name and then he steeled himself as she fired off a round of questions about how long Laura had stayed and what they'd talked about and why he even wanted her to rent that little bedroom again. "Look, Lucy," he told her, after her questions petered out. "You really have nothing to worry about."

"From you maybe."

"What's that supposed to mean?"

"I've seen the way she looks at you."

"But I'm not looking back. Not that way."

"Not yet, you're not."

"Lucy!!"

"Well if you're allowed to get upset about that State Patrol man getting too friendly with me when the Pinto stalled on the freeway last week, I'm allowed to get upset about Laura getting too friendly with you."

"But you said he was coming on to you."

Lucy snickered, remembering how the good-looking young officer had fixed his blue-eyes on her, slipped her his card, and suavely told her she could call him anytime. "He was."

"Well Laura isn't coming onto me."

"She looks like she is."

"That's just her way."

"Okay!" Lucy snapped. She was angry but knew she was angry at herself, for even feeling this way.

There was an uncomfortable pause and then Joe decided to change the subject. "You think the Pinto's going to make it up here tonight?"

"I hope so. I'm really looking forward to seeing you."

Joe knew that was the real problem; they weren't spending enough time together. "I'm looking forward to seeing you too," he said.

"If it stalls again, I'll just sit and wait for it to start back up, like it did last time. At least I'll have Sol with me, if anything does go wrong with the Pinto."

"Yeah, I don't think Sol knows much about cars though."

"Well then he can just protect me from unwanted attention from the State Patrol."

"Could he do that for the rest of us too?" Joe joked.

They both laughed and hung up on a good note. Joe looked at the clock again. Now it was lunchtime. He made himself a cheese sandwich, the same thing he made himself almost every day for lunch, poured himself another cup of coffee and sat in the armchair, next to the table, to eat and read his book for a while. Now that the power was back on, Garrison Keillor accompanied him on the radio with one of his rambling soliloquies but Joe was lost in the heavy snow of the Ardennes Mountains, gripped by the movements of the Allied troops in the Battle of the Bulge.

Half an hour later he reluctantly put down his book. Revived and replenished, he made his way through his own snowy forest back over to the studio. He threw some more wood on the stove, to keep a certain amount of heat in the space while the door was open, and inventoried the shelves of pots in a glance.

He liked to start with lidded casseroles when he was loading so he walked over to a ware board with a piece of paper folder over its end, on which he had written 9". This held casseroles and small jars, items that would fit under a 9-inch lift without wasting space.

Joe picked it up in one decisive move and balanced one end of the ware board on his shoulder. The middle of the board rested on the palm of his right hand as his left balanced the far end. He walked

at a steady, determined pace, out of the studio, down the steps and
along the path he had made in the snow, his eyes focused down on
the ground a few feet ahead of him. Usually he walked a little faster
than this but today he had to be careful not to slip.

Once he reached the kiln shed he lowered the ware board onto
the arms of a wooden patio chair that he used when firing his kiln,
swung around and switched on the radio. Count Basie was playing
"Satin Doll," one of his father's favorites and Joe sang the words
when the horns came in. "Cigarette holder, which wigs me, Over my
shoulder, she digs me......." He turned the volume up and the sound
of Basie's crisp piano playing tinkled out from under the metal roof
to fill Joe's snowy hollow in the woods.

He began lifting the objects off the ware board and carefully
placing them in the bottom of the kiln, making sure that the distance
between each pot was small enough to maximize use of the space
but large enough for them not to touch. Touching pots meant they
fired as one and Joe had an example of a small teapot with a coffee
cup attached to its spout hanging on one of the kiln-shed posts. He
liked to tell visitors they could have the pot if they could make it
pour tea into the cup.

He transferred the pots from the ware board to the kiln at an
assured, steady pace, partly because he had done this once a month
for the last eight years so it was pretty much habit for him and partly
because he didn't want to give himself time for second-guessing.
Loading a kiln was like packing a suitcase; you had to decide which
items were going with you and then make them fit. Now and again,
he stopped to check the height of his pieces with a cut off length of
measuring tape. The last thing he needed was to set the 9-inch kiln
posts, on which he would balance the next level of shelves, and find
that one of the pieces was too tall. Backtracking frustrated him even
more than second-guessing.

Satisfied that he'd got the bottom shelf right, Joe spun around
and picked up some 2 by 2 bricks, 9-inches long, from a shelf behind
him. He placed them in the back, middle and front on one side of the
pots, then did the same through the center and down the other side.
He topped each post with a generous wad of soft clay that would
crumble easily when he took the shelves apart after the firing.

Benny Goodman replaced Count Basie and Joe swung his head
a little to the music as he rubbed a handful of dry kiln wash on the
surface of a shelf, to stop the pots from sticking. Boy, this big band
music made him think of his parents, how they liked to go out

dancing to this kind of stuff. Maybe he'd call them later, find out what the weather was doing in the Spa. He placed the shelf over three of the kiln posts and pushed down into the wads of clay. He picked up another kiln shelf. Right now his dad was probably sitting in his recliner, smoking a cigarette and watching college basketball on the television. Or maybe the football playoffs. Joe didn't have TV and wasn't much of a sports fan so he wasn't sure. Sonny would know. It always amazed Joe that he and Sonny got along so well despite the fact that Sonny was into organized sports and Joe wasn't. Of course, they argued regularly about the value of sports versus arts in a person's life but that never stopped them from wanting to hang out together. Joe leaned into the kiln and placed the second shelf so it spanned another quarter of the kiln. Joe's dad, on the other hand, was not so easy with his son's preference for the arts, being a high school football coach himself. "Only faggots go to art school," was his less than salubrious comment when Joe announced his plans as a 19-year old. "Then I guess I'll get all the girls," Joe shot back.

Joe rubbed wash on a third shelf as he thought about how far his dad had come in accepting his chosen career. He wasn't making much of a living as a potter, not yet, but his dad had come to see that drive comes in many forms, with or without a goal post to shoot for. And his mother, who had nurtured a love of art museums in him as a child and left him discreetly alone when she'd caught him practicing life drawing using the nudes in his dad's Playboy magazines, paraphrased William Randolph Hearst time and again: "If you make a good enough product," she told him, "the public will beat a path to your door."

Joe placed the third kiln shelf in the left front corner of the chamber and then prepped the final one for this lift. The news headlines came on the radio; Anglican Church envoy Terry Waite taken hostage in Beirut, President Reagan's prostate surgery raising questions about his physical fitness for the Office and England in the most intense cold spell of the 20th Century. And the local weather report forecast more snow in Seattle. Joe placed the fourth shelf in the kiln and stood back. Now he was ready for more pots. Maybe he'd do a 6-inch lift this time. He walked back towards the studio. If they were calling for more snow in Seattle then they were likely to get dumped on up here tonight. Oh well, all he really cared about was that Lucy get up here safely and that they plow the highway so she could get back down again safely tomorrow. Once she was back there, she was on her own because Joe knew the City of Seattle didn't plow the roads. They used the buses to do that for them. And that just left endless puddles of slush. He lifted a shelf with mugs, honey pots and cereal bowls onto his shoulder and made his way back over to the kiln as Frank Sinatra crooned, "I've got you under my skin."

❀

"So what do we do now?"

Sol and Lucy were sitting in the Pinto close to the Conway exit on the freeway.

"Now we wait for about 20, 25 minutes and hope it starts back up again." Lucy had been driving for just over an hour when the Pinto suddenly died on her and she had to coast to a stop at the side of the road. The timing was pretty consistent with the last time this happened, down by the Marysville exit on the freeway when she was on her way into Seattle, only then Lucy had got out of the car and had started walking off the freeway to call Joe. That's when the State Patrol man spotted her and offered to drive her to the gas station. He waited while she tried, unsuccessfully, to get through to Joe and then drove her back to the Pinto, which, miraculously, started back up when she turned the key in the ignition.

"Too bad we didn't make it as far as that 7-Eleven," Sol remarked, nodding in the direction of the exit. "I see a sign that says home-baked berry pies." He smacked his lips together gleefully. "I do like berry pies."

"Are you hungry?" she asked, genuinely concerned about him.

"Oh no! I just think I am," Sol answered. He ran a hand over his protruding belly. "And I certainly don't need to be feeding this any more baked goods. That's why I want to go down to see Ramon. There's no bakery with cinnamon buns and honey rolls close by down there. I've eaten *way* too much of that stuff at Pedro's these last few months." He turned and scanned the landscape outside the window, obviously contemplating something while chewing on his false teeth. Lucy checked her watch. It was 6:20. She'd wait until 6:30 before trying the car again. Sol noisily sucked his teeth back into place and, without missing a beat, took the conversation back to what they'd been discussing before the engine had stalled. "Does Joe have *any* of the materials yet to build this new kiln?"

"No. We've got to get the money together first. If we'd've been able to buy those firebricks in Eastern Washington, we would have had a bit of a head start. But, you know, that didn't pan out."

Sol grunted and crumpled his lips disdainfully. "I remember *that* story!" he remarked.

"Anyway," Lucy went on, "Joe prefers castable for the construction of the kiln. And he told me he doesn't want to use recycled materials this time – that's what he used for the last two kilns. He wants to use new."

"Because the kiln will last longer if he uses new?"

Lucy shrugged. "I think so." She yawned and stretched her arms forwards, across the steering wheel. At least it was warm in the Pinto.

"How much is it going to cost to build this kiln?" Sol asked.

"About $5,000."

Sol shook his head decisively. "Oh no, I can't do that much."

Lucy did a double take in his direction, wondering what he meant by that comment. They hadn't asked him for any money. "Oh, it's not an issue," she said. "We're going to borrow the money from the bank and add it onto the mortgage."

Sol looked at her, narrowing his eyes like he was thinking about her statement. "How much is your mortgage payment?"

"$200 a month."

He perked up. "Oh, now that I can do." He leaned forward and picked up a small, zip-up pouch that he carried around with him. "When's the mortgage payment due?"

"The 15th of each month. Why?"

He unzipped his pouch and got out his checkbook and a pen. "And who would I make the checks out to?"

Lucy didn't understand. "What are you doing?" she asked.

"I'm going to give you enough checks for $200 a month to cover the cost of the kiln. I'll make the first one for February 15th and then one a month every month after that for two years." He stopped and thought for a moment. "That should be enough, shouldn't it?"

Lucy was embarrassed. "Sol, you don't have to do this…"

"No," he said, raising his left hand up in the air to stop her. "I like to help." And he bent over his checkbook and began writing. "I guess I can leave who it's payable to blank. You can fill that out. But make sure you let me know because Pedro gets very upset with me if I don't fill out my check book correctly."

Lucy didn't know what to say. She turned and let her eyes blur on all the vehicles rushing past them on the freeway. She wanted to say something, something about how it was okay, that they'd make the mortgage payments, that they didn't need him to spend his pension on the kiln; but she knew that once Sol's mind was made up, there was no changing it. So she just sat in silence, listening to the sound of his pen scratching on the surface of the checks and thinking about what a wonderful, generous-spirited man he was. Joe wouldn't know what to say either, she was sure of it.

A few minutes later Sol turned to her and handed over a short stack of checks. "Here," he said.

Lucy took them feeling completely humbled. Sol turned back to putting his checkbook away in his pouch but Lucy stopped him, with a hand on his forearm, and made him look at her. "Thank you," she said.

She slipped the checks into her purse and leaned forward to try the ignition. "Think good thoughts," she instructed Sol.

"Always," he declared.

And the Pinto lit right up.

❀

Joe had about half the kiln loaded when he got stuck. He was looking at his orders on the board over by his glazing table, a board that he'd asked Lucy for because he so liked the first one she'd got him. With two, he reasoned, he could have one by his wheel, for making the orders, and one where they needed to get glazed, streamlining his commission work perfectly. The trouble was, once the pots were glazed, it was hard to tell them apart because they all looked like they were covered in whitewash. Joe knew he'd made the four cereal bowls on the order he was staring at and he remembered putting a clear glaze on them but he didn't know if he'd already loaded them into the kiln or not.

He spun around and looked at the remaining shelves of bisque ware, mentally scratching his head. He couldn't dedicate much more space to cereal bowls because he'd already got quite a few in and needed to load more mugs. Suddenly his brain felt too logy to make a decision. It had been a long day, starting with an interrupted night; maybe it was time to light the sauna. He glanced at the clock above his clay mixer and saw that it was almost 4 o'clock. Definitely time to light the sauna.

He switched off the lights and headed out, rolling the door to the studio closed behind him. He whistled for the dogs as he walked back to the kiln shed to turn off the radio. He was going to need their help again, making a path in the snow up to the sauna.

They came up behind him and panted expectantly. He threw his right arm out in front of him. "G'won," he said and walked forward with the two of them leaping ahead of him. They tumbled and scrambled and jumped their way through virgin snow that came up to their shoulders, encouraged by the thought that Joe was going with them. All three labored uphill, past the garden and the dome house, until their footing became easier under the cover of trees on the short trail between the dome house and the sauna.

Joe stopped alongside the 10 by 12, chalet-style building and grabbed an armload of firewood that was stacked under a loose piece of sheet metal. From there he took a step up onto the covered porch and made his way around the cedar-shingled building to the woodstove. Joe and his hippie friends had built this sauna so that the big woodstove with the heat exchanger on top of it was inside the building while the door for lighting and stoking the fire, remained outside. Joe dumped the firewood then walked around to the front of the building again. The porch on this side had a long cedar bench with hooks above it for clothes and towels. Old-fashioned candleholders with ornate, glass panels held together in blackened, rectangular, metal frames hung from knots in a log beam under the eaves to provide light in the winter months.

Joe pulled open the old, wooden door that somebody had donated to this project, and took two steps inside the building to adjust the damper on the heat exchanger. There were two windows to his left, one on either side of the stove, and the light from the windows fell on the slatted, cedar bench seats with triangular back rests which filled the small space to his right. It smelled like eucalyptus in the shadowy interior, from the oil Joe dropped on the stove each Sunday to cleanse his lungs of clay dust. Much better than smelling like sweat, he thought to himself as he backed up out of the space.

Joe slammed the door shut again and followed the porch around to light a fire in the stove. He split one of the rounds of firewood into kindling and used the pieces to build a tripod inside the stove. He carefully added larger and longer lengths of wood onto the stack and then held a sliver of flaming pitch wood to the bottom. The fire took off instantly. Joe split the remaining rounds of firewood in half and waited for the fire to get going completely before placing them in at the top. He had built the sauna next to a creek that crossed his property and at this time of year, it was boisterously turbulent. As he waited, he looked down at the water, frothing its way through the thick banks of snow, and heard the unmistakable sound of rocks from its bed clunking and knocking their way further downstream. He shivered, thinking about the icy precipitation against his bare neck in the middle of the night. It would feel good to sit in the sauna tonight. He looked out towards the trees covering the steeply graded land on the other side of the creek, and saw tiny flakes of fresh snow drifting down from the sky in the gathering twilight. Yep, it would definitely feel good to sit in the sauna.

Lesson 12

Firing

A wood-firing kiln is often likened to a fire breathing dragon; no matter how much you try to meet its needs you will find, firing to firing, that you are just along for the ride.

Lucy marched right up the hill to the kiln shed as soon as she knew Laura was in the house. She'd just driven two hours from Seattle to be with Joe and she had to turn around and head back down at 7 o'clock tomorrow morning; the last thing she needed was a third wheel to their few precious hours together. Particularly a third wheel that was so good at creating a burn inside of Lucy the likes of which she had never experienced before.

"I think you might have a chimney fire up in the studio," Laura had called down anxiously as soon as Lucy opened the door to the house.

Lucy felt like she'd been smacked in the nose. What was this woman doing up in the bedroom at 6 o'clock on a Sunday evening? Didn't she have all day to make art?! "It's the kiln," she answered snottily and slammed the door without going into the house.

Of course, the fact that Laura didn't know that Joe was firing the kiln might be an indication that she wasn't really hanging on his every word, Lucy thought to herself as she picked her way past the potholes in the driveway so as to avoid getting her high heels stuck in them. And it wasn't as if she even suspected Joe anymore of responding to this woman's flirtatious manner, although he could be so irritatingly encouraging, with that warm charm of his. No what got her, Lucy thought, ignoring the dogs who had run down from the kiln to greet her, was that it seemed like every time she'd come up to be with Joe in the last month, Laura was there, in the house, effectively blocking their chance to be alone together. It was as if she were deliberately trying to sabotage their relationship.

She got to the mouth of the kiln shed, fully intending to accost Joe on this subject, only he was engrossed in some dog-eared, used paperback, the only kind of book he read while firing the kiln because his hands got so sooty they inevitably discolored the pages, and she knew that his time to be lost in a book was very limited. Not only did he have to stoke both fireboxes every three to five minutes, he had to pay attention to the sounds and signs of the kiln, the smoke, the flame, the backpressure; consequently he had very little time to decompress. If she said something now, Lucy was sure she would startle Joe. And if she startled him, well she might just get smacked in the nose for real.

Not that she expected Joe to smack her in the nose but Lucy *had* found herself testing him recently. As if she were wondering just how far he would go when provoked. He always said he wasn't the hitting kind because his hands were his tools but what did he know? Maybe she just hadn't got to him yet. After all, she didn't think she'd provoked her father all those times he'd hit her when she was a kid, but apparently she had.

And watching Joe explode after a couple of the visits they'd had with Maddie, she'd certainly seen him angry. It didn't have anything to do with her, fortunately, or with Maddie for that matter, but it still scared Lucy. Enough that she'd considered putting an end to the visits, if that's what being around Maddie's mother could do to Joe.

"Oh no, don't give up," her friend, Pete, had begged when they were talking about it on a shared ride down into Seattle one day. "That's what I did when I could see my ex was using our kids to punish me for breaking up with her. I couldn't stand to see them being hurt like that, so I backed off. Which is what she wanted. But all they learned from that was that I didn't want to see them. And they thought that meant I didn't love them." He pushed open the little triangular window beside him in his VW bus and threw out the toothpick he had been chewing on.

Lucy noticed the curl to his upper lip, a sign of the bitterness he still felt after all these years over not getting to spend time with his children. She remembered Mr. Tall and Lanky, the man sitting next to her on the flight out to Washington from New York; how his eyes had clouded with pain when he showed her a photo he carried in his wallet of a baby girl that he hadn't seen in too many years. Lucy remembered wondering why he'd shared that with her. Maybe it was so she would hear what Pete was saying to her now.

"Whatever you do," Pete added. "please don't give up. Maddie loves her daddy and it's obvious to me that he thinks of her as one of his greatest creations."

Lucy told Joe about Pete's advice and they decided to take the problem to Brenda, an aging, retired, psychiatric social worker, one of the many part-time residents of the Upper Skagit. She helped them work out a visitation schedule that didn't involve the parents spending any time together and so far, Lucy hadn't seen any more outbursts on Joe's part. But she still couldn't help wondering.

She looked at him now, an island of quiet concentration, seemingly detached from the popping and roaring of the kiln by pulp fiction and the radio, and wondered just what it would take on her part to make him snap.

Joe had read the same sentence about five times now, twice before he jumped up to stoke the kiln a few minutes ago and three times since then. Not only was he busy listening to the kiln but his mind was working the problem of how to design a form for the new kiln that would allow him to pour the back wall at the same time as the arch, so they would be one piece instead of two. He was pretty sure that the reason today's firing stalled on him earlier was because he was losing heat between the arch and the back wall and he'd love not to have that problem in the future. There must be some way to have a piece of free-floating back board that he could put behind the arch and pour castable clay down between it and the front of the catenary arch. Or arches, because he'd already decided on a double chamber, climbing kiln, where the waste heat from the first chamber would preheat the second, for fuel efficiency. Joe was all about fuel efficiency.

He heard the thundering of the flames slow down and looked up at the mirror he had on an artist's easel in the clearing beyond the kiln. He could see the flame coming out of the chimney in the mirror and right now, it was about a foot above the top. After stoking, the flame burned a good three feet above the top of the chimney so it was almost time to stoke again. Almost.

His eyes scanned the clearing under the easel. Yep, that would make a great spot for the new kiln. He'd pour a concrete slab and build a post and beam kiln shed with a sheet metal roof...... His peripheral vision caught sight of Lucy standing behind him and to the right. He was hot and tired from spending 10 hours trying to meet the needs of the kiln so she snuck into his consciousness like a breath of fresh air. "Heeeeyyyyyy, when did you get back?" he shouted excitedly and jumped up from his patio chair, propping the paperback over the arm.

Lucy noticed his huge smile and his obvious enthusiasm at seeing her and she instantly regretted the flare of temper she'd just had towards him. "About 3 minutes ago," she answered after they kissed. "I saw the smoke coming across the highway as I pulled in and thought I'd come right up."

"Smoke?" questioned Joe. "Can't be. I finished body reduction about an hour ago and I've been pushing for temperature increase ever since. So if you saw anything you saw the flame...." He stopped suddenly, as if realizing something. "Oh no, you know what you saw? You saw the smoke from the sauna. Skye went up to light it a little while ago. She was hoping you'd get back in time to take one with her."

"Maybe after I change," Lucy contemplated. She didn't want to pick across the wet grass between the kiln shed and the sauna in her high heels.

Joe looked her up and down. "Yeah, how come you're so dressed up?"

"I had that audition in Everett this morning...."

"That's right." He leaned to his left and turned the radio down.

".....and I didn't have time to change before today's matinee."

"How'd it go?"

"What?"

"The audition."

Lucy shrugged. "It felt okay." Then she shrugged again. "But you know what they say about auditions....."

"Do them and forget them, right?" Joe stepped away and glanced in the direction of the mirror again. He quickly removed a brick from the mouth of one firebox, sank a poker down into it and stirred up the glowing, almost molten-looking embers. Tiny sparks spat into the air around him and he backed his face away instinctively.

Lucy looked at her watch. "Body reduction?" she asked, mystified.

Joe turned to his pile of mill waste and grabbed a two-handed load of the 24-inch long by 4-inch wide ends of cedar. This was wood that would have been incinerated to no purpose or left to rot in great piles by the shake mills; although when Joe first moved to the Upper Skagit, he'd even found some mills buying undeveloped land to give them a place to dump their waste wood. Joe much preferred the idea of transferring the energy trapped in the wood into his pottery.

He shoved the cedar into the firebox and it dropped down onto the grate bars, crackling loudly as it spontaneously combusted. Flames shot out of the stokehole and Joe quickly replaced the brick over the mouth to contain the fire. He moved to the other firebox and began repeating the process. "Body reduction's when I starve the kiln of oxygen," he told Lucy, "to make a smoky atmosphere so I get a good, dark clay body. Least, that's the theory."

"I know what body reduction is. I just thought you did that earlier in the firing than this. Did you start late or something?"

"No, I started at 8 this morning, like I always do, but for some reason she decided to stall on me mid-day. She seems to be going up in temperature now though."

He finished stoking and immediately slipped his glasses up over his head to wipe the sweat off his brow on his upper arm. When he propped them back in place he noticed that Lucy was gazing distractedly at the kiln.

She was thinking about the fact that she had to go back down to the house and see Laura again. And probably have to talk to her. And she really couldn't see herself being anything other than rude to that woman. "Are you okay?" Joe's question effectively interrupted Lucy's thought process. She pulled her coat tighter around her, protecting herself against the chill of the early March evening. "I'm fine," was all she said.

"Skye was looking pretty grim when she stopped by earlier. I think she was hoping to get some time alone to talk with you. Maybe that would be good for both of you," Joe suggested, sensing that something was bothering Lucy.

"Maybe. How much longer have you got up here?"

"I don't know. I'll check the cones in a few minutes but a good hour at least, I suspect." He stepped in closer to kiss her once more, thinking that might make her feel better. "Say body again," he teased.

"What?"

"Go on, say it. Say body." He grinned at her. She wrinkled her brow, confused. "It's my favorite thing to hear you say," he explained.

Lucy let out a long, "Ooooohhhhhh." Now she got it. It was the way she said it that he liked, not the actual word. "You're as bad as the director at the audition today. He wanted me to say mum like you say it in American only I couldn't hear the difference. He kept saying, "mom," very slowly and distinctly and I'd say, "mum," and he'd shake his head no and laugh. So then I tried saying it the way it's written here, like "mohm," only that wasn't right either. Finally he said, "Try, M-A-H-M, mahm," and I did. And I got it right." She raised an eyebrow in irony. "Who would have thought I'd have to learn English all over again." She started to walk away, then glanced at Joe once more. "Body," she tossed out in her best British accent.

He heard that luscious O sound that she made at the front of her mouth with her lips and smiled. "Body," he said, trying to imitate her. Then he bounced hastily to the right to check the flame in the mirror again.

❦

Lucy opened the sliding glass door slowly and quietly, just wide enough to slink in sideways without being heard. Both dogs panted against the glass on the outside, wondering if they were going to be let in too but Lucy decided against that. She closed the door behind her and bent down to take off her shoes, then she tiptoed furtively across the wood-floor, wincing here and there at the tiny pieces of gravel that had been walked in from outside and were now stabbing the undersides of her feet. For all Joe's pride in his $25, garage sale vacuum cleaner, he certainly hadn't learned to use it! She sneaked around the stairwell to the front entryway of the house and began climbing the stairs with great stealth. She could see the light streaming out of the small bedroom at the top of the stairs so she knew the door was open but she hoped that Laura was so involved in her painting she wouldn't notice someone approaching from behind. If she was quick, Lucy could whip past that door and into the big bedroom on the right, change her clothes and head back down without having to say two words to Laura.

She got about half way up the stairs and Laura came into view, standing at her easel. She was sideways on to Lucy, her left hand propped on her hip as her right made loose brush strokes on the canvas. Maybe, Lucy thought, if she folded herself flat against the inside wall coming up the stairs, she could slide up them unseen. She took one more step, then swung her left shoulder around to place her back against the wall. "Woo, woo, woo, woo, woo, woo, woo!" Maggie started on the front porch. "Ruff, ruff, ruff, ruff, ruff, ruff, ruff," Max joined in. Lucy swung around, furious with them for giving away her position, but they weren't even paying attention to her. They were barking at a little pick-up that had pulled into the driveway.

"Oh hi," came Laura's voice from the top of the stairs.

Lucy turned back around and saw her standing there, pushing the hair out of her eyes with a paint smeared hand. "Hi," she snapped over the noise of the dogs.

Heavy footsteps on the front porch made her turn back towards the commotion and, just as she did, a lumbering, non-descript male opened the front door and called out, "D'you know you have a chimney fire out back!"

"I guess you get that a lot, huh?" laughed Laura.

"Uh, not really," Lucy stammered. "It's the kiln," she told the guy who was peering around the front door.

He looked up and saw her on the stairs. "Oh. Is that where Joe is?"

"Uh huh."

"Okay, I'll go up and see him..."

"And you are....?" Lucy called out before he closed the front door.

"I'm your neighbor. Ricky. Joe helped me out a month or so back when I got my pick-up stuck and I wanted to tell him about this firebrick supply house I found down in Seattle that's going out of business."

Lucy thought quickly; this must be the fellow that startled Joe out of bed that one time. Apparently Joe's having a gun hadn't put this Ricky off randomly opening the front door. But then again, he was trying to be conscientious about a possible chimney fire.

"Do you know where the kiln is?" she asked.

"Just follow the flame, right?"

"Right," said Lucy, and let him go.

She watched the dogs barrel down the front steps to follow Ricky to the kiln before she turned around again.

"Sorry if I panicked you earlier," Laura offered. "I had no idea the kiln created such a huge flame and I was looking out the bedroom window thinking, oh my god, Joe's studio's on fire, when you walked through the door."

"Mmmm," was all Lucy said as she blithely climbed the last of the stairs, swinging her shoes in her hand as if that's what she had been doing when Laura first noticed her.

"How much longer will Joe be up there?"

Lucy shrugged. "As long as it takes. That's what he always tells me."

"Oh." Laura stepped to one side, and Lucy slid past her and went into Joe's big bedroom. "Because we're supposed to have dinner with you and Jimmy was wondering when he should come over with the kids."

Lucy felt her face flame up at this news and she was glad she had her back to Laura when she received it. She set her shoes down slowly on the floor and composed herself before swinging around to look at Laura through the doorway. "You're having dinner with us?" The words sounded casual enough but Lucy felt the stricture in her voice.

"Yes, but Jimmy's made everything, so you don't have to worry. He slow-cooked a big pot of his Tex-Mex beans and he's bringing a salad and some bread. Joe and I got the idea earlier, when I was visiting with him up at the kiln…"

"I thought you didn't know he was firing the kiln."

"Well I knew, I just didn't know it made a big flame like that…"

"Oh."

"We were thinking that this way, you wouldn't have to cook. And I'd get to leave the kids with Jimmy a little longer so I could keep painting."

Lucy wasn't listening to her rationalizations; she was too busy fuming over the thought of Laura hanging out with Joe up at the kiln, finagling an invitation to dinner out of him. "Well," she said finally. "He told me he'd be at least another hour. So I'm going to change and join Skye up at the sauna..."

Laura eyes popped. "Skye's up at the sauna?"

"Yes. She lit it for us."

"That's great. I'll come up and join you guys in a while..."

Lucy sputtered; this wasn't what she wanted to have happen at all. "Well no.....Joe thinks she needs to talk to me."

"Oh I'm sure she won't mind if I'm there too. Skye and I are pretty good friends."

Lucy stuck her chin out pugnaciously. "I thought you wanted more time to paint?"

"Not a whole other hour..."

Lucy wanted to explode, to tell this woman not to try honing in on her friendship with Skye too, but she couldn't. That just wasn't her way. Instead she looked at Laura, not really believing the circumstance she was finding herself in. "Whatever," she managed to toss out, over the mix of anger and jealousy she had broiling inside of her. "I'm going to change." And she let drop the curtain that was acting as a temporary bedroom door.

Five minutes later Lucy re-emerged from the bedroom wearing jeans and sneakers and charged down the stairs at high speed. She grabbed one of Joe's wool jackets off a hook under the stairs, bobbed into the bathroom for a towel and thumped across the wood floor on her way out of the house. She banged the sliding glass door closed, hoping she'd make Laura jump so she'd make a big splotch on the Georgia O'Keeffe-style poppy she was painting upstairs.

She tugged the jacket up over her arms and slung the towel around her neck as she took the steps down onto the grass at the back of the house and began a forward charge up the trail towards the kiln shed. Now she wouldn't get a chance to talk to Joe before she headed up to the sauna because he'd be busy with that Ricky. She heard a car door close and an engine start up and swung around to see the dogs chasing up from the front of the house to join her. Maybe Ricky hasn't stayed so long, she thought to herself, before turning around to continue her journey. Dusk was descending on the valley and the thick coating of snow on the top of Sauk was bathed in the soft rose of alpenglow. Looking up at that took some of the steam out of Lucy's bad mood. Plus the dogs were demanding that she pay them at least a modicum of attention, forcing her to slow down and caress each of them behind an ear. When she sped up again, her eyes took in the intense flame coming out of the kiln's chimney. It was like looking at the sun, it was so bright, except instead of being a circle it was a tall point of yellow and orange, tipped in red, progressing to clear, colorless undulations of heat that disappeared into the atmosphere. She could see, as she got closer, that Joe had just stoked the kiln because carbon-rich flames escaped from every available opening. They blew around the mouth of both fireboxes, lingered in cracks in the walls of the chamber and licked in and out of the gaps above the peepholes in the door. Lucy wished she could vent what was inside of her this way.

Joe was standing in front of the chamber, his hands on his hips, intent on everything that was going on with the firing. Lucy watched him bend over suddenly, and pull out a brick that he was using as a peephole in the bottom part of the chamber. Flames followed the brick out of the 2-inch by 2-inch square opening and turned up, in the direction of the top of the door. Joe blew on them, forcing them back into the chamber and squinted hard into the white heat to see the pyrometric cones. The cones were narrow, ceramic posts, pyramidal in shape and about 3 inches tall, that were designed to melt and bend at specific temperatures. Joe always put a line of 4 pyrometric cones behind peepholes in the bottom, middle and top of the chamber to give him an idea of the temperature inside the kiln during the firing.

"What's it look like?" Lucy asked, as he pushed the bottom peephole back into the place.

Joe jumped at her voice, not having heard her approach over the roaring and snapping of the kiln. He turned around to answer. "Cone 4 is flat, and cone 6 is hooked." He looked at the flame in the mirror again.

"What does that mean?"

"It means the temperature in the bottom has reached 2125 degrees Fahrenheit and it's getting close to 2175, otherwise cone 6 wouldn't be hooked. But I need cone 7 to bend for the glazes to melt and nothing's happening with cone 7. Not at the bottom anyway." He pushed his lips together, dissatisfied but resigned.

"How much hotter does it have to get for cone 7 to bend?"

"It has to reach 2200 degrees."

"Oh, so not much hotter then?"

"Yeah, but those last few degrees mean the difference between the pots being fired out or not. And you know if they're not fired out, I have to re-fire them."

Lucy did know this. And she knew how frustrating it was for Joe to work so hard only to have certain parts of the kiln not get to temperature. Joe turned away from her, checked the mirror once more, then pulled the peephole from the middle of the kiln. He blew on the escaping flames and peered into the heat, bobbing his head slightly from side to side to see the cones. "Okay, all the cones are bent there, including 7," he announced. He pushed the peephole back into the opening and climbed up onto the 4 by 12, to look in at the top. Flames poured out of this peephole and Joe leaned back away from them and quickly stuffed the brick back in place without trying to see the cones. He jumped down and slapped the soot on his hands onto the sides of his jeans. "Too much backpressure," he told Lucy. "I'll check again in about 15 minutes."

He walked around the kiln to push the damper in on the chimney, hoping to force the heat down in the chamber. "Now I play the guessing game," he said.

"The guessing game?" Lucy shouted, competing against the constant sounds of the kiln and the radio in the background.

"Well if the bottom doesn't catch up pretty soon then I'm going to have flat cone 7 in the middle. Which means I have to decide how much longer to push it to catch the bottom up without over-firing the middle."

"I thought over-firing was good. I thought that's when you got those rich, drippy glazes?"

"Yeah but if I push them too far they can drip onto the kiln shelves and stick. And sometimes that means I lose entire pots. It's better to have the pots under-fired because I can re-fire them."

Lucy groaned inwardly. The last thing they needed right now was an unsuccessful firing. And a lot of re-fires would mean it was unsuccessful. Not that re-firing was hard on the pots; on the contrary, often that led to them being even more beautiful, slathering them in well-bronzed wood-ash. But it was awfully hard on sales. And even though it was still only March, Joe was voicing a lot of needs for the upcoming summer season in the pottery. He needed clay and glaze making materials, new brushes for his slips, a tune-up on his chain saw and he'd been working on her to get a lawn mower to make the place look more presentable. "I've got 5 acres," he complained, "and only a weed whacker to keep the grass down.

Trust me, you'll think a lawn mower's a great investment." But with nearly all their savings depleted at the end of the long winter, the only chance they had of affording any of this was if Joe had a firing good enough to tempt the few stragglers into the shop before the Pass reopened. Lucy looked at the flames breathing out of the peephole in the bottom of the door again. "Heat up," she willed it. "Heat up, heat up, heat up!"

"So, hey, did you see Ricky Weaver pull in?" Joe said, interrupting her mantra. He turned down the radio so they could talk more comfortably and threw himself into his chair, rocking it backwards with his weight. It was dark around them now, and the disappearance of the daylight had made it colder.

"Yes, he came into the house," Lucy answered, stepping a little closer to the kiln. "Isn't that the guy…?"

"…that I pulled out of the ditch that night. Yeah. I think he just paid me back *big* time for helping him out because he told me about this firebrick supply house down in Seattle…"

"…that's going out of business. I know. He told me too."

"Well he said they have kiln shelves for $5 a piece. $5, Lucy! Do you know how cheap that is? I paid $150 last time I bought a kiln shelf…."

"$150?!"

"Yep. And I'm going to need a stack of them for the second chamber of the new kiln, which I didn't think to add in when I got the loan. So I'm going to drive down there tomorrow…."

"To Seattle?"

"Uh huh. To check them out before they sell. And see what else this guy's got. Then I'll come over and hang out with you after your shows."

"Why don't you just ride down with me and use the Pinto after you drop me off."

"But he might have more than just kiln shelves on sale."

"You could always go back down with the truck."

"That's true." Joe did his visual check; fireboxes, peepholes, chimney in the mirror. "I might get to see you twice this week," he said with an encouraging lift of his eyebrows.

"Three times if you come for the final performance on Sunday."

"Yeah, well I don't know about that yet."

"Hmmmm."

They both stood silently gazing at the kiln, mesmerized by the heat, the glow, the smell of the cedar and the snapping of the wood as it burst into flames.

"You heading up to the sauna?" Joe asked.

"Uh huh."

"And Laura?

"Laura what?"

"Is she going too?"

"I hope not."

"Don't be like that, "Joe chided. "She's entitled to take a sauna. She's paid her dues." The rule was that anyone who put into the sauna, time, labor or materials, could use it, so Jimmy and Laura had brought over wood from their property, to fuel the stove.

Lucy shrugged. "I didn't say she couldn't sauna. I'd just prefer she did it after Skye and I were finished."

"Well maybe she doesn't want to wait that long because Jimmy's coming over with dinner."

"So I heard." Lucy's tone was icy.

"You don't like that idea?"

"I don't see why you want her around all the time….."

Joe bolted upright in his chair. "We're going to go through this again?! Now?! When I'm trying to fire the kiln?"

"I wasn't the one that invited them…"

"I thought I was doing you a favor…"

"Oh sure."

"What's that supposed to mean?"

"It's all about *me* and has nothing to do with you, being Mr. Charming so Laura will fawn all over you…"

"I can't help being charming. I thought you liked that about me."

"I did. Until…." She stopped abruptly.

"Until what?"

She clenched her teeth, stubbornly refusing to meet his gaze.

"Until *what*?!"

Lucy wanted to let it go now that she'd got this close to provoking him but she knew he'd never let her off the hook. She snapped her lips together irritably and threw him a petulant look. "Until my father told me that was an indication of how much you liked the girls."

Joe levitated out of his seat like a man on fire. "This is about something your father said?!"

He was standing just a few feet away from her, his hands splayed taut in front of him from exasperation. Lucy instinctively arched backwards. "He said he watched you talking to some lady from the Forest Service one day and he could tell from your manner how much you liked the girls." She looked down at the ground miserably. "I was humiliated when he said that."

Joe sloughed off her reply with a quick toss of his head. "Because that's what he wanted you to be." He stepped towards her, all anger gone with the toss of his head, and spoke holding his thumb pressed against his forefinger in front of his face for emphasis.

His voice was softer, gentler, but his tone was pointed, like he wanted her to get this. "This is the man who told you that the reason he hits your mother is because she knows when he's tense and deliberately provokes him to make him feel better. You didn't believe him when he told you that; what makes you think you should believe him when he's telling you I'm some kind of womanizer?"

Lucy gazed into his eyes, as if she could see the truth reflected in them, then she looked across at the kiln. Joe spun around, climbed up onto the 4 by 12 and pulled out the highest peephole once again. Ribbons of incandescent blue heat whispered around the top of the opening, all the carbon atoms having been devoured by the kiln in the last few minutes. Lucy let herself stare at the flickering blue flames while her mind churned what Joe had just said. She'd left England at the age of 22 because she didn't want her father controlling her anymore, and now here she was, six years later and 6,000 miles away, and he was still controlling her. And she was blaming *Laura* for trying to sabotage her relationship with Joe?

"Okay, I've got cones 6 and 7 down in the top and I know they're down in the middle. So let's check the bottom again." Joe stepped off the 4 by 12, folded himself in half and pulled the bottom peephole. He scrunched his face up, peering into the heat. "Alllriiiiiiiight!" he yelped excitedly. He pushed the peephole back in place. "6 is down and 7's not far behind." He hustled around to the chimney and pushed the damper in three quarters of the way.

He hustled back, driven by the fact that the end of the firing was now in sight, and plugged the intakes at the bottom of each firebox by 50 percent. Then he pulled the brick covering the mouth of one firebox and threw in a half a dozen lengths of resin-rich Doug fir followed by as much cedar as would fit through the mouth. He replaced the brick and repeated his actions in the second firebox.

Lucy watched all this with admiration. Joe could have an

electric or gas kiln, both of which just needed switches to be adjusted to change the temperature, but he chose this, this sweat-drenched, labor-intensive way of firing his pots, partly because the wood was readily available but also, Lucy suspected, because he wanted to be fully involved in the culminating stage of his pottery. "Like natural childbirth," she joked with customers.

Joe raced around to the porch of the studio and switched on a halogen work light aimed at the mirror in the woods, so he could see what was going on now that it was dark. Lucy peered through the kiln shed out to the mirror and saw black smoke pouring out of the kiln's chimney. Joe had started glaze reduction.

"Why do you use the pitch wood again?" she asked as Joe dropped more of the resinous Doug fir into one of the fireboxes.

"Because it's full of long chain hydrocarbons and you saw how I closed the damper and intakes?" Lucy nodded. "Well, that starves the kiln of oxygen so the long chain hydrocarbons can move in and fill it with smoke and carbon atoms. And at high temperature that draws the oxygen out of the clay and glazes and changes the color response." He crossed to the other firebox. "So reduction makes the reds and purples and deep blues that I like. But what's really cool," he added, his eyes shining with enthusiasm as he removed the brick from the stoke hole, "is that a reduction atmosphere will make a glaze that is glossy in the electric kiln come out matte in my kiln. And I have no idea why."

He stoked the second firebox, replaced the brick, glanced at the mirror and then pulled a dark blue and white bandana out of his back pocket. He drenched it in a 50-gallon rain barrel that he had next to the kiln shed and wiped his face with the wet cotton cloth, smearing soot from his forehead over his nose and cheeks. He moved it around to the back of his neck and doused that too and finally, he folded it into a long length and tied it around his forehead like a sweatband. He looked quite the sight, tired, grimy and drippy from the water on the bandana, but Lucy felt suddenly very tender towards him. "I'm sorry," she said as he moved towards his chair.

"'Bout what?"

"About earlier."

"Ach!" he puffed dismissively as he sat down. "It wasn't your fault." Then he tipped his head down and looked at her over his glasses. "It was your father's."

Lucy nodded. She knew he was right.

"Forty minutes, then I'm done," he told her as he picked up his book. "So you'd better go take your sauna."

"Okay. But first I'm going to get Laura."

"Sounds like a plan," Joe looked at the mirror one more time then looked down at his book.

❧

There was renewed joy in Lucy's step as she picked her way across the graveled lane and the grass in the dark, heading for the house. The dogs cavorted beside her, glad that her spirit was back, and barked and jumped at each other in their excitement. She didn't get as far as the back porch before Laura appeared in front of her, carrying a towel over her right arm. "I was just coming to get you!" Lucy exclaimed.

"Perfect timing then," replied Laura with her usual warm smile. "I borrowed a towel. I hope that's okay?"

"Of course. And Joe said he's 40 minutes away from finishing the firing."

"And Jimmy said he's going to feed the kids now and bring the food over here right after."

"Great. Let's go and sauna then."

Lucy turned and the two women fell in step behind the dogs. Part of Lucy wished that Laura had grabbed a flashlight as well as a towel but the dark was not unpleasant and the sky was beginning to fill with a myriad of tiny stars, prelude to the arrival of the moon no doubt, which would light their way back down to the house after the sauna.

"Can I ask you something?" said Laura.

"Okay," agreed Lucy.

"Are you jealous of me?"

Lucy was grateful for the dark now, hoping that it was hiding any outward sign of shock she might have on her face as a result of this question. Her mind raced the choices she had for a reply. She could just not answer, she could lie, she could rebuff the accusation, or she could be honest and get this over with. "Yes," she said finally.

"Well you've no need to be," Laura assured her. "I love Jimmy with all my heart and there have been many times when I've been jealous of other women's intentions towards him, so I know where you're coming from. But he's proved to me, over and over again, that he's just a faithful, loving soul mate - you know, real true blue – even though he's good looking and a lot of women notice him. And

I'm sure that's true of Joe too. Which means that even if I were interested in him romantically – which I'm not – he wouldn't be interested in me. So you have no reason to be jealous."

Lucy's emotions spun like a whirligig at a fair, from feeling awkward about the conversation to feeling complete awe for this woman who was trying to alleviate her fears without sounding judgmental or superior. She wondered if she would ever be so self-assured to do that for another woman. "I know," she admitted, looking Laura directly in the eye.

"And to be honest, you're all that Joe talks about."

Lucy laughed. Some part of her knew this to be true but she was flattered nevertheless. "How boring," she joked.

"Sometimes, yes," Laura joked back.

"Well," declared Lucy. "I suppose we'll just have to go and purge all this nonsense in the sauna and see if we can't help Skye do the same thing with whatever's bothering her."

Joe glimpsed them passing by the kiln, their body language a refection of their reconciliation, and he felt relieved. Neighbor problems were rife in the Upper Skagit and it would be too bad to have one based on something that wasn't even true. Plus he didn't like to think of Lucy as the jealous type; he hadn't expected that of her and it made him wonder what else she might be hiding that he wasn't expecting. He looked back down and read a sentence in his book but the words didn't register. He thought about the design of the house Jimmy and Laura were building. Then he thought about his new kiln again.

Two chambers, for sure, with a firebox at the entrance to the first chamber that would be arched instead of rectangular. He'd start the fire down in the ash pit and keep stoking there until the temperature reached about 1,000 degrees, then he'd switch to stoking on grate bars. Drafts at the side of the firebox would pick the flames up and push them through the chambers and if his math was right and he built it correctly, he'd have a 40-foot flame from firebox to chimney at the height of the firing. He glanced down at the words on the page in front of him, then back up again. He couldn't wait.

He let his book drop down onto his lap and thought about how many times he'd fired this old kiln over the years. It had to be about once a month for eight years. And it held approximately 150 pots.

So that would make how many hundreds of pots that it had fired for him? Joe worked the problem for a couple of minutes then decided that nope, he wasn't gonna do that kind of math after almost 11 hours of constant stoking. He looked at the kiln, silently belching sooty plumes of smoke like a geriatric with indigestion and he knew it was time.

The only thing worrying him was that the new kiln would have its own set of idiosyncrasies, and Joe knew he'd have to learn those before he could get the results he wanted out of it. And he didn't know what that would mean for his pottery. He stood up to stoke and felt the inside of his stomach clench.

The unexpected at work *and* at home; what in the world was he getting himself into?

Lesson 13

Unloading the Kiln

After all the hard work that went into creating your pots, what will you find when you open the door to your kiln? A good surprise or a not so good surprise?

Spring came shyly to the Upper Skagit, like a young girl unsure of her beauty. A few crocuses here, the fleeting glimpse of a robin or two there and a yeasty scent to the earth that suggested new life fermenting. Then she gathered her courage and burst onto the scene with pom-poms of bright green at the ends of all the branches on the conifer trees, sunny yellow daffodils and elaborate white and pink blossoms on the apple and cherry trees.

Further down river, in the rich agricultural soil of the valley basin, spring came in fields of glorious, colorful tulips and brought people from all over to gaze in admiration. Joe's parents, Frankie and Betty, had come this year to see their son and join in the festivities surrounding this season that for so many, meant a fresh start and a new beginning. For Lucy it meant the time had come.

"Are we ready?" Betty asked, with the same wide, warm smile that Lucy saw so often in Joe. The older woman's hair was a billow of white on top of her head and she was diminishing in size as she slid towards her seventies yet Betty could still soften hearts with that smile. And she was definitely the source of Joe's good looks.

"Almost," Lucy answered as she dashed across the living room to Joe's cash jar. She took off the lid and pulled out a handful of dollar bills, then counted them. $9 in all. Oh well, at least she'd have something with which to make change if anyone bought pots today. Betty was wearing a loose, blue cotton skirt and flowery blouse and Lucy glanced out the picture window at Sauk Mountain as she slipped the money into her purse. The sun was gaining height over the mountain and filling the valley with an alluring April radiance but that didn't necessarily mean it would be warm today. "I've heard it can be very windy down in the fields," she warned Betty.

"Well, I've got my raincoat," Betty responded, lifting a summery-looking piece of outerwear off one of the stairwell hooks and folding it over her arm. Then she bent forward and picked up her camera and purse from the bottom of the stairs.

Lucy discreetly grabbed a second wool jacket. Betty was soft-spoken but she was also somewhat indomitable and Lucy didn't want to waste time arguing. Plus she really wasn't sure that she was right about the weather in the tulip fields since she'd never been there before either.

The truth was that this was an excursion for both the ladies, although Lucy would be working while she was down in the fields. Joe's artist friend, Luther, had won the inaugural Tulip Festival poster art contest and, as a result, had been selling posters and t-shirts from a table in one of the tulip fields for the past 19 days. He'd included some of Joe's pottery on his table but hadn't had any luck selling them and with this being the last weekend of the Festival, he'd approached Lucy about coming down to sell the pots. Since Betty was an ardent gardener and lover of flowers, Lucy agreed and offered to take her down too, so she could tour the flowers while Lucy sat with the pots.

"Should I bring my umbrella?" asked Betty, again with that same smile. Lucy looked at her; she had no idea. "It is April, after all," Betty added.

"Yes," nodded Lucy, "maybe you should." Umbrellas had really become a thing of the past for her, since Joe favored fedoras against Washington's constant drizzle and had taught Lucy to favor them too, but she could imagine that Betty would not want to wear anything that might affect the bouffant nature of her hairstyle.

Running through a mental list to double check she wasn't forgetting anything, Lucy slipped the strap of her purse over her head to hang at a diagonal across her torso and picked up both the jackets. She threw a last eye across the room and saw the notebook sitting on the table under the picture window; she would need that for recording sales. She crossed quickly to pick it up and then hesitated, thinking, wondering, enjoying the warmth spilling onto her face through the window from the sunshine. She looked up at the fresh bud burst on the cedar trees behind the house. Yes, she told herself determinedly, if this weekend proved to be good for them financially out in the tulip fields, then she'd definitely put her plan into action.

Joe pulled a peephole from the door of his wood-firing kiln and the heat came out with a quiver to meet the April morning. Stepping up onto his 4 by 12 he raised a flashlight level with his eyes and shone it down through the empty peephole to glimpse portions of the newly fired objects. He could definitely see glassy surfaces, suggesting the pots were fired to temperature. "Those don't look so bad," he muttered. He tipped the flashlight and his eyes up to see the unglazed foot of a cereal bowl. "Little under-reduced in the clay body, but still…." He raised himself up on tiptoe and brought the left side of his face even closer to the inside of the kiln, tucking the flashlight under his nose as he pointed it down and to the right. The light caught the curve of something in porcelain, something that looked good and fired-out, as far as Joe could tell, and had maybe just a hint of….yep, just a hint of red. "That's got potential," he told himself.

He tried shining the flashlight further down into the kiln but couldn't see anything other than the dark. He really wanted to find out whether that ominous sound he had heard towards the end of the firing was a kiln shelf collapsing – or worse – a kiln shelf collapsing on the little pinch pots he'd had a group of preschoolers make on their field trip to his studio. But the kiln was too hot to be opened yet and the peephole didn't give him access to anything more than was what directly behind it so he'd just have to wait.

He leaned right and picked up a half size firebrick he had sitting on top of the firebox, then pushed it into the peephole. Now the kiln could vent, but not too quickly. He stepped down off the 4 by 12 and slapped at his thighs, to remove some loose soot that had landed there. The slapping liberated an accumulation of clay dust from his jeans but basically just smeared the soot deeper into the weave of the fabric and allowed the black on his fingertips, that he'd got off the peephole, to add to the general broad-stroke smudge. Joe glanced at the tips of his fingers then rubbed them on the loose folds in the back of his jeans. "May as well make it even," he said to no one in particular.

"Your mother will have a fit when I tell her."

Joe had been so absorbed in his early morning aloneness that the sound of his father's voice caused him to jump. He swung around to find the tall, white-haired, ex-football coach taking a long drag on his cigarette as he pointed at the kiln. "She wanted to be here when you opened it," he explained.

"I'm not opening it..."

"Oh."

"I'm just helping it vent so I can open it tomorrow. It takes a good 36 hours for the kiln to get cool enough for me to open it without breaking all the pots. I told mom that already. Besides, I thought she was going to the tulip fields with Lucy today?"

"Uh huh. They left already."

"Oh. You didn't want to go see the flowers, huh?"

Joe's father made a face that suggested that wasn't it. "The Queen decreed," he explained.

Joe laughed. He could imagine his mother telling Frankie what to do with his day.

"I would have thought she'd want you there to chauffeur her around and take her out to lunch."

His father exhaled long and contemplatively, letting the fact that he would never argue with a decree go unspoken.

"Did you get any breakfast?" Joe asked, spitting down onto the gravel a few inches away from where his father was in the process of extinguishing his cigarette.

"I got my coffee at the motel," replied the coach. His voice was gravelly, from years of smoking, and even though he was still tall, taller than Joe by a good 4 inches, he was stooped, from age and from the weight of the belly he now carried around. Joe was a very visual person and preferred to think of his father as the paragon of athleticism he had been during his childhood. He hated what age and retirement had done to the old man.

"I'd say we could go for a ride up into the mountains but I'm not sure we'd get too far," Joe mentioned, glancing up at the snow-covered top of Sauk as they strolled alongside each other back towards the house.

"I thought you'd have to work."

"Nope. Typically I take the day after firing the kiln off."

"Well, I'm happy sitting on your front porch, counting the cars going by with campers on them. Where're they headed this time of year?"

"Over to Eastern Washington now that the Pass is open. To go fishing."

"Fishing," Frankie repeated, stopping to catch his breath. "You don't want to go fishing?"

"Yeah, but nothing's open around here yet. And I'm not driving over to Eastern Washington." He looked at his dad, who was pulling his cigarettes out of his shirt pocket. "Not unless you want me to," he offered.

"Noooooo," his father assured him. "We'll do that when Mame's around." He released a cigarette and tapped the filter end on the box before putting it in his mouth. He nodded towards Joe's house. "I had no idea it was going to be so big."

"Doesn't seem that big when I'm inside though," said Joe.

His father lit his cigarette, inhaled deeply then pulled it out of his mouth to speak. "Maybe it's the shop, taking up some of the downstairs."

"Yeah. That could be."

"It's impressive," his father remarked.

Joe accepted the compliment without comment, knowing this was his father's way of saying he was proud of him. He waited patiently for Frankie to build up the strength to walk again. Frankie was the same age as Betty, 66, but years of abusing his body with alcohol and tobacco had certainly taken their toll.

"We could go to the grocery store in town," his father suggested. He began moving towards the house again. "Get some lunch meats."

"You might have to front me the money till Lucy gets back from the fields."

"I'm paying," his father stated.

Joe opening his mouth to speak then thought twice about it. He wasn't going to argue with that.

※

When Lucy turned into the Van Daveers' tulip field she and Betty had the same response to the blaze of color in front of them. "Ohhhhh," they sighed. It was like a sand painting made out of row upon row of orderly flowers opening their petals to the sun to form a wide swatch of red, next to a swatch of soft pink, then purple, yellow, lavender, ivory, until the colors became just a hue on the horizon and Lucy knew they would have to get out of the car and walk to see the rest of the painting. It was nothing short of breathtaking.

Sunlight filled the field and Mount Baker sat in the distance, white and flat-topped, like a beacon over the many-colored carpet of flowers, but the ocean air coming in from the San Juans was definitely crisp and cold. "The tulips prefer the cold," Julia Van Daveer explained to Lucy as she walked her into the field to show her where she might set up for the day. "They're a very hardy flower so the colder it is, the taller their stems and the bigger their blooms. See these," she said, stopping at the flower booth and pointing at a bunch of classically fluted, orange tulips, with petals as long as Lucy's hands. "These are our Temple of Beauty and they grow 3-feet tall in the field." Lucy looked at all the different varieties of tulips being sold on the flower stand; not only did they each have their own, very distinct color but the shape of the flowers differed in ways that Lucy had never seen before. Some had petals with pointed, star-like tips while others were alluringly plump and curvaceous. And there were tulips that didn't even look like tulips. "That's Angelique," said Julia as Lucy gazed in amazement at the smallish, pink and white blossoms that looked like a cross between a rose and a peony. "It's a double ruffle tulip and our most popular seller."

Lucy caught Betty's eye and grinned. She'd never thought of herself as much of a flower person but this was great. "I think I'd better get to work so I can buy some of these before we leave today."

"How about I buy the flowers in exchange for you lending me one of those wool jackets," said Betty with her winning smile.

Lucy slipped her arm around Betty's shoulders and pulled her close. "I'd lend you a wool jacket even if you *didn't* buy us flowers," she said.

"If you want something specific," warned Julia, waving her hand over the bunches of field-fresh tulips on the stand, "I'd buy it now." She turned to face the line of vehicles waiting to pull into the parking area. "Otherwise you might be too late." And then she was gone.

❀

Lucy had a splendid day. Everyone seemed in such good spirits being out in the flowers, even though most of them had to wait to park and then got their feet muddy and wet, picking across puddles in the rutted topsoil surrounding the bulbs. But they couldn't have cared less. The tulips screamed springtime and being there at the peak of their bloom on one of the first sunny days of the month just perked everyone up.

Betty spent most of the morning out in the field, photographing the different varieties of tulips. She came back to share lunch with Lucy and then declared she was going to walk down the road to explore an art show in a barn. Lucy was pleased that Betty was enjoying herself, particularly since she'd been too busy with customers to entertain her. And when she wasn't busy with customers, she spent her time people watching. The women selling Luther's poster art had lent her a card table for the pottery and Lucy set it up at a diagonal, a few feet away from their stand. From this position she could see the people coming into the field to her right, the flower booth directly opposite her and the field of flowers to her left. People would walk into the field and Lucy would watch their faces light up immediately at the sight of so much color. Some would venture over to the sales booths or the port-a-potties but most would head straight out to the tulips as if hypnotized by their beauty. Eventually, after they'd had their fill of walking around the perimeter of the flowers, taking photographs and jotting down the varieties that appealed to them most so they could order bulbs for their own gardens, the people would head back towards the booths and shop. Lucy made $100, had some great conversations and was pretty sure she secured potential customers for the shop upriver, even though she only had a dozen or so pots on her little card table. There was one piece, a teapot, on which Joe had drawn tulips and everyone wanted to look at it. Nobody bought it, probably because they wanted pieces to hold their just purchased, cut tulips, but it certainly drew their attention. Lucy made a mental note to let Joe know as she packed up the pieces that were left at the end of the day and carried them back over to the t-shirt stand. "Are you coming back tomorrow?" one of the ladies asked.

"Oh yes," Lucy replied. "Definitely."

But when Lucy went down the next day, somebody had set up her little table a long way away from the t-shirt stand, putting her out in a place where nobody really saw her. She sat all morning, watching people do their thing of coming into the field, glancing at the booths, heading for the flowers, then coming back later to shop. She waited, thinking that as the numbers grew, somebody would come over and look at the pottery but when noon rolled around and nobody had even glanced her way, she packed up the pots and headed back upriver. At least she'd had one good day.

While Lucy was driving back upriver, Joe was starting to unload the kiln. The first thing he had to do was take the door apart, brick by brick. He worked quickly, removing the bricks in pairs and knocked them against each other to get rid of the clay that he'd pushed between them before the firing to hold them in place. Then he stacked them in groups, according to size, on a shelf to his right. The pots tinkled as the cold air from outside rushed in and touched their warm surfaces and Joe stopped every now and then to peer inside and see what was waiting for him.

"D'you have to do that every time?" his father asked, nodding at the bricks in Joe's hand. He was sitting on an upturned milk crate, smoking a cigarette, while he watched his son climb up and down on the 4 by 12.

"What? Brick and unbrick the door of the kiln?"

His father nodded.

"Yep. Every time I fire her up. And it's a pain in the butt....." Joe stopped talking to look down deeper into the kiln but it was still too dark to see anything. "...all the up and down and back and forth."

"Will you have to do that twice in the new kiln if you have two chambers?"

"Maybe." Joe scrunched up his face as he looked towards the back of the shelves that he'd already exposed. Frankie watched the dogs sniffing across the surface of the gravel outside the kiln shed. "My friend, Pete, has been talking to me about that. Turns out he put himself through school working as a welder and he thinks he can weld me some frames that I can fill with firebricks so I'll have doors that'll swing open and closed on the new kiln."

Frankie contemplated this as he inhaled one last time. He flicked the end of his cigarette out onto the gravel and both dogs looked up, then decided against going over to investigate. "You got what you need to build that kiln?"

"I've got a lot of it. That firebrick supply business that I was telling you about had insulated firebricks for thirteen cents apiece, so I loaded up. They're all arches, which means they narrow at one end, but I can just put two together to make a regular shaped firebrick and use those for the doors. And he *gave* me two palettes of hard bricks."

"I saw them."

"Plus I got a bunch of kiln shelves..."

"That's what those white slabs are?"

"Uh huh. You should have seen Lucy's Pinto when I had it loaded with those. It came home like this...." and he put his forearm in the air, sloping sharply down from the hand to the elbow to demonstrate the angle of the weighted trunk of the car. "For five bucks each I bought every one he had."

Frankie laughed and the laugh turned into a cough and the cough started to rack his body. He reached into his jacket pocket, pulled out an inhaler and spritzed it into his mouth. The coughing subsided.

"You okay?" Joe asked, a brick in each hand as he stood and watched his father.

"I'm fine," Frankie snapped back, returning the inhaler to his pocket.

"I just need the castable," Joe went on as if their conversation had not been interrupted. He was down to the bottom half of the door now. "And this guy in Seattle, even though he's going out of business, he says he can order it for me at a discount. So I'm going to......" Joe stopped, seeing something in the kiln. "Aw, shit!" he groaned.

"What?"

"I think I've found out what made that noise." Joe's head bobbed this way and that, trying to get a better angle on the collapsed kiln shelf, but it was no good. He was just going to have to wait until he unloaded down that far. At least it was below where he'd put the preschoolers' pots. "Wouldn't you know it," he muttered, turning to shelve the bricks in his hands.

Frankie made a "huh?" sound, like he had no idea what Joe was talking about. But he didn't ask. He pulled another cigarette out of his pack and lit it.

Suddenly both dogs perked up their heads, looking down towards the front of the house, then took off, barking. "Is somebody here?" Joe asked of his father.

Frankie peered down the graveled lane towards the front of the house. "Could be your mother, coming up for the unloading."

"Finally. I thought for a moment you'd forgotten to tell her."

"Noooooo," Frankie exclaimed. "She just had to finish her lunch, is all. And do her hair. Her lipstick. Use the powder room." Frankie paused, tipped his head down and looked at his son over his glasses. "You know how it goes."

Joe nodded. He only had two more rows of bricks and the door would be off. He looked down towards the house, trying to see what had set the dogs off. "I don't think it's Mame they went after. I think someone may have pulled in." He listened for a moment. "I'd better go check it out."

He jogged down the hill to find the dogs hovering at the door to the Pinto as Lucy tried to get out. Joe scooted them out of the way opened the door and immediately leaned down towards Lucy. Her green eyes searched his face for some sign of trouble, he seemed so anxious to see her. "The preschool pots are fine," he reassured her.

Lucy had forgotten about Joe's fears for the preschool pots but she was glad that they had come to naught. "That's good," she told him. "So you opened it already?"

"I'm still taking the door off. But I can see in to the little pinch pots and they all seem fine."

"And that noise?"

Joe backed up to give Lucy room to get out. "Yeah," he admitted, "there's definitely a kiln shelf that's tipped but I can't see what that means for the pots yet. I'll find out once I start taking the shelves apart."

Lucy pulled a sleeveless down jacket off the passenger seat of the Pinto and slipped it on, popping four buttons towards the bottom closed in preparation for following Joe up to the kiln. "I'm not too late then."

"For the unloading? No." Joe slammed the door of the Pinto closed. They fell in step beside each other, the dogs trotting ahead of them. "Isn't this kind of early though for you to be finished in the fields?"

Lucy wrinkled up her nose as she looked at him to answer. "I wasn't doing any business."

"Really?!"

"No. Nobody was even coming over to my table."

"Huh." Joe looked up towards the mountain, but it was hidden completely by mist. The air felt cool too, like it was going to rain again. "Was it cold down there?" he asked.

"Not too bad. But I just didn't want to sit there getting bored so I thought I may as well come and give you a hand with the unloading."

"I'm glad you did."

"Are your parents up at the kiln?"

"My dad is." Joe bent over on the fly and picked up a short length of vine maple that was lying in his path. He flung it far across the rose garden, towards the woods and both dogs gave chase. "But Betty still hasn't showed up. My dad says she's on her way though."

And Betty was on her way, in a manner of speaking. She'd just slipped her camera strap up onto her wrist and was about to open the sliding glass door when she saw Lucy and Joe walking up the driveway together. Lucy was wearing her green jacket and Joe had on one of his wool shirts. Betty glanced at the sky; it did look a little overcast for a cardigan, particularly one as thin as the one she was wearing. She walked over to the stairwell, took down her raincoat, pulled a silk scarf out of one of the armholes and looped it around her neck, crossing it in the front. Then she slipped on the raincoat and buttoned it.

She picked up her camera and was heading towards the back door again when the tulips that she and Lucy had brought back from the fields the day before caught her attention. There were two varieties, the pink and white, double ruffle Angeliques and a lavender tulip with white tips called Catherine's Radiance, both of which Betty had arranged in a bulbous, blue and green stoneware pitcher that Joe had made, one which reminded her of a milk pitcher in a Vermeer painting. The flowers were sitting in the center of the table under the picture window and had opened to the light, revealing their inner petals and stamen. Betty decided she needed a photograph. She held the camera up to her eye and pushed the shutter release but nothing happened. She looked at the image counter on the back of the camera; sure enough, she had used up all thirty-six on this roll of film. She must have taken more pictures down in the tulip fields than she realized.

She spent the next few minutes changing the film in her camera and then went back to snapping the flowers on the table. When she was satisfied she'd got at least one good photograph, she made her way out to the back porch to go up to the kiln. She took the first of the four steps leading from the porch to the ground and stopped to admire the cherry blossoms on the tree right in front of her. They were magnificent. She lifted the camera up to her eye once more and was about to take a picture when she glimpsed a tiny bird, frolicking in a thimbleful of rainwater on an upturned bucket. She held her breath in wonder as he hovered in the air, dipping and dragging his feet, then splashing the moisture over the rest of his petite frame with what could only be described as euphoric flapping of his wings. This is what she needed to photograph but would the click of her camera disturb his bathing activity and cause him to flee?

Betty stood holding her breath, completely enraptured by the little bird. She realized she was smiling, amazed at the gravity defying act of physics happening in front of her. What it must be to be a bird. Although she imagined she'd rather be a peacock with those highly decorated feathers that she could strut around and show off to people than this little house finch or whatever he was. Didn't Joe have a book of birds? Specifically birds of the Northwest? Maybe she could look this one up.

Just as Betty was preparing to risk it and take a quick photo of the bathing beauty she heard a noise that caused her to jump and the little bird to head for the trees. It sounded like a cross between a pop and a small crash preceded by what may have been an angry utterance. Her head swiveled automatically to the left, suggesting that the noise had come from a place close to the kiln shed. Betty waited, wondering if the noise would repeat itself, or if the bird would come back. When neither happened, she made a gentle smacking sound of resignation with her lips, for the moment that was now lost to her, and climbed down one more step. Then she remembered the cherry blossoms. She looked up at the exquisite, multi-petal, white blossoms and wondered if this might be the best angle for her snapshot. Maybe she could take a close up from here and then another one, of the entire tree, from further up the path. She also liked the daffodils in the rock planter that Joe had created around the base of the tree. If she stood far enough back, she could capture the cherry blossoms *and* the daffodils.

But as soon as she lifted her camera up to her eye again, she heard the second yell/pop/crash. "What *is* going on?!" she muttered.

Abandoning her photographic aspirations, Betty climbed down the last two steps and began walking towards the sound, having determined that it was, indeed, coming from Joe's kiln. She'd only gone about a dozen steps when she heard what sounded like a curse and then she saw something fly through the air and land with a loud pop and crash on the ground about a hundred feet ahead of her. Betty stopped, to ascertain that there weren't going to be any more flying objects, and then continued forward, curious about what lay broken on the ground. She got as far as the connection between the footpath from the house, the graveled lane and the fence at the bottom of Joe's garden when she realized, with horror, that it was a pot! A pot that Joe must have just taken out of the kiln and decimated without even wondering whether she, his mother, might like to look at it. This was not good.

Betty started forward, hopeful that she could retrieve the pieces and glue it back together when she was halted again, this time by a stream of foul words coming from her son's mouth, words that he had most definitely *not* learned from her. She watched another pot careen through the air to land with that heart wrenching pop crash sound on the ground, and then another. And another.

Fixing her eyes on the broken pots, Betty pushed her lower lip up as she quietly considered the situation. The dogs trotted over to her, glad to escape all the commotion at the kiln and, without taking her eyes off the pottery shards, she reached her hand out to scratch Max on the head. His coat was thick and soft, a collage of brown and white patches over his chunky part-Pit Bull, part-Chow frame. He was one of the gentlest dogs Betty had ever met yet Joe told her that many of his customers pulled in, took one look at Max and were instantly intimidated. So Joe had taken to drawing with colorful markers on Max's head and the drawings made people shelve their prejudices and warm immediately to the friendly dog. Today, Max was sporting an orange tulip with green leaves on the wide expanse of white above his eyes. Betty smiled indulgently down at the artwork and caressed the underside of the dog's jaw then jumped as she heard another pot crash to the ground. Maybe she wouldn't go to the kiln opening after all, she thought to herself. She made another soft smacking sound with her lips and turned to head back towards the house with the dogs. Maybe she would sit and read the Sunday newspaper instead.

❦

Frankie and Lucy waited silently as Joe pulled one damaged pot after another out of the kiln and hurled them into the air behind him. Lucy flinched every time his arm swung and jumped when the pot hit the ground but that was just reflex on her part. She didn't blame him. She could imagine his frustration; all that work for nothing. Part of her wished he would at least let her look at the damaged wares, in case she could salvage them somehow. But if the finished product aggravated him enough that he felt the need to toss it, then she should let him vent and keep her mouth shut. Sol had told her that it was best not to argue with an artist over how they chose to deal with their work and she had taken that advice to heart.

While she waited for Joe to get past the damaged pots, Lucy turned and picked up one of the small, jagged-edged bowls made by the preschoolers. It was about as wide as the palm of her hand, with sides about 2-inches tall and the clay on the outside was lined with flattened creases. Frankie watched as she turned it over and around in her hand. "See these marks on the outside?" Lucy said to him when she realized he was watching. "I bet they came from the plastic wrap that Joe put inside the little yogurt cartons so he could get the pots out once the kids had finished making them. He showed them how to roll out coils and dots of clay and then push them into the yogurt cartons and pinch them into a bowl." She held the little pot on the palm of her hand in front of him. "That's why they're called pinch pots."

Frankie acknowledged this with a flick of his eyebrows then put his cigarette to his lips and inhaled.

"Hey, make sure those stay together," Joe said, nodding at the preschool pot as he hustled past Lucy, heading for the studio.

Lucy peered into the kiln now that Joe was out of the way.

"Did he get all the damaged pots out?" Frankie asked.

"It looks like it," she replied, "but I can't really tell. Sometimes if a pot bursts during the firing, he finds little pieces of it stuck to other pots that weren't even close to it in the kiln, so who knows what else might be in there. He's got two lifts left to unload."

"I don't think I'd be able to throw the pots away like he did if I'd made them," Frankie remarked.

"Nah," was Joe's comment as he strode back into the kiln shed carrying a piece of paper with an order written on it. Lucy moved out of his way and Joe straddled the 4 by 12, sat down on it and placed the order on the plank in front of him. "You're not supposed to be attached to the object, only the process," he told his dad, "because the object can come out disappointingly – like you saw," he waved his hand towards the broken pots on the gravel. "Or it can be taken away from you." He reached into the kiln. "But the process can't."

He pulled out a mug with a name carved on it and put it on the 4 by 12 next to the order. Then he looked up at his dad. "And I bet you went to plenty of games where your team lost. But did you let that stop you from wanting to coach?"

Frankie shook his head; nope. "Do you often get that many total losses?" he asked, nodding towards the pots on the ground.

"Not usually, no." Joe crossed his fingers *and* his arms in front of him as he said it then went back to pulling mugs out of the kiln. "But I get a lot of pots that don't come out the way I want. Like that bowl I had Lucy put on the bench seat over there...." They all looked to Lucy's left, at a large, shallow serving bowl that was a dirty, mustard yellow in color. "I pictured that way different when I made it than it came out. But...." He tipped his hands up into the air. "Oh well." He took another named mug out of the kiln. "I'd say a good firing is when twenty percent of the pots realize the potential I saw for them in my mind's eye."

"Twenty percent," mused Frankie. "That's not that many."

"Yep. And that's a good firing. I get a lot of firings that I consider not so good." He reached deep into the kiln once more with his left arm. "Fortunately my customers don't see it that way because everything sells."

Joe looked down at the accumulation of mugs in front of him and then at the order. "Wouldn't you know it," he grumbled. "I've got three Freds and no Mary or Theresa."

Lucy looked over his shoulder at the names written on the piece of paper, then at the mugs. "And one of the Freds has got a goober on the inside of the lip," she remarked.

"It does?" Joe leaned forward and saw the offending shard. He picked the mug up and tossed it out onto the gravel. "Not any more it doesn't."

❀

The next day, Lucy and Joe worked alongside each other to clean up after the firing. Joe removed shelves from the kiln, knocking off bits of melded clay and glazes with a wide chisel as he found them, while Lucy priced the new wares and stacked them in fruit boxes ready to take down to the shop. The sun was out, making it warm and full of the sharp, tangy scent of cedar in the small space under the metal roof. Lucy was enjoying herself but she wasn't so sure about Joe. He had a subdued look to him today, with a slump to his shoulders that wasn't usual. "Are you all right?" she asked, glancing in his direction as she set a mug down on top of another in one of the boxes.

"Yeah," he sighed. "I just go through letdown after a firing, is all. And not because it was good or bad but because it's over."

"I know that feeling," Lucy sympathized. "I get it after a show comes down."

"Yep." Joe leaned the shelf he'd been working on up against the others he'd already taken out of the kiln. "And then you go onto the next show and I go back to throwing pots and we're over it, right?"

"Usually, yes." She looked at him then took two steps across the dirt floor of the kiln shed and straddled the 4 by 12 behind him. She sat down and slipped her arms around his waist, clutching him in a hug as he rested one of his hands on her forearms. His back was broad and muscular and she turned her head to lay the side of her face up against it, enjoying the feel and smell of him. "Are you going to throw again tomorrow already?"

"No. I thought that since you're here till Thursday I'd take a couple of days off and we could maybe drive over the Pass with my folks."

Lucy squeezed him tighter. "I like that idea."

"And then I pick up Maddie on Thursday. She always seems happiest when she's hanging out in the studio with me, maybe because that's where we bonded when she was a baby." He ran his hand once up and down her forearm. "Maybe. So I figured I'd go back to making pots when she was here, that way my parents can see their son *and* their granddaughter playing in the clay."

Lucy sat up and gave him a loud kiss between the shoulder blades, then rubbed her hand over the spot where she'd kissed. She stood up and went back to the mugs she'd been pricing, leaving Joe to extract the final shelf from the kiln and run a chisel over it.

Once he'd leaned that shelf up against the pile, Joe stood up to help Lucy put pots into the garden cart. This was his preferred way of transporting his pots down to the shop, in a square, 4-foot by 3-foot wooden cart on two big, bicycle wheels. "You ready?" he asked.

Lucy nodded. Joe stepped out of the kiln shed onto the graveled lane and Lucy passed him boxes of priced objects until he indicated that he had enough of them stacked in the cart. Then she handed him baking dishes, large bowls and planters, filling the free space around the boxes until they had their first load.

The cart had a strong, metal handle bent into a 3-sided square. Joe tipped this up just enough for the wheels to want to start drifting down the graveled lane towards the house and the shop. The lane wasn't very steep but Joe used his upper arm strength to hold the downhill motion of the cart in check so the wheels wouldn't turn too fast. Lucy walked slowly beside him, listening to the pots rattling noisily against each other, a sound that could still make her nervous even though she knew nothing would break. Joe had done this too many times to allow that to happen.

"When do you have to take Maddie back to Everett?" Lucy asked as they crept down the hill.

"Everett?"

"Yes. Isn't that where you meet up with her mother? At the entrance to 405 off the freeway by Everett?"

"Oh yeah, sure. Now I know what you're talking about. Sunday evening," he replied.

"I rehearse in Everett till five on Sunday. Maybe we could meet up for dinner before you drop her off."

"Okay," agreed Joe. "I think my parents would be into that too."

"Do you think they'd be into letting us go out to dinner tonight?" Lucy asked.

"All four of us, you mean?"

"No, I mean just you and me."

Joe glanced in her direction. "You want to take me out to dinner?"

"I was hoping to, yes."

"Why?"

"Why not?" She didn't want to tell him that she had something important to discuss with him because it would ruin her plan.

Joe navigated the cart around a treacherous pothole in the lane. "Okay," he said. "Let me ask my folks if they're good with getting a meal at the restaurant next to the motel tonight." He stopped, obviously thinking about what he'd just said. "That's not where you were planning on taking me, was it?"

"No. I want to go up to Bellingham."

Joe moved on again. "Where exactly?"

"I don't know," Lucy replied. "Since we only made sales the one day down in the tulip fields I don't want to go anywhere too expensive. But I would like to go somewhere nice. Somewhere we'd both enjoy."

Joe glanced at her again and could tell by the look in her eye that she was plotting something. "There's a great little spaghetti place up on the hill, overlooking Bellingham Bay," he told her.

Lucy nodded. "That sounds good."

They rounded the corner by the front of the house and the dogs, who had been keeping Frankie company on the porch while he smoked and counted camper-vans on the highway, leapt up and began to bark.

"Yeah, way to act like you were working," Joe scoffed.

"It's just us," Lucy put in, "bringing fresh pots to market."

"I see these campers going by," Frankie stated, like he was midway through the conversation already with Joe, "towing Jeeps or cars, with bicycles hanging off them, and I say to myself, there goes $30,000, there goes $50,000 and I wonder how people afford it."

"Yeah, I wouldn't be the one to know," Joe remarked.

Frankie chuckled and coughed, then took another drag of his cigarette. "Your mom went for a walk down by the river," he informed them, then fixed his gaze back on the highway while Joe and Lucy went up and down the front steps, carrying pots from the cart to the shop. The dogs lay at the far end of the steps, Maggie with her eyes almost closed as she nodded off while Max kept watch. And then they both leapt up barking again, this time at a station wagon that was slowing down to pull into the driveway. Lucy looked over her shoulder and peered into the car at the driver. "I think that's Julia Van Daveer," she told Joe.

Sure enough, the cherry cheeked, bulb farmer's head appeared over the top of the station wagon after she'd climbed out of the vehicle and petted the dogs. She was laughing as she called out, "I see someone other than me likes to wear tulips."

"What's that?" Joe said, lowering a box of mugs back down into the cart.

Julia came around the back of the car pointing at the tulip on Max's head. She laughed when she saw Joe smile at his drawing.

"You like that?" he asked.

"Oh yes," agreed Julia. "You should have him try out for Tulip Ambassador next year." And she fell about in giggles once more. She stopped laughing as soon as she and Joe got close enough to shake hands. "I'm Julia Van Daveer, from Skagit Tulip Farm...."

Joe nodded. "That's what Lucy said."

"And I was hoping to get a moment of your time."

"I'm impressed that we're getting a moment of *your* time," was Joe's rejoinder. "Isn't the festival still going on?"

"No, it ended yesterday..."

"But the flowers...."

"Oh yes, they're still blooming," Julia finished for him. Then giggled as Joe's jaw dropped. "They didn't consult the farmers when they set the dates of the festival," she explained, shaking her head as if this had been a big mistake. "We would have told them it was too early."

"Leave it to the politicians, eh?" Joe quipped and Julia laughed again. "Would you like to go inside?" he offered, stretching his hand out towards the house.

"No, I don't want to interrupt you too much," Julia said, glancing across at Frankie. Joe's dad acknowledged her with a smile and a nod, then went back to watching the highway. Julia looked at the pots in the cart and then at Lucy. She smiled and Lucy was impressed yet again with how Julia Van Daveer's eyes could convey such warmth and sincerity when she smiled. The bulb farmer turned her attention back to Joe. "I really came up to tell you that after your girlfriend left yesterday I was approached by another potter about setting up in my field. I looked all around but couldn't see the table with your pots on it and I asked the women at the t-shirt stand who told me that Lucy had left so I told this potter okay, that would be fine. He sold his pots from the back of his pick-up truck, right next to my flower booth – a big box of pitchers and vases that ranged in price from about thirty to seventy dollars - and he sold out. Which was great, I was very pleased for him. But the thing is, I like your work better and I wondered if I offered you the chance to set up in a booth right next to my flower stand, would you agree to bringing your pottery down to my field next year for the festival?"

"You drove all the way up here to ask me that?" Julia Van Daveer nodded. "Well I'm flattered," Joe responded. He pointed at Lucy. "And if I can talk my lovely assistant into helping me out next April then I'd love to have my pottery in your tulip field. I'd have to make a booth, right?"

"Yes. But you can build it in the barn on our property and store it there and my husband will move it with his tractor to whichever field we rent for our tulips next year."

Joe looked at Lucy and they nodded at each other. This was sounding like a great idea. "Okay then, sign me up," Joe told Julia. She clapped her hands gleefully. "I'm just sorry you had to drive all this way to tell me that," Joe added. "You could have just called."

"Well there was another reason I wanted to come here," Julia said, her eyes roving playfully over the pots in the garden cart. "You had a teapot down in the field, with tulips on it. Do you still have that teapot?"

"Uh huh," replied Lucy.

Julia withdrew some cash from the front pocket of her jeans and held it up grinning. "Can I buy it?"

"Twist my arm, why don't you?" Joe wisecracked.

And Julia laughed like this was the funniest thing she'd ever heard.

Maybe it was Julia Van Daveer's obvious enjoyment of life that set the tone for Joe and Lucy's dinner out or maybe it was the life-affirming feel of spring and the little bit of spare cash they now had in their pockets. Whatever it was, dinner in the homey spaghetti place in Bellingham was more fun than they'd had in a long time. They laughed and flirted, told stories and made plans as they coiled noodles thick in Bolognese sauce on their forks and pushed them hungrily into their mouths. Lucy had ordered them each a glass of red wine and when they'd finished their entrees, she took another sip of hers, sat up straight and decided the time had come.

She let the inexpensive house red sit in the back of her throat, to fortify her courage, before she swallowed, wiped her mouth with the starchy cloth napkin and looked out the window at the lights twinkling on the bay. "So," she said to Joe, batting her eyelids back in his direction. "I've found myself wondering these last couple of weeks why I got so jealous over Laura and it came to me the other day that it's because I love you. I mean, *really* love you. Enough to care about losing you. And when I knew that I didn't want to lose you, I knew I wanted to share my life with you. Soooooo," she said, running her fingers up and down the stem of her wine glass, "I asked you out to dinner tonight to tell you that if your offer still stands, I will marry you."

Joe's mouth dropped open and he sat back in his chair putting a little distance between them. Lucy had expected him to jump all over her with delight and now that he hadn't, she felt a little embarrassed. She let go of her glass and also sat back in her chair.

"Well I don't know," Joe replied finally. "I guess I'd gotten myself used to the idea of us *not* getting married, 'specially since we seem to be making it work this way. And it's made me think about all the couples we know that have relationships that are different. Like Tony and Bev. She has her own house and works here in Bellingham and he has his own house and works upriver but they're definitely committed to each other. And Dave and Shana, look at them; they lived together for 20 years before they finally tied the knot."

Lucy nodded. She was beginning to regret the wine because she was worried it was making her face flush.

Joe could see he was upsetting her and he didn't want to do that, but she had made him rethink his preference for marriage. He slipped his left hand over hers on top of the table. "I love you, you know that, but I've had one marriage go sour on me and I guess you making me wait has given me time to think. I don't want to end up with a pig in a poke."

Lucy withdrew her hand. "What does that mean? A pig in a poke?"

"You've never heard that expression? That's when someone goes to buy a pig from a farmer and the farmer has the pig in a sack, so the buyer can't really see what he's buying until the deal's done and then it's too late."

"Oh please!" scoffed Lucy. "It's not like you don't know me."

"Well I think I do…"

They looked at each other over the table. Lucy could definitely have let herself get upset at his poor choice of analogy but she knew that this was just Joe, blurting whatever first came into his mind. Besides he was right; she had made him wait. A long time. Without even an answer to his many proposals. She deserved it if he'd changed his mind. She let her eyes steal away, to a couple talking animatedly at a table alongside the wall, and somewhere behind the disappointment that was churning on the surface of her emotions, she felt a tiny glimmer of relief. Maybe it was for the best.

Joe saw her face soften as these reflections passed through her mind. He loved that about Lucy; that she would listen and think about what he'd said. He loved Lucy. And he wanted to marry her very much.

So why, all of a sudden, was he hesitating?

Lesson 14

Find Someone to Sell Your Wares

If you want to make a living at your pottery consider having someone else in charge of sales. Preferably someone who has a deep admiration for your work. And for you.

July came around and with it the urge to backpack into the high country. Lucy had a visitor from France staying with them – Véronique - an ex-student from Lucy's days of teaching English as a Foreign Language to adults in Strasbourg, and this young woman apparently loved to hike in the mountains. The two girls hadn't been that close when Lucy lived in Strasbourg but when she moved to New York, Véronique had started a correspondence with Lucy. And when Lucy moved to Washington State, Véronique had written and asked if she could come and visit. She had never had much interest in the city, she told Lucy, but she lived in the Vosges, vacationed in the Alps and would love to see the Cascades. Now Lucy and Joe, and their friend Pete, were going to try and show her the heart of the

Cascades; the wilderness.

Lucy and Véronique were all about the hiking but Joe and Pete wanted to fish, and taking a game trail across a densely wooded ridge at 4,200 feet of elevation, then side hilling down into a seldom visited cirque lake would assure them of catching as well as fishing. Pete was also interested in Véronique, although he hadn't figured out yet whether she was interested in him, but he was motivated to come along and find out. The four of them had been planning this overnighter since the weekend, when the temperature in the Upper Skagit had moved into the mid-80s, and as well as discussing how many tents they would need and who would carry what, Joe had asked Lucy repeatedly to make sure that Véronique understood just how wild the trail was. "Ah yes," the French girl assured them. "I hike many times in the Alps."

But when she came down dressed for departure early on Wednesday morning, Joe looked at her aghast. "You're not going like that!" he objected.

Véronique turned her blue eyes towards Lucy, the pale skin of her brow furrowed above an inquisitive smile. She had never been one of Lucy's best students, managing to express herself a little in English but having a lot of trouble understanding it, and the way Joe spoke obviously confused her even more. Lucy explained in French. "You can't wear shorts on this trail, it's too brushy. You'll get all scratched up."

"But I will get hot," Véronique replied, pointing out the door at the promise of another 85 degree day.

Lucy was crouched down by her backpack, tightening the front straps over her bulging sleeping bag. "It will be hot here," she grunted, pulling down hard on the straps. "But we'll be high up in the mountains. It won't necessarily be hot there. And anyway, you can take the shorts with you and change at the lake if it's hot but, honestly, you don't want to walk the trail with your skin uncovered. You should even wear a long-sleeved shirt for the hike in."

"Nooooooo," protested Véronique.

"Yeeeeessssss," protested Lucy right back. She stood up and hefted her backpack onto one shoulder. "You wait till you see the brush at the start of the trail. We're going to end up wearing gloves too."

Véronique pouted, waving her head from side to side as if she thought this was a lot of fuss over nothing, but she went back upstairs to change. Lucy and Pete carried the backpacks down from the house and handed them off to Joe, who secured them in the bed of the pick-up with bungee cords hooked onto the metal rack behind the window of the cab. It was only 7 o'clock in the morning but Véronique was right, the day was definitely beginning to heat up. "Did you get the water bottle I put in the freezer last night?" Joe asked Lucy. She raised her index finger at the reminder and jogged back towards the house. They weren't on any fixed schedule so she didn't need to hurry but there was an excitement that came with going on an adventure in the woods, an excitement that made at least the three of them keen to leave.

Véronique seemed excited for the adventure too because she came down the stairs a second time wearing jeans, a long-sleeved shirt, a straw hat and a smile. Lucy looked at the hat, wondering how it would fair if it got snagged by a branch on one of the downed trees they'd have to fold themselves and their backpacks under, but she didn't say anything. Véronique must have picked up on her reservations though because she pointed at the hat and asked, in her broken English, "Too much?"

Lucy grabbed one of Joe's baseball caps off the hooks by the stairs and held it out to Véronique with a suggestive smile.

"But my hair," the French girl groaned. Véronique's hair was a mass of short, tight, blonde curls on top of her head and Lucy couldn't imagine how one hat over another would alter their arrangement but she didn't argue the point. "You look fine," she told her friend, putting the baseball cap back on the hook.

They walked together down to the truck and joined Pete and Joe at the tailgate. Véronique pointed at the dogs. "We take?" she asked Joe.

"Oh yes." He turned towards the dogs; "Hup," he said. Max and Maggie leapt into the truck, their tails and rear ends wagging vigorously with excitement. They knew they were going somewhere fun and they couldn't wait. "We ready?" Joe asked Lucy.

"Yep," she replied.

All four of them moved towards the front of the truck and pulled themselves into the cab. Joe took the driver's seat, Lucy climbed in first on the passenger side to put herself next to him, then came Véronique, then Pete. "Everyone okay?" Joe asked, realizing that even though Lucy and Véronique were both slim enough not to take up too much space, it was still a squeeze for the three of them on that side of the bench seat.

Pete folded down the brim of Véronique's hat to make himself visible to Joe. "Yeah," he replied. "But I might ride in the bed with the dogs once we get on the logging road."

"Wait, please," said Véronique suddenly and flapped her hand at Pete to indicate that she wanted to get out again. Pete obliged, tumbling easily out of the truck as he pushed the door open, and Véronique ran up to the house and in through the front door. Just as quickly she was back out, wearing the baseball cap Lucy had offered her earlier. She ran down the front steps, across the driveway and threw herself with a big bounce back into the truck. Pete climbed in after her and pulled the door closed against himself. Véronique looked at Joe with a crooked smile. "Now we ready," she announced.

It took about an hour to drive up the narrow, winding, logging road to the trailhead; an hour of squeezing the truck past the occasional boulder that was too big to move by hand, putting it into four-wheel drive to climb over water bars and coming around corners where there were million dollar views of the mountains around them. Joe was very cavalier in his driving style, taking his hands off the steering wheel whenever he wanted, to point out a particular peak, and his eyes off the road to look up or down the mountain in search of wildlife. More than once the truck veered precariously close to the edge, threatening to pitch them all over the side, but none of the occupants of the vehicle seemed worried. Joe was used to driving these logging roads and always corrected before any of the wheels went too far from center. And Maggie, in the back, loved it because it gave her a chance to snap at leaves and branches on the trees that came too close, tearing them off with her teeth to drop into the bed of the truck.

Lucy, Pete and Véronique tumbled gratefully out of the truck once they got to the trailhead, however, mostly because they'd been so cramped, they couldn't wait to straighten out the kinks in their bodies. It was incredibly quiet at the end of the road, with a sweet, almost edible smell of warm flora, and the three of them followed Joe to stand and stare at the ridges opposite. The dogs bounded out of the truck and raced a certain distance down the logging road only to turn around and sniff their way excitedly back up, as if hoping to learn which creatures had been there ahead of them.

Pete and Lucy ambled away after a few moments, each in

search of a discreet place to water a plant, and Joe led Véronique around to the back of the truck to get the packs. He pulled himself up into the bed and kicked out all the leaves and twigs Maggie had dropped there. "Why she do?" Véronique asked as she scraped some of the foliage off the tailgate onto the ground. Joe shrugged. "I have no idea. But she's done it ever since she was a puppy."

He freed the packs from the bungee cords and moved them, one by one, to sit on the tailgate. Véronique turned around and slipped her arms through the straps of her pack. Then she took two steps forward and bounced it into position before clipping the waist strap closed. She stood, her eyes roaming every inch of the perimeter of the wide spot at the end of the logging road. Lucy was walking back up the road, Pete a few steps behind her. "Where do we go from here?" Véronique asked Lucy in French.

Lucy walked her around the truck and pointed at the basin below them at the end of the road. It was completely filled with tag alder, salmonberry, elderberry, thimbleberry and countless other wild berry bushes and brush. Lucy walked around the truck again and pulled two pairs of gloves out of the front pocket of her pack. She slipped one pair on and held the other out to Véronique, The French girl took the gloves and tucked them into the top of her jeans. Lucy hoisted her pack onto her back and turned to look at the men. They were ready.

Joe walked the width of the road and found the little piece of orange ribbon that a thoughtful hiker had tied to a branch to indicate the start of the trail. "Here we go," he called out to the others and stepped down into the brush. Both dogs hustled after him, then Pete, Véronique and finally Lucy.

It was gnarly stuff, the thicket of berry bushes; much of it was thorny and grabbed at their clothing as they walked through it, and the tag alder had roots that went down, then back up, forming hooks that tripped them if they weren't careful. And it was easy not to be careful since they couldn't see down to their feet nor the ground ahead of them for an indication of just where to put their feet. Plus the basin sloped downhill at this point, causing all four of them to stumble again and again as they'd reach a foot out to where they thought they would meet ground only to have the ground be a few inches lower than expected.

"Aiee!" cried out Véronique as the skin on her hand got bitten yet again by a prickly branch that she'd grabbed to steady herself. She stopped, examined her hand carefully for stray thorns, then put on the gloves that Lucy had given her.

"Everyone okay?" Joe called out to them.

"We're fine," Lucy called back.

They pushed on through the brush and 10 minutes later emerged into an old-growth conifer forest covering the ridge they needed to cross to get to the lake. There was undergrowth here too but, shaded by the trees, it wasn't nearly as compact as what they had just come through. Joe pointed at a leggy plant with broad, palmate leaves. "Whatever you do, don't touch that," he told Lucy and Véronique. "That's called Devil's Club and it's covered in brittle spines that break off under your skin when it's touched. And there's hell to pay trying to get them out."

He turned and began to lead them all through the woods. The path was convoluted and completely undefined other than the odd scuffing of the earth here and there where a human or maybe a deer had gone before them. Then it would disappear altogether under a downed log that they would have to climb over or crawl under to get to the next section of the path. Periodically a glimpse of orange in a tree would verify their route but really it was Joe's knowledge of the trail that was carrying them forward.

Forward and up, although not very steeply up. That was one of the saving graces of the trail. It was filled with obstacles but that just meant the four hikers had to control their balance with their packs. And it was almost entirely in shade because of the thick canopy layer of the forest, which protected them all from becoming completely overheated by the rising temperature of the day.

After about 20 minutes of steady hiking, Joe stopped by a gully where they would need to walk a log to cross and waited for the others to catch up. He took off his pack, stripped off his long-sleeved shirt and looped it through one of the straps on the pack. "Me too," said Pete when he caught up. Joe pulled out a water bottle and took a few sips while Pete shed his outer shirt. "Want some?" he asked, offering Pete the bottle.

Pete took it and tipped his head back, letting the cool water trickle slowly down his throat. "Ahhh," he breathed.

Joe stood quietly alongside Pete, his eyes cruising the forest around them for signs of wildlife while his heartbeat slowed. He heard the girls approaching before he saw them. "Everyone doing okay?" Joe asked, as they got closer.

Lucy nodded from behind Véronique. "I think I'll take my shirt off though," she told him.

"Yeah, we just did that." Joe held the water bottle out to Véronique. She took it and drank thirstily before handing it off to Lucy. Then she followed everyone else's lead and took off her long-sleeved shirt, wiping her face with it before she tucked it in her pack.

The quiet around them was broken by the sound of the dogs pushing through the brush on their way back up the side of the gully. They arrived panting and eager to lead the way on for the humans. "We're coming," Joe told them as they looked at him hopefully.

"How is this called?" Véronique asked, pointing at the lichen hanging down from a tree.

"Moss," Lucy told her.

"It is so much," her friend exclaimed. "Everywhere."

Lucy, Pete and Joe all nodded. "Welcome to the rain forest," Pete informed her.

Joe got them moving and waited to make sure everyone made it across the gully okay. Once they were all safely on the other side, he set the pace again, to move on to the top of the ridge. There was more climbing over and under logs, more pulling themselves up through rock chutes, using trees for leverage, and one long stretch of side hilling across loose dirt that threatened to slip out from under them with each step. But once they got past this, it was just a short climb before the trees became sparser, the ground softer and they were moving downhill. Rays of sunshine slipped between the trees and lit their way through the shady forest like emergency lights in a theatre. Since the trees were thinner on this side of the ridge, the undergrowth was more prolific but it didn't stop them from gaining speed as they moved downhill in anticipation of reaching the lake. An explosive beating sound startled them all into a halt and they spun their heads right to see a grouse taking off in a panic from the base of a tree. Joe looked at Lucy and nodded towards Maggie, who was pointing gracefully in the direction of the grouse, her jaw quivering. This was what he liked to see, nature in action. He clicked twice in the side of his cheek and Maggie pulled her nose reluctantly away from the direction of the departing bird and trotted to Joe's side. "Good girl," he told her, stroking her head. Then he threw his arm forward to indicate they should move on.

Forty minutes after starting out on the hike, they felt their legs brushing against low-lying, wild blueberry bushes. Joe, Pete and Lucy all recognized this as a sign that they were close to the lake. The ground in this section of the trail was pretty much flat and had a well-marked path so even though their packs were creating a burn across their shoulders and they were tired and hot, their stride took on the jauntiness of almost being there.

And then they saw it, the deep blue green of the water, like a tourmaline gemstone suspended in a setting made of rocks and trees. They arrived in a small rugged glade, with the lake up against a sheer escarpment to the left and the forest to the right and behind them. The glade was divided in two by a creek, with the area closest to them having a slightly elevated flat spot in the center of which was a campfire pit. Here was where they would pitch their tents. A couple of straggly paths led the few feet down through wild rhododendron bushes from the camping area to the lake and the perimeter of the water was almost entirely edged in crisscrossed graying logs.

Joe and Pete stood watching the lake while Lucy and Véronique went on up to the fire pit and let their packs, then themselves, slip down to the ground. The dogs were already at the creek, getting a drink. Lucy closed her eyes and tipped her head back into the sunshine. "Did you see that bear scat over by the blueberry bushes?" she heard Joe say quietly to Pete.

"I sure did."

"Pretty big pile, eh?" There was a pause, while they obviously watched the lake.

"Don't mention it to Lucy though, okay?"

"Okay."

A loud plopping noise echoed through the glade. Lucy opened one eye and watched. She heard another plop, then another and saw the men turn to each other, their jaws wide open with excitement.

"Let's go fishing!" they agreed in unison.

They each caught some trout and that evening they fried the fish in a pan over a good hot fire after Joe coated each one in a pre-mix he'd made of flour, breadcrumbs and spices. He showed the fish to Véronique before he coated them and explained that they were called Cutthroat trout because they had bright orange slashes on their gill slits that made them look literally like they had cut throats.

"I'm not sure she understands," Lucy told him, "and I don't know how to translate Cutthroat."

Pete laughed. "It's simple," he said. He looked at Véronique and made a slashing movement across his throat with his index finger. "Cut throat," he explained.

"Ahh!" Véronique's brow cleared and her face opened up as if she understood.

"She seems very interested," Joe told Lucy, lifting another fish out of his bag of flour mix and lowering it gently into the sizzling oil. Véronique was bent over beside him, her hands on her knees, watching attentively.

"That's because she's hungry, love." They'd eaten sandwiches that they'd packed in for lunch, after the guys had fished for a while and Lucy and Véronique had set up the tents, but the hike in, together with being out in nature, fully exposed to the elements, was definitely making their stomachs rumble.

"So what kind of fish is this?" Joe asked Véronique, holding up a trout before dunking it in the flour mix.

"Is good fish," Véronique replied. Then she stood up and rubbed her belly. "Good fish for me."

Joe laughed. "That'll do," he concurred.

"I can use this now, right?" Pete asked, pointing at the pot full of boiling water on the fire.

"To add to the pasta? Sure," Joe replied. "Should be perfect timing." He edged a fork around the four plump, white-fleshed trout in the pan, and the aroma of fresh fish turning crispy in hot oil hit all of their palates. Joe saw the hungry glances. "I'll cook the rest of the fish once we've had the first serving," he assured everyone.

Pete drained the boiling water into two freeze-dried pouches of pasta primavera and then refilled the pot and put it back on the fire. "For hot drinks later," he told Lucy.

"Did anyone get the plates out of Veronique's pack?" Joe asked, looking up at the French girl as he flipped the fish in the pan.

"What is?" she asked.

"Things for us to eat off? Plates," he articulated.

"Ah yes," she responded. "I have." And she picked up a small pile of mismatched metal plates, bowls and utensils that she had sitting beside her.

"I guess you were right," Joe told Lucy. "She is hungry."

"Ah yes," beamed Véronique.

❧

Someone had placed short logs on two sides of the fire pit and they ate perched on top the logs, then slid down in front of them as the evening grew cooler and the mosquitoes fiercer. They sipped hot chocolate and apple cider watching the color of the lake deepen as the sun began to move slowly behind the escarpment on the far side of the water. A pika whistled and both dogs turned their heads towards the sound, then lowered them back down onto their paws, Max groaning softly in pleasure. They had also eaten dinner; dog food that Joe had carried in for them, sprinkled with the oil from the fish frying pan.

Lucy stretched her legs out away from the fire, enjoying the inner tranquility she felt from the exertion and accomplishment of a good hike. Joe turned towards her. "Pete and I were thinking that tomorrow, if you guys are into it, we'd like to hike into the lake that's just over the next ridge. Make kind of a day hike of it from this camp, then come back, fish this lake a little more, pack up all the gear and hike out. What do you think?"

"Sounds like a plan," Lucy agreed, even though what was "just over the next ridge" to Joe was often quite the hike for everyone else. But that's what she enjoyed most about these adventures in the woods; the hiking. And she assumed the same was true for Véronique.

The morning mist was still hovering over the lake when they set out from camp the next day. Joe had risen early and practically stumbled over the dogs sleeping at the entrance to his tent. He had packed in two long lengths of rope and used them to tie the dogs to a tree for the night, so they wouldn't wander off, but looking at them sprawled out as close to him as they could be without being inside the tent, he doubted they would have gone anywhere. He was in the process of untying them when he noticed, out of the corner of his eye, that they had company. Two deer were down in the lower part of the glade, getting a drink from the creek. Joe stayed the dogs silently with his hand and stood watching the deer for what seemed like the longest time. Then one of the dogs began scratching and both deer lifted their heads, their ears flickered and turned, like radar antenna detecting a signal, and they were gone. It made Joe's day though, watching those deer be completely oblivious to his presence.

He looked for their tracks as he led the others across the creek at the start of the hike. "Yep, here they are," he told Pete. Lucy and Véronique bent forward also and saw the cluster of two pronged hoof marks in the soft, marshy ground at the side of the creek.

"They look like they were big," Pete commented.

"Pretty good size, yeah. For Blacktails."

"Did they have horns?"

"Yep. Both of them."

"Argh," groaned Pete. "That's what I get for sleeping in until I smelled you cooking the bacon."

"Maybe we'll get lucky and they'll be back for a late afternoon drink," Joe suggested as he straightened himself to a stand.

They all pushed on over the lower section of the glade and began the climb up over what was essentially a rocky cornice to the top. This definitely wasn't as easy as coming through the forest on the other side. All four of them had to be careful to lodge their feet in the crevices between the rocks and make the most of the few trees growing at odd angles on the precipice for leverage but Lucy and Véronique didn't have packs and the climb, though demanding, only took about 15 minutes.

And then they moved downhill for a similar amount of time, through terrain that was grassier, with salmonberry bushes growing here and there, until they dropped down into a long, narrow clearing that offered views of the ridges around them. Joe pointed to a big, alpine shoulder in the distance to their left; "That's where we're going," he told them.

It was warmer on this side of the ridge. Lucy and Véronique both took off their long shirts and tied them around their waists while Joe wiped the sweat off his neck with his bandana. He looked up at the sky; it was a perfect, robin's egg blue without a cloud in sight. They weren't going to get any relief from the heat today unless they found it under the trees. "Anyone need a drink?" he asked. The others shook their heads no. "Okay, then let's go."

They walked another 20 minutes in the clearing, heading southwest from where they were camped towards the ridge that Joe had pointed out. The quiet was punctuated by the sounds of insects and flies, buzzing and whirring through the brush, and the occasional trill of a songbird looking for love. Lucy let her mind wander to the guys who had stopped in the pottery shop on their way up to hike Cascade Pass a couple of days ago. Joe helped them while Lucy was upstairs, sitting on the floor of Joe's bedroom, sorting through a box of her old notebooks that her mother had sent her. Some were composition books from her English classes in high school, others were things she'd written in at home. With the theatres dark for the summer Lucy had decided to fill her time around making sales in the shop by writing, something she'd been toying with for a while now. A long while if the scribblings in the notebooks were to be believed. There were mini-plays that she'd written when she was 16, poems, ideas for stories. Lucy didn't remember any of this. Letters, that's what she remembered writing, lots and lots of letters. Lucy loved letters.

She heard Joe downstairs, asking the guys where they were from and what they did for a living and when he found out they were psychiatrists, from the East Coast, he launched into his favorite question for psychiatrists: "How come some people can carry in a six-pack of beer to a high country lake, but they can't carry out the empties?"

She heard the guys laugh then offer a disclaimer about how they didn't really do that kind of psychiatry, more the kind that would medicate the person so they wouldn't take in the six-pack in the first place, which made Joe laugh too, and she could tell that a good time in the shop was already underway.

The visitors talked about how they were a couple, but one of them was moving to Seattle and hadn't convinced the other to leave the East Coast and join him. Hence the hiking. "If I can just get him up into the woods, he might fall in love with the area and be willing to leave the rat race for here," explained the one guy. Lucy smiled to herself; he sounded like Joe. Hadn't that been part of his ploy, to get her to come out to the Skagit so she might fall in love with the area as well as him? And to a certain degree it had worked. More than once she'd found herself gazing at the mountains as she drove upriver to be with Joe, completely awed by their splendor. There was none of the elaborate, centuries-old architecture that she so loved about London but there was also none of the grime; instead the landscape was lush and pristine and had forced her, by its very beauty, to start paying attention to the natural world.

And if it weren't so hard to make a living in this area she might even consider settling here. But now that she and Joe were no longer talking marriage, she had to think of the long term and how she would pay her way through life. Here, she was a British actress looking for work in American regional theatre; in England she'd be just another British actress. What the advantage was between them she couldn't be sure but she had a suspicion she'd get more work in England. Plus there was the question of how long she and Joe could survive the rhythm of her going down to Seattle for three month acting contracts and spending just one-day a week with him. But if she weren't doing that, then what would she be doing?

She took another brown-paper covered notebook out of the box and looked at the ornate cursive on the neatly drawn line across the top; English, 1st Form, it read. She would have been eleven when she wrote in this book. She ran her fingers softly over the paper that she'd used to cover the book, still so clean and tidy, and tuned into the conversation down in the shop again. They certainly didn't seem to be any closer to talking about buying pots. Maybe she should go down and try to help Joe close the deal. Or at least meet these guys since they sounded so interesting. That was one of the things she liked most about Joe's little pottery shop; for a tiny business in the middle of nowhere it certainly drew an eclectic mix of people. And the stories they told her about their lives were often very inspiring. So inspiring that she found herself repeating them, so that others could enjoy them too.

There was definitely a connection between that and her acting because what was she doing if not telling other people's stories when she was up on stage. What she'd found stirring in her recently, though, was a desire to have the telling of the stories last more than three months. She wanted them to resonate forever. Film might answer that stirring in her but in order to act in films, she'd have to move to Los Angeles. Or back to London. And if she moved to either of those places she'd have to leave Joe. And Maddie.

Lucy sighed as she opened the notebook and began leafing through the essays. And then there was that other stirring, the one that she'd thought she'd never have. It was only faint but she'd felt it enough times since they'd been seeing Maddie for regular visits that she couldn't ignore it. It whispered her desire for a family. And the only person she could imagine having a family with was Joe. But Joe was still raw from the time he lost with Maddie and was pretty sure he didn't want to go down the parenting path again and Lucy wasn't sure that every other weekend would appease what she felt stirring inside her. Which put them where? She lifted her head and looked out the back window of Joe's bedroom at Sauk Mountain; nowhere that she could picture. She shook her head faintly as Joe and the customers laughed together down in the shop. It wasn't easy, this game of life.

She turned another page in her notebook and found an essay she'd written entitled *Love*. What could she possibly have known about love at the age of eleven, she wondered. She read the first line:

"People in families show they love each other by hitting each other."
She gasped. An icy cold touched the back of her neck and suddenly
she knew, as clear as the water that came out of these high mountain
creeks, that she'd dodged a bullet when Joe had changed his mind
about marriage. It was only a matter of time before he hit her; she
had the proof right in front of her. And when he did, that would be
her cue to leave.

Lucy read the essay, a clear, childlike account of her father
hitting her for falling down the stairs, and it made her sad. She was
such a good kid; why hadn't he been able to see that? She listened to
the guys down in the shop, laughing and joking about situations
they'd got themselves caught in when they were hiking. They were
having a really good time. Maybe she'd go and join them.

She closed the composition notebook and put it on the stack
with the others, stood up and started across the wood floor, towards
the door. She heard Joe's voice - "Quick, my girlfriend's coming –
pretend we're talking about pottery!" - and she couldn't help but
smile. He was joking of course, but then again, they had had their
share of conversations in which she had counseled him that if he
wanted to make more money in the pottery he should let the
customers shop while they talked. Or at least talk about the pottery
every once in a while. "Nah," he rebuffed. "I don't want to talk
about the pottery. I know about the pottery. I want to talk about them
and what they do. I might learn something new that way."

"But that's why they stopped," she countered, "to learn about
your art form."

"So you tell them about it."

Lucy let it go. Joe definitely had his style and it was a style
that many people enjoyed. Her mind flashed through all the people
she'd met this past year that had bought pots or befriended her or
supported Joe in one way or another. He was doing something right.

The sounds around Lucy changed suddenly and she glanced up
to see that Joe and Pete had stopped, along with the dogs, who
seemed to be looking up at Joe for a signal as to where to go next.
There was a steep ascent to their right and Joe pointed up it. "That
way," he told the dogs as Lucy and Véronique caught up to the men
and stopped. "Anyone need some water before we head up?"

"Not for me," answered Lucy. She had that gentle burn
beginning in her lungs and wanted to keep moving.

Pete shook his head no.

Véronique pointed up through the trees. "We go that way?"

she asked.

"Yep," replied Joe.

Véronique shook her head no. "I stay here," she said.

"What?" Joe was thinking that maybe he hadn't heard right.

"Is good. You go. I stay here." And she sat down, cross-legged, on the ground.

"She can't stay here!" Joe told Lucy.

"It's not safe," Pete agreed.

"We can take a break for her if she wants. For as long as she wants. But we can't leave her here."

Lucy looked down at Véronique; she was as shocked as the men at what her friend had just said. "What's going on?" she asked her in French.

"I don't want to walk anymore," Véronique replied in her native tongue. "Yesterday's hike was already too much for me and I'm tired and I don't want to go any further."

"Well you can't stay here. Not all alone."

"Why not?"

"We're in the middle of the wilderness, Véronique! What if a bear comes along?"

This French girl made a little O with her mouth. "There are bears?" she asked uneasily.

"What's she saying?" interrupted Joe.

"That yesterday's hike was harder than she expected and she doesn't want to hike anymore today," Lucy translated.

"Why didn't she say that this morning?" Pete complained. "She could have stayed in camp."

"I thought she was used to hiking," interjected Joe. "I thought she had all this experience in the Alps."

Lucy shrugged. She looked down at Véronique who was looking up at her, waiting to hear what the men had said. Her face was blotchy from the heat and her eyes had a glint of steely determination. She wasn't going up that ridge.

"I guess we thought this would be okay for you," Lucy said apologetically, "because of all the hiking you said you've done in the Alps."

"Ah yes!" Véronique bristled. "But in the Alps the paths are paved and if you get tired you wait a while and a bus comes along to take you to an inn where you can eat and rest and spend the night if you want!"

"What did she say?" Joe asked.

"Nothing," lied Lucy. She thought quickly; she couldn't leave Véronique here and she didn't want to ask the guys to give up their day hike into the upper lake. "Why don't I just take her back to camp?" she suggested.

Joe and Pete looked at each other, seeing this as a possible solution. "You sure you're okay with that?" Pete asked.

Lucy nodded; she didn't mind.

"And you know how to get back to the camp?" Joe asked.

Lucy made a little grimace of uncertainty; here was that direction thing again. She *thought* she knew the way back to the lake but she wasn't sure. And if she doubted herself, she almost certainly wouldn't find her way back. But really, how hard could it be? She knew they'd walked along this clearing since dropping down through the grass and salmonberry bushes on this side of the ridge and she was pretty sure she remembered the place where they had stopped and she had taken off her long shirt. They hadn't traveled that far from camp. Plus she would have Véronique with her, who undoubtedly did know the route. "I think so," she offered.

"It's easy," began Joe, his enthusiasm for the idea growing as he launched into a narrative about the layout of the land. He made a circle out of the fingers of both hands. "You've just got to picture the lake as sitting in the center of a bowl and you need to climb up and over the edge of that bowl. So you go back the way we came and start angling up and to your right." He emphasized the direction with his hand, curving it up onto its side and flexing the fingers back a little. "Once you're at the top of the ridge you should be able to look down and see the lake. Then all you've gotta do is keep it to your right at all times, and you'll walk into our campsite."

Lucy nodded; that made sense.

"Whatever you do," Joe cautioned strongly. "Don't go down into the creek bed drainage behind where we're camped. The creek that comes out of the lake, where I saw the deer drinking this morning – you know the one I mean?" Lucy nodded. "That's some of the worst real estate you ever want to meet down in there. I know because I've hunted it. It's steeper than a cow's face and the brush is thick enough to choke you."

Lucy was surprised he even brought this up. She could picture the cirque, holding the lake, and there was no way they needed to end up down behind where they were camped.

"Here," said Joe pulling off his pack and searching in one of the front pockets. "Take this whistle with you and if you run into any trouble, just stay where you are and blow the whistle until we come." He passed a red whistle on a length of dark, narrow rope to Lucy. "And you can take the dogs if you like."

"No, that's all right," said Lucy. "I'd be worried they'd go chasing off after a deer or a squirrel or something and I wouldn't be able to call them back. They should stay with you."

"What are we doing?" Véronique asked, seeing Lucy loop the whistle over her head so it would hang around her neck.

"I'm going to hike back to camp with you," Lucy told her. She pointed at the whistle. "And I'm taking this just in case we get lost."

Véronique absorbed this information then asked wearily, "Can you carry me on your back?" But the glint in her blue eyes had turned into a twinkle so Lucy knew she was glad of this decision. She reached her hand out and offered it to Véronique, who grabbed a hold of it and allowed Lucy to help her get up from her sit. She brushed down the back of her jeans and flitted her hands around her face to get the bugs away from her.

Joe stepped forward and slipped his arm around Lucy's waist. "You be careful," he warned softly.

"Mmm hmm."

They kissed and the men took off up the ridge. "Catch a lot of fish," Lucy called after them.

"Cut. 'Sroat," Véronique added in her stilted English.

The guys looked back, smiling. Lucy was surprised. "Good job!" she conceded. Then she took Véronique by the arm. "Let's go."

It seemed longer, hiking without Joe, maybe because Lucy had to pay attention to where she was going and maybe because she had to chat, instead of losing herself in her daydreams. Well, she didn't have to chat but Véronique was curious about Lucy's roll in the pottery and Lucy decided it might make the distance seem shorter for her French friend if they talked.

"No, I don't make any of the pottery," she answered in reply to Véronique's first question, a question that she'd been asked many times in the shop. "It's not really my thing, playing in the clay."

"Really? I think I would love it."

Lucy sighed. She heard that from a lot of people and she never really knew how to explain that it just didn't interest her. "I like selling it," she said finally after swatting at a particularly obnoxious horsefly that was intent on buzzing around and around her head. "I like feeling the customers listen to me as I describe the techniques that Joe uses in his pottery making. And I like watching their faces as I take them on the tour of the studio and kiln and they see just how much is involved in the process of making a pot."

"It's a role for you?"

"Yes," agreed Lucy. "That's *exactly* what it is. And a role I love playing because I believe in the work."

"Would you ever do it full-time? Say, when you marry Joe?"

"We're not going to get married," Lucy rebutted quickly. "And even if we did, I don't know that I'd *just* want to sell his pottery."

"Why not?" Véronique was surprised.

"Because selling the pottery isn't a living for me. It's Joe's living."

"Does he think of it this way?"

"Not most of the time. Most of the time he brags about my prowess in selling his pottery and taking his income to the next level and tells me that the money is mine as well as his. But when we fight....." Lucy looked across at her friend. It was hot and Véronique's face was red from the heat but her blue eyes were full of curiosity. "When we fight that's always the sensitive spot. The place that either of us can touch and cause the other to yelp."

"What do you mean?"

"Well, he tells me that without the artwork there would be nothing to sell and I tell him that without the sales, the artwork is moot."

Véronique tipped up her head in acquiescence. "Ahhhhh," she said, long and slow in that special way the French had of agreeing without words. "Which comes first, the chicken or the egg?"

"Exactly." Lucy stopped for a moment and looked around. This was not the place. She moved on. "Sometimes I want to leave him after one of those fights, so he can figure it out for himself," she grumbled.

"Why don't you?" Véronique asked. She had never been one to stay in a relationship for long, not since the marriage of her youth had failed.

"Because I think that the fight is just a beard for my need to get centered and I don't think running from it is the answer."

Véronique blew a noisy puff of air out from between her lips. "I think you're perfectly centered," she shot back.

If only she knew, Lucy thought to herself.

They walked another dozen steps before Lucy stopped again. Something seemed familiar. She looked at the view of the ridges to her left, then she glanced back, at the distance from where they were now to the alpine monument Joe had pointed out when they first came over the ridge. She was pretty sure they had walked far enough to start climbing the ridge now. "Okay, let's go this way," she instructed, veering off to the right and looking for a way up through the salmonberry bushes.

"No," she heard Véronique protest from behind her. Lucy stopped, instantly doubting her sense of direction, and looked at Véronique.

"I don't think we go up here," the French girl argued. "I think this is too soon. See those trees over there," she said, pointing at a thick grove of trees further along and to their right, "that's where we cross into the lake."

"Okay," agreed Lucy. That's why she'd been so willing to go back to camp with Véronique; she knew her friend would remember the way. She looked at her watch; it was almost 10 o'clock. They'd be there well before lunchtime.

They pushed on until they were among the trees, as Véronique suggested. It was cooler under the trees and darker. Veronique sat down for a break, leaning her back up against a cedar tree, while Lucy tried to get the lay of the land. Her eyes were having trouble adjusting from light to dark but she could see that the land sloped gently up in front of them. "We've just got to go up this way," she told Véronique, pointing ahead of them, "and then we'll be able to drop down to the lake."

"Go up. Go up!" grumbled Véronique. "I don't want to go up anymore. My legs ache too much. I want to go down."

"No it's okay," Lucy reassured her. "We won't have to go up for long by the looks of it."

Véronique dragged herself to a reluctant stand and took a deep breath. "Okay," she grumbled. "I'm ready."

Lucy led the way, leaning into the slope and trying to make sure that none of the brush she was pushing out of her way snapped back onto Véronique. She kept glancing up at the top of the ridge, hoping that it was indeed the top of the ridge and not an illusion. She remembered the first date she'd gone on with Joe; that had also involved climbing a ridge to drop down into a lake. But that ridge, it turned out, had a series of ridges on it, all of which looked like they were the top of the climb until they got to them. Then they'd see that it was just a plateau and they had yet another section of straight up. They never did make it to the lake that day, it was just too hot and buggy, and they weren't really sure of the trail in the first place. But Lucy remembered getting a great workout and having fun in the process. She wasn't sure Véronique would feel the same way if an identical geological deception was going on here. And Lucy wasn't sure she had it in her to keep encouraging the French girl.

Fortunately, she didn't need to. They reached the top of the little hillock and the land sloped down, gently at first but then it curved to their left and the gradient became quite sharp. Lucy tried to walk it, grabbing the green growth around her hard to stop herself from pitching forward but when she felt her feet slide out from under her she yielded to gravity and plunked down on her bottom. "When in doubt," she called back to Véronique, "use your bum."

Véronique followed this advice immediately and both girls began to slide downhill on their rear ends. "This is better," Véronique said, the lift in her spirits evident in the lilt to her voice. They used their hands and their feet to plow their way through bushes with endless prickly burrs that kept catching at them, clawing any morsel of exposed skin. They stopped now and then, to assess whether they could really fit between certain root wads or if they had to slide around them and when they stopped they could hear nothing other than the sound of each other's breathing. The temperature was close, sticky even, under the thick canopy of trees and Lucy could feel herself sweating. She thought she heard water at one point but Véronique said no, she didn't hear it, so Lucy gave up her hope, yet again, that they were getting closer to the lake.

But it didn't stop nagging at her. She kept asking herself why, after all this traveling downhill, why weren't they seeing the lake? Joe had said specifically that the lake would be on their right as they moved towards the camp but all Lucy could see to her right was more undergrowth and trees. And the slope felt wrong compared to what they'd climbed up earlier.

Then suddenly the downhill stopped for a moment and they were in a flat spot that was wide enough for them to sit alongside each other. Lucy looked at her watch again. It was 11:20 already. She was hot, sore in so many different ways from the attacks of the undergrowth on her skin, and more than a little frustrated that they weren't at the lake yet. "Why aren't we seeing the lake?!" she whined, out loud this time, to no-one in particular.

"You know," said Véronique slowly. "I've been watching the sun. It's been in front of us, moving higher in the sky, the whole time we've been coming down this hill and I remember noticing last night that the sun set behind the rocks on the other side of the lake from our campsite. Which would mean," she said, getting up and straightening out slowly, as if every part of her ached. She turned 180 degrees. "We need to go back up this hill to get to the lake."

Lucy twisted around and looked at the steepness of the slope they had just come down. "*Now* you want to go up?" she complained.

"No," confessed Véronique. She flopped back down onto the ground beside Lucy. "If you want to know the truth I had a feeling we were heading in the wrong direction when we started down this slope but I didn't want to say anything because I just didn't want to climb anymore. And now, ironically, the climb is much worse than anything I rejected earlier."

Lucy didn't care about the irony of their situation, she just cared that they figure out where they were exactly. And since she knew she didn't have any idea and since she wasn't sure she could trust Véronique to be telling her the truth, despite what sounded like an accurate solar compass, Lucy did the only thing she knew to do. She stood up and blasted on her whistle.

"What are you doing?!" protested Véronique. "We're not lost."

"You may not be, but I am," admitted Lucy. "And I know when to stop guessing and stay put."

"But I'm not guessing," Véronique went on, throwing her hand into the air above her. The heat was getting to both of them. The heat and hunger and frustration over having taken a wrong turn. "I can tell by the direction of the sun. Can't you?"

"No," Lucy admitted again. "I would never think to follow the sun."

"I can't believe you're that ignorant," Véronique commented. "Don't you know *anything*?"

Her words stung but Lucy felt the truth of them. She really didn't know anything about directions; what on earth made her think she could lead Véronique back to camp?

She was about to apologize when Véronique jumped in. "What did Joe tell you about how to get back?" she asked.

Lucy felt that icy cold on the back of her neck again. She looked down the slope behind her, then up it in front of her, while Véronique's assertions about the direction of the sun rang in her ears and she knew, she *knew* they were exactly where Joe had told them not to go. They were in the creek bed drainage. She blew the whistle again.

Now she was going to get it. This was the moment she'd been waiting for, expecting. Dreading. When Joe found her, if he found her, he would be so angry. He had told her specifically not to get down into this mess and look what she'd done. A gunshot rang out, somewhere above their heads. Lucy tipped her head back and blasted three long whistles into the air. Another gunshot. He'd found them. And she was sure he would come and get them. And when he did, there would be hell to pay.

Her mind flashed back to the fancy department store in London with its twinkling lights and happy carol music. Christmastime, in a place of wonderment and surprise, at least for her, as a six-year old who'd never been to such a place before. And her older brother, who'd discovered the delights of the elevator, the magic box that went up and down and up and down, until he couldn't stand it, he was having so much fun. And her father, who couldn't find her brother and started turning this way and that, fear gripping him like an angry claw, until he suddenly knew where that child was. And then he was just angry. He waited, teeth clenched in fury, outside the elevator, a crowd building around them. And the doors opened and the little boy came out, his face split from side to side in a grin of delight, and their father stepped forward and slapped him so hard across that face, the little boy flew sideways into the crowd. And the crowd gasped but nobody stepped forward to help the little boy.

This was what she had coming to her, Lucy knew it. She braced herself, preparing for the blow. She could hear Joe thundering down through the brush, getting closer and closer; her eyes darted to the right to see where she would land when she fell.

The dogs got to her first and a deep sadness washed through Lucy. She would have to leave them too, when she left Joe. Them and Maddie and Skye and Pete. And Sol. All the people she had come to care about, people that had trusted her not to ruin this wonderful thing she had going with Joe. How could she be so stupid?

And then he was there, exploding out of the undergrowth like a bear on the run. Joe lunged towards her. Lucy felt her weight rock back into her heels as she steeled herself physically. He fell to his knees in front of her and lifted up her left hand, slipping a metal fishing ring onto the fourth finger. "Will you marry me?" he asked.

Lucy gasped, her fears hissing out of her like air from a balloon. She reached out and touched his face with her hand. "Oh yes," she replied softly. Then she threw her head back and shouted, for all the world to hear, "Yes."

And the word flew up the ridge and spun around the lake like a pot on the wheel.

"Yes, yes, yes."

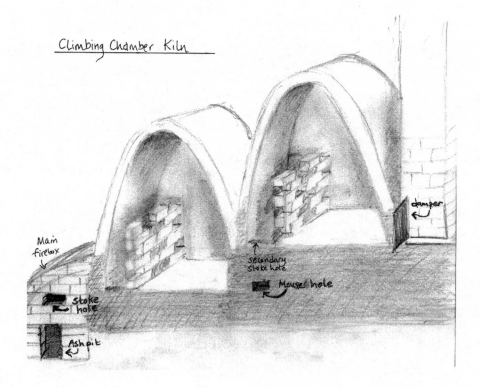

Climbing Chamber Kiln

Main firebox

damper

secondary stoke hole

Mouse hole

stoke hole

Ash pit

Made in the USA
Lexington, KY
08 August 2017